THE CHRONICLES OF

THOMAS BRIGGS

WORLD OF THE DAMNED

D.K. NEVILLE

D.K. Neville

The Chronicles of Thomas Briggs by D.K. Neville ISBN 978-0-9845362-6-9

Published by Fire Pit Creek Publishing, 31208 E Heidelberger Rd. Buckner, Mo 64016 US.

Manufactured in the United States

Acknowledgments

  Just like *The Fall*, I started writing this with no intention of publishing it. In fact, I wrote only a couple of chapters before abandoning it in favor of finishing *The Fall*. It turned out to be a good decision, I think, because *The Fall* was a good book to start with. It engaged readers in a way that I never would have expected. It left people longing for more (or so my readers tell me). Most importantly, it was nearly half completed before I was ever talked into publishing it. Had I only been a couple of chapters into it (like I was with *World of the Damned*), I can fully imagine myself getting fed up, discouraged, and abandoning it. That would have been unfortunate, because much to my surprise, I thoroughly enjoy other people reading my work. Sure, I have always liked writing. But previously I rarely let anyone read what I wrote. I always thought that whatever it was would never be good enough for someone else to be genuinely interested in.

  With all of that being said, I cannot express just how excited I am for *The Chronicles of Thomas Briggs* series. I ended the book in a totally different way than I had intended, starting out (just like *The Fall*). I think it will give readers a different take on the zombie apocalypse genre, and hopefully the apocalypse genre as a whole. Something more than hacking apart the undead. Don't get me wrong...the old "hack and slash" style is definitely cool. I wanted, however, to convey a much more fundamental element of surviving in an undead wasteland. I think *The Walking Dead* TV series does an incredibly good job with this, but I wanted to do a different take on it. Most certainly not a *better* one, just a *different* one. Most of all, I wanted to mostly focus on one character, and limit how much I "sidetracked" with other characters. Why? Because the inner workings of a person's mind are obviously very complex. Instead of conveying the very *fact* that a character is changing, I wanted to intimately show *how* the character is changing. What is going on inside his head while he endures certain experiences? How does a certain situation affect how he thinks about this or that later on? Is there any one moment when the character dynamically changed, or was it a slower evolution from what *once* was, to what now *is*? Also, I want to emphasize what this book really is: A starting point for the series. It is not intended to be read and put down. Admittedly, it is written in such a way that you will (hopefully) want to read the other books in the series when they come out. And that isn't just because I want to sell books. Don't worry, I'm not trying to sound righteous—I *really* want to sell books—but I also want to give my readers the best possible experience I can give them. To do that, I believe it is necessary to leave certain things out, or leave questions unanswered. The reason for this is twofold: For one, as previously said, I want you to buy my other books. Two, I want the reader to elaborate on the story in their own way. I want it to become *yours*. Does that mean that these questions will forever remain unanswered? No, of course not. It just means that I want you to put your wonderful imagination to good use. As always, my primary goal is to inspire. If I did not feel I was doing so, my work would have no meaning.

Now I would like to thank certain individuals for assisting me, in some way, with the creation of this book:

My wife, Sarah, for (usually) understanding when I would spend hours and hours in front of my computer. She also gave me good feedback about certain parts of the book, in addition to telling me what she thought of the book cover ideas and promotional pictures.

My good friend Simon Spiers, for inspiring a character in my book. He also assisted me with the photography portion, helped me with book signings for *The Fall*, and offered ideas for crucial elements of this book's plot.

The following individuals, who did an amazing job posing as zombies for promotional pictures (and probably mostly for fun), as well as those who helped with makeup and organizing the whole thing:

Jamie Yung
Bill Fricke
Taylor Davenport
Emily Nordsieck
Austin Vance
DeHavan McCrary
Curran McCrary
Abby Beach
Morgen Nicodemus

The awesome cover on the front of this book, as well as the promotional pictures, were made possible due to the great work of the aforementioned individuals. Jamie Yung and Bill Fricke both do a wonderful job directing the students and helping them grow theatrically. They all are (or were) Thespians, and I have had the great pleasure of seeing them in action. Their performances are fantastic, and I wish all of them great success.

Of course my last thanks is to you, dear reader, for taking the time to read my work. This world is a busy place, and our lives are growing more hectic by the day. As always, my greatest aim is to inspire. If I can succeed at that, then I believe I know my place in this world. I hope you enjoy *World of the Damned* as much as I enjoyed writing it, and further hope that you enjoy it enough to follow the whole series of *The Chronicles of Thomas Briggs*.

--Dylan Neville

D.K. Neville

<u>Prologue</u>

In the beginning, most everyone believed it could be contained, overcome...extinguished. After all, they were slow, dumb, and dead. Throughout the ages, mankind has overcome terrible diseases and great catastrophes. Why should this one be any different?

It all started as one might imagine...with strange reports on the news. Thomas Briggs was an architect, and he had been at work when he heard the very first news report on TV. A man in Canada had reportedly collapsed in a grocery store, and later died in a hospital from some unknown disease. He supposedly "came back" within minutes of his death, and attacked one of the nurses. After that report, the media began digging for strange stories all over the world. As best as anyone could tell, it originated in Nigeria. Or at least that's where the first incident had occurred. Soon after the incident in Canada, people started dying from some strange disease at an increased rate. Then they came back...as something quite different. It was like something out of a horror movie. Thomas Briggs was terrified, having never seen anything so disturbing. But who had? Thomas had been a "clean" person his whole life. He was a straight A student, went to college, graduated at the top of his class, and was now a 32-year-old architect living in Seattle.

Thomas's sister, Mindy, was now living with him. She had moved in about a month after the first reports. It was now six months later. The world had gone to shit fast, and the dead seemed to be everywhere. Most of the city was quarantined, and only certain areas were considered safe enough to inhabit. But nowhere was truly safe. Someone could die from this strange sickness at any moment and come back to life. From what doctors and scientists could tell the disease was airborne, but only certain people could get it that way. The other way was to get bitten by one those...things. If a person died and was infected, they would certainly come back to life. If they bit someone, that person would surely become infected and eventually die and come back as well. It was a vicious cycle. The worst part was that these..*things*...had one goal, and one goal only: to feed.

The news networks were still on TV, although they only reported about every other day. There was only one grocery store and one gas station in Thomas's area of Seattle, and neither could keep up with the number of customers. Eventually, the government created a ration system to prevent violence. It was only mildly effective. Inevitably, people would fight and even kill to get their hands on more meal or fuel cards. Fortunately, most people didn't need much fuel.

In the bad parts of the city, the number of hungry dead was worse. The few humans that were still alive fought as hard as they could to keep the zombies at bay, but they weren't capable of sustaining themselves forever. The poorer and higher population areas had been hit the hardest. Thomas and his sister were lucky, because they lived in a higher-end apartment complex and most of the people there were fairly civilized. The police and National Guard had so far done a good job of keeping the infected out of his part of the city, but Thomas knew that wouldn't last forever. The number of walking dead were growing every day, and it almost seemed like they were getting *more* violent, if that was possible. Who knows, maybe the zombies could actually starve? Who knew what they felt, if they felt anything at all? Thus far, Thomas had no contingency plan. What plan could he have? The rest of the nation wasn't doing much better. The northern states were the worst—for now—and every single state was having the same problem to some degree. The southern coastal states were the safest right now, but they still had to deal with the problem as well. Maybe he could load up and they could try to get to Mexico? Thomas knew that was an unrealistic idea, no matter how comforting the thought was of escaping this madness completely.

Currently, Thomas and Mindy were a little better off than most because Thomas assisted the local authorities in effective ways to keep the zombies out. Being an architect, he knew the best and most cost effective ways to build walls, towers, outposts, etc. He was one of the few people who still had a job, and was paid with extra food and fuel for his help. Mindy had been a nurse, and was assisting in any way she could. Most of the hospitals and clinics were closed down, and poor medical care was a growing concern. Public utilities were still functioning, but barely. There were frequent blackouts, and the water was only on three times a day for an hour each time. It could certainly be worse, and Thomas was almost positive it would eventually get to that point.

"So what do we do when this problem doesn't get fixed?" Thomas asked Sergeant First Class Ben Anderson, a National Guard platoon sergeant and currently the non-commissioned officer in charge of security.

"It'll get fixed. We've been doing a mighty fine job so far, and the rest of the military is conducting operations to take out the largest populations of dead," Sergeant Anderson told him.

"Just not here..." Thomas mumbled.

"Not yet. Places like Washington D.C., and the military bases are the primary concern. There's a lot of cleaning up to do." Anderson and Thomas stood in one of the towers next to the gate, and the rough sergeant first class brought his binoculars up to his eyes to scan the perimeter.

"It's only going to get worse, Ben. Anyone with half a brain can see that. The dead are relentless. They don't need to sleep, they don't get scared, and they have one mission: to eat *us*."

There was a long silence, and Sergeant Anderson pulled his binoculars away from his eyes.

"Want my advice? Learn how to use a gun. Take your sister and head South. Don't get me wrong...you two have been invaluable these past few months. But if you're worried about

3

everything going to shit, get out while you can." Anderson turned to look Thomas right in his eyes.

"Our mom and dad live in Albuquerque. Heard it wasn't too bad down there yet. I've been wanting to go down there to be with them—we both have—but honestly, I'm scared of the trip. It's not exactly like going on vacation. What will we find between here and there? Will other places be as heavily fortified as this? What if it's a lot worse than we think? What if..." Thomas paused and looked down at his feet, "What if they're dead, Ben?"

"I don't know what to tell ya', son. But you gotta do what you think is best. I can help you prepare and get the things you'll need, if you want to leave."

Sergeant First Class Ben Anderson was a good man. He was 45 years old, and he was an MP in the Washington Army National Guard. His full-time job had been a foreman for a construction company. He had been in the National Guard for twenty years, was an active-duty Marine before that, and had been deployed to Iraq twice since joining the National Guard. He was tough as nails.

"I'll talk to Mindy about it and let you know in the morning. Thanks Ben."

Thomas climbed down the ladder and headed down the block to his apartment. The moans of the dead outside the walls were ever present, but the sound had become strangely familiar. It was the middle of July, so the Washington weather was quite comfortable. It was about 70°, partly cloudy, and humid (as always).

Thomas unlocked the door to the apartment complex and walked up the stairs to the second floor. His apartment was quite spacious, with a large, combined living room, kitchen, and dining room, and two bedrooms, a full bathroom, a study, and a medium-sized balcony. His sister Mindy was sitting on the couch, playing a game on her tablet.

"Anything interesting happen today?" she asked.

"Not really. Reinforced part of the wall around the neighborhood. Talked to Anderson about maybe leaving..."

"Leaving?" Mindy turned her attention away from her tablet

and sat straight up.

"Yeah. Things aren't always going to be this way, Mindy," Thomas said.

"Well then we'll deal with it then. Right now we're safe..."

Mindy was 26, six years younger than Thomas. She was a highly intelligent girl, and very beautiful. Her long, dirty blonde hair and bright, blue eyes always captured the attention of men. Luckily, they lived in a good part of town. Otherwise she might have become a victim several times over.

"Mindy, I didn't tell him we were going to do it. But I *did* tell him I'd talk to you about it again. He's actually the one who suggested it, and said he'd help us get what we need to make the trip to Albuquerque." Thomas sat down next to her and ran his fingers through his dark brown hair.

"I don't want to."

Thomas could hear the fear in Mindy's voice. Neither one of them had experienced too many terrible things since this all began, and neither one of them wanted to change that. The worst thing they had seen thus far had been a man put a bullet through a zombie's skull. A pretty mild experience, considering what was going on around them.

"To be honest, I don't really want to either. But we've got to do *something* soon. It's not going to stay this way forever, and I don't want to wait until dead people are knocking on our door to do something about it." Thomas slouched down into the couch and leaned his head back.

"Well what will the Army guys do without us? And the police? They need our help." Mindy was thinking of everything she could to use as an excuse.

"The walls are fortified better now, and you've done a good job at training other people in first aid. Besides, we have to look out for *ourselves*. I don't like the idea any better than you do, Mindy, but we've got to make a decision. What about mom and dad?" Thomas stood up and walked into the kitchen.

"They're fine. I know they are. New Mexico hasn't been hit all that hard..."

"That's what we *think*. What if the news is wrong? Accurate reports aren't exactly in abundance these days." Thomas opened the top on a jug of water and poured himself a glass.

Mindy didn't reply for some time. Somewhere deep down, she knew Thomas was making sense. Even though their current situation was safe and comfortable, it could only last so long. And with the current rate of walking dead increasing, it didn't seem like it would last much longer. It was only a matter of time before there were so many zombies outside the walls that they would simply crash through due to sheer weight, or perhaps even climb over mountains of their owns bodies and fall over the wall.

"So what would we do?" Mindy finally asked.

Thomas finished his glass of water and sat it on the counter.

"I'm not sure yet. I'd like to take a Humvee, but I seriously doubt that's an option."

"Has anyone else left?" Mindy asked.

"In the beginning. No one's left recently." Thomas walked back over to the couch and sat down next to his little sister.

"What all would we need to bring?" Mindy curled her legs up on the couch.

"The basics. Food, water, some miscellaneous survival stuff, and only the personal items we can't live without."

Mindy felt a knot form in her throat. She knew all too well that her brother knew nothing about surviving without the conveniences of modern life. What would they do if their vehicle broke down? Or if they got overran by zombies? Or if they were attacked by bandits? There were surely criminals out there taking advantage of this terrible situation, weren't there?

"It'll be alright, sis," Thomas said as he placed a hand on Mindy's shoulder. Mindy forced a smile and took his hand in hers.

After several minutes of the two of them sitting in silence, Mindy finally piped up.

"Let's go," she said.

"You sure?"

"Yep. Let's go be with mom and dad."

Thomas gave her a reassuring smile, then got up from the

6

couch and walked into his study. He was a very organized person, and everything demanded a system. Thomas sat down at his desk and began writing out a list of items he thought would be invaluable.

1

The next morning, Thomas made his way to the National Guard and police tent to see if he could find Sergeant First Class Anderson. After asking around, he located the grizzly senior NCO sitting on his cot.

"Mornin'," Anderson said.

"Good morning, Ben." Thomas pulled up a crate and sat down in front of Sergeant Anderson.

"So what did you decide?" Anderson asked.

"We're going to do it."

Anderson pursed his lips and nodded his head.

"Hate to see you go, son. But you gotta do what ya' gotta do." Anderson stood and pulled his shaving kit out of his duffel bag.

"You said you would help me. What kind of help can you provide?" Thomas asked him, following him out of the tent and over to the shower area.

"Well, I have a squad of men going out a little later to scavenge. I might be able to arrange for you to go with them. Maybe pick yourself up a good SUV or something."

"Out...there...??" Thomas pointed toward the wall.

"Yeah. You'll be in vehicles, of course. And we always create a distraction. The guys are never gone more than an hour or so. Sometimes more if they're looking for something specific."

Thomas was missing his personal vehicle right about now. It was sitting on the other side of the city, on 32nd Avenue. But a Prius wouldn't exactly be the best escape vehicle, so maybe it was for the best. Sure, it got great gas mileage, but the thing fell apart if you hit a pothole.

"There's nothing inside the walls I can use?" Thomas asked him.

"Not that I can think of. In case you didn't notice, the only vehicles inside are ours or are owned by locals. I doubt they'd be willin' to part with any of 'em." Anderson lathered his face up with shaving cream.

"Alright. What else do you think I'll need?"

"A gun. Something simple, something that uses a common type of ammunition. I can help you out with that. You'll also need a way to carry water and food. Who really knows what's going on out there? You might not see another person for hundreds of miles. Well, not one that's alive, anyway." Anderson dragged the disposable razor across his face, playing close attention in the tiny mirror. It was funny, really...after all that had happened, he was still stuck in his ways. Always the respectable NCO.

Thomas tried to swallow the knot in his throat. The more he thought about this adventure, the less appealing it seemed. But he was committed. His reasons for leaving were sound, and no amount of fear could change that fact.

"Obviously, you'll want to leave out of the south gate. Less dead over there. I can provide an armed escort until you get out of town. After that, you're on your own." Anderson's gravelly voice somehow wasn't helping Thomas's gut.

"Do you think I should see if there's anyone else around who wants to leave with us?" Thomas asked.

"Up to you. I wouldn't. There's strength in numbers, but more people equals more mouths to feed, increases the chance of disagreements, or someone doing something stupid. If everything goes to shit out there, I'm guessing it's not going to matter if there are two of you or twenty. The dead will keep on comin'."

"Thanks for your help, Ben. We really appreciate it. Let me know when you guys are going out. I'll be at my apartment."

Thomas walked off and stuck his hands in his pockets. The more real this was becoming, the scarier it was getting. Sure, he had always been well aware that there were dead cannibals on the other side of the walls, but he hadn't gone out there with them. The past six months hadn't been too bad for him. He had never even been closer than ten feet or so from one of those things. Now he was throwing himself out to the wolves.

After getting back home and talking with Mindy again, Thomas reaffirmed his decision. This is what they needed to do. Seattle was getting progressively worse, and reports from around the nation weren't much better. The rest of the world was having problems, too. Thomas wasn't a religious man by any stretch of the imagination, but it was as if some malevolent god decided to exterminate humanity in the most gruesome way possible.

* * *

As the day went on, Thomas collected various items that they would need along the way. He had two five gallon water jugs that he kept in his apartment, and those would be going with him. He put together a bag of junk food (which was what it seemed like people mainly survived off of nowadays), as well as a few MREs he had been lucky enough to acquire over the months. He plotted out their expected course on the map. It was over fourteen hundred miles to Albuquerque, and they would need lots of gas, water, and food, as well as a lot of luck. Thomas kept two ten gallon gas cans out on his balcony, which he used to fuel his personal generator if they happened to need electricity during a blackout. Those would be coming with him. He seriously debated taking the small generator as well, but it was heavy and took up a lot of space. It would have to stay behind.

Mindy spent her time folding clothes for both of them and packing them away into two travel bags. Thomas periodically checked on her out of the corner of his eye, and she seemed to be doing alright. She stayed silent, emotionless.

At around 3pm, there was a knock on the door. It was one of Anderson's men, telling Thomas that they were heading out in an hour to scavenge. Thomas changed into some more rugged attire, and grabbed the only weapon he had in the apartment: an old wooden baseball bat. Thomas had never used the bat for baseball, oddly enough. In fact, it had never been used for anything except decoration. It had been given to him by his father when he was 16, in an attempt to get Thomas more interested in sports. It didn't work. Thomas remained a bookworm, and his father loved him just the same.

"You ready?" Anderson asked.

"I guess. You going out, too?" Thomas tucked his shirt in, even though it was unnecessary. It was a nervous habit.

"No. Gotta stay behind. Listen...my guys will take care of you out there. Just make sure to keep your eyes open. Look for anything you could use on your journey. When choosing a vehicle, make sure it's tough, has lots of space, and preferably has a full tank. Something like a Suburban might be a little much, especially with how much gas they consume. Maybe a crossover or something like that." Anderson placed his hand on Thomas's shoulder and gave him a reassuring pat.

The group of five National Guardsmen, four police officers, and one architect loaded up in the Humvee and big deuce-and-a-half truck. Thomas rode in the Humvee with two guardsmen and a police officer. The two vehicles lined up at the south gate and waited for the distraction.

After about five minutes, fireworks could be heard coming from the other side of the compound. The group waited another ten minutes, to make sure all of the dead were heading that way, and then the gates opened. Thomas felt his heart speed up, and there weren't even any zombies in sight. For the first time in six months he was leaving the safety of the fortified camp that used to be his neighborhood. Once outside the walls, Thomas took Anderson's advice and continuously scanned the area. After only driving about a block away from the gate, Thomas could see the walking dead scattered throughout the streets. Abandoned cars were everywhere.

"Sarge said to help you find a vehicle. You leavin' us?" one of the Guardsmen asked Thomas.

"That's the plan. After seeing this though, I'm not too sure." Thomas tried to wish away the knot in his stomach.

"Ah, it shouldn't be this bad outside the city. Gotta remember that the number of dead directly represent the number of living that used to be here. You get out in the country and it shouldn't be all that bad." The Guardsmen spoke with conviction, and it reassured Thomas.

"Of course, I haven't seen it first hand, so I could be completely wrong. Just a theory," he added.

The knot formed in Thomas's stomach once more.

"After driving for only five minutes, the two vehicles stopped in the middle of the road. The police officer told Thomas that they were going to check out the strip mall, maybe there were useful items inside.

Now Thomas was really worried. He saw two zombies down the street, and had no idea how they planned to scavenge here without drawing attention.

"You can stay in the Humvee if you like, but then you'd miss your opportunity to gather supplies for your grand adventure," the police officer said.

Thomas reluctantly exited the Humvee. The driver stayed inside, as did the driver of the deuce-and-a-half. Everyone else got out and quietly made their way to the small strip mall that contained four businesses. They weaved in and out of vehicles, moving in a crouched position. Thomas held his baseball bat firmly and close to his chest. Most of the troops had switched to their sidearms, but a few carried melee weapons like crowbars, axes, machetes, and one even had a samurai sword.

The group made it the fifty feet or so to the strip mall without incident. Two of the Guardsmen—who were still using their M4's—stopped in the parking lot and kept watch. Everyone else went to the closest business in the strip mall, which was a hunting supply store.

The door was already partially open, which was a bad sign. It meant that it had probably been scavenged by someone already, and there was a good chance of zombies being inside. Thomas stayed in the middle of the group, well aware that he was not suited for zombie killing. Best to leave that sort of work to the professionals.

Inside presented no obvious indication that the dead were in there. Items were scattered around the store, and it was very obvious that someone had already been here. But there were still things of value left. Right away, Thomas spotted a couple of machetes, camping gear in one aisle, and a few handguns in a broken display case.

"I'm surprised there's anything left in this place," one of the Guardsmen whispered, "Usually these places and grocery stores are the first to go."

Thomas pulled the duffel bag off his back and grabbed a few items. A two-person tent, two sleeping bags, a machete, and a kerosine lantern. Then he went over to the display case with handguns inside. There were only three left.

"Which one should I grab?" Thomas asked.

"Hell, grab all of them. We'll sort them out back at base," the cop told him.

Thomas grabbed a small snub-nose revolver, a semi-automatic handgun, and a full-size revolver. He didn't know what any of them were, but it didn't matter right now.

"There's a little ammo over there. Grab all of it," a Guardsmen told him.

Thomas walked over to the shelf behind the counter and pushed the five boxes of various ammunition into his duffel bag. The other guys were gathering up items as well. All in all, Thomas felt like he had been lucky already. The items he had taken would certainly prove valuable during his trip.

Then there came the moaning. Thomas heard it coming faintly from the back room. At first he froze up, staring at the doorway with a sign above it that read *Employees Only*. Another long moan emitted from the room.

"Did...did you guys hear that?" Thomas asked quietly.

"I did," the police officer said.

"Best we leave now. No need to draw any attention to

ourselves," one of the Guardsmen said.

The group exited the building and moved onto the next one, which was some sort of spa. After peeking in and not immediately seeing anything of value, they moved on. Their next place to check in the strip mall was an office supply store. The team went in and gathered up pens, paper, pencils, and other miscellaneous office items. When they exited the business, Thomas caught movement out of the corner of his eye.

Stumbling through the doorway of the hunting store was a zombie, presumably the one they had heard in the back room. The two Guardsmen keeping watch at the edge of the parking lot had their backs turned, watching the perimeter.

"Shit..." one of the guys said.

"I'll get him," the cop volunteered.

The zombie spotted the two Guardsmen at the edge of the parking lot, and immediately took interest. The creature started heading their way at a fast walk (for a zombie). One of its feet dragged behind it, its arms moved in a most unnatural way as it walked, and it snarled as it approached. It was still about forty feet from the Guardsmen, and the cop who had volunteered to take it out was now jogging toward it as discreetly as he could.

"Hey!" the cop said, somewhat quietly when he was about fifteen feet away. The rest of the team looked on, ready to offer aid if it was needed.

The zombie slowed down and turned toward the police officer. It looked back at the Guardsmen, then back to the officer, almost like it was momentarily confused. It seemed to be making a decision: who to eat.

The cop brought up his crowbar and took two steps toward the zombie. The zombie snarled loudly and advanced, reaching out as he did so. When it got within striking distance, the police officer swiftly swung his crowbar, striking the dead creature square in the head. It fell down and snarled, apparently still alive (or as alive as a zombie can be). The cop delivered two more punishing blows to it's cranium, finishing the thing off for good. The two troops on watch turned toward the commotion, and watched the officer beat the hell out of the thing.

"I think we should move on, just in case that drew any attention," one of the Guardsmen suggested.

The group made their way back toward the vehicles. Thomas looked at the zombie as they walked past. It had once been a living man, with a life and a story and a family. Its skin was pale gray, wrinkled and torn in places. Its clothing was so dirty and covered in blood and tissue that Thomas couldn't discern what color it had originally been. The skull of the monster was cracked wide open, and its black, mushy brain was now oozing out onto the pavement. Maggots crawled out of its mouth. It was hard to tell how long it had been since the person turned. Judging by the decomposed brain, Thomas guessed it had been at least a couple months.

The group moved on down the road, passing by a small group of zombies that took interest in the noise and movement of the vehicles. As they past, Thomas saw them turn and move toward the vehicles as quickly as they could. As soon as they were down the road a ways, the beasts apparently lost interest.

Their next stop was a small convenience store. Inside was practically barren, but the group managed to scrounge up several bags of chips, a few bottles of water, and a six-pack of beer. They found two zombies in the back room, and the group of soldiers made short work of them. Thomas didn't personally witness the slayings this time. He opted to stay in the front of the store, deciding he would just be in the way anyway.

The team had only been gone for about half an hour, but Thomas remembered Anderson say the scavenging teams usually didn't stay out more than an hour. He needed to find a vehicle soon. So, as they made their way to their next destination, Thomas paid special attention to the vehicles they past by. One in particular caught his eye. It was a brand new black Dodge Durango. Thomas wasn't a car expert, but he new that "manly men" often were. Manly men also often became soldiers or cops.

"Any of you guys know a lot about cars?" he asked his fellow passengers in the Humvee.

"I do. I was a full-time mechanic," one said.

"I saw a new Dodge Durango back there. Think it would be a good pick?" Thomas asked.

"Sure. It comes in V8 or V6, and it's all-wheel drive. I think they have a 24-gallon tank, too. Pretty good gas mileage, I think I remember reading. Pretty spacious, good storage space. Definitely a good pick with everything going to shit. Better than some tiny economy car or a giant gas hog."

Thomas briefly thought it over, and before they reached their next stop, he had made up his mind. Hopefully the keys were in it.

After killing four zombies and picking through the hardware store, the team loaded up and headed back the way they came. Thomas had grabbed a hammer and nails, a hacksaw, and some other miscellaneous items that he couldn't really think up a use for, but could certainly see putting them to use for *something* in the future.

The team stopped right next to the Durango Thomas had picked out. It was parked in the middle of the street, so the chance of the keys being inside were pretty good. The team walked around it, checking it for damage. The inside looked clear, so they opened it up and found the keys still in the ignition. They popped the hood and the mechanic checked it out.

"It's a 2013, R/T. Looks like a beauty. Probably just bought the damn thing right before all this happened. Only has 13 miles on it. Tank is three-quarters full, too," he said.

Thomas grinned slightly, happy that he was lucky enough to find such a reliable ride. The interior was clean, even. He tried not to think about the circumstances surrounding its owner abandoning it.

"I'll ride with you," the mechanic said.

Thomas got in the driver's seat and turned the key. The crossover started right up, and the sound of it made Thomas happy.

"Better get out of here," one of the Guardsmen said through the window, and pointed down the road. A fairly large group of zombies was making its way toward them, about a hundred feet away.

Thomas adjusted the seat and steering wheel just in time to

16

turn around and get behind the deuce-and-a-half as it was leaving. The vehicle drove like a dream, and it still had the "new car" smell. The Guardsman riding with him checked the glove box and center console, looking for anything useful.

"Well would you look at this," he said, "They left us a present."

The Guardsman pulled out a semi-automatic handgun and an extra loaded magazine, as well as a wad of cash held together with a rubber-band.

"Is that a good gun?" Thomas asked, barely taking his eyes off of the road.

"Decent. It's a .40 caliber Taurus. Says '840BC' on the barrel. Never heard of that model. Holds 15 rounds, so that's a plus. Not too big, either, so you could easily tuck it away. I like it."

"Great. I guess just leave it in the console in case I need it," Thomas told him.

Honestly, the fact that he would have firearms in his possession scared Thomas a little. He had never fired a gun in his life, and knew nothing about them. He didn't know what ".40 caliber" meant, or how to load it, or even how to keep it on his person without accidentally shooting himself.

About halfway back to the camp, Thomas heard a strange noise coming from the back. Both he and the Guardsman turned and looked in the back seat at the same time without saying a word to each other.

"What the hell was that? See anything?" Thomas could only glance for a second at a time, not wanting to take his eyes off the road for too long. With zombies walking around aimlessly and cars parked all over the place, it wasn't like driving down the road before all of this happened.

Thomas felt the adrenaline pumping through his veins already.

"I have no idea. Don't see anything."

Then the Guardsman moved his gaze from the backseat to the cargo area in the back. He couldn't see what was back there, but if there was anything in the cab with them, that's where it had to be. The third row of seats wasn't folded down, so he couldn't see anything that might be back there.

"Shit...stop!" he said loudly.

It scared Thomas so bad that he slammed on the brakes, causing the vehicle to screech to a halt.

The Guardsman hopped out of the passenger seat and ran around back. Thomas craned his neck around to look. The hatch popped open, and Thomas could see the look on the Guardsman's face.

"Holy shit...you have to see this..."

Thomas jumped out and ran around to the hatch. What he saw inside made him gasp in horror.

"Oh...my...God..." he managed to spit out.

A zombie was lying in the cargo area, its hands and feet bound together and duct tape wrapped around its head. His eyes were gray and obviously lifeless. Dried blood covered its neck, but its clothes were surprisingly clean. Scattered around it were air fresheners.

"What the fuck, man!?" the Guardsman exclaimed, completely taken aback by the sight.

"What do we do?" Thomas asked.

"Fuckin' push him out!" the Guardsman said as he reached to grab the monster.

He abruptly stopped when he heard the noises coming from their left. Stumbling out of an alley was a large group of the dead. They flooded out of the narrow alley, bumping into each other and letting out terrifying moans and snarls. They had found food.

"Shit! We gotta go!" the Guardsman shouted as he grabbed the M4 that was leaning against the back of the Durango.

Thomas locked up for a brief moment. The sight of the zombie horde overwhelmed him.

"We have to go! Now!" the Guardsman yelled, and smacked Thomas on his shoulder.

The horde was closing the gap between the sidewalk and the Durango with surprising speed, and the further the front of the group got from the alley, the larger their number seemed to grow.

Thomas jumped into the driver's seat and put the Durango in

gear. About that time, they saw the deuce-and-a-half turning back toward them off of a side street. Apparently they had turned around to see if they needed help.

"Fuck!" the Guardsman yelled.

The street was two lanes, but there wasn't enough room for the Durango to squeeze past the deuce-and-a-half with all of the vehicles blocking off a good portion of the road. Thomas only made it about a hundred feet before having to stop in front of the big truck.

The driver of the truck opened the door and leaned out, presumably to ask what was going on. Then he saw the horde closing in behind them. He cursed and slammed the door closed, then began backing up.

The deuce-and-a-half was slow and cumbersome, and the narrow street wasn't making things any easier. There were no parking lots to back into, so the driver was forced to continue in reverse until he got to the street he had originally turned off of. Thomas and the Guardsman were cursing and yelling, paying close attention to the horde behind them. They obviously weren't moving as fast as the Durango and deuce-and-a-half were, but the fact that they were still advancing was cause enough for concern.

The deuce-and-a-half finally made it to the street it had turned off of, but as the driver cut the wheels to turn, the Humvee appeared on the same street. It had apparently turned around to help as well. The large truck almost backed into the Humvee, but the guy in the passenger's seat yelled for the driver to stop.

"Shit! Get the fuck out of the way!" Thomas's companion yelled, although the windows were up and no one could hear him but Thomas.

Thomas gripped the steering wheel so hard his knuckles turned white, though he didn't notice. His eyes were frantically bouncing back and forth, the sense of urgency growing inside him. He checked the rear-view mirror, and the horde was now about twenty feet away. It wouldn't take them long to close that distance.

After what seemed like an eternity, the Humvee backed up enough for the deuce-and-a-half to back down the street. Thomas zoomed by, knowing that nothing he could do would be of any use to the two vehicles and eight troops that were in them.

After he got past the deuce-and-a-half, Thomas slowed the vehicle to a crawl and watched the events unfold in the rear-view mirror. The deuce-and-a-half was slow, and as the driver switched gears to drive forward, the guys in the Humvee opened fire on the horde of walking dead. The zombies were now close enough to touch the deuce-and-a-half as it pulled away, the Humvee close behind it.

"That was way too fuckin' close," the Guardsman said as he slammed his head against the headrest and let out a sigh of relief. Thomas was still freaking out inside.

"That was a lot of them," Thomas said.

"Yeah, no shit. I've never seen them in a group that big. I mean, I've seen a bunch of zombies wandering around, but those guys looked like they were moving as a unit. Maybe it was just coincidence because they were all packed together in that alley, and they all saw food at the same time."

"Maybe. But why were they packed into the alley?" Thomas asked, although it was rhetorical.

Several moments passed before the walls of the camp came into view.

"What about the zombie package we're bringing in?" Thomas asked.

"We'll deal with it when we get inside. He's tied up, after all."

The three vehicles drove through the south gate and pulled over as soon as they got inside. Everyone got out of their vehicles and huddled together in a group. Sergeant First Class Anderson came over.

"Everybody okay? I heard gunshots," he said.

"Everybody's fine, I think," one of the Guardsmen said.

"Saw a big horde of 'em. They got a little too close for comfort. What were you guys doin' back there?" the driver of the deuce-and-a-half asked Thomas and his passenger.

"We heard a weird noise coming from the cargo area. You

20

gotta see this," the Guardsman said.

The group walked over to the hatch of the Durango, and the Guardsman opened it.

"Shit! You brought him inside!?" one of them yelled.

"Didn't have much of a choice. Besides, he's all tied up. Not sure why," the Guardsman/mechanic answered.

"Family member, maybe?" Anderson offered.

"Perhaps," Thomas said, "Maybe they didn't want to kill him. Maybe they were trying to wait for a cure."

"Well, guess we better deal with him," Anderson said.

"Shouldn't we tell Top about this before we do anything? I mean, this is the first time we've captured one of 'em alive like this," one of Anderson's men said.

"Good point. Rodriguez, go fetch First Sergeant Cooper," Anderson ordered. The Guardsman ran off.

"Fuck! Look out!" someone said from behind everyone.

Thomas looked past the group and saw a zombie crawling out from under the deuce-and-a-half.

"Must have gotten stuck," the driver of the deuce-and-a-half said, and then stomped on the zombie's head several times. After about six stomps, brain matter started oozing from its ears.

"That's not good enough," Anderson said as he grabbed the baseball bat from Thomas's hands, "Better make sure it ain't comin' back."

Anderson walked over to the thing, raised the bat high above his head, and swung hard. It's skull cracked open and the black goo that used to be a brain squirted out onto the pavement.

That night, Thomas went through all of the things he had collected. Anderson had advised him to keep one of the handguns he had found, an M9 Beretta. It was a 9mm semi-automatic, and was the same type of sidearm most of the military used. Anderson was nice enough to give Thomas two loaded magazines to go with it, as well as a box of ammunition. He said the gun was shit, but since he had extra magazines and ammunition for it, it was the best choice. The handgun only jammed "every once in awhile". That was reassuring.

Thomas told Mindy the story of what had happened out there, and showed her the Durango. Minus the zombie prisoner, of course. First Sergeant Cooper had ordered the thing to be taken somewhere "secure" so it could be studied. He believed that studying the thing might help them figure out how to deal with them better. Thomas agreed...research was always invaluable. But he didn't like the idea of letting one of those things "live" inside their secure walls. Oh well...they were leaving tomorrow.

<u>2</u>

Thomas and Mindy loaded everything up early the next morning. Their supplies took up most of the space in the Durango, but he made sure to leave a little room in case they acquired anything else along the way that they couldn't live without. Anderson gave them a full ten gallon gas can, in addition to what Thomas already had. Thomas topped off the Durango's tank and double-checked all of his supplies. It wasn't much, really. They had enough food to get them through a week, maybe. The water should last them for about a week as well, probably more if they were careful with it. Sergeant Anderson showed Thomas how to siphon gas, since Thomas would certainly need to acquire more along the way. He gave him a few more pointers about survival, and "loaned" him one of his personal fire starters. After Anderson went over the steps to load, unload, and fire a handgun, Thomas felt a little better about using one. Mindy was another story. She was even more unsure about guns than Thomas was. Thomas still hadn't fired one, but hopefully he wouldn't need to.

Thomas did some rough figuring, and concluded that they would need approximately 100 gallons of fuel to make it to Albuquerque. They would certainly consume less than that, but Thomas wanted to plan for more than they would need. After asking around, Thomas found someone in the camp who had owned a 2013 Durango before everything went to shit (not the same one, of course). The man told him that it got about 15mpg in the city, and 20mpg on the highway. Fortunately, most of Thomas's driving would be on the highway. But to play it safe he used 15 miles per gallon in his math. Even if they consistently got 15 miles per gallon throughout an entire tank, that would enable them to travel about 360 miles or so. They would probably consume about 85 gallons, but there was no harm in having more than they needed. And with abandoned vehicles everywhere, it shouldn't be much of a problem. Thomas would just have to think ahead and take advantage of his 140 IQ.

Mindy cried a bit before they left. Thomas almost did, if for no other reason than because Mindy was crying. He tried not to think about what was ahead of them, or worst-case scenarios. He said his goodbyes to everyone, made sure he had everything he needed or wanted, and drove the Durango toward the south gate.

"Good luck out there, Mr. Briggs," a Guardsman said as the gate opened. Thomas waved to him and drove through.

Mindy was in charge of the map, and Thomas had instructed her to take them a different route than the one he had been down yesterday. He didn't think the horde would still be around, but with how little anyone knew about the behavior of zombies, he didn't want to take any chances.

As Thomas drove through a different part of the city, he found himself remembering the place as it used to be. People who were actually alive strolling down the sidewalks, heavy traffic, clean business fronts and traffic lights changing. None of that existed anymore. Thomas and Mindy saw one small group of living people on their way out of the city, and they were rummaging through a dumpster. The group of two men, a woman, and two small children stopped what they were doing and stared at the vehicle as it drove by.

"So what do we do about other people?" Mindy asked as they followed Interstate 90 out of the city.

"What do you mean?" Thomas relaxed a little as the building faded away and the countryside opened itself up to them.

"I mean, what's our policy going to be? Do we help them? Do we ignore them? What's expected of us?" Mindy was always thinking about things like this, and it was good that she did.

24

Thomas was more introverted, and his way of thinking generally centered around himself and his sister more than anything else. That's not to say he was unkind or didn't want to help people. Thomas had a soft heart and always wanted to help those in need. But problems like the one Mindy just brought up didn't usually make their way into Thomas's mind until the situation was upon him.

"I'm not real sure. I don't think it's a good idea to put ourselves in harm's way," he said.

"But don't we have an obligation to help people?" Mindy asked.

"I suppose, under certain circumstances. But what if the people we help are only nice while we're helping them, then they rob us blind or kill us afterward?" Thomas countered.

"True. I guess people are more desperate and will probably be more inclined to do bad things to feed themselves. Especially if they have a family. Hopefully we don't have to worry about that." Mindy reclined the seat back and peered through the passenger side window.

Thomas was almost positive that they would be faced with that type of situation at some point in time. They had a great journey ahead of them, and one would think that fact alone increased the odds of something like that happening. But really, what help could they provide? Neither Thomas nor Mindy had any training in the use of firearms, and certainly no self-defense skills. They were just genuinely good people who had always relied on the good nature of others, always giving people the benefit of the doubt. So far this crazy world hadn't changed that about them. They had been comfortable, safe. Now they were on their own. For a moment, Thomas questioned his decision. Was it fair to persuade Mindy to do this? He didn't necessarily force it upon her, but he certainly swayed her opinion. What if something happened to her? Would it be his fault? Of course it would be. But what if he had decided to stay, and the base became overrun?

"Can you hand me a bag of chips, sis?" Thomas asked. He knew he couldn't clutter his mind with paradoxes.

"Sure."

Mindy grabbed a bag of pretzels, opened them, and stole one before handing the bag to Thomas. Her brother chuckled at her before shoving a handful in his mouth. The two of them had always been close. Most siblings fight all the time, especially when they're younger. But not Thomas and Mindy. Thomas vaguely remembered learning about his mother's pregnancy. Even at five years old, he had been eager to help her pick out decorations and arrange the baby's room. He clearly remembered the arrival of his little sister. They had been inseparable since her birth. Their classmates always commented on their closeness, how it was "weird" because siblings were supposed to hate each other. Thomas and Mindy went to the movies together, ate out together, and watched movies at home together. Neither one felt the contempt that was so common among other siblings.

After a couple of hours had passed, the pair turned off onto I-82, now heading directly southbound. Thus far they had seen few vehicles on the side of the road, and even fewer roaming zombies. Mindy was keeping count, and they had only passed six since the Seattle city limits. Thomas was reassured by this, and thought that maybe...just maybe...things would continue to get better the further South they went. But he also realized that they were in a very rural area now, with a much lower population density. Things might be just as bad as Seattle in high population areas. With any luck, those places would also be as "lucky" as Seattle and have established safe zones.

After about another hour they were passing the Richland exit, a city that had about 48,000 people. Off in the distance, well off from the highway, Thomas saw smoke rising. He had no intentions of getting off the highway, and as they passed by the city on I-82 he was even more glad he didn't have business in Richland. To the left of the interstate was a large suburban area, and it was literally crawling with undead. From the interstate, Thomas and Mindy looked on at the massive hordes of zombies roaming the streets. Thomas found himself unconsciously letting off the gas, but

26

quickly sped up as soon as he realized it. Richland was now a wasteland, or so it appeared. Of course, parts of Seattle probably looked that way, too.

"I think we should top off the car's tank and the gas can when we get a chance. The interstate looks safe enough," Thomas suggested once Richland was in the distance behind them.

"Sounds like a good idea to me," Mindy said.

"I want you to stay in the car while I siphon the gas and look through the vehicle for anything useful. Crack the window and yell if you see anything coming, even if it's another car. I'll stop what I'm doing and hurry back." Thomas was beginning to feel more comfortable with their situation. He had made the dreadful drive from Seattle to Albuquerque a couple times before, and it took about 21 hours or so. However, he didn't plan to drive straight through. Something about flying down the highway at night with dead people walking around aimlessly didn't sound like a good idea to him.

Kennewick was right next to Richland, but sat a little further off the highway. But it seemed to have fallen victim to the same fate as Richland. Smoke rolled up from several areas of the city, although the town sat too far off the highway for Thomas to see any dead walking around. In just a few minutes Kennewick was completely out of sight, although plumes of smoke could still be seen in the rear-view mirror.

About ten minutes later, the siblings came upon an old Ford truck—probably used on a farm—sitting on the side of the interstate. Thomas pulled over, scanned 360° around the Durango, and got out. In his left hand he held a tire iron, in his right was the 9mm Beretta. After approaching the truck and seeing no one inside, and looking around him once more, Thomas put the Beretta in his waistband and slipped the tire iron through one of his belt loops. He looked back at Mindy, who was vigilantly looking around the Durango in all directions and turning her gaze toward Thomas every couple of seconds.

Thomas went back to the Durango and retrieved the gas can that was missing about half its fuel. He decided to siphon gas first, since it was the most important. After slipping the hose into the truck's gas tank, he began sucking on the other end to create the vacuum necessary for the siphoning process to work. Once the taste of the god-awful gasoline entered his mouth, he quickly pinched the hose and stuck it in the gas can. When it was full, he stopped the siphoning process by pulling on the end of the hose that was in the truck's gas tank. He then brought the can over to the Durango and poured the gas through a funnel into the SUV's tank until it was full. Then he went back to the truck and started the siphoning process once more. He was only able to fill the can about halfway, but the act had certainly been worth it. The Durango's gas tank was now completely full, and he had about twenty-five gallons of fuel on hand, more than enough to completely refuel the Durango.

After storing the gas can in the cargo area of the Durango, he proceeded to search the old truck's cab for anything useful. Inside he found an old tool bag, which he decided was worth the space it would take up. He also found some gun enthusiast magazines, which might prove informative when he had some time to read them. Underneath the seat was a flashlight with working batteries, and they were added to his collection as well.

Thomas loaded the new items into the Durango without incident and took off down the road. Mindy breathed a sigh of relief once they were moving again, and so did Thomas. Even though they had been in a wide open area with no zombies in sight, the fact that he had been out on his own was unnerving. Perhaps he would get used to it.

* * *

They had left Seattle almost four hours ago and were now coming up on the Columbia River, also the Oregon state line. Less than a mile on the other side was Umatilla, Oregon, a small town of less than 7,000 people. Even the size of the town didn't reflect how many people inhabited it, encompassing less than five square miles. It was so small that if you blinked while driving down I-82, you would surely miss it. Thomas had never stopped in Umatilla, except maybe once to get gas on the ride back from Albuquerque (surely the only gas station in town). It was a pleasant little town, with seemingly friendly people. Now it appeared that times had changed.

The impact of the plague was immediately apparent in Umatilla. While there were no plumes of smoke rolling out of the town like in the previous two cities, the town's demise showed in a different way. Many of the dead were walking around in identical clothing: dark blue coats or long-sleeve shirts and pants, and light blue undershirts.

"What the hell?" Mindy sat up straighter and looked out Thomas's window.

"Prisoners. Umatilla has a prison. That's not a good sign, if everything has gone to shit so bad that the prisoners are out walking around. At least they're dead...I think." Thomas looked at the huge number of identically-dressed zombies scattered across the landscape. Some of them had made it up on the highway, and Thomas swerved around them quickly to avoid hitting them (or them throwing themselves at the SUV). Scattered amongst the prisoners were what looked like average townspeople, as well as some prison guards. Some of the guards were dressed in normal uniforms, while others were dressed in riot gear. All were presumably fighting for the same team, now.

In only a minute, Thomas and Mindy were away from the town proper and the number of dead was decreasing. The realization of Umatilla falling completely into the hands of the dead was unsettling. One could only imagine that most smaller towns like Umatilla had met a similar fate by now, although the fact that there was a prison in Umatilla might have had something to do with its apparently complete downfall. Thomas couldn't imagine how anyone could be left living in such a small town with so many dead roaming around, and if there *were* survivors, there couldn't be many.

A few minutes later, Interstate 82 ended and Thomas turned East onto Interstate 84. It was about 5pm now, and Thomas was beginning to wonder what they would do for the night. Obviously he had already decided that traveling at night was out of the question. It just seemed insane to him. With his luck he would come around a curve and mow down a horde of zombies, leaving him and his sister vulnerable in the middle of the night without a vehicle. And to be perfectly honest, he really liked the Durango.

"Think we should pull off onto a small road and sleep in the Durango for the night?" Thomas asked his sister after they had been driving down I-84 for a few minutes. He had expressed his concerns to her earlier about driving at night.

"I'm not really sure. If you think that's best."

Mindy routinely followed her brother's lead. Most of the time it was good, because Thomas largely got to do whatever he wanted. But now it seemed like he wanted her to be a bit more opinionated. He wanted to make a decision *together*, so it didn't feel like the weight was solely on his shoulders.

"Pendleton is the next decent-sized city, and it's less than 20 minutes away. It has a prison, too. No stops there under any circumstances." He looked down at the gas gauge, which was barely below full. They had only been driving about forty-five minutes since he topped it off.

"I don't think I want to stop in any big city. And after seeing Umatilla, I'm not so sure about smaller towns, either," Mindy said.

"Agreed. La Grande is about forty-five minutes from Pendleton, and it's slightly smaller. What's after La Grande?" Thomas glanced over at Mindy, who was pulling the map out of the glove box.

"Umm...Baker City," Mindy said.

"That's right. It's been awhile since I made this trip."

Thomas briefly thought about how long it had been since he had seen his parents. Neither him nor Mindy had seen them since Christmas last year, just before everything went to hell. Thomas and Mindy had both moved to Seattle together four years ago, although they hadn't lived together until just after the first reports of the plague. Both of them had spoken to their parents off and on until about four months ago when the phone lines went down. At least they had lasted longer than cell phones, which proved useless after barely a week.

"I'm guessing that the sun will be going down not too awful long after we get into Idaho. I'd like to find somewhere off the beaten path to crash for the night. Or, even better, a building that's off the beaten path and has an easily accessible rooftop. I picked up a tent and sleeping bags for us." Thomas felt a little proud of himself for thinking ahead. It wasn't a great feat, but he had never done anything remotely close to this before. He wasn't doing too bad, in his humble opinion.

The siblings drove through Pendleton, and La Grande, and Baker City, and Ontario and Fruitland, which both sat on the Idaho state line (Ontario was in Oregon, Fruitland was in Idaho). All of them looked decimated. Caldwell, Idaho, was the next large town, with about 46,000 people, followed by Boise, which had over 200,000. Caldwell and Boise were basically merged together. Thomas sped through them as quickly as possible, as the dead were literally everywhere. He saw only one indication of survivors in Boise: a giant flag made out of a bed sheet or something, erected on top of a building, and the word "HELP" had been painted in big red letters. But who knew how long that had been there? He briefly thought about the survivors that may still be alive inside, how much food they had, how much water, how many of them there were. If they were a collection of families with children, or maybe elderly people. And if they had long since died, were they now roaming aimlessly in search of human flesh, or had they been consumed and were saved that horrible fate? He shook the thoughts from his mind as he felt tears forming in his eyes, and did his best to stay focused.

They traveled south of Boise about 20 minutes, just before reaching Mountain Home, Idaho. The Durango was sitting on about a quarter tank of fuel, and the sun's light was fading. Along the way, Thomas had been looking for a suitable spot to sleep for the night. About three-fourths of the way to Mountain Home from Boise, the pair came upon a strange-looking community of houses out in the country. From the interstate, Thomas could see bunch of roads and quite a few houses. The area was obviously very rural, and it wasn't a town of any sort.

Thomas pulled over on the highway and completely refilled the Durango's gas tank. He now had about half a can of gas left. With the sun's fading light, Thomas was able to see the occasional zombie roaming around between the closest group of houses and the highway. Several of the houses had lights on.

"Think we should take our chances over there?" Thomas asked his sister as he gazed over at the houses.

"I'm not sure. At the beginning of this trip we were talking about how crazy people might be," Mindy replied.

"Yeah, but these people look like they're doing alright. I mean, some of them have power. They obviously aren't hurting too bad. Maybe one of them would take us in for the night? Or at least let us park our car in a garage or shed and sleep in it? Anything to get us out of the open."

Thomas pulled the Durango back onto the interstate. There was no exit or road connected to the highway that led to the community, but Thomas saw a road going underneath the interstate ahead a little ways. Once he got there, he put the Durango into 4-wheel drive and went down the gradual slope to a paved road named "Ditto Creek Rd". He drove up around the curve, turned left onto "Faulkner Ave", and pulled into the driveway of the first house that had lights on. The home had a two-car garage, as well as a large detached garage next to it, and it looked like the perfect place to pull the Durango in for the night. Assuming the garage wasn't already full, and assuming the people were nice enough to let them.

Thomas stashed the Beretta in his waistband and covered it with his shirt. He certainly didn't mean these people any harm, but he wanted to be as safe as possible.

The sun had set, and the only remaining light was the dim, gray color that the last of the sun's rays bathe everything in just before total darkness. Thomas approached the door, breathed a heavy sigh, and knocked softly three times. Mindy was waiting in the Durango.

Thomas saw the curtains move, followed by some muffled talking on the other side of the door. Pretty soon the front door flew open wildly, and a big, burly man in his fifties wearing overalls and a straw hat was pointing a shotgun in Thomas's face.

"Whoa!" Thomas said as he threw his hands up and stumbled backwards.

"What the hell do you want?" the man asked, although his voice was surprisingly calm.

"Please, sir...the gun...I don't mean you any harm...please..." Thomas stuttered.

The man peered out the front door, past Thomas. He then lowered the shotgun, but still kept it gripped firmly in his hands.

"I don't mean to frighten you," Thomas began, "But my sister and I are traveling south from Seattle. I would really like to get out of the open for the night, even if I could just pull my car into a shed or something and sleep there. I understand if you..."

"You came from where?" the man interrupted.

The man in front of Thomas was probably just over six feet tall. He had a burly build, a pot belly, a long gray beard, and straw hat on top his head.

"Seattle, sir. Seattle, Washington." Thomas tried to swallow the knot in his throat, and noticed that his hands were still half raised. He slowly lowered them, but his eyes were still peeled wide.

"Just your sister in the car, there?" the man asked.

"Yessir."

The old man squinted as if he was thinking, then a woman's voice came from behind him. Thomas couldn't understand her, but she sounded friendly enough.

"Alright. Go get your sister and come on inside. Quickly, now. Don't want the dead to get interested." The man closed the door until it was only open a crack.

As Thomas walked down the sidewalk from the house to the driveway, he saw a woman looking out through the curtains. Thomas's legs felt a little weak, and he was still shaking. That man could have easily shot him dead, and who would've stopped him?

There was no law now, no one to deal out punishment.

"Alright sis, let's grab our bags. They want us to come inside," Thomas said as soon as he opened the car door.

Thomas looked around as Mindy grabbed their things, then made sure the Durango was locked before following her up to the door.

"Keep quiet, please. This guy almost blew my head off..."

"And we're going inside!?" Mindy said, a little too loudly.

"Shh! I think he was just being cautious. Come on."

Even though the door was cracked still, Thomas gave it a gentle knock. The man's rough voice bellowed from the other side with a simple, *Come in!*

Thomas and Mindy stepped inside the house, and Thomas made sure to close and lock the door behind them. The older man was standing in the doorway to the kitchen, shotgun still in hand. The woman—presumably his wife—appeared to be tidying up the kitchen.

"You got a gun?" the man asked.

"Yes I do. You're more than welcome to hang onto it for the night. I completely understand." Thomas lifted his shirt and revealed the Beretta stuck in his waistband.

"Sit it on the table, there," the man said calmly.

Thomas gently grabbed the handgun by the end of its grip and sat it on an end table, then stepped away from it.

"So what are your names?" the man asked.

"I'm Thomas. This is my sister, Mindy."

"Thank you so much for taking us in," Mindy said, "I understand how uncomfortable it must be to take in strangers, especially in these times."

The man walked over to the table and grabbed the handgun. He disappeared around the corner, and Thomas could hear what sounded like a small cabinet door or a drawer open and shut. When the man came back, he leaned his shotgun up against the wall next to the fridge.

"I'm Mark," the man said.

"And I'm Virginia, his wife," the woman said from the kitchen as she poked her head around the doorway. She had a very pleasant, friendly face, and her tone of voice was welcoming.

"Nice to meet you both," Thomas said.

"Alright, so here's how I reckon we ought to do this," Mark began, "I don't have any problem with you all staying the night inside the house, but I don't know you. We haven't had supper yet, so let's sit down and eat. If I still think you're alright folks, I'll let you stay inside. If I don't like ya', you'll be in the garage. And if I really don't like ya', neither of those things are gonna happen."

"That sounds more than fair to us, sir, but you all don't need to feed us. We have our own food. Wouldn't want to take anything from you." Thomas relaxed a little after he saw that Mark was a completely reasonable man.

"Oh, nonsense!" Virginia said as she walked into the living room. She was a smaller-framed woman, probably in her fifties as well. She worse a dress with an apron, and her silver hair was up in a bun, "You're guests, and our guests eat!"

"Well we appreciate it greatly, ma'am," Thomas said, trying to have the best manners possible. He knew how much country folk valued manners, especially the older ones.

Mark and Thomas sat quietly in the living room while Virginia finished cooking supper. Mindy tried to help her, but the older woman insisted she relax instead. Mindy stayed in the kitchen and kept her company anyway.

When supper was finished, Virginia and Mindy brought the food into the adjoining dining room while Mark and Thomas laid out plates and silverware. Before getting any food, Mark and Virginia bowed their heads while Virginia said a prayer. Mindy didn't have a problem with it, because she was religious. Thomas always found such things to be a waste of time, but he slightly bowed his head anyway out of respect.

Supper was beef stew, mashed potatoes and gravy, and green beans. It was absolutely wonderful. One thing about country folk...they knew how to preserve food and cook. About halfway through the meal, Thomas decided to express his gratitude.

"We really appreciate this. This supper is the best we've had in months. Tastes better than anything I've ever had before."

"That's probably 'cause you ain't never had this before," Mark said as he continued eating.

"It's beef stew, right?" Thomas asked as he shoveled a spoonful into his mouth.

Without missing a beat and with a completely serious face, Mark said, "You're eatin' a person."

Thomas almost choked. He spit out his food on the floor and started coughing uncontrollably.

"Oh Mark, stop it! It ain't no person!" Virginia said as she slapped her husband on the arm with a cloth.

Thomas covered his mouth and stared at Mark, who finally chuckled wryly. Thomas breathed a sigh of relief—as did Mindy—before laughing.

"Glad to see you still have a good sense of humor in times like these," Thomas said. Then, just to clarify, "It's not a person right?"

"Of course it isn't! Mark's just ornery!" Virginia said as she frowned at her mischievous husband, who was still grinning slightly.

"I could just beat you with a whip sometimes," she added.

The siblings looked at each other and smiled, somehow feeling a bit more at ease after the incident.

"Let that be a lesson to ya'. Food might not come so easy in parts of the country, with everything going on. You better believe that some people will eat each other, and I don't mean the dead things walking around outside." Mark was serious this time.

It made sense. Thomas just hadn't considered that anyone other than the walking dead might eat their fellow man.

"So how many others are there?" Thomas asked once everyone had finished their dinner.

"Four other families," Mark answered.

Thomas had seen a lot of houses on his way in. Only *four other families*?

"What happened to everyone else?" he asked.

"Got eaten. Or moved away. Everyone seems to think it's not

36

as bad elsewhere. Guess they just tell themselves that so they have *some* amount of hope to cling onto." The older man wiped his mouth off with a napkin.

"We're headed to New Mexico. Albuquerque, actually. That's where our parents are. Hopefully it's not that bad down there. Seattle was horrible." Thomas leaned back a bit in his chair and stretched out his full belly.

"Don't got no idea how bad it is that far south," Mark said, "How bad was Seattle?"

"Pretty bad. We were lucky enough to receive aid from the National Guard. They established safe zones in the city to keep the dead out."

"Heard all the towns around us were pretty bad, too," Mark said.

"They are. At least, the towns we went through were. We crossed over the state line at Ontario and Fruitland. Both of those places are gone, from what we could tell. Caldwell and Boise, too." Thomas looked down at the table after putting it all into perspective.

"Best we just stay put," Mark said.

"I honestly don't know what the best thing to do is," Thomas said, "Everywhere we've been so far is just...dead."

"Are ya'll full enough?" Virginia asked abruptly, changing the topic. Her face now conveyed a sense of uneasiness and despair, instead of friendliness and hospitality.

"Oh yes, thank you ma'am," Thomas said.

"Definitely, thanks," said Mindy.

"It was wonderful. We greatly appreciate your kindness," Thomas added.

Virginia retained the sad look on her face as she began picking the plates up off the table. Mindy helped her. Thomas walked into the adjoining living room and sat down on the couch, across from Mark and his rocking chair.

"Just don't know what to do," Mark said, almost to himself.

Thomas didn't say anything.

"I don't want to leave my home, put my wife in any danger,"

he continued, "But stayin' here might be just as dangerous. So far, the dead have—for the most part—stayed a good distance away. The neighbors who got eaten were the ones who tried to go out and scavenge, or take a look at what was going on elsewhere."

"How much food do you all have stockpiled?" Thomas asked.

"Not much, son, not much. Got some corn bagged up in the shed yet, and one more sack of potatoes in the cellar. Got a couple shelves full of canned goods, so I guess that's good. Chickens out back provide us with plenty of eggs, and we've got several dozen stored away, though I'm havin' some trouble findin' feed for 'em. There's some cows in a field down the road."

"That doesn't sound too bad," Thomas said before leaning forward, "Ya know Mark, I saw a few dead scattered around between your house and the highway. I'm not sure why they haven't taken an interest in this area yet...maybe it's just luck...but before long the dead are going to start moving out of the cities."

"I figured as much. Killed one the other day, over by the well. Shot 'em with my .308. Apparently those things take an interest in noise, because I saw a whole bunch of 'em comin' over the hill when I was gettin' back in my truck." Mark continued rocking slowly in his chair, staring down at the floor.

"How far away is the well?" Thomas asked.

"Ol' Ran'l had a well on his property, about a mile or two down the road. That's where we've been gettin' our water."

"Maybe it's time to leave, Mark. I know you don't want to leave behind the comfort of your home, but..." Thomas stopped and chose his words carefully. He didn't know Mark, although he seemed like a good enough guy, "I don't know everything about what's going on. To be honest, all I know is what I've seen between Seattle and here. But it's bad, Mark. Real bad. I'm an architect, and I helped the National Guard fortify their safe zones. I heard a lot of their reports, and the northern states are the worst. Down South has it bad, too, but not nearly as bad as up here. We might have a chance if we go far enough south. Perhaps it's something you and your wife should talk about."

"Maybe you're right."

The rest of the night was full of quiet conversation. Thomas and Mark conversed, but it was mainly Mark telling hunting stories and Thomas listening, or Mark telling funny stories from years ago. Virginia and Mindy sat together on the couch and talked about "girly" things. Virginia showed her some of her quilts she made, and even gave one of them to Mindy. Mark and Virginia were great people. Virginia was a very pleasant woman who never liked to talk about the bad, and Mark was a generous man and a little rough around the edges. Thomas liked both of them a great deal, and after some thought, he decided to ask them a big question.

"Mark," Thomas said after Mindy and Virginia had left the room, "I want to ask you something, and you don't have to answer me right away. How would you feel about maybe heading south with Mindy and I?"

"I'm glad you asked, son. It sounds like a good idea to me. Have to run it past the ol' lady, of course. But how long are ya'll willing to wait? It'd probably take us a couple days to get everything together, and I know you kids want to get on down the road and see your folks."

Thomas thought about it for a second, and considered what him and Mindy had discussed at the beginning of the trip about helping strangers.

"We can wait. You all are good people, and you've been so generous to us by not only letting us stay here for the night, but feeding us a great supper. And you two have some great skills. Virginia is an amazing cook and can sow, among other things. By listening to your stories, I've gathered you're a pretty good hunter and know a lot about mechanics, farming, all that country stuff. I'd be honored if you all went with us." Thomas smiled at the end, to let Mark know his words were true.

"Alright. I'm gonna turn in for the night. Virginia and I will discuss it in bed, and will hopefully have an answer for ya' in the mornin'. You kids get some sleep, too. Feel free to lay your head wherever ya' like. On the couch, floor, guest bedroom, wherever."

Mark slowly stood, stretched a little, then headed off down the hallway. When Mindy and Virginia came back, Virginia said goodnight and Mindy sat down on the couch next to Thomas.

"She's such a lovely lady," Mindy said.

"Yes she is. They both are, really. I asked Mark if they wanted to go with us." Thomas wasn't sure how Mindy would react.

Mindy pursed her lips, something she had done ever since she was little when she was thinking about something.

"I like that idea," she said after a few seconds.

"Mark is a tough guy, he's good with a gun—from listening to his stories—and he has a lot of knowledge about rugged survival. How to fix things, how to grow food, stuff like that. Virginia is obviously a good cook, seems like a strong woman, can sow, and is very pleasant to be around. I think they'll make a great addition. And if we find somewhere safe along the way, we can drop them off before we get all the way to Albuquerque."

"Sounds good to me," Mindy said.

The siblings slept in the guest bedroom that night. The bed was all made and nice-looking, as if it hadn't been used in years. It was fairly comfortable, too. The two slept very soundly, without all the dead moans and snarls they had grown so accustomed to.

3

The following morning, Thomas and Mindy got up early as soon as they were woken up by the sounds of Mark and Virginia moving throughout the house. They got dressed, ate a good breakfast of farm fresh eggs and friend potatoes, and then were told that Mark and Virginia had decided on going with them. Both Thomas and Mindy smiled, happy that they wouldn't be alone in the journey.

Thomas helped Mark load up his old truck, and Mindy helped Virginia pack bags and food. Overall it was a pleasant day, and they only saw the occasional zombie roaming between Mark's house and the interstate.

Mark's truck was a 1999 Chevrolet 1500, and had a camper shell on the bed. That was quite convenient, because they didn't have to worry about strapping things down or covering them to avoid them getting wet. Virginia was an excellent organizer, and Mindy was awed by her ability to gather things up and consolidate them in an efficient manner. Both Thomas and Mindy were organized people—especially Thomas because of his mild Obsessive Compulsive Disorder—but Virginia was certainly one of the most tidy people either of them had ever met.

"You're sure this is what you want to do?" Thomas asked as he helped Mark load some boxes into the back of the truck.

"I'm sure. It's true, we've got a fairly good supply of food and water here, but for how long? How long's it gonna be before them dead things mosey on through here and break into the house, or catch me while I'm out gettin' food? We don't really have any neighbors nearby, and I don't really like any of the ones we do. The only family we were close with moved away." Mark looked a little sad as he loaded up the truck.

"Our last name's Briggs, by the way," Thomas said, kind of out of the blue.

"Ours is Johnson," Mark said.

Nearly everything was ready to go by that afternoon, and the group had a late lunch of vegetable soup to fill their bellies. Thomas and Mindy rearranged some of the stuff in the back of the Durango to make room for some of the Johnson's items. They certainly weren't taking any useless things—they just had more useful stuff to take with them. Tools, canned food, firearms—Mark took two hunting rifles, two shotguns, four handguns, and plenty of ammo for all of them—and various bags of miscellaneous items that the group figured they might find a use for in the future.

After getting everything loaded up, the small group sat around and made small talk. Occasionally one of the Johnsons would think of something they needed to take with them, or one more thing they wanted to do before leaving the next day. Virginia went through every cabinet and drawer in her kitchen while preparing supper, mostly just looking at the things she had collected over the many years they had been in the house. Mark spent some time in the shed, recalling all of the vehicles he had worked on, all of the things he had built. Mindy spent a good chunk of her time reading a book she had found in Virginia's collection. Thomas mostly sat on the couch and thought about random things, as he usually did. At one point he pulled out his map and refreshed his memory about the best route to take. Albuquerque was still a very, very long way.

That night, after supper, the group sat together in the living room and discussed their trip. Virginia stayed relatively quiet, and Mindy spoke up only a couple of times. It was mostly Mark and Thomas doing the talking.

"You think it's a good idea to go through Salt Lake City?" Mark asked.

"I really don't know. From what I've heard, the further south you go, the better it gets," Thomas said.

"Sure are a lot of people in Salt Lake." Mark rubbed his hands together and stared at the floor.

"Yes there are, but I'd like to stay on the highway as much as possible because of fuel consumption. We can play it by ear, and if it still looks bad as we get closer, we'll change our route and go around it. Sound good?" Thomas asked. Mark nodded his head.

"How long is this going to take?" Virginia asked, her only question thus far.

"About another day and a half, probably. Under normal circumstances, we could make it there by driving all day tomorrow. But we don't exactly have gas stations and diners to stop at along the way, and driving after dusk is far from advisable." Thomas leaned back and relaxed on the couch a little.

"Sure hope there aren't many dead out there," Mark said.

"I hope so, too. So far it hasn't looked promising. The last reliable report I heard about the situation around the nation was about a week ago. The news was still on in Seattle, but those reports aren't exactly credible."

"Hate to bring up somethin' like this," Mark began, "But what do we do if we get to Albuquerque and it's overrun?"

Thomas and Mindy looked at each other for a moment. Thomas let out a long sigh.

"So you plan to go all the way with us?" Thomas asked.

"Might as well, I reckon. Unless we find some kinda' paradise between here and there," Mark said.

"I honestly don't know for sure what we'll do if that's the case. There have *got* to be survivor groups scattered about all over the place. I suppose we find one and settle in."

Mark didn't sleep well that night. Thomas kept waking up to the floor creaking under Mark's footsteps, the older man repeatedly going to the kitchen or the bathroom. The last time Thomas was awakened by Mark was 3:30am. He didn't wake up again.

* * *

The group was up and getting dressed at about 6:30am the next day. Except for Virginia, who was already dressed and had breakfast halfway ready when Thomas woke up. He woke up his sister, and about that time Mark came walking down the hallway. He was fully dressed in his overalls, long-sleeve shirt, boots, and straw hat.

"Forgot to give this back to ya'," Mark said as he walked over to Thomas and handed him his Beretta.

"Oh, thank you. Honestly, I had forgotten about it, too."

Perhaps if Thomas had been more used to firearms it wouldn't have slipped his mind. If he had been a soldier, or a police officer, he surely would've been constantly remembering that the old man had taken possession of his weapon.

"Is that the only one you have?" Mark asked.

"No. We've got a .40 caliber semi-automatic in the Durango, as well as another semi-auto, a snub-nose revolver, and a full-size revolver. I don't remember what those are."

"How much ammo?"

Thomas had to think for a moment before answering.

"Got an extra magazine for the .40, and two extra mags for the 9mm and a box of ammo. Think there's 50 rounds in the box. I don't know anything about the other guns, but one of the Guardsmen back in Seattle went through all of the ammo I scavenged and left me with the appropriate kind," he said.

"Well, at least you got *some,* I guess," Mark said, "Ammunition goes quick."

"Have you ever..." Thomas hesitated, "Have you ever been in...well...combat, I guess?" Thomas asked him.

"Nope. You?" Mark replied.

"Never even fired a gun," Thomas told him.

"Uh oh. Well, I guess we all have our roles. Just wish we were more prepared."

Mark sat down at the kitchen table, and Thomas and Mindy joined him. Virginia brought over the large plate of scrambled eggs and toast, and the group dug in after saying grace. They ate every last piece of food that had been prepared, well aware that this could possibly be the last hot meal they would have for some time. Mark had packed a camp stove, but who knew when they would have an opportunity to use it? Everyone was well aware that the journey might take a lot longer than a day and a half, depending on what they ran into. Especially if they had to take a detour *and* ran into problems. With any luck, everything would go smoothly and Salt Lake City wouldn't be that bad. There would surely be dead there, but hopefully nothing like Seattle or any of the previous towns Thomas and Mindy had been through thus far.

After everyone had finished and taken about a twenty minute break to let their meals settle, they loaded up and left the house behind. Thomas took the lead, and pulled over at a house down the road that Mark had said was abandoned. The home had a large shop and a large gasoline tank behind it. After breaking the lock on the gas tank with a pair of Mark's bolt cutters, Thomas proceeded to top off the tanks on the Durango and Chevy, and fill up the three gas cans he had. He also filled up the five ten gallon gas cans that Mark had brought along.

They finally got on the highway at about 7:40am, which wasn't too bad of a start. Mark had a couple battery-powered walkie talkies lying around, and he had smartly thought to bring them along so the pair of vehicles would have a link to one another. Each walkie took four AAA batteries, and fortunately Mark and Virginia had a stockpile of batteries in their house. The group had unanimously voted to bring along every single battery the Johnsons had, including two car batteries Mark had out in the garage (just in case). They had enough AAA batteries to replace both walkie talkies two times. Luckily, the walkies were fairly new and had a power save feature. They should easily make it to Albuquerque.

Mountain Home was only a few miles away from the Johnson residence. The population was only just over 14,000, and as the group got closer the town's small number of inhabitants became more apparent. They had only seen two zombies between the Johnson residence and Mountain Home city limits. As they passed through the small town, they saw several small groups of zombies scattered about. Only a few had been in the road.

"Sure does look pretty bad," Mark said over the radio.

"Oh, this is nothin'," Thomas replied, "You should've seen the larger cities. This looks like paradise."

* * *

A little less than an hour later, the two pairs of survivors were entering Jerome, Idaho. This town was even smaller than Mountain Home, with just 7,000 inhabitants. However, the tiny town of Jerome and the larger city of Twin Falls with over 44,000 people were basically one in the same. They were mostly separated by the river, but for all practical purposes they were two cities in one.

The walking dead were literally everywhere. The two vehicles were constantly forced to weave in and out of abandoned vehicles, occasionally speeding up to avoid zombies in the roadway. At one point a zombie even slapped both hands against the Durango, attempting to grab on and somehow get to the food inside. Both Thomas and Mindy jumped in surprise, and Thomas instinctively mashed his foot against the accelerator to get away. He constantly checked his rear-view mirror to keep an eye on Mark and Virginia. Mark was keeping no more than two car-lengths from Thomas's Durango.

After getting out of Twin Falls without further incident, the team sped up to make up time. Technically, they had never gone through Twin Falls. The highway passed just north of the city. However, the populations of Twin Falls and Jerome had mixed together to form one city of the dead. Apparently the dead residents of Twin Falls had found their way over the bridge and onto the highway.

The journey through Twin Falls/Jerome had taken almost a

whole hour, due to the slow pace and numerous obstacles they had to get around. Thomas and Mark drove side by side down the highway, unless they came upon the occasional abandoned vehicle parked in the middle of the road. They quickly made their way through the small town of Burley, which was also completely dead. Driving down a highway certainly had its advantages; it was almost always above the towns and cities they were driving through, lifted up above the local roads. But Thomas had a fear that they would not always be so lucky.

The area between Burley and the Utah state line was exclusively rural, with no cities or even towns between them. There were very few vehicles on the road, and the group took comfort in the solitude. But about ten miles from the state line, Thomas began cursing at what was ahead of them.

Right in the middle of the median, covering both lanes going both North and South, was a crashed airplane. Not a small, private airplane. No, of course not. This was a huge Boeing 747. Debris covered the entire highway. A gigantic rut ran east to west, showing the path of the crash landing leading up to the interstate.

"Shit!" Thomas cursed. He stopped the Durango just short of the crashed jet, and briefly scanned their surroundings before getting out.

Mark met him halfway between the vehicles.

"Well?" the older man asked.

"I guess go off-road, go around..." Thomas said.

"Wouldn't recommend it. That crash probably left debris a mile West. And going East around it obviously isn't an option. Its path runs for almost a mile that way. I just don't feel safe going off-road around it and possibly blowing a tire."

Mark had a good point.

"Well what about taking a back road? I saw one a couple miles back. I just don't know if it goes across the state line." Thomas ran his fingers through his hair, his nerves starting to take the best of him.

"Got a map?" Mark asked.

"Yeah, but it's useless right now. It's a nation-wide map. Doesn't show back roads." Thomas slowly paced back and forth.

"Well, I guess go back and take the road. Head south."

"Thomas," Mindy said as she got out of the Durango, map in hand, "There's a highway just south of the state line. Highway 30. It runs east to west, and connects with I-84."

"There we go. We just head South until we hit the highway. Might have to go off-road a time or two, but it'll sure beat doing it here. I just don't feel comfortable going off-road anywhere around that thing." Mark pointed to the aircraft.

Thomas walked over to Mindy and took the map from her. He placed it on the hood of the Durango, double-checking before they took off.

Mark leaned up against his truck and crossed his arms, taking the opportunity to relax and take in the country air. The wreck was a sad sight. The airplane was in a million pieces, with the nose of it surprisingly being the only thing still partially intact. Who knew how many people had died? People...dead...what if...?

"Thomas! We need to go!" Mark abruptly shouted.

"What?" Thomas asked, startled. He quickly looked around him and saw nothing.

"Go! We need to get away from here!" Mark shouted once more.

"What's wrong, Mark? There's nothing around us?"

Whether it was coincidence or Mark's loud voice alerting them, several mangled bodies began moving amongst the debris. Most were torn to pieces so bad that they could barely move. Some were mostly intact but missing limbs. Two sat up in the ditch right next to the group of survivors, as if on cue.

The bodies were horribly deformed. Some of them were surprisingly intact, but most were terribly gruesome. Burned faces and bodies, limbs dangling, large gashes across their faces and torsos. One's jaw was barely attached to its head. Another was so twisted that its lower half was turned around nearly backwards. If it had been in a movie, it would've been a comical scene. Somehow, the zombie still had partial control of its legs. While its one remaining arm was extended out and its teeth were mashing, it was actually stumbling backwards away from its prey. It only made it a few steps before falling down.

Almost instantly, fifteen to twenty zombies had materialized from the wreckage. Some were in the wreckage that spanned across the interstate, others were in the ditches and fields, obviously hurled away from the airplane during the crash. In actuality, they had probably been hurled long before the airplane came to rest on the highway, their bodies flung great distances through the air before coming to rest.

Thomas, Mindy and Mark almost fell down as they scrambled to get in their vehicles. The closest zombies were the two that had been in the ditch directly to the right of the road, one only about ten feet away now. The other was just now crawling out of the ditch, its lower half nonexistent.

Tires squealed as both vehicles were thrown into reverse and the accelerators were hammered. Thomas nearly ran into Mark's truck as they turned around about twenty feet down the road. Once they were turned around and driving back the way they came, Thomas slowed after realizing he was doing 105mph. Mark was in the distance behind him. Thomas pulled the Durango over, and within a few seconds Mark pulled up beside him and rolled down the window.

"Holy shit..." Thomas managed to spit out, still breathing heavily.

"I didn't see one until after I told you we needed to get out of there. I just put two and two together. Airplane crash, lots of dead people..." Mark was breathing heavily as well, although not as bad as Thomas.

Virginia had her hands clasped together against her chest. Mindy brushed her hair out of her face and let out a quick exhalation of air. Thomas touched his forehead against the steering wheel and let out a sigh.

"Alright, I think we passed the exit that takes us to that back road," he finally said.

"I'd say so, son. You left me in the dust," Mark chuckled.

"Let's get turned around and take the exit. Then we can stop and top off our tanks."

"Sounds good to me."

The group turned around and got off on the paved back road. After a few miles it turned to gravel, and that's when they decided to stop and fill up their tanks.

"That could have ended badly," Mark said while filling up the tanks of their vehicles.

Thomas let out a long sigh, "Yep."

"We need to be more prepared. Make some protocols for different situations." Mark emptied his gas can and put it in the bed of his truck.

"Agreed. We'll work on that tonight when we stop...wherever that will be."

Thomas noticed a couple of humanoid silhouettes walking toward them in the far distance. Their sluggish, uncoordinated movements were obvious. Zombies, presumably from the crashed airplane just a couple miles east of where they currently were. Probably some of the same ones who took notice of them and tried to eat them only moments ago. But the zombies were barely moving, and they were still over a mile and a half away. It would take them hours to reach the small group of shaken survivors.

The group mounted up once more and drove for only five minutes before coming to a fork in the road. They were currently facing almost directly south, and the state line couldn't be more than a few miles away.

"Which way?" Thomas asked over the walkie.

"I guess left," Mark suggested, "It'll take us back toward the interstate. At least then we'll have a sense of where we're at and can use that map of yours."

Mark was naturally more at home on gravel roads than Thomas was. To Thomas, it was a very helpless feeling driving on these unmaintained, unpredictable back roads. They curved all over the place, meeting up with other gravel roads like a maze. It was easy to get turned around. Luckily, they had Mark to give them a sense of direction. And the compass on the Durango's rear-view mirror.

After a few more minutes of driving they came to another intersection, and the interstate was in view again. The group turned south, following the interstate. They gradually got further and further away from the main road, as it glanced off in more of a southeast direction. The gravel road they were currently on was taking them due south. Pretty soon, a small sign nailed to a telephone pole read, *Entering Utah*. Thomas breathed a sigh of relief, though his anxiety was unneeded. All of the data indicated they had been going the right way, and with the interstate in plain view most of the way, they weren't exactly lost.

Before long at all, Highway 30 came into view. It was a welcomed sight. Thomas was ready to get back on a paved road, the open highway, the comfort of familiarity.

"Alright Mark, we're turning left up here. We should hit I-84 again in just a few minutes," he said over the radio, a smile on his face.

After connecting with I-84 and finally getting back on track, Thomas realized that it was already after noon. What should have been a three hour trip had been over four and a half hours. Salt Lake City was only about an hour and a half away, but Thomas decided to stop in the middle of the interstate and have a little pow wow. The spot he had chosen was completely devoid of any signs of human activity, living or dead. No vehicles, no buildings, not even any houses off in the distance. They had just passed a sign that said the city of Tremonton was 12 miles away.

This time, everyone got out of the vehicles to stretch their legs. They all gathered in a little circle between the truck and SUV, everyone scanning their surroundings a bit just to be on the safe side.

"What's goin' on?" Mark asked, though not in an irritated manner.

"I've been thinking...that airplane crash back there?" Thomas started.

"Yeah?" Mark crossed his arms and spit on the pavement. Thomas noticed for the first time that he had a wad of chewing tobacco in his mouth.

"Well, if everything around these parts was decent—if there were any safe, organized groups of survivors—wouldn't someone have gone to the crash and, ya' know, taken care of the dead ones?" Thomas posed a good question.

"Maybe they didn't know it crashed?" Mindy suggested.

"Maybe, but I find that hard to believe. If there was any organized resistance, they'd have the military or at least local law enforcement in charge, and they'd be in touch with NATO and all that, wouldn't they? I mean, if NATO's still around. And you'd think we would be seeing more human activity. Hell, any human activity at all would be nice. The occasional car, perhaps? It's just not very indicative of human life."

Thomas's concerns were valid, but not comforting in the least. It was supposed to be *better* further south, not the same or worse as up North.

"Who knows," Mark finally said, "but where else do we have to go? I mean, shit...everything's gone to hell. If we don't go south, then we go north, and we all know what that's like. If we don't go north *or* south, then we go to the east or west, and why should we believe those directions are any different?"

It seemed to hit everyone in the group all at once after Mark spoke: The overwhelming weight of absolute fear and helplessness. It really seemed like the incident had crossed over the point of no return. Who was left to correct the situation? From what they had seen, there were far more dead than living. Hell, as far as they had seen, *they* were the only ones alive between Mountain House, Idaho, and Tremonton, Utah. Of course that couldn't be true—there had to be patches of survivors here and there—but the fact that there had been no *obvious signs* of human life was very disturbing.

"I guess we stick to the plan, then," Thomas said after several moments of silence, "We continue on south. It can't be this bad everywhere, right? I mean, how could it be? It's a plague. It can't just mysteriously manifest itself *everywhere* all at once. And if it's this bad further south, then we'll just keep driving south. All the way to Mexico if we have to, after we find our parents. They shut down the borders, didn't they? Surely the plague hasn't made it that far, if it started in Canada?"

"Unless...," Virginia spoke, one of the few times during their short trip today, "Unless it's the wrath of God."

"I don't mean to offend you, Ma'am, but I'm not religious. I can't accept that." Thomas ran his fingers through his hair, a nervous habit.

"The dead rising up, consuming the earth...sounds like a prophecy foretold, to me," Mark chimed in.

"Alright, so what if it is? It changes nothing." Thomas got a little agitated and stepped away from the circle.

"Well, I guess we should get back on the road, then," Mark said.

They made the short jog to Tremonton, which, as expected, looked like every other town and city they'd been through. Consumed by the dead. From the relative safety of the interstate, the small group could see walking dead everywhere they looked. A few had even stumbled up the on-ramps and were scattered amongst the abandoned vehicles.

Cars...lots of them...

Thomas and Mindy both gasped as they came upon the largest collection of abandoned vehicles they had seen yet. All of them were facing south, out of the city, taking up all lanes on both the southbound and northbound sides of the interstate. It made their hearts sink.

"Uh...Mark, you seeing this?" Thomas asked shakily over the walkie.

"Yep...what now?"

Thomas brought the Durango to a halt, about a hundred yards shy of a small group of zombies stumbling through the blockade of cars.

"This is not good..." Mindy said.

"No, it's not. The interstate isn't an option."

"We can't...we can't go through the city..." Mindy snapped her gaze toward Thomas, who was still staring at the virtual wall before them.

"What else can we do, sis?" he asked her.

"Well?" Mark said.

"Guess we'll have to go through the city," Thomas said, reluctantly.

In hindsight, he should have seen this coming. They had just passed the junction of I-84 and I-15, and the number of abandoned vehicles had been steadily increasing. Now they were at one of the major on-ramps just outside Tremonton, and it appeared that everyone had gotten the bright idea to take refuge in Salt Lake City. The only question was...what had stopped them? Why the major traffic jam? Tremonton only had about 7,500 people. Surely they hadn't all tried to leave at once?

Thomas carefully exited the Durango, against Mindy's pleas, and climbed up on top of the SUV. Above the vehicles in front of him, he saw a horrible sight. An overturned semi...and too many zombie heads to count. It looked like something had caused the semi to wreck, which blocked off all the vehicles in the southbound lanes. People were forced to drive southbound in the northbound lanes, but the semi partially blocked those off, too. It created a choke point, slowing down the survivors' escape. Then something must have gotten them. Car doors were open everywhere, a sign that occupants had decided to flee on foot. But from what? Were the zombies Thomas was seeing the occupants of the vehicles, or were they the reason the occupants freaked out?

"Shit..." he said to himself before jumping down and getting back in the Durango.

"Well? Turn around and get off in Tremonton?" Mindy asked.

"Yeah...guess so..."

Thomas notified Mark of the plan, and they turned around. The Tremonton exit was only a couple of miles back the way they came, just before I-15 and I-84 merged.

For such a small town, Tremonton was now a hotspot for the dead. The group got off the on-ramp and blindly made their way through the town. They were essentially driving based on direction, using the highway as one long landmark. Thomas had never been in Tremonton before. Luckily, a lot of the dead were now on the interstate, and not very many vehicles blocked the roads. It was a tiny town, which possibly made it even harder to navigate. Not many options.

Thomas came upon a tight squeeze. A sedan and full-size truck were blocking the road, almost longways. They had to take the sidewalk to get around them.

"Are you sure we're going to fit?" Mindy asked.

"It'll be close, but we'll fit," Thomas told her, though the confidence in his voice was not exactly very representative of the confidence he felt inside. He did not, however, want to waste more time going back the way they came to find another route.

"I think we'll both fit," Thomas said over the walkie.

He slowly edged the Durango forward, judging the distance he had on both front corners. To his right was a brick building, to his left was a newer model Ford truck. He popped up on the sidewalk, gently navigating the SUV between the two obstacles. As the nose of his vehicle crossed the threshold between the two, he realized he would have about a foot of room on either side. He relaxed a little, and put his foot down on the gas a little more.

Being an architect, Thomas should have seen it coming. After all, he worked with angles all the time. But this time he hadn't compensated for it. He had pulled the Durango between the two obstacles at an odd angle, and while the nose of his SUV cleared them, he still needed to cut the wheels to get all the way through without hitting the building to his right. This was the problem.

About midsection, the side of the Durango gently pumped into the rear bumper of the truck. The Ford's alarm began to sound, its lights flashing with the beat of the horn. Thomas and Mindy both jumped, startled by the loud honking of the truck's horn.

"Jesus...that scared me..." Mindy said, placing her hand against her chest.

"Not a big deal."

Thomas backed the Durango up a bit, readjusted, and pulled it between the truck and the building with no problem. Mark, having a little more experience driving vehicles, working with tractors and using narrow back roads, passed between the two just fine.

What Thomas hadn't thought of, however, was the possibility that the Ford's alarm was not simply an alarm, but a dinner bell.

Zombies flooded out of broken storefront windows, alleys, and from underneath cars. Thomas cursed loudly, Mindy screamed, and Thomas was pretty sure he could even hear Mark yelling behind them.

"Go! GO!" Mindy shouted.

Thomas floored it, unintentionally side-swiping a zombie as he left the scene. He glanced in the rear-view mirror and saw Mark hot on their tail.

If they had thought there were a lot of zombies before, then there would be no words to describe what they were seeing now. As if they had been in hiding, or sleeping, the walking dead manifested everywhere. Every road they turned down was now filled with them. They had to stop and back up several times, only to find that the next road was just as crowded with zombies as the last one. Where the hell were they all coming from? And how could a town so small have so many?

"I hope you have a plan," Mark's shaky voice said over the radio.

"Not really!" Thomas yelled, swerving around zombies, "We just need to get the hell away from here! Anywhere! Where the hell is the edge of town!?"

The Durango crashed into zombies left and right, though the damage had to be minimal since Thomas was only doing twenty or thirty miles per hour. Some roads they turned down were so congested with rotting, walking corpses that they were completely impassable. It was like a nightmare.

Finally, the group found a road—presumably the main drag, of all places—that was largely clear of any walking dead. They drove down it for only a minute before an entire horde of zombies flooded out from a side street. The horde instinctively turned their attention to the two vehicles driving toward them, and filled the main road completely.

"Shit!" Thomas yelled as he slammed on the brakes.

"Back! Go back!" Mindy yelled into the walkie talkie, which Thomas had thrown in her lap a couple minutes before.

Both vehicles were now driving in reverse, but the worst possible thing imaginable happened. One of the roads behind them—the next block down, actually—had a horde coming out of it as well. Quicker than Thomas ever would have thought zombies could move, the dead filled the street and made that way impassable as well.

In front of them and behind them, gigantic walls of zombies at least ten rows deep were closing in on their position. The snarling, hungry beasts were now close enough that Thomas could see the black slime coming from their mouths. Most of them were wearing clothes torn to rags. Some were dragging a foot behind them, clumsily making their way toward their new food source.

Just as Thomas was getting ready to floor it and hope for the best—knowing neither his Durango or Mark's truck would make it through the giant horde of walking dead—a miracle happened.

An explosion, behind the horde in front of them. Thomas and Mindy saw multiple zombies in the back fly through the air, mostly in pieces. The zombies toward the front stopped and turned, curious as to what the loud noise was. At this point, they probably hadn't actually seen the humans in front of them. But to the primitive mind of the zombies, the vehicles made noise...and noise meant potential food.

Another explosion, also in the back. More zombies were torn to shreds. The ones in the front continued staring, unsure of what was going on. They heard noise, but saw nothing creating it. Then Thomas saw something fly off the roof of a building the next block over. A small amount of smoke rolled off of the object as it flew through the air, landing on the sidewalk just past the intersection. The object erupted into bright colors and loud pops. Fireworks...

Thomas watched as the zombies in front of them began walking toward the firecrackers, absolutely enthralled by the movement, bright colors, and loud noises. The horde behind them was still coming, but now they had an escape route. The horde in front had moved past the intersection, allowing them to turn onto a street that presumably led them out of town.

Thomas hit the gas, but not enough to make the tires screech. He didn't want to take any chances. Again, he saw more fireworks get launched from the top of the building and erupt into a fountain of colors and (apparently) attractive noises. But who was doing it? As Thomas turned left onto the street—Mark close behind him— he looked up and saw the silhouette of a human on top of a building. He only caught a glimpse, but it appeared to be a man.

Thomas drove about a hundred feet down the road, then brought the Durango to a stop. The building the man had been on top of was on this side of the main street, which meant he could come down and meet them. As long as he did it before the zombies lost interest in the fireworks, of course.

"What the hell's goin' on?" Mark asked as he pulled up beside Thomas and Mindy.

"I don't know, but it looks like we might have a friend."

Thomas turned around and looked through the back windshield. A few of the zombies had lost interest in the fireworks, recognizing that they weren't a source of food. Some of them took notice of the two vehicles sitting in the road—the same two they had been pursuing earlier—but others apparently had no memory and wandered off in a different direction. The horde, though, was still largely intact.

After about thirty seconds, Thomas saw the back door of the building fly open. A man ran out, full tilt. He appeared to be a fairly large guy, and he was wearing what looked like tactical gear. A black tactical vest, with magazine pouches and equipment on it. As he neared, Thomas saw that he had an assault rifle in his right hand, a canvas bag in the other and a backpack over his shoulders, and a sidearm strapped to his thigh. Thomas quickly unlocked the doors on the Durango, and waited for the man to get in.

"Who the hell is that?" Mark asked.

After only a few seconds, the man had closed the gap between the building and the Durango. The slow, clumsy zombies were getting closer now. The man tore open the rear passenger side door, tossed the bag in, and literally threw his whole body into the back set.

"Go!" he shouted in a deep, gravely voice.

Thomas floored it as the man closed the back door. He checked to make sure Mark was following. He was. As they pulled away from the town of Tremonton, Thomas adjusted his rear-view mirror to get a better look at their savior. The man appeared to be in his late thirties or early forties, and his face was rugged and seemed to be carved from stone—a dark shadow wrapping around it from several days of not shaving. His hair was so dark brown that it was almost black, and it was obvious that it was normally kept as a military-style high and tight, except it hadn't been touched for several weeks. He had dark sunglasses on, so his eyes weren't visible. Even so, Thomas had a feeling that the man's eyes would be cold and cunning. He was wearing tan BDU pants that were tucked into his black combat boots, and beneath his black tactical vest was a charcoal gray t-shirt. His biceps filled the entirety of his shirt's sleeves. The man's neck had a small scar on the right side. Thomas could tell that this man was not to be trifled with under any circumstances. He had noticed a handgun in a holster on the man's thigh as he had been running toward the Durango. The man had also been carrying an assault rifle, which was now between his legs with the muzzle pointing toward the vehicle's ceiling. He also had some sort of sword attached to his backpack. It was pretty obvious that he was military, or at least former military.

"So what were you doing up there?" Thomas finally asked the man.

"Well, I *was* out scavenging for supplies. That is, until some dumb ass set off a car alarm. That wouldn't have been you all, was it?" the man asked stoically as he stared Thomas in the eyes through the rear-view mirror.

Thomas adjusted the mirror back the way it was, so he could no longer make eye contact with the scary guy in the backseat.

"Um...yeah, that was us. An accident," Thomas finally said.

"Well I didn't figure you did it on purpose. I mean, not unless you specifically *wanted* to be torn to pieces by dead people."

The man's voice was deep and slightly raspy. He spoke slowly and enunciated his words very carefully. Just the sound of him talking—regardless of what words came out—was terrifying. It was almost as if Thomas could sense that he was a cold-blooded killer just from hearing his voice.

"What's your name?" Thomas finally asked.

"Vance," the man replied, but his gaze remained directed out of the window.

"Nice to meet you, Vance. And thank you, for what you did back there. We would have died for sure," Thomas told him.

"I know."

Thomas paused for a moment, wondering if this Vance fellow was going to ask them their names.

"I'm Thomas Briggs, and this is my sister Mindy," Thomas finally said.

"Nice to meet you," Mindy said with a smile as she turned around in her seat.

"Yep, it's a fuckin' pleasure," Vance grumbled, still looking out the window.

The two vehicles turned down a gravel road once they were a couple miles outside of Tremonton. Thomas had absolutely no idea where he was going anymore. His sense of direction was all turned around, and even though the Durango had a compass, that did very little to actually help him ascertain where they needed to go. After driving about a mile down the gravel road until they were away from any houses, Thomas stopped and got out. The newest addition to their group instinctively hopped out of the Durango with his assault rifle at the low-ready, scanning their surroundings. Thomas and Mindy walked to the back of the Durango as Mark and Virginia got out of their truck and met them.

"Who's our guardian angel?" Mark chuckled as he approached them. Vance was still on the passenger side of the Durango, scanning the perimeter.

"His name's Vance," Thomas told him.

"Vance? And what's your full name, Vance?" Mark asked.

"James Vance. Everyone just calls me Vance," the newest member said quietly, his eyes still focused on the landscape around them.

"He's a hell of a social butterfly, ain't he?" Mark said softly as he leaned toward Thomas.

"I don't know where to go," Thomas said, getting straight to the point, "I have no idea what to do."

"Well, I'd say we need to go back the way we came. The same direction, anyway. At least then we'll be goin' the right way." Mark crossed his arms and leaned up against the Durango's rear hatch.

"What about you, Vance? You have any idea where we should go?" Thomas asked as he walked around the vehicle and behind Vance.

"Nope. I've been wandering for the past couple months. Going from one group to the next, one town to the other. I'm from Albuquerque. Don't know shit about this area."

"You're...you're from Albuquerque?" Thomas stuttered as he asked the question.

"Yep," Vance replied. He still had his back turned to the others, remaining ever vigilant.

"Is that where you came from?" Thomas asked.

"No," was all Vance said.

"So...you don't know what Albuquerque is like?"

"Not at all."

"Are you trying to get back there?" Thomas walked in front of Vance so he could talk to him face to face.

"Nope."

"Then what the hell are you doing?" Thomas was close enough now that he could just barely see through Vance's dark sunglasses. Through the lenses he could see the man's right eye, and even though it was like looking into a dark corner, something cried out to Thomas that the man was a pit of pain and despair.

"Surviving," Vance said, turning his head to look at Thomas for the first time.

4

"Don't you have any family? Anyone to go back to?" Mindy asked Vance once the group had gotten back on the road.

Vance stared out of the window, still keeping his mind in soldier mode.

"No."

The group had decided to go back toward Tremonton and avoid the town by traveling down gravel roads whenever possible. With any luck they would bee able to reach the interstate again without incident. Eventually.

"There must be someone who cares about you, someone who..."

"Sis..." Thomas said quietly as he patted his sister's leg, "Leave it alone."

The group traveled on, south around Tremonton. They continued mostly on back roads, trying to find a good place to get back on the interstate. After another couple of hours, the sun was beginning to set and the group was running out of daylight.

"Are we going to keep going through the night?" Vance asked, breaking the uncomfortable silence for the first time since Thomas had told his sister to stop interrogating Vance.

"No. I don't feel safe driving at night. We need to find somewhere to stay," Thomas told him.

"At least you have some sense, then," Vance replied, mostly to himself.

The group spotted a white, two-story ranch-style house about five minutes later. It had a large, modern barn beside it. There was a single truck sitting in the driveway. Thomas stopped on the gravel road about twenty feet away from the estate's driveway.

"What do you think, Mark?" Thomas asked into the walkie.

"Up to you, I guess. It could either be really good or really bad. No way of tellin' if someone's in there or not...dead or alive."

Thomas slowly pulled the Durango down the driveway, Mark following closely behind him. He did his best to scan the area around the house, but it was becoming difficult in the low light. He finally turned on the vehicle's headlights to see better.

"Well, if anyone's inside, they definitely know we're here now," Vance said from the backseat.

Thomas felt his stomach start to knot up after Vance's comment. He was right, of course, but it was too late now. Thomas had already shined his lights almost directly on the house. Might as well keep going and take advantage of his increased visibility.

Thomas brought the vehicle to a stop beside the truck that was already sitting in the house's driveway. He looked around some more, mostly just dreading getting out of the vehicle. Finally Vance reached up and switched off the Durango's interior lights, then opened the car door and hopped out.

"Wait!" Thomas whispered, but it was too late. Vance was already in soldier mode with his M4 against his shoulder, scanning from left to right around the yard.

"Stay here, and lock the doors. If anything bad happens, honk the horn," Thomas told his little sister before grabbing the crowbar out of the backseat and exiting the Durango as well.

Thomas gently touched the Beretta that was tucked in his waistband, mostly just to make himself feel a little better. He had little belief that he would actually be able to hit anything with it, even if he had to use it. For that reason, he kept the crowbar gripped tightly in both hands. He was now about ten feet behind Vance, and Mark was walking up beside him.

"So what do we do if someone's inside?" Mark asked quietly.

"Do we knock, or what?" Thomas whispered.

"Shh!" Vance looked over his shoulder just briefly enough to give the two men behind him a menacing stare, even if they really couldn't see his face very well in the grayscale environment created by the last of the sun's ambient light.

Vance carefully stepped up onto the porch. Thomas watched as the soldier placed his foot on the first step ever so carefully. Barely moving, as if time had been slowed down. Thomas had always enjoyed movies and books that centered around time and the possible manipulation of it.

Thomas shook his head a little, trying to get rid of the distracting thoughts that had absolutely nothing to do with their current situation. It was a defense mechanism of his, though, to always think about familiar things that were somewhat connected to what he was currently experiencing. After all, he was a complete stranger to situations like these. Death and having to react quickly to avoid it, people trying to hurt or kill him. Those things were all new to him. He was no stranger to stress, though. Thomas Briggs had been a worrier his entire life. He could always remember feeling overwhelming anxiety about almost everything. His mother used to tell him that it would give him an ulcer someday.

Vance peered through the dark windows on the house's porch. The terrifying man was perfectly still for a moment, as if he were listening for any movement. He apparently didn't see or hear anything, because he quickly but quietly turned his attention to the front door. After giving the handle a fast turn, he discovered that it was unlocked and turned his head back to Thomas and Mark, who were still waiting on the sidewalk directly in front of the porch's steps. Vance motioned with his head for them to come up on the porch, then turned the handle on the door and took two quiet steps inside. Mark and Thomas were only a couple of feet behind him, but had not yet stepped inside the house. Vance turned on the flashlight that was attached to his assault rifle, and pulled the beam of light back and forth across the room a couple of times.

The house appeared to be well kept. The first room was a living room, with two nice couches, an entertainment center, and a glass display case full of trophies of some kind. Vance walked behind the first couch and away from the front door, his attention now on the dark hallway that turned to the right out of the room that they were currently in. He stepped out into the hallway and directed his flashlight's powerful beam at the other end. Then he turned the light off and walked around to the front of the couch.

"What are you doing?" Thomas asked him, but his voice was barely a whisper.

Vance ignored him, and instead pulled his sword from its makeshift sheath on his backpack. It was a shorter sword—probably a little less than two feet long—and was almost perfectly straight. Thomas had seen that style before, and remembered that the blade was called a "tanto". He looked on as Vance turned the light on his M4 back on, then gently slapped the sword against the couch cushions. Dust flew up, and it was immediately noticeable in the artificial light provided by Vance's weapon. Particles danced all around through the stale air.

"Nobody's been here for awhile," Vance said, "At least no one living."

A floorboard creaked, somewhere deep within the house. Vance turned his head toward it, but the rest of his body stayed frozen.

"What was..."

"Quiet," Vance said to Thomas, before he could get anymore words out.

The same creaking noise could be heard again, coming from the depths of the large house. Vance and Mark appeared to be frozen in time, but Thomas couldn't help but look back and forth between the two men. The look on Mark's face was radiating fear, his mouth hanging open slightly and his eyes wide. Vance's face, however, was as stone cold as ever. The small amount of moonlight coming in through the south window was just enough to see his sharp-looking eyes, almost halfway closed. His jaw was rigid and frozen along with the rest of his body. The only thing his expression revealed was that he was unwavering and strong.

"Do you feel that?" Vance asked in his raspy voice, barely above a whisper.

"What?" Thomas asked.

"Airflow. There's a window or door open somewhere."

Even though he was in the middle of a situation that made him anxious beyond belief, Thomas couldn't help but look in awe at James Vance. The man was a machine, perfectly equipped to handle any situation. At least, that was Thomas's impression of him. Perhaps inside the man was terrified. Somehow, Thomas found that very hard to believe.

Vance moved forward slowly without notice. Mark and Thomas watched him for a brief moment before falling in line behind him. Vance's sword was still gripped firmly in his right hand, his M4 was hanging from its combat sling. The three of them moved down the hallway, and soon they came upon the kitchen. Vance stopped in the doorway, carefully looking around. Their eyes had adjusted to the darkness now, so it was slightly easier to see. Thomas had to take off his glasses after they started fogging up, and that was when he noticed the back door standing open. The three of them stared at it before Vance quietly but quickly moved across the kitchen to shut and lock the door. Thomas turned toward the living room that they came from, remembering that he should probably stay alert and watch for things that intended to hurt or kill them...whether alive or dead. Without his glasses on things close up would be fuzzy, but he really didn't need to make out any close details in a situation like this.

Another creaking noise, this time from seemingly right above them. Vance looked up and stared at the ceiling, as if he had x-ray vision. Then one more loud creak, followed by a large crash. Something or someone fell and/or knocked something over.

"Better go check it out, then we'll come back down and clear this floor," Vance said.

Mark and Thomas both nodded without saying a word. After all, wouldn't a man like James Vance be the expert on such things? He stepped past them casually, heading back to the living room. Once there, he poked his head through the doorway of the next room over and discovered the stairs. Mark and Thomas followed closely as Vance made his way up, slowly and carefully. One of the steps squeaked a little, but Vance immediately froze in mid-step as soon as he heard the noise, so as not to put anymore weight on it. He then skipped the step and gingerly placed his foot on the next one. Thomas and Mark did the same thing, trying their best to put their feet in the same places that Vance had.

"I wanna be your friend..." a small, high-pitched voice said from somewhere upstairs.

All three men froze instantly. The voice had been muffled, but they were able to hear it well enough to know it sounded like the voice of a small child. Just then, all three men noticed a bad odor hanging in the air. An odor that smelled rotten and oddly sweet. Mark and Thomas reared back slightly at the smell and covered their noses. Strangely, Thomas noticed Vance perk up a bit and sniff at the air. The smell apparently only intrigued him, and didn't seem to phase him a bit.

"Do you think a kid's..." Thomas began.

"That tickles!" the same voice said, interrupting Thomas. It was still muffled.

Vance walked up the top two steps and then stopped once more. There was a single hallway that went from the top of the stairs to the other side of the house. Four doors were down that hallway, two on either side. The three men slowly walked down the hall until they reached the first set of doors. They were single file again; Vance was on point, then Thomas, then Mark.

"I like hugs..." the small voice spoke once more, this time a little more clearly.

It was coming from the first door on their right, which was closed. Vance turned his attention to it, staring for a long moment before looking down the hallway once more. The other three doors were closed as well. Vance touched the doorknob—his tanto sword still in his hand and hanging by his side—and slowly turned it. He quietly cracked the door open, peering inside. The smell became stronger now, and Thomas could hardly stand it. Vance, on the other hand, looked as if he couldn't smell anything at all.

"See anything?" Thomas whispered through his hand, just barely loud enough for even Vance to hear him.

Vance shook his head, still staring into the room. His field of view was miniscule through the small crack, so he slowly pushed it open more. The door slowly swung on its hinges. Halfway through, one of the hinges quietly squeaked. Vance took a step away from the room and stared down at the floor, taking a deep breath as he did.

"Well?" Thomas asked, anxious. Mark stepped closer to the room as well, but neither could see into the room at all.

Vance pointed into the room with his sword. Thomas peeked around the corner, and what he saw made his heart ache. A small child—a little girl—was standing with her back to them, as if she was gazing out the window. In her right hand was a small teddy bear, and she was holding it by one of its arms. The little girl was obviously dead, her stance awkward and unbalanced. Her hair was a mangled mess, and the back of her shirt was torn. The room was decorated in pink wallpaper with butterflies on it. Light pink covers were on the bed, and the carpet was a very light purple color. On the nightstand was a porcelain ballerina, possibly a music box. Scattered about the room were cups of yogurt, empty bags of potato chips, and numerous bottles of water.

"I love you..." the teddy bear said as the girl moved away from the window and inadvertently smacked it against the windowsill.

"Christ..." Thomas gasped. His eyes grew large and his stomach twisted.

"Watch my back. Mom and Dad are bound to be around, too," Vance said somberly.

"What is it?" Mark whispered, still unable to see. He could have easily squeezed past the two men to peer into the room, but it was quite obvious that he would rather be told than see for himself.

Vance stared into the room quietly, then slowly entered. Thomas watched him approach the little girl—or what *used* to be a little girl—who was now staring blankly at the closet with her back still to a potential food source. Thomas looked away as Vance grew nearer, and instead focused his attention down the hallway. Even though all the other doors were shut, and Thomas and Mark could both see all of the exposed areas on the second floor, it was easier to pretend they were doing something productive. Something other than slaughtering a little girl...a little girl who was no longer a little girl.

A sick smacking noise could be heard coming from the little girl's room, followed by a soft *thump*. Thomas cringed when he heard it, and momentarily squeezed his eyes shut as tight as he could. When he opened them, a single tear ran down his left cheek. He didn't even wipe it away. He let the tear dry up on its own, as if doing so symbolized the passing of the little girl. Realizing that she had actually passed long ago, Thomas looked down at the floor briefly and inhaled deeply. He then turned around as he heard Vance's boots slowly making their way out of the room.

"Well...?" Thomas asked, although he didn't know why.

"She's been dead awhile. I'd say at least a month." The soldier stepped past Thomas and made his way down the hallway.

Vance stopped at each door and placed his ear close to them, listening for any movement. He gave two quick knocks on each door, and no life at all became apparent to them. Neither did any death that might not have resembled death as much as it should. Vance slowly pushed open the first door on the left, directly across from the little girl's room. It was a bathroom, and it was obvious that it was empty. He then moved on to the last door on the left. After trying the door handle and finding it locked, Vance abruptly kicked it open. Part of the frame broke as the door flew open and hit the wall inside, and a horrid smell poured out of the room. It was ten times worse than the smell in the little girl's room. Actually, it was only twice as bad...

Inside were two adults—a male and a female—both lying in bed completely motionless. They were both dressed in wedding garb. The man was on the left side of the bed, in a full tuxedo, and the woman had on a brilliant wedding gown complete with a veil and gloves. Between them, in the middle of the bed, their hands were joined together.

"I need to leave," Mark said.

"No. Go out in the hall, but don't leave," Vance barked,

slightly above a whisper.

Vance and Thomas approached the couple, although Thomas was more hesitant than Vance. The soldier appeared to be unperturbed by the gruesome scene. As they approached—one on either side of the bed—they noticed the holes drilled into both heads of the dead bodies. The woman had a small hole on her right temple, and a larger one on her left. The man also had a hole on his right temple, but the trajectory had been quite different. The bullet had exited through the top-left portion of his skull, creating a rather large hole and quite a mess on the bed and wall.

"Looks like they...opted out..." Vance said calmly.

"Jesus..." Thomas said as he stared. That was twice in so many minutes that he had called out the name of a deity which he did not believe in.

"Jesus ain't got nothin' to do with it," Vance said casually after a brief moment of silence.

The lifetime soldier—most likely all too familiar with pain and death and horror—leaned in closer to inspect the bodies. He grabbed some sort of revolver out of the man's right hand and shoved it into his pocket. Thomas continued staring in shock until Vance broke his trance. But it wasn't his words that shook Thomas awake. It was his actions. He watched as Vance leaned over the dead man and grabbed something out of the woman's left hand that was only barely visible from under the sheets. It appeared to be a card of some kind, as best Thomas could tell. It was awfully dark upstairs, and Vance was not using his flashlight at all.

"Happy 10th anniversary," Vance read, "Love...David."

Vance placed the card on the dresser, which also had a piece of paper with writing on it. Vance took it to the end of the bed with him and read it to himself, but not out loud. Thomas stared at him, completely taken by the moment. Several seconds later, after Vance had read it, he handed it to Thomas without looking at him and slowly made his way out of the room.

To whoever finds us, if anyone finds us at all, please read this...

I write these words with an unspeakably sad heart. The date is June 1ˢᵗ, 2014. Today is my wife and I's anniversary. We have chosen this day to end our lives. My wife Wendy is very ill and has been for several days now, and I am starting to feel a little sick myself. Pamela, our seven year old daughter, seemed to be doing just fine at first. But she became very sick two nights ago and died in her sleep last night. It was not peaceful. I can still hear her screaming out in pain. I held her as she thrashed about, trying to shake the evil from inside her. ~~She was...~~ ~~It was...~~

I know it is not fair to leave her like she is now, but I can't bring myself to harm her. I've seen what those things out there can do. I've seen how people can turn into them when they die. Even though she has turned into one of those...things...she is still my Little Pamela. Please...if you find her, let her be. Please do not kill her. I can't bear the thought of anyone.... Why do I feel this way? My head hurts... ~~my throat is dry~~... every joint in my body feels like it has broken glass inside it... What is this ~~sickness~~ plague?? My mind is scattered, like it has been   Who am i and why do i here this whay
           kiill whaats Insite me

Tears dripped from Thomas's face and landed on the letter he was holding. Reading it was painful. He folded it up and placed it in his left back pocket, although he wasn't sure why he felt compelled to keep it.

Vance was standing in the doorway, his back turned to Thomas and the dead couple. Thomas stared at the back of his head, hoping that some of the man's emotional strength could somehow be siphoned off and used for himself. After all, he seemed to have a surplus of it. Or did he? Thomas looked closely at Vance's left hand. Through the small amount of moonlight coming in from the window at the end of the hall just a few feet away, Thomas could see some sort of toy or display item in Vance's left hand. Thomas took a couple of steps closer and could see that it was the porcelain ballerina from the little girl's room.

"You okay?" Thomas asked. He had no idea why Vance might

have taken the item from the child's room.

"We should clear what's left and then search the house for anything useful," was all Vance said before pushing open the fourth and final door in the hallway. It was a spare bedroom, which had been used for storage after the plague broke out. Cardboard boxes filled the room.

The three men cleared the remaining rooms downstairs that they had skipped over when they went to investigate the strange noise. After that they escorted the two ladies inside, taking only the bare essentials in case they needed to make a hasty escape and wouldn't have time to grab everything.

Inside the home they found a small jackpot of canned goods and a whole case of bottled water in the storage room upstairs, clean blankets in a linen closet, and a ten gallon can of gasoline on the screened in back porch. The small group of five set up in the home's living room. No one had even said anything about sleeping in the same room because it was safer...it seemed to be something that everyone just wanted to do. And who wouldn't? In this new world, where the safety and familiarity of human contact was a rare commodity, no one had any qualms with it. Both of the couches had fold out seats that reclined back. Virginia sat down on one and leaned back, covered up with a blanket, and fell asleep within minutes. Mindy sat on the second couch but did not try to go to sleep yet. Mark and Thomas sat at the kitchen table, a small kerosene lantern gently burning between them. Vance had pulled a chair out of the kitchen and into the hallway, where he could see both the living room and the kitchen. He took off his tactical vest and pulled out his combat knife to clean under fingernails.

"I don't even know what to say about today," Mark said.

"Neither do I. It was a gruesome sight," Thomas replied, rubbing his face as he did. He was truly exhausted, but today's events had him worked up still. Mostly the little girl and her parents.

"I don't know what I would do, if I had a child and I had to watch as they turned into one of those...things." Mark stared at the hardwood floor and shook his head.

"I think my fate would be the same as the two upstairs," Thomas said somberly.

"Let's change the subject," Vance quickly said, his quiet but deep voice cutting through the air, "We haven't told either of the girls about what happened. I think it's best it stays that way."

"Yeah...you're probably right," Mark said, but Thomas knew there was more to it than that. He could look at Vance's face and was able to tell that much.

"Do you think I could get another bottle of water?" Mindy asked as she appeared in the kitchen.

"Sure," Thomas said to her.

Mindy walked over to the counter where the full case of water was. She pulled one out, anxiously broke the cap's seal, and started drinking. Thomas could see her hand shaking as she held the bottle to her lips. He glanced over at Vance, and saw that he had noticed it, too. But who could blame her? Who wasn't a bit shaken up? Before now, Thomas would have said that Vance was not bothered at all. But he had been naïve. Vance was a soldier through and through, but he was also a human being. He might not wear his heart on his sleeve, but he still very much had the same struggle with emotions. Thomas could see that now. How foolish he had been, to judge a man so quickly.

"Do you think..." Mindy began, almost as soon as the bottle left her lips, "Do you think this thing is as bad as it looks?"

Thomas looked over at Mark, who made a sour face but continued looking at the floor. Looking over at Vance, he found that he had no expression at all even though he, too, was looking at Mindy.

"I think it's probably worse than it looks," Thomas answered honestly.

Mindy took another quick drink of water.

"What are we going to do, Thomas?" she asked, this time a bit more nervously.

"I don't know, sis."

There was a long pause.

"We survive," Vance said. His voice seemed decisive,

steadfast. It wasn't shaky or hesitant. It was as clear and steady as a voice had ever been.

Mindy went back into the living room just a couple minutes later. After ten minutes or so of complete silence, Thomas went to check on her to see if she was sleeping yet. She was, although he could tell it wasn't a very sound sleep. Her legs were curled up beneath her, and she was mostly in a sitting position. Her head was resting against the back of the couch, and every once in awhile her hand or leg would twitch. It was something she did whenever she had nightmares, ever since she was a baby. Thomas left her alone. Whether it was good or bad sleep, it was still sleep. He walked back into the kitchen, and saw Mark digging around in the pantry.

"Well now...would you look at this?" the large man said as he pulled out a bottle of champagne.

"No thank you," Thomas said with a slight laugh as he sat down at the kitchen table.

"I wouldn't advise drinking it," Vance suggested.

"Why not? I'm sure it's still good," Mark replied, sitting down at the table with his new found treasure.

"If you get drunk, you won't be able to defend yourself very well if it comes down to it. Which means you won't be able to protect your wife. You won't just be a liability to yourself, but to all of us, too."

Vance's words were true, and Mark knew it. He stared at the bottle briefly and nodded in agreement before sitting it down and turning his attention away from it.

"You're right. Glad someone around here has a level head. I still can't get over..." Mark hesitated, "...what we saw earlier."

Thomas and Mark spoke for a few more minutes, mostly making small talk. Then Mark got up and said goodnight before sitting down on the same couch as his wife and reclining back. Thomas leaned forward and placed his elbows on the table, resting his head in his hands. Staring at the speckled tabletop, he replayed the day's events over in his head. The dead towns, the airplane, the horde of walking dead in Tremonton, Vance saving them, the little girl, the parents...it was all almost too much to bear. Thomas's thoughts faded off as his eyes got heavy and he finally fell asleep.

* * *

Thomas woke up to find the lantern missing. It was still very dark, save the little bit of moonlight coming in through the small window above the sink. He got up from the table and looked around the kitchen, but found no one. Vance's chair was still sitting in the same spot in the hallway.

Thomas walked into the living room and saw that the other three were still sound asleep. From a small room set to the side of the living room, Thomas noticed a soft yellow glow coming from it. He walked quietly to the doorway and barely peeked his head through to look inside. The room almost looked like a study, with a desk and computer, bookshelves, and a large painting of a lake scene on the back wall. Sitting at the desk was Vance, who was leaned forward studying the ballerina he had taken from the little girl's room. His hard hands that had surely brought death upon countless men were gently gripping the porcelain ballerina, turning it around so he could stare deeply into it as if it somehow contained the cure to the plague. He gingerly gripped flipped the ballerina over, winding it up underneath. He then sat it down on the table while the ballerina turned slowly, and a quiet, gentle—and also creepy, given the circumstances—tune came from it. Thomas looked on, a dark sadness rushing over him even though he had no idea what the whole thing was about. Just the thought of that poor little girl, and the sight of a man like Vance in obvious pain, was enough to bring tears to his eyes. Or perhaps his emotions were just on a roller coaster at the moment because of everything going on.

Vance suddenly snapped his gaze to the doorway, and Thomas almost reeled back to avoid being seen, as if he were breaking the law. But instead he slowly stepped into the room and sat down in the soft chair in front of the desk. Vance pushed the ballerina over to the side and leaned back in the padded leather computer chair.

"Sometimes I wonder if there is any hope for us left," Thomas began. Vance stared deeply into his eyes, but didn't say a word, "I don't know a thing about surviving. I've never had to. I'm an architect, for Christ's sake."

There he was, referencing a divine entity again.

Thomas continued, "I don't want anything to happen to my parents, and that's why I'm going to Albuquerque. But what can I do to protect them? I'm worthless in this type of situation."

Vance continued staring at him with piercing yet oddly soft eyes, his chin resting on his hand. Then he leaned forward and said:

"Sometimes you just have to keep going. Sometimes...you just have to have faith that hope is still there."

"Pfft..." Thomas guffawed, "Faith. I don't have any of that."

Vance actually smiled, but it was a smile of empathy.

"It's not about the faith itself. It's about fooling yourself into believing that hope exists. Otherwise, why keep going?" he said.

"Wise words. But why *should* we keep going? We can't beat this." Thomas rubbed his face in frustration and exhaustion.

Vance squinted at him for a moment before calmly speaking.

"Just like we couldn't beat all the other horrible things throughout our dark history? We made it through the Ice Age, which would seem impossible now. Millions upon millions of people were killed, tortured, and otherwise punished during the Crusades and Medieval Inquisition, all in the name of God. We thought we couldn't beat the Black Death, which killed over 30% of Europe's population. World War I seemed to move us toward self-destruction, and if we include those who died from the Spanish Flu in the number of casualties—and believe me, it played a huge role because of the frequent movement and close quarters of human beings on a massive scale—then at least 65 million people lost their lives. World War II was even worse, and killed about 75 million people—*without* a worldwide flu to facilitate a large portion of the deaths. 45 million people died in China because of communist policies, while their leaders dined on expensive imported alcohol and cuisine. Pol Pot killed off over 20% of

Cambodia's population. Thousands of animal species and whole races have been wiped out because of humanity's curiosity, greed, and envy. And you know how most people survived these terrible things? They waited. Yes, a lot of people died. And a lot of people have died during this thing. But humanity will survive. We'll overcome it eventually, if not through action then from *inaction*. From sheer willpower and determination."

Thomas nodded his head, staring at the bookshelf in the corner of the room. So it seemed that James Vance was not some mindless killing machine, not simply some jarhead who only knew how to end life.

"I hope you're right. But you know the difference between all those things and what's happening now?" Thomas asked, before answering his own question, "Humanity isn't as tough as they used to be, and no one is coming to our rescue. There's no help, there's nothing at all that we can do. You're right...the only way we can beat this is to wait. But how long will it take? Will we be able to wait long enough without being eaten? What happens when the last humans on Earth are hunkered down in a hole in the ground, and the dead come pouring in to consume them? Then this will no longer be our planet. This giant hunk of rock we call home will belong to the dead."

Vance smirked and leaned forward, sticking his neck out slightly to get as close as he could.

Whispering, he said, "It already does...and it always has. The deeds of dead men have influenced this world more so than any living person ever could, for better or worse."

Thomas stared into his eyes and thought deeply. He really had no rebuttal to that. But something inside him made him curious. Why would a man like James Vance seem to have such a positive outlook on everything? Or perhaps it wasn't a positive view...perhaps it was simply the proverbial dark tunnel with a dim light at the end. But how long was this tunnel? Or maybe Vance was just fucking with him.

"Tell me, Vance," Thomas began, "How does a man like you make it through this post-apocalyptic world?"

"I do what I must, and refrain from doing the things I don't have to."

Vance leaned back in his chair once more.

"Explain that, if you don't mind." Thomas thought he knew what Vance was saying, but wanted it to be clarified.

"I eat, drink, sleep, seek shelter, kill those who threaten my existence...the things that keep me alive. I don't do the things I want simply to gain pleasure—or the things I could otherwise get by without doing—because that is how you get killed. The exception is when I see an opportunity I could greatly benefit from, so long as the benefits outweigh the risks."

"So why, then, did you go out of your way to save us?" Thomas asked.

All emotion drained from Vance's face. He looked down at the floor, then slowly rose from his chair.

"Because my ride was two blocks away, and hundreds of living dead were between me and it," he said, and left the room.

Thomas thought about that briefly. The words made him feel unsettled. Had Vance truly done that only because he stood to gain from it? Had he still saved them if he had been able to get out and get back to his own vehicle?

5

Everyone woke up the next morning at about the same time. Thomas woke up with Mindy's head resting on his shoulder. Virginia had just gotten up, and Mark was sitting on the couch rubbing the sleep from his eyes. Vance was not in the living room. Thomas nudged his sister awake before getting up and making his way into the kitchen. There he found Vance, who appeared to be cooking scrambled eggs.

"Eggs?" Thomas asked as he sat down at the table.

"There's a chicken coup out back. Most of the chickens are still alive. The house has a propane tank, so the stove still works," Vance replied.

"Think we could take the chickens with us?" Thomas asked him.

"Probably could, but it wouldn't be very practical. Chickens are messy and smell bad, not to mention they die pretty easily. They'd take up a lot of space during transport. I think we could find another farm that still has free range chickens, if we have to."

"Smells good," Mark said as he walked into the kitchen, hooking the last strap on his overalls.

Vance scraped the large pan of eggs onto a plate so everyone could get a scoop. Their breakfast consisted of scrambled eggs, some yogurt they found in the pantry, and water.

"What I wouldn't give for just one glass of orange juice," Virginia said when everyone was about halfway done eating.

A faint voice interrupted their meal. It sounded like it was coming from out back. Everyone but Vance froze, not even chewing the food in their mouths. Thomas stared at the back door as if it would reveal to him what the noise was. Vance was already across the kitchen, picking up his M4 from the counter. He didn't yet have his tactical vest on, so he only had his sidearm in its thigh holster and his assault rifle in his hands.

"See anything?" Mark asked.

"Not yet. Quiet," Vance quickly replied as he pressed himself against the frame of the back door, out of sight.

Thomas watched as Vance carefully peeked through the back door's window. It was obvious he hadn't seen anything yet.

"Well...?" Mindy shakily asked.

"Quiet!" Vance said, this time sternly.

Thomas got up and pulled his Beretta from his waistband before standing behind Vance, waiting for him to give some sort of order or at least some sort of description of what he was seeing.

"Son of a..." Vance began, but was cut off by a terrifying scream.

"Help!" a female shouted, "Is anyone there!? Help me!"

Thomas stepped around Vance and looked outside. A girl who looked no older than 13 or 14 was walking through the field behind the house. Her legs looked shaky, and they moved awkwardly over the rough terrain. Her shirt was half torn, exposing her bra. Something red—presumably blood—coated the right side of her face and stained a portion of her shirt.

"What the fuck..." Thomas said to himself.

"Mark! Thomas! Grab your weapons and go out with me! Watch my back!"

And that was all the soldier said before he ripped open the door and rushed outside. Thomas followed him, and saw Vance with his M4 shouldered instinctively and scanning his surroundings for any signs of danger. Mark came out just a moment later, a shotgun in his hands.

"Help me!" the girl said, now much closer.

"Have you been bitten!?" Vance yelled to her.

The girl was now only about twenty yards away.

"No...people did this to me!" the girl said, then tripped on a small hill of dirt and tumbled to the ground.

She laid there in agony and pain, staring up at the sky. She was crying so hard that she began coughing, letting out long moans of despair in between. Vance removed his M4 from his shoulder and carried it in his left hand. He jogged toward her slowly. Mark and Thomas were behind him by about twenty feet, both looking around them to make sure there weren't any zombies or people around.

"What happened?" Vance asked as he approached her. Thomas picked up his pace and was now directly behind Vance.

"Please...just help me!" the girl cried.

"Take this," Vance said to Thomas before quickly tossing his M4 at him.

Thomas barely caught it. He watched as Vance picked the girl up in his big arms and took off running back toward the house. Thomas followed him, running as well. Mark was overweight and had a large build, so he was moving at a very slow jog much further behind.

"Clear the floor in the living room," Vance said as he rushed through the back door.

Virginia and Mindy had already been looking out of the door's window. They both moved quickly into the living room and began pushing bags and blankets over to the side. Vance gently laid the girl down and started looking her over. Thomas and Mark came in just a brief moment later.

"What happened?" Vance asked her again.

"I'm a nurse," Mindy said as she fell to her knees beside the girl and started looking her over.

"These men...they did," the girl paused and held her eyes tightly shut as she fought back another crying fit, "...they did horrible things. Please...just help me!"

"What's your name?" Mindy asked her.

"Samantha," the young girl said through the frantic coughing.

"Samantha, my name is Mindy. I'm a nurse. Can you tell me what happened and where it hurts?"

Thomas looked on, in awe over his sister's caring nature and ability to stay calm during medical emergencies.

"They...they raped me," the girl clenched her teeth together and shut her eyes, "They hit me in the head, and punched me all over. I...I don't remember everything."

"Okay Samantha, I need to remove your shirt. Is that okay? I won't take your bra off."

Mindy was so good at her job. So compassionate and thoughtful.

"Okay," Samantha said.

Mindy gingerly unbuttoned the shirt and opened it up. Beneath it was a sports bra. She delicately touched her fingertips to the girl's right side, checking for broken ribs.

"Ow!" the girl cried out when Mindy touched her side.

"I think you have one or two broken ribs," Mindy said.

Mindy looked at the girl's head next. Virginia—in all her wisdom and foresight—had already filled a small bowl with water and brought it into the living room. She also pulled out a new bar of soap and several rags and hand towels.

"I have some medical supplies in one of my bags, in the truck," Mindy said as she looked at a small cut on the right side of the girl's head.

"Which bag?" Thomas asked.

"The red one. I think it's in the back seat," his sister replied.

Thomas rushed outside toward the Durango. He unlocked it remotely with the keys and threw open the back door. Inside was one of Mindy's bags of junk food, and also a medium-sized red bag. Thomas dragged it from the driver's side of the back seat and slung the strap over his shoulder. As he backed up and placed his hand on the door to close it, he noticed something very disturbing on the road.

"Are you hurt anywhere else?" Mindy asked.

"I don't think so. I...I hurt down..." Samantha looked around the room in embarrassment and humiliation, then pointed to her pants, "I hurt down there, but I don't think anything's wrong."

"Okay. Well as soon as my brother gets back I'm going to patch you up good as new. Then I'll need to take you into a more private area to check elsewhere to make sure nothing serious is wrong." Mindy smiled and gently placed her hand on the girl's face. Samantha smiled briefly for the first time before taking Mindy's hand in her own and gripping it tightly.

"We need to go! NOW!" Thomas shouted as he barreled through the front door.

It startled everyone, even Vance. The old soldier immediately jumped to his feet and rushed off to gather up what they needed. Everyone just stared at Thomas, confused.

"What's wrong?" Mindy asked.

"There's a whole army of undead coming this way. We've gotta get out of here right now," Thomas said.

"Holy hell..." Mark said as he looked through the curtains.

Vance ran back into the room with his M4, tactical vest, and backpack. He threw on his vest and put the sling on his M4, then rushed over to the window.

"We need to move...now," he said, surprisingly calm, "We have maybe two minutes before a horde is upon us that's large enough tear this house down."

Thomas wasn't sure if it was an exaggeration or not, but he got the message: They were going to be shit out of luck if they weren't loaded up by the time the horde got there.

"Did they see you?" Vance asked.

"I'm...I'm not sure. I couldn't tell," Thomas replied as he ran over to his one and only bag.

The five people picked up what they could as quickly as they could. Mindy helped Samantha to her feet and put her arm around her.

"There's no time for that. Pick her up!" Vance ordered.

Mark stepped over to the girl and bear hugged her. Samantha wrapped her arms around Mark's neck, and he carried her like she was a toddler. Virginia had a single bag slung over her shoulder and Mark's shotgun in her hands. Vance peeked through the curtains once more, and saw that the horde was now veering off of the road and moving toward the house. Whether it was because they knew there was food inside or because it was a house that potentially had food in it was irrelevant. Now was not the time to analyze the behavior of the walking dead.

"Move your asses!" Vance roared.

Everyone moved a little quicker, hastily picking up what they could. Vance threw open the front door and rushed outside with bags in his hands and his M4 hanging freely. Thomas was right behind him, and Mindy was behind him. Mark—with Samantha in his arms—and Virginia brought up the rear.

"Shit!" Vance cursed as he saw the zombies in the front of the pack getting close to the vehicles. Some of them were faster than others. The ones that were almost to the vehicles were the quick ones, and the main group was about a hundred yards away still.

Thomas stared at the massive horde as he rushed to the Durango. It was like a sea of death. Their incessant moans and sneers were now a roar, their hands stretched outward at the sight of living flesh. Their jaws hung open and their teeth gnashed, viscous black fluid dripped from their mouths. Thomas was now only a few feet from the Durango with Mindy right behind him, but a zombie was now on the driver's side, trying to lean across the hood and reach for Thomas. Thomas pulled out his crowbar and walked around the front of the Durango while Mindy quickly hopped into the passenger side. He felt his heart pounding, and the adrenaline was coursing through his veins. He had never killed a zombie like this before. The Durango had hit and ran over quite a few zombies along the way, but he had never had to deal with one so directly.

The creature lifted itself off of the Durango's hood as its food source got closer. It stumbled in front of the car, and Thomas could see its eyes very clearly. They were gray and lifeless, with a milky film coating both of them. Thomas swung the crowbar and hit it in its jaw. The creature's head jolted to the right from the blow, and the left side of its mandible was now hanging freely, but it recovered and kept advancing. Thomas gripped the crowbar with both hands, raised it above his head, and brought it down with all his might. The end of the crowbar crashed through the top of the zombie's skull, shattering it. The lifeless creature tumbled to the ground, black fluid and gray brain matter pouring out where the crowbar had caved the skull in.

Thomas ran around the Durango to hop in the driver's seat and looked back at Mark's truck to see how they were doing. Mark was pushing Samantha into the truck, and Virginia was already inside. Vance was between the two vehicles, his M4 up and his finger pumping the trigger. The closer zombies were dropping like rag dolls as the veteran shot them through the head. Thomas was in awe at his precision and proficiency, but he would have time to admire James Vance's ability later. Instead of jumping into the Durango, Thomas summoned his hidden courage and sprinted toward Vance. He grabbed the bags Vance had been carrying and opened the Durango's hatch, hastily throwing them inside. Vance fired a few more rounds, but the larger group of zombies was now dangerously close. The soldier stopped and ran toward the Durango with Thomas, who hopped in the driver's seat. Vance jumped in the backseat, and both vehicles spun their tires and threw gravel as they quickly backed out of the driveway. The horde was massive. Where the hell were they all coming from?

Countless hands slapped the Durango's windows and streaked across as Thomas continued in reverse as fast as he dared. Him and Mark both ran over several zombies along the way, making their vehicles bounce and their steering wheels fight against them. Both of them got onto the gravel road, threw their vehicles in drive, and took off as fast as they could. Had Thomas been thinking clearly, he would have realized how dangerous it was for a guy like him to be traveling this quickly down a gravel road. He would have remembered that he had no experience driving on such rough and unpredictable terrain. But he wasn't thinking clearly, and he didn't remember that very important detail.

The Durango's rear end slowly started sliding, its tires desperately trying to gain traction on the loose gravel but failing. Thomas was not an incredibly good driver anyway, and he had never had to maneuver a vehicle that was fishtailing so bad. He jerked the steering wheel a little too much, trying to correct the vehicle's current trajectory. It started sliding sideways down the road, before its back end fell off into a deep ditch. Fortunately, it didn't roll over and no one was injured.

"Shit!" Vance shouted.

Thomas slapped his hands on the steering wheel in frustration. Mark slid his truck to a stop directly in front of them. They were about two hundred yards from the zombie horde. It wasn't a good situation.

"Get in the back!" Mark shouted as he rolled down his window.

"No!" Thomas yelled as he got out, frustrated and terrified and helpless, "We have too many supplies in here to leave behind!"

"Those supplies will be worth nothing if we're all dead!" Mark argued.

"He's right," Vance said as he climbed out of the back, only a slight hint of anxiety in his voice, "We need those supplies. Do you have a chain?"

"Somewhere in the back, but you better hurry!" Mark shouted.

Thomas and Vance ran around to the back of Mark's truck and opened the hatch on the camper shell. After digging through a box, Thomas finally found a heavy logging chain. He muscled it out and ran over to the front of the Durango. Mark pulled his truck forward so the chain would reach his hitch.

"Where do I put this?" Thomas asked as he crawled under the front of the Durango.

"Anywhere that's sturdy, preferably the frame!" Vance yelled to him, turning to look at the zombie horde that was quickly approaching. He brought up his M4 and started shooting the closer zombies.

The faster ones were of course way ahead of the main body of countless dead beings lumbering toward them. None of them were running, obviously, but it was a brisk walk. Almost like they were only moving quickly because their bodies were leaned over so far that they threatened to fall over, and their feet were just barely fast enough to keep advancing so their own momentum wouldn't pull them over.

"Hurry up!" Vance yelled, now with a little more urgency in his voice.

"I'm trying!" Thomas yelled back.

"Well try faster, because we're going to have company soon and I don't think they're coming to help," Vance replied.

Thomas finally got the chain wrapped around the axle, and crawled out from under the vehicle. Mark slowly rolled forward until the chain was taut. It wasn't going to be easy to pull it out because of the angle. The Durango was perpendicular, relative to the road. It's front tires were barely touching the road, and its rear end was deep in the ditch. It almost looked like it was high-centered, but Thomas couldn't tell for sure because the grass was high.

"Hop in and put it in four-wheel drive!" Mark yelled.

Thomas hopped over the chain and climbed into the driver's side. He turned the knob to the "4H", and gave Mark the thumb's up. The old farmer gently tugged on the Durango, getting a feel for how this whole thing was going to go. Thomas gently gave his own vehicle some gas, but didn't feel like he was contributing at all. Mark revved his engine up, and all four of his tires started spinning. Thomas and Mindy felt the Durango get yanked forward a few inches, but still not enough for it to get out on its own.

"Get that thing *out! Now!*" Vance roared.

Mark slammed his foot against the accelerator, yanking the Durango even harder. Thomas pulled the steering wheel back and forth and continued pushing his foot down with the hope that all the tugging might allow the Durango to get itself out.

The faster zombies were now close enough to be a threat, but they were few in number (comparatively speaking) and were scattered out at different distances. Vance pulled his tanto sword from his back and let his M4 hang by his side. At this close range, he would be more deadly and a lot faster with a melee weapon. Thomas watched him as he swung his sword left and right, slicing and stabbing through the zombies' heads. He took down four of them within just a few seconds.

Mark backed his truck up a couple feet, and the chain went slack. Thomas was slightly confused, until Mark hung his head out and said, "Hold on!" Thomas and Mindy braced themselves, unsure of how bad it was going to be. Mark slammed on the gas and the truck flew forward, jolting the Durango so hard that Thomas felt like he had whiplash. The Durango's front passenger tire jumped up onto the road, and the vehicle was now sitting at a more diagonal angle. Thomas hurriedly mashed down on the gas. The Durango slid so that it was parallel to the road, with both of the driver's side tires still in the ditch but both of the passenger side tires now on the gravel road. Thomas drove it forward a couple of feet, and felt it starting to get more traction.

"Hang on!" Mark shouted, "The chain's still on!"

Vance must have heard Mark, because after slicing apart two more zombies he ran to the back of Mark's truck and removed the chain.

"Go!" he yelled, then went back to playing defense.

Thomas gunned it, and for awhile just drove the Durango straight through the ditch. But the ground started to level out a bit, and soon he was able to crawl back onto the road. He hit his brakes and turned around to look behind him.

"He's out! Let's go!" Mark shouted.

Vance was starting to run out of the quicker zombies to kill. He was jumping back and forth across the road, swinging once or twice to dispatch the closest threats. But soon he would have too many zombies on top of him to count. After stabbing one zombie up under his chin and through his brain, and momentarily getting his blade stuck in the skull of another after he tried to cut it in half, Vance hauled ass back to the Durango. He threw the door open and dove inside. Thomas was moving before the door was even shut all the way, the sound of the chain still clanking against the ground as he went. Mark drove closely behind them. Everyone in both vehicles let out a sigh of relief, knowing that they could have very easily died. Especially if it hadn't been for James Vance buying them an extra minute or two.

Thomas looked back briefly and saw Vance's shirt covered in

dark, viscous blood. At first he was alarmed, but decided to not mention it until they were in a safer location. Could you get the sickness from their blood? Or did it have to be saliva? Finally, once they were far enough away that the horde was no longer in sight, Thomas asked the question.

"Can you...is it possible..." he hesitated, trying to find the right words without sounding rude to the man who had saved their lives not once, but twice.

"No," Vance said before Thomas could find the words, "At least, not from what I can tell. Seems to just be when their saliva enters the bloodstream. But I'm not a scientist."

"What if you have an open wound or something? Is it possible then?" Thomas asked.

"Not from their blood, I don't think. But I still wouldn't recommend testing that theory. Regardless, I don't have any open wounds."

"What about hangnails?" Thomas was anxious now, thinking of the worst possible scenarios. Their recent brush with death was starting to make him feel rather helpless.

"Again, I don't think so. I've gotten their blood and fluids on my hands before, and I'm still here." Vance stared out of the window as he spoke, his words quiet and devoid of any emotion.

"So...I've been thinking about that letter we found..." Thomas began.

"The one back at the house? The suicide note?" Vance asked.

"Yeah. They didn't make any mention of them coming into close contact with those things. Didn't say anything about anyone being bitten. Yet they all got sick. How..."

"Best not to think about things like that," Vance interrupted.

"I remember the news reports...they said that some of the scientists believed it could be airborne, but only certain people could get it..." Mindy added.

"Yeah, but after that everyone in Seattle thought it was false. Literally no one got sick and died without being bitten," Thomas said.

"Perhaps we should focus on driving, since we nearly got

everyone killed not long ago..." Vance said dryly.

* * *

The group traveled for just over half an hour before nearing the Hill Air Force Base in Clearfield. As they got closer they saw the exit sign for Clearfield, and written on the green sign in big red letters were two words: "SURVIVOR COLONY". Thomas slowly brought the Durango to a stop, staring at the red letters with his mouth hanging open.

"Holy shit..." Mindy said. It broke Thomas from his trance because his little sister rarely cussed.

"You think it's like the one we had in Seattle?" Thomas asked.

"I thought we were going to Albuquerque?" Vance asked them.

"We are. But this would be a great place to stop and resupply, catch some sleep and not have to worry about security," Thomas said.

"Or it could be a fucking hell hole," Vance quickly replied.

"Am I seeing that right?" Mark asked over the walkie.

"Yep," Thomas said.

The group looked around them, inspecting the surrounding area. It really looked no different than all the other towns they had been to: dead. Zombies roamed around sluggishly, bumping into each other and falling down. Then off in the distance, east of the interstate, was the military base. They couldn't see much from the road, but they saw enough to know that the sign was telling the truth. A truck was driving around a building, and it looked like people were moving about doing very "human" things. They were loading things into trucks, standing in groups. Definitely not zombie behavior.

"How's our newest member doing?" Thomas asked Mark through the walkie.

"She's doing okay. Shook up, but nothing serious."

"Let's go," Thomas said, though it was so quiet that Mindy and Vance barely heard him.

Thomas slowly pushed his foot against the accelerator and took the Clearfield exit. The ramp was relatively clear, but at the bottom there were about a dozen undead walking around. Thomas slowed down even more, pushing his way through them. The Durango bumped into several and knocked them over, and once the others took notice they were quickly on the Durango like it was a giant steak. Six or so sets of hands slapped against the Durango, but Thomas was going about 5mph so they didn't have time to do anything more than that. Mark was following behind him closely as they turned left and headed toward the base.

Clearfield was a large town, with over 30,000 inhabitants. Now there were no signs of life, besides the Air Force base. The dead were everywhere, but their numbers seemed surprisingly small compared to the previous population. Perhaps the troops at the base had thinned them out considerably? Or perhaps a lot of them had joined together to form those herds or hordes—whatever they were called—and moved on? Most of the vehicles that littered the roads had been forcibly moved to the sides, presumably by the military to clear a path. As the group got closer to the base, they saw yet another sign with the same big red letters on it that said, "HILL AIR FORCE BASE – SURVIVOR COLONY".

Thomas turned down the road leading to the base. He could already see guards at the gates, patrolling in a routine manner. Several of them had now obviously turned their attention to the two vehicles heading toward them. Thomas slowed down to a crawl, so they wouldn't think he was some sort of threat. Well...as much as a Dodge Durango could be a threat to men carrying assault rifles with a tank parked behind them. As they neared, three men behind the safety of the large chain link gate held up their hands to tell them to stop. Thomas and Mark complied, stopping about six feet before the fence. Two men slid the gate open, and four others calmly came out to greet their new visitors.

"Where did you folks come from?" the first man asked as he approached the driver's side of the Durango.

"Seattle," Thomas told him, slightly nervous.

"Damn...that's a long way. What are you doing in Utah?" the

man asked. He was wearing ACU pants—indicative of an Army soldier, not Air Force, although only Vance noticed this—and only a tan t-shirt, no rank or insignia.

"We're on our way to Albuquerque to find our parents. At least, my sister and I are. Everyone else is just along for the ride," Thomas answered.

"Go ahead and pull in where it's safe. We'll need to ask you a few questions."

Thomas and Mark pulled their vehicles in, and were directed to park them on the side of the drive just inside the gate. No one got out yet. Vance had warned them to only do what they were told and nothing more.

"Step on out, and if you have any weapons leave them in the vehicle," the same soldier told Thomas. Another soldier apparently told Mark the same thing, because Thomas saw them slowly getting out.

Thomas left his crowbar and Beretta in the Durango before opening his door and stepping out. Mindy and Vance did the same thing, although Vance left his sidearm in its holster.

"He said to leave your weapons in the vehicle," Thomas heard another man say on the other side of the Durango.

"I'm never unarmed under any circumstances," Vance told him calmly, "Least of all when the threat of being eaten is all around us."

The soldier raised his M4 a little, not quite pointing it at Vance but enough to make Vance unsettled.

"If you point that weapon at me, you alone are responsible for the outcome," Vance said.

"Hang on!" the soldier who had been talking to Thomas said loudly. He was obviously in charge, "What's your rank?"

Vance gave him a piercing glare.

"Come on, now. I know you're military. Or at least former military."

"I got out a couple years ago," Vance said, "I was a private contractor when all of this went down."

The man in charge gave him a strange smile.

92

"I see. One of those special forces guys, huh? What was your branch, rank, and MOS?" he pressed.

"Army, Sergeant First Class. I was an eighteen-foxtrot. Before that I was an eighteen-bravo, and before that I was infantry." Vance's voice was calm and quiet, but it was still deep and raspy. It sent chills down Thomas's spine, mostly because he had seen him in action and knew what he was capable of.

"Eighteen series, huh? Interesting," the guy in charge said, "He can keep his weapon."

The soldier who had been arguing with Vance eased up and took a step back.

"Everyone else...the rule still applies to you," the leader said, "I'm Staff Sergeant Overfield. Follow me."

"Who are you guys? I don't see any Air Force personnel around," Vance asked as the group was leaving their vehicles behind to follow Overfield.

"My unit and I were in the area when shit got real bad. Originally we had search and destroy orders. Cleansing the area, if you will. But none of us could have anticipated how quickly this whole thing would take off. Before we knew it, those things were literally everywhere. We barely made it back to the base here. The Air Force guys are doing what they do best: support. What's left of 'em, anyway. They let us take care of security, which is what we're best at. Everyone here has their roles."

"What unit are you—were you—with?" Vance asked as they neared the building.

"Army National Guard 118th Sapper Company, out of Blanding. Long way from home, I know, but we were given orders to haul ass to the Salt Lake City area. Spent a couple weeks moving around and trying to contain this...thing. At first we had high hopes, but it didn't take long for the problem to explode and become uncontrollable." Staff Sergeant Overfield walked at a brisk pace as they neared the doors of the visitor's center.

"How many men do you have left?" Vance asked. Overfield paused as he touched his hand to the door.

"Not many. We had a bunch not show up to begin with, and

we lost quite a few along the way. Most of our casualties occurred the night before we made it here. We're down to just 29, now."

Overfield opened the door and allowed the small group to walk inside, including Samantha, who seemed to be doing better now that her nerves had calmed down some. The group was led by Overfield and two others to a cafeteria, which now had boxes stacked all around and cots set up, but no one in sight.

"How many civilians have you taken in?" Thomas asked him as they were seated at a table.

"Not many, considering the population of the area. Just under two hundred, I believe. But that isn't my area."

Overfield stepped away from the table and placed his hands together in front of him, as if he was waiting on something. Soon another man and two more following him entered the cafeteria from another door. The man walked with an obvious sense of authority, but he wore no clothing indicative of military service. For pants he had black jeans, and his shirt was a gray thermal with the sleeves pulled up to the elbows. On his right hip he had a handgun holstered, but no other obvious weaponry was on his person. His hair was jet black and long—long enough that it was pulled back into a short ponytail. The two men accompanying him appeared to be more like guards than assistants. Neither wore any military clothing, nor did they have a military presence about them, but both were armed with handguns. As the man got closer, Thomas could see that he had a scar on the left side of his face that ran from his temple to just below his cheekbone. His facial features were very Anglo-Saxon, despite his black hair. He was clean-shaven, and besides the large scar, fairly handsome. A strange conveyance of courage and strength was prominently displayed on his face. The man grew even nearer, and Thomas saw that his eyes were dark blue, like his own. He was a tall man, maybe an inch or two taller than Vance, and appeared to be in good shape. He was lean and had large forearms, like those of an iron worker or blacksmith. There was not a speck of dirt or grime on any of his exposed skin, and his hair even had a slight shine to it.

"It's always nice to see new faces," the man said as he pulled a chair up to the group, although he didn't sit down on it. Instead, he leaned over a bit and supported himself by putting his left hand on the back of the chair.

"My name's William McCoy, and I'm mostly in charge here," he said with a friendly smile.

"Mostly?" Vance asked.

McCoy gave him a piercing look, but the smile never left his face.

"Yes, mostly. Everyone here has a job...and an opinion. I run the day-to-day business of this place, but I allow those with qualifications better than my own to take care of the details when it comes to things like security and scavenging." McCoy spoke with a very authoritative tone. His voice wasn't necessarily deep, although it could be if he tried. It was assertive and confident, regardless of how high or low it was.

After looking over each member of the group with the same welcoming smile, he asked, "I'm assuming you all plan to stay?"

"Not all of us," Thomas said, "My sister and I are going to Albuquerque. The others in the group might want to stay, though. We're only going down there to find our parents."

"Albuquerque...that's a heck of a long way," McCoy said, the smile fading and a look of concern replacing it, "Places like this base are few and far between. I'd reconsider, if I were you. But you can decide all that later. For now, let's get you all cleaned up and have someone look over the girl."

Samantha was obviously in need of medical treatment. The area around the laceration on the side of her head was now swollen up pretty good, and the girl clutched her injured right side. A permanent expression of pain was on her face.

"I'm a nurse," Mindy said to McCoy, "As long as I have what I need, I can take care of her."

McCoy's smile came back as he nodded to her.

"Fantastic. Medical professionals are something we're short on," McCoy told her, "Now you folks go with Sergeant Overfield. He'll take you to the showers, and then you'll need to come back so I can ask you a few questions."

Overfield escorted the group to a large shower area. It was very clean, and the base still had power so they didn't have to fumble around in the dark. It was fairly open, with no private showers. Just a small wall on either side of each shower head, so at least no one could see you unless they were in the shower directly across from yours. The group split up, spreading themselves around the shower room so they could get as much privacy as possible. Vance was the only exception, who chose the shower right next to Thomas.

"So what do you think?" Vance asked as he peeled his clothes off and hung them over the back part of the divider. He also placed his Glock on the wall, even though he was in the shower.

"About this place?" Thomas asked, peering at Vance over the short wall.

"Yes."

"I think it looks great, so far. And I wouldn't blame you if you guys chose to stay here. But I...we...we just can't. We're halfway to Albuquerque. I can't stop. We *have* to find our parents."

Strangely, Thomas didn't feel weird about showering with another guy in the very next stall. Perhaps it was because the only things visible over the wall were the very tops of shoulders and up. Except for Vance and Mark, who were both about the same height. For them the walls exposed everything from just below the armpit on up. Not that any of them cared *too* much. They were bonded with each other now on a very fundamental level, regardless of how little time they had spent together.

"I didn't ask if you'd stay," Vance said, "I asked what you thought about it."

"Too early to tell, I guess," Thomas replied.

The group enjoyed their hot showers immensely, and no one's shower lasted any less than twenty-five minutes. Being able to wash the grime off with hot water in a real shower was an extreme luxury. The group even cracked a few jokes while showering, but nothing too bad. None of them had known each other very long, and Mark and Virginia were good Christian people who didn't normally discuss anything too inappropriate.

Once they were done, they walked out of the shower room with fresh clothes on and met Overfield in the hallway. The staff sergeant and the other two armed men escorted them back to the cafeteria. After sitting them down, Overfield left the two armed soldiers with the group and went through the same door that McCoy had come through earlier to greet them. After only one or two minutes, McCoy came back out.

"Hello again," he said cheerfully as he entered, that same friendly smile on his face, "I bet you're feeling a lot better. It's amazing how much something like a shower can improve one's mood, isn't it?"

"We greatly appreciate the hospitality," Thomas said.

"Not a problem at all. Hospitality is growing increasingly rare these days, so I always try to remain as accommodating as possible," McCoy said, followed by, "I have a few questions for you all. Which one of you is in charge?"

The group (except Vance) looked around at each other for a moment. Finally, Mark raised his arm and pointed a quick thumb toward Thomas.

"Guess he is. We've been following his lead, mostly," the old farmer said.

"Alright, then for the sake of simplicity, he'll be the one to answer. Don't worry, my questions aren't difficult and they aren't riddles." McCoy chuckled slightly.

"Alright then," Thomas said, feeling a little nervous.

"Where did you all come from?" McCoy asked, placing his hands on his hips.

"Seattle," Thomas quickly replied.

"All of you?" McCoy asked.

"My sister and I. Mark and his wife lived in Mountain Home, Idaho." Thomas looked over at Mark and Virginia. Mark appeared calm, but Virginia looked a little uneasy.

"And what about your other member of the group?" McCoy asked Thomas, nodding his head in Vance's direction.

"I'm...I'm not real sure," Thomas answered.

97

"You don't even know where a member of your group came from? That is very unwise, my friend. Especially for a leader."

"Well, I'm not really a leader. Not in any official capacity. And I don't make it a habit to pry into people's lives, especially when a person has only been with us for a couple of days. Vance saved us. Without him, we'd all likely either be walking around searching for human flesh or in the bellies of the undead right now." Thomas straightened his posture a little, not wanting to appear foolish to McCoy.

"I see," McCoy said, looking at Vance out of the corner of his eye, "So then—Vance—where are you from?"

"New Mexico," he answered calmly.

"Why'd you travel North?"

"New Mexico is where I used to call home. That's not where I was when all of this started," he told him.

"So where were you?" McCoy pried, a slight smile forming on his face.

Vance paused for a brief moment, staring back at McCoy.

"I'm not at liberty to discuss that, at the moment. I don't make it a habit of telling strangers everything about myself all at once."

McCoy chuckled quietly and looked down at the tile floor of the cafeteria.

"I respect that. In time we'll learn to trust one another. That is, if you decide to stay. That's entirely up to you."

"Noted," Vance said. He was perhaps being a little too confrontational for a first meeting, but Thomas didn't really blame him.

"What are your names?" McCoy asked, "We haven't been properly introduced."

"Thomas Briggs, and this is my sister Mindy. That's Mark and his wife Virginia. This is Vance."

"Good. So now I just have one more question." McCoy took a couple steps closer to the group, but he did so calmly and slowly so it didn't come off as threatening or uncomfortable.

"Okay..." Thomas felt uneasy, for some reason.

"Have you killed anyone? Living, I mean?" he asked.

"My sister and I haven't. I don't believe Mark and his wife have." Thomas looked over at Vance.

"Well?" McCoy turned his full attention to Vance.

"Yes," Vance said coldly.

"How many?" McCoy pried.

"A few."

"And what did they do to deserve death?"

Vance glanced over at Thomas, but still had a stoic, indifferent look on his face. It seemed to be his natural, neutral expression.

"They threatened my chances of survival," Vance said dryly.

McCoy's smile grew a bit, and he glanced around at each of the survivors who made up the small group.

"Alright. Overfield and his men will show you to your quarters for the evening. Tomorrow, if you decide to leave, then so be it. If you decide to stay, then after you've been here for a couple of days we will return all of your weapons and supplies to you."

"Wait...why can't we have our supplies?" Thomas asked.

"You'll have no need for them. We have everything for you. And frankly, we don't know any of you from Adam, and my people don't have time to sort through your things in detail. Standard safety precautions. Also, you might be less inclined to steal from us or harm one of us if we have possession of your belongings. As I said...you all are strangers here. It's nothing personal, I assure you. Mr. Vance here is only able to keep his sidearm because Sergeant Overfield personally vouched for him. Besides...what can one man with a single handgun possibly do, when I have a whole platoon of soldiers on my side?"

McCoy gave the group one last friendly smile before turning and leaving the cafeteria. Thomas looked around the group and saw that his sister looked a little uncomfortable. Vance still had the same emotionless stare, but somehow Thomas got the vibe that he was suspicious and perhaps a little annoyed. But for all he knew, that's how Vance was all the time. He didn't exactly know the guy very well, and he had to remind himself of that. He could easily throw the group under the proverbial bus for his own benefit, or steal from them, or hurt one of them, and there wouldn't be a damn thing any of them could do to stop him.

"Well...now what?" Mark asked, staring at the floor.

"Now we go with Staff Sergeant Overfield so he can show us to our 'quarters'," Vance said quietly. Thomas looked over and saw that Vance was giving Overfield a cold stare.

"Right this way," Overfield said with a forced smile after looking away from Vance's stare.

Overfield escorted the group out of the cafeteria and up a flight of stairs to the second floor of the visitor's center. After rounding a couple of corners, he opened a door and flipped the light on. Inside were eight twin-sized beds, but they only had mattresses on them.

"Here you are," Overfield said.

Everyone but Vance stepped inside.

"I'm not going in there," Vance said sternly.

"Come on, buddy. Don't turn this into an ordeal," Overfield said amiably.

Vance glanced over his shoulder and noticed the two armed men standing behind him. He reluctantly stepped inside the room and looked around, but didn't move more than ten feet from the doorway. Overfield and one of the guards stepped inside as well.

"This is where you'll be calling home for the night. Our medical staff should be up here shortly to look you guys over and make sure no one needs any medical treatment." Overfield still sounded friendly. He even had a welcoming smile on his face.

"Got any bedding?" Mark asked as he looked around.

"Yes. You'll find all of that through the door on the other side of the room, in the bathrooms," Overfield replied.

The group—except Vance—got their blankets and pillows and started making their beds. Vance remained close to the open door, staring at Overfield nearly the whole time. It was blatantly obvious that he made Overfield uncomfortable. Mindy sat a blanket and pillow on Vance's bed and gave him a quick smile. He didn't thank her, or even give any indication that he had noticed. Another minute or two passed before two more people who were unarmed entered the room. They both had stethoscopes around their necks, and one of them carried an orange gym bag.

The two medical "staff" checked everyone over, and after Mindy insisted on treating Samantha herself, they gave her the supplies she requested and left the room. Thomas was beginning to feel uneasy, mostly because of Vance's piercing glare. It was directed at Overfield, and Thomas wasn't sure why. Overfield had been friendly, and had even allowed Vance to keep his weapon.

"Thank you for your patience and understanding. See you in the morning," Overfield said before turning and heading through the door.

"But it's one o' clock in the afternoon," Thomas said, looking at his watch.

Overfield paused and gave him a quick nod before closing the door.

"What the hell?" Mark asked.

"Why didn't you want to come in here, Vance?" Thomas asked, now feeling like perhaps Vance had a very valid reason.

A loud *clank* emanated from the other side of the door. It echoed throughout the room, and the whole group stared at the door.

"That's why," Vance said.

"What the fuck?" Thomas stood and walked toward the door.

"I saw the latch on the door frame. We're prisoners now," Vance said as he turned and began making his bed.

"Fuck that!" Thomas said before approaching the door and banging on it twice with his fist. Then he yelled at the top of his lungs, *"Hey! You can't do this!"*

"They can, and they did. Now stop before you turn this into an 'ordeal'," Vance said calmly, mocking Overfield even though he was no longer there, "Besides, you're scaring the girl."

Thomas turned around and saw Samantha huddled in Mindy's arms, obviously worried.

"Why didn't you say something?" Thomas asked Vance in a quiet voice.

"And then what, huh? You suddenly nut up and fight your way out of here?" Vance asked him, throwing his pillow on the bed and turning toward Thomas.

"We could have done *something*," Thomas replied quietly.

"Yeah...'something'. That's awfully fuckin' descriptive. Hell of a plan you have there, chief," Vance told him as he sat down.

"Well it's better than staying quiet like a good little boy and letting them lock us in here to do God knows what!" Thomas said to him, raising his voice slightly.

"Whatever. Calm down and ride it out," Vance said.

"How the *fuck* can you be so calm about this? We just got locked in a room!" Thomas threw his hands in the air.

"Again...what would you have done if I had told you?"

"Protested! Refused! *Something!*" Thomas was shouting now.

"Oh, there ya go!" Vance actually chuckled, "Passive non-compliance works well on soldiers with assault rifles. You're right, I should have told you. Then we wouldn't be in this mess. Thomas Briggs would have saved the day with his stern refusal to follow their orders."

"Fuck you!" Thomas roared, pointing his finger at Vance, "Are you telling me you couldn't have done something to avoid this!?"

Vance jumped up from his bed and took two large steps toward Thomas, stopping less than a foot away.

"Sure I could have," Vance said sternly, but not loudly, "and I would have made it out of here alive. But what would have happened to your helpless ass? Or your sister? Or the injured girl who was just raped? Or Mark or Virginia? Think about more than just the next two minutes. Not doing so will only ensure your death in this world."

Vance glared at Thomas briefly before turning and sitting back down on his bed. Thomas felt a little dumb, perhaps a little ungrateful. He had just openly expressed that he didn't have faith in Vance, which wasn't true at all. He was just so mad at the whole situation. It had been his idea to come here, after Vance expressed his apprehension.

"Besides, there's a single bolt keeping that door locked. I can kick it open if we need to," Vance said calmly, staring down at his hands, "There will be at least one guard sitting outside—who undoubtedly just heard all of our arguing, by the way—but as long as there aren't more than sixteen of them, we'll be okay. That's how many bullets I have in my Glock."

Thomas looked down at the floor for a moment, searching for the appropriate words.

"What makes you think it will all be okay?" he asked Vance, this time quietly.

"I didn't say it will all be okay, but I don't think they're going to hack us up into little pieces and eat us or anything like that," he said, "Regardless of what kind of people they are, what they're doing is the smart thing to do. They don't know us, nor do they know if one of us has been bitten and is maybe hiding the mark. Think of this is an observation period. There's no way they're going to risk us stealing their shit, or infecting others and making this place unlivable. No matter how much it sucks, this is necessary, and I would do the same thing. Assuming I would be taking in survivors at all, of course. In any case, the worst thing you can do right now is make them think we're bad people, or uncooperative, or dangerous. So just sit down, shut up, and don't go all in until you know what cards you have in your hand."

Vance got up and dragged one of the unused beds over to his, pushing them together to form a much larger bed. Then he sat down and smacked his pillow a couple of times before kicking his feet up and laying down on his back. He crossed one foot over the other, placed his hands on his stomach and interlaced his fingers, looking calm and comfortable. Thomas shook his head slightly in frustration and walked over to his own bed. He sat down quickly, looking for all the world like a defeated child who just got grounded.

"It just sucks, ya know?" Thomas said.

"Mm-hm," Vance groaned, but it sounded like he was just doing as little as possible so that Thomas would get the message that he didn't want to speak.

Thomas looked over his shoulder at the others. Mark was running his fingers through his hair, sitting next to his wife. Virginia was sitting quietly with no expression on her face—her posture was impeccable—and nervously smoothing out her dress with her hands. Mindy was holding Samantha, who was quietly crying into her shoulder like a daughter would a mother. But even from across the room Thomas could tell that Mindy's eyes were full of tears. Hell, he felt like crying himself. But Vance's ass-chewing had woken him up a little. *What would have happened to your helpless ass?* The words seemed to be hanging in the air, even now. Thomas wanted to smack himself, or punch something, just to let out some of his anger and frustration and confusion. Was he really helpless? Of course he was. What could he do to a soldier armed with a gun? What could he do to *anyone* armed with *anything*? He knew he had no training, no proficiency in anything that could hurt or kill someone. Worse than that, he had no mental fortitude when it came to tough situations like these. No reserve of rage or ruthlessness to equal the playing field. After all, he could almost feel an ulcer forming every time he had to make a simple decision. Could he strangle a man to death with his bare hands? He didn't know the real answer, no matter how much he wanted to be able to say that he could if he had to.

Thomas got up and walked past the other group members, toward the bathroom door. He didn't look at anyone, instead focusing on the door like it was all he was capable of seeing. After calmly opening and closing the door, he walked over to one of the stalls and stepped inside. His hand shook as he turned the lock on the door. Then his body fell straight down onto the toilet, and he began crying. Tears fell from his face and dripped down between his legs, hitting the gray tile floor and forming tiny puddles of sadness and frustration and anger. His jaw fell open on its own, his mouth twisted into a horrible sign of despair, his shoulders heaved as he bawled his eyes out. At this point he physically hurt inside because of how terrible the world around him had become. It was like a nightmare that he had been trapped in for months. But it had still seemed surreal while he had been behind the relative safety of the walls that surrounded his Seattle apartment. Now it was all hitting him at once. He had thrust himself into a markedly different world than the one he had been in just a few days prior. Now it was all catching up to him. The reality of the situation was crashing down on him like a ton of bricks. How was he going to continue on? He had only been away from home for four days and he was already regretting his decision. Of course he was concerned for his parents, especially now that he saw what everything was like. But what the hell could he do for them? He couldn't even keep himself alive, let alone his sister, and certainly not his parents who were both in their fifties.

The bathroom door creaked open. Thomas immediately froze with his face buried in his hands, then he grabbed some toilet paper and wiped his eyes and nose. He took a deep breath and quietly exhaled, not wanting to let anyone know his current state.

"Thomas?" Mindy's familiar voice asked from the other side of the stall door.

"Oh, Mindy, it's you," Thomas replied. His voice was shaky.

There was nothing he could do to hide his sadness from his sister. Even if he had the capability to magically remove the puffiness around his bloodshot eyes, completely remove every noticeable feature of despair, his sister would still be able to tell. They had always been amazingly close, and could read each other like a book. They had both been depressed messes around each other before.

"You okay?" his sister asked.

"Yeah...yeah, I'm fine," Thomas said as he stood up and snorted as he wiped his nose once more. He then opened the door and stepped out.

"Oh, Thomas..." Mindy immediately said once she saw her brother, then wrapped her arms around his neck and hugged him tightly. In truth, she had already known he was in a bad way by the way he looked when he walked to the bathroom. Then his voice...she knew something was very wrong.

"I don't know what to do," Thomas told her, tears running down his cheeks once more. His voice was starting to crack, the knot in his throat growing larger and more unmanageable.

"Everything will be alright," she told him, her own voice sounding a little shaky.

"What the hell do we do?" Thomas asked, mostly rhetorically. He was now crying so hard that his vision was completely blurred.

Thomas removed his glasses and let them hang from his hand while he hugged his sister. He was farsighted, so he could see everything clearly until his sister pulled away from him and held his face in her hands. Her features were slightly blurry through Thomas's bad, tear-filled eyes. He wiped his eyes off, squeezing the tears out of their corners. Mindy's face was still blurry. Thomas couldn't make out the little details of her face, but he didn't exactly need to. She was his little sister, and the image of her face was forever ingrained in his mind.

"Listen to me," she said with a shaky voice and glossy eyes, "We will figure this out. We'll make it to Albuquerque and find mom and dad, and find somewhere safe."

Thomas turned his head and wiped his face on his shoulder and bicep. He was an absolute mess. His little sister was consoling him. He was the man...he was supposed to be tough and carry his sister through hard times. Now she was picking him up from the ground. Metaphorically, of course. Thomas wasn't a large man, by any stretch of the imagination, but Mindy was a very petite girl and had very little upper body strength.

"I just feel lost, sis," Thomas began, his eyes drying up a little and his voice returning to a more normal tone, "I'm completely lost in a world like this. I can't keep you safe. Or mom, or dad. Hell, I can't even keep myself safe."

Thomas threw his hands up and took a couple steps back before turning to the sink.

"That's not true, Thomas," Mindy said.

"Oh come on, Mindy. Who are you kidding?" Thomas slapped his hand on the counter and turned on the sink's faucet, "You heard Vance. I'm helpless."

Mindy crossed her arms and looked up at the ceiling for a brief moment.

"You're an architect, Thomas. You've never had to do any of...'this'. But you're also a genius. A very capable genius, at that. Smart enough to realize what's going on around you and what

106

needs to be done to stay alive. You're right...you're no bad ass. You're not a soldier, or a cop, or a biker, or some gang member. But that doesn't mean you have to *stay* 'helpless'. I have faith in you. Whatever you set your mind to, you can do."

Mindy's words were heartfelt and encouraging. Thomas threw water on his face and turned toward his sister.

"Do you really think we have a chance? Without someone like Vance on our side, I mean?" Thomas asked her. It wasn't rhetorical, or sarcastic. It was an honest question.

"Of course. You're my big brother. You can do anything."

Mindy gave him a warm smile before stepping over to him and giving him one more quick hug. She stood on her tip-toes and kissed him on the cheek, patted him on the chest, and walked out of the bathroom. Thomas leaned up against the bathroom counter and let out a heavy sigh as he looked up at the ceiling.

<u>6</u>

It was now eight o' clock at night. Two guards had opened the door at around six o' clock and shoved a meal cart through, then quickly closed the door again. Supper was actually pretty decent; it consisted of instant mashed potatoes, canned peaches, and peanut butter and jelly on homemade bread. An odd combination, to say the least, but with things as they were no one complained at all. Now the group was bored out of their minds. Mark had been napping for the past hour. Virginia spent a lot of time in the bathroom, and the time she spent out with the others she was off to the side by herself, sometimes humming a little tune while cleaning her nails or quietly listening to the others talk. Mindy sat with Samantha most of the time, who was wrapped up in a blanket and leaning against Mindy. The girl's attitude was a bit better, and she had even giggled a few times at things Mindy had said. Vance's earlier nap had only lasted about half an hour, and Thomas doubted that he had actually been asleep during that time.

"How long do you think they'll keep us in here?" Samantha asked. Thomas was now sitting across from them on the next bed.

"Well, Overfield said he would see us in the morning. That doesn't mean they'll let us out of here, but I hope they will." Thomas had his elbows resting on his knees, and he felt much more relaxed now than he had earlier.

"I'm starving," Samantha said.

"There's still some peaches left. I'll get you some," Mindy said with a smile. She got up from the bed, caressing Samantha's face in a motherly way as she did, and walked across the room to the food cart.

Thomas noticed Vance walk past and into the restroom. It was the first time he had gone since they had been put in this room. Thomas took the opportunity to speak to Vance in private. After Mindy came back with the peaches, he waited another few moments before getting up and going in.

Vance was at the sink, washing his hands vigorously. He had enough soap that both of his hands were lathered up and completely covered with white bubbles. He gave Thomas a glance out of the corner of his eye as he rinsed the soap off.

"I'm..." Thomas began, but then paused, "I apologize for how I acted earlier. I had no right to talk like that, especially to you. You saved our lives more than once. I owe you...everything. Thank you for that. And I'm sorry for making a fool out of myself and disrespecting you like that."

Vance dried his hands off with paper towels, not immediately answering. When he was finished he threw the paper towels away and turned to face Thomas.

"No, Thomas, you *did* have a right to talk like that."

Thomas was a little surprised.

"You had just been locked in a room, in a place where you had expected to be welcomed with open arms as a fellow survivor. You did nothing that any normal human being wouldn't have done in the same situation." Vance leaned against the counter and crossed his arms.

"So..." Thomas searched for the words, "But, what I did wasn't right. I shouldn't have done that."

"What you *should* or *shouldn't* do is completely irrelevant. The point is that you acted according to the situation you had just been thrown into. That doesn't mean it was the right way to act, but it means that you have nothing to be sorry for." Vance nodded his head as he spoke. His words were calm and quiet.

"Okay, well..." Thomas hadn't expected the conversation to go this way. He had fully expected Vance to grunt in response and then walk out.

"That being said," Vance started, his voice a little more stern, "Don't be such a fucking pussy. Stand up for yourself. Do what needs to be done."

Now Thomas was really confused, but Vance's directness made him let out a chuckle.

"You're a man, for fuck's sake. I don't know anything about you, but you don't seem like you've done so much as rip a band-aid off a kid. I bet you've always followed the rules, always met the expectations that were set for you, always played nice." Vance smiled a little.

"Well...uh..." Thomas chuckled again, "Yeah...I guess you're pretty spot on."

"So man up!" Vance growled as he jolted forward away from the counter. Thomas jumped back a little, his eyes wide.

"Hold your head fucking high and show the world that you've got a pair of balls!" Vance told him, his voice still sounding more like the growl of a drill sergeant, "It's not about being a tough guy. It's about surviving. Do whatever you have to do to ensure you make it out alive, and that your sister makes it out alive, and that whoever else looks to you for guidance makes it out alive. You owe that to yourself and to those who depend on you. Now I don't know why, but Mark and Virginia and your sister look to you to make the decisions for the group. And since they do, then most likely whoever else joins you along the way will as well. Like it or not, that means you have to be a certain kind of person. Who you are right now is unacceptable. If you stay how you are, you *will* die. Your sister *will* die. That much I can guaran-fucking-tee you."

"So...what do you suggest?" Thomas asked cautiously.

Vance smacked his hand on the counter. The loud slap echoed throughout the small bathroom.

"See! That's what I'm fuckin' talking about. You just automatically default to subservience. You're so used to rolling over and letting life pound you in the ass that you don't even know what it's like to be your own person. Stop doing exactly what others want you to do and do what you *need* to. Whatever it takes to survive, at any cost. Start with changing yourself a little. Right

110

now you look like a goddamn high school math teacher!"

Thomas looked down at his clothes. He had on blue jeans and a green and brown plaid button-up shirt tucked into his pants nice and neat. He was wearing a pair of cheap, brown, business casual shoes. His hair was still trimmed nice and neat and brushed to the side, and he only had a little stubble on his face from a couple days of not shaving. His glasses just added to the dorky *come steal my wallet* look.

"I guess I see what you mean," he finally replied, "So..."

"No!" Vance interrupted as he stuck his hand up, "Don't even ask me what I think you should do or any bullshit like that. There's no dress code in the apocalypse, but shit...at least make yourself look a little rough. Make people hesitant to approach you. And it's not just what kind of clothes you wear and how you wear them. You've gotta change up *here*..."

Vance poked Thomas in his head with his index finger.

"Get in touch with your instincts. Find that primal side and bring it closer to the surface so you can use it when needed. Don't look so goddamn friendly all the time."

And at that, Vance turned around and walked out of the bathroom. Thomas was left a little bewildered. He finally sighed and chuckled slightly.

* * *

Another two hours passed, and Virginia was now asleep. Mark had woken up long enough to use the restroom, then went back to sleep about twenty minutes later. Mindy was awake and laying on her bed, but Samantha was curled up in her arms and sleeping deeply. Vance was sitting on his bed at the end of the row, his back turned to everyone. Thomas quietly crept into the bathroom. Mindy took notice, but only because she could tell that Thomas was making it a point to be quiet.

Thomas entered the bathroom and went over to the small closet, where they had gotten their blankets. Inside were a couple more blankets,a few bars of soap, a couple bottles of disinfectant, some cleaning supplies, and an unopened package of disposable razors. No shaving cream, though. Thomas pulled out the package of razor blades and went over to the sink. Staring at himself in the mirror, he looked himself over and sighed. He was really quite a handsome man, but any strong features he might have had were constantly concealed by his more..."nerdy"...aspects. His hair was always kept brushed over to the side. When it fell, he had a habit of always pushing it back to its "proper" position. His glasses were definitely chosen for their cost effectiveness and practicality, not appearance. They weren't large glasses, but they were brown and ugly. They were actually bifocals, and he really only needed them for reading. Wearing them constantly had become a habit while Thomas had been in college, when he needed to wear them much more often than not to study and do his schoolwork. He also had a habit of losing them if they weren't on his head, and the last thing he wanted to do while studying for a final was to take the time to go buy another pair. He also continued using them a lot when he became an architect, constantly pouring over blueprints and forms and research. Again, it only reinforced his habit of wearing them constantly. He usually only took them off when he was tired or had a headache, besides the obvious times like when he was showering or sleeping.

Thomas removed his glasses and placed them on the counter. He hardly needed to wear them constantly nowadays. He ran one of the disposable razors under the hot water and brought it to his neck. Within a few short minutes, all of the stubble on his neck was gone. It was a little dry, but he didn't exactly have any lotion, shaving cream, or aftershave to put on. Instead, he turned the cold water on and dampened his neck completely. That would temporarily solve the dryness problem and hopefully help prevent razor burn. He decided to leave the stubble on his face; never before had he had a beard, so he wasn't sure what he would look like. Now to deal with the hair. There was very little he could do with it, and he desperately wanted a pair of scissors. Currently his hair was about two inches long on top, maybe an inch and a half on the sides and back. It all laid down completely flat, except his bangs which were slightly fluffy. All of the hair on top of his head was parted on the left side and brushed over to the right. Thomas actually shook his head in disapproval. How did he allow himself to walk around like this? It was no wonder people always took advantage of him, or talked down to him, or stole his lunch money. He looked like someone who lived in his mother's basement. Not that there was anything wrong with middle-aged basement dwellers, but it wasn't exactly the best look to have in this world. He had never played any of those online multiplayer role-playing games, but he imagined that he probably looked like he did. Or used to, anyway.

He finally got the idea to pull the small razor blade out of the razor he just used and try to shorten his bangs a little so they didn't look quite so ridiculous. Popping the blade out proved sort of challenging, but he eventually got it without breaking it or slicing one of his fingers open. He brushed his bangs straight down over his forehead with his fingers and gently grabbed the ends of a few strands of hair. Using the razor blade, he carefully cut off about half an inch from his bangs. He was meticulous while doing this, ensuring the length was uniform all the way across. Then he leaned down into the sink and threw warm water all over his hair with his hands. He vigorously ran his fingers back and forth, trying to get all of the hair wet so it could be worked with. It also felt amazingly good on his scalp, the warm water running down his face and the back of his neck. When he was satisfied, he dried his hair most of the way with a towel and then ran his fingers through it, making sure none of it was still trying to lean sideways across his head. When he was done and his hair was almost completely dry, the part that used to run down the left side of his head was no longer visible. His bangs parted in the middle and hung down around either side of his forehead. The rest of his hair laid down forward, and had a slightly more "messy" look. Thomas actually kind of liked it. His dark brown hair was not too thick and not too thin, so it was easy to work with and laid how he wanted.

The next thing to go was the plaid button-up. It was a

comfortable shirt, but hardly appropriate zombie killing attire. Perhaps for a big, muscular man who was an iron worker or logger, but not Thomas and his thin frame. He unbuttoned it and pulled it off. Beneath was a light gray undershirt, which he pulled out from his pants and let hang down over his belt. There was nothing he could do with his jeans or shoes. They would have to wait until he had his belongings back. If he ever got them back, of course. Thomas looked in the mirror once more, and realized that he looked like a whole new person. Not his basic features, obviously, but the vibe he gave off was undoubtedly completely different than before.

Thomas exited the bathroom, feeling a little more confident for some reason. There was something about his new casual look that made him feel a little more loose and no-nonsense. It wasn't to impress anyone, but it was to get rid of the, "I'm a pushover," look he previously conveyed. He walked out into the sleeping area with a little more pep in his step. Mindy gave him a strange look and smiled.

"What do you think?" he whispered quietly.

Mindy smiled and gave him a thumbs-up. Thomas then walked toward Vance, stopping about ten feet away from his bed.

"Hey Vance," Thomas said in a loud whisper.

Vance slowly turned and looked at him.

"Fuck you," Thomas said playfully after Vance got a good look at him, then turned and fell down onto his bed.

Vance turned back around and chuckled to himself. He wasn't yet sure if what he had said to Thomas would turn out to be a good or bad thing. He finally laid down and placed his handgun under his pillow before covering up with his blanket and closing his eyes for the night.

* * *

"Well, what's your official report?" William McCoy asked Staff Sergeant Overfield during their usual morning briefing.

"The guard on watch all day yesterday had nothing to report.

114

He listened in on them periodically and said they seemed like normal people. They weren't plotting anything, didn't try to escape. In fact, Vance—the special forces guy—he said to wait it out because quarantining new people was a wise thing to do. I heard that myself. They got into a bit of an argument as soon as the door shut and I locked it. That's expected, though." Overfield stood firmly in McCoy's personal quarters, his hands held behind his back in a very military manner. He stood this way every morning.

McCoy poured himself a glass of water and sat down at his desk, which was right outside his bedroom. He had claimed a small office area and converted it into a bedroom/office/living room. It was nice, because the smaller office—like where a high-ranking officer might be—was big enough to keep his bed in. Directly outside that was a slightly larger office, like where the officer's secretaries/assistants would sit and work. Then there was yet another room attached to that one that was fairly large, and it had previously been a conference room. There were plenty of those on base, so McCoy had taken the table and chairs out and made it more like his personal lounge. These three rooms made up McCoy's personal residence, which was much more than anyone else had. Even Overfield stayed in what had previously been a small storage area, even if he *did* have the tiny room all to himself.

"So you don't suspect we'll have any problems out of them?" McCoy asked him, his elbow resting on his chair and his hand covering his mouth in a thoughtful manner.

"No, sir," Overfield responded.

"And this Vance guy...he can be trusted?" McCoy asked.

"I can't answer that for sure, sir. I don't know him," Overfield said.

"Well you trusted his appearance enough to let him keep his weapon," McCoy said, sounding slightly agitated, "And now you're telling me you don't know if he can be trusted?"

"I suppose he can be as much as the rest of them."

"Goddamn it!" McCoy shouted abruptly, slamming his fist down on his desk, "Give me a straight answer! Is the man going to kill one of us in our sleep?"

115

His long black hair wasn't up in a ponytail yet, and he hadn't shaved since yesterday morning. He had just woken up not long ago, so his usual morning agitation was still present.

Overfield was unperturbed. His face remained stoic, and his tone was still calm and business-like. After giving McCoy a couple of seconds to calm down, he finally answered his question.

"No, I don't think he's going to kill one of us in our sleep. Not unless we give him a reason to."

McCoy finished his glass of water and got up. He walked over to the window and looked out over the airstrip from his second story window. Survivors were moving around below, tending to their daily tasks.

"What did he do? In the Army, I mean?" McCoy asked after a long while.

"He was in the special forces," Overfield answered.

McCoy rolled his eyes, although Overfield couldn't see it.

"I mean specifically...what did he do?" McCoy spoke slowly to express his foul mood and current agitation.

"He was an Intelligence Sergeant. Before that he was a Weapons Sergeant."

"Explain to me what those roles do in a little more detail," McCoy told him, but he wasn't being difficult. Overfield knew that McCoy had very little knowledge when it came to military details like job descriptions.

"A Weapons Sergeant is proficient in both light and heavy weaponry, as well as the use of all kinds of explosives. The job description is a lengthy one. They are tasked with going behind enemy lines, performing recon, infiltrating high security areas, remaining completely undetected, destroying enemy resources, supplies, weaponry, buildings—whatever—with both standard and improvised explosives. They also sometimes recruit and train nationals from whatever area they are operating in, so they can fight for our side." Overfield was very knowledgeable, even if he was just a lowly grunt in the National Guard. He had been active duty Army many years ago, and had been around long enough to know a thing or two.

"And the other one? The Intelligence Specialist or whatever?" McCoy asked.

"Intelligence Sergeant. He's like the NCOIC," Overfield began.

"The what?" McCoy interrupted.

"Sorry. The Non-Commissioned Officer In Charge. He's responsible for the special forces operators beneath him—making sure they are properly trained, equipped, all that—as well as planning operations and processing intelligence that has been gathered. He's also in charge of establishing security protocols, keeping all classified documents secure, leading interrogations and interviews with enemy prisoners of war and local informants, and briefing everyone on operations. To put it simply: He's the senior NCO in charge of pretty much everything, but not so high up that he isn't directly involved in it and never gets dirty."

"And he was a Sergeant First Class, you said?" McCoy asked after thinking for a moment.

"Yes, sir."

"Interesting..."

"Sir..." Overfield began, "While I don't think this guy is a direct threat, I think it's important to note that his capabilities have to be incredible. He could kill someone in so many different ways, it would make your head spin. And the scariest thing about it is that he would probably do it without thinking twice. Guys like him can kill a man with one hand while eating a sandwich with the other and be okay with it. He is not to be underestimated, and he's not the kind of person..."

Overfield stopped and cleared his throat, then stared at the floor. After a long moment of silence, McCoy turned away from the window and looked at him.

"Well? He's not what?"

"He's not the kind of person to manipulate, sir. I know what you're thinking: We could use a guy like him. And you're right. I'd love to have a guy with his abilities on my side. But men like Vance need to be handled very carefully. He needs to decide on his own that he wants to help us. Waiting until he's comfortable here is strongly suggested, assuming he stays. Trying to trick him or persuade him simply won't work. If he was really a Weapons Sergeant and Intelligence Sergeant, then he has extensive psychological training in addition to extensive training in every imaginable—and some unimaginable—ways to kill people."

"Thank you for the advice, Sergeant Overfield, but I don't need a lesson on how to deal with people," McCoy said hatefully.

"I know, sir. Just...tread carefully. That's all I'm saying."

"Let them out. They're free to go, but don't give them their gear or any weapons unless they want to leave. If there's nothing further, you can go on about your day," McCoy told him as he turned back to the window and looked out, far above the airstrip. His mind was completely lost in thought.

* * *

Thomas was pacing in the open area between the two rows of beds. He had been awake for over two hours now. Vance was awake before he was. Samantha was sitting on her bed rubbing the sleep from her eyes, and Mark and Virginia were washing up a bit in the bathroom. Mindy was running her fingers through her tangled hair and stretching out her back after sleeping on the uncomfortable mattress.

"What the hell could they be doing?" Thomas asked himself out loud.

"Probably forgot about us," Vance said jokingly. At least, Thomas hoped it was a joke. It was hard to tell, since Vance rarely showed any emotion.

"It's 9:30 and no one has been up here. Not even to serve us breakfast, and I'm sure everyone is starving. I know I am." Thomas stopped pacing and placed his hands on his hips.

About five minutes later, they heard the latch on the door slide and the door flew open. Overfield appeared in the doorway with a friendly grin on his face.

"Alright guys, you're free to go. Thank you for your patience and cooperation. I hope you understand that it was nothing personal," the staff sergeant said.

"Thank God," Mindy said as she jumped up.

Vance slowly rose from his bed and turned to face the others. Mark and Virginia were coming out of the bathroom together, and looked a little confused when they saw Overfield standing there.

"We can go," Thomas told them.

Everyone walked out of the room in a single-file line. They followed Overfield, who took them down to the cafeteria. Even before going through the double doors, the group could hear what sounded like a large number of people talking. They stepped into the large room and saw countless people sitting at the tables eating breakfast. Steam rose from the serving area. The group was a little taken aback by it all, since they hadn't seen this many people all together for quite some time. Not ones who were alive, anyway. It almost resembled normal life, like it was just another day and the world wasn't burning to the ground on the other side of the large chain link fences that surrounded the base.

"Go ahead and eat, and then I'll take you to your gear so you can get clean clothes out. Sorry, but you won't be able to take all of your stuff with you just yet. Unless you want to leave, of course." Overfield stood with his hands on his hips, smiling at them.

"I don't think we're going to complain too much anymore. Thank you for the hospitality," Thomas said, staring at the large group of people.

A fair amount of the base's survivor population had taken notice of the new faces. Some of them were smiling, obviously happy that a few more people made it to the colony alive and in good health. Some of them looked a little shady and spoke amongst themselves very suspiciously. All types of people in the world, right?

Thomas led the group over to the serving line. Two people were sitting behind the polished steel warmers, relaxed and eating breakfast. When they noticed Thomas and his group they both quickly jumped up and started putting food on plates. Scrambled eggs, some sort of sausage links, and biscuits. They were very obviously from a can, but no one cared.

"Welcome to The Hill," one of the servers said with a smile as he handed Thomas his plate of food. Thomas smiled back. *The Hill?*

Thomas waited for everyone to get their food before finding a place to sit. The only available area was in the far back corner. Half of the table was empty. Three strangers occupied the table, but scooted around to make room when Thomas and his group sat down.

"Always nice to see new faces," one of the guys said.

"Likewise," Thomas replied. Then, "So everyone calls this place 'The Hill', huh?"

"Yep," the same guy said, "It just kinda stuck. Doesn't really feel right to call it 'Hill Air Force Base', ya know?"

"Yeah, that makes sense," Thomas said through a mouthful of eggs.

The food was amazing. The buttermilk biscuits were a little slice of heaven. Thomas didn't know what the sausage links were made out of at first, but Vance quickly told him it was deer sausage after seeing his look of confusion. The eggs were definitely powdered, but they tasted wonderful nonetheless. After a short time, the three strangers finished their food and left the table.

"So are we staying?" Mark asked his wife, but he said it loud enough for everyone to hear.

"That's up to you, dear," Virginia answered. It had been one of the only things Thomas had heard her say during the whole trip.

"I guess we don't have to decide for sure just yet," Mark said, "How about you guys?"

"We can't," Thomas told him, "We have to find our parents."

"I know, but it's an option. You don't know what Albuquerque might be like. This place seems great." Mark shoveled another big bite of eggs in his mouth.

"We were prisoners not that long ago," Samantha chimed in. Thomas was actually a little surprised.

"Can't really blame 'em, I guess," Mark said.

"What about you, Vance?" Mindy asked, "Are you staying?"

Her eyes looked hopeful, although Thomas couldn't figure out exactly what it meant. He was hoping that she wasn't starting to take exception to Vance. He had noticed her staring at him quite frequently when she thought no one was looking, but it didn't bother him much. Mindy was his little sister, but Thomas didn't fool himself into believing that his little sister didn't have hormones. She was a human being, and Vance was a handsome and well-built guy. He was confident and mysterious. Not to mention the fact that he had saved their asses more than once. So Thomas didn't have a problem with his sister finding Vance attractive, or intriguing, or whatever. He just didn't want her making any moves on him anytime soon.

"I don't know yet," was all Vance said in response to her question.

"Well what's your initial impression of this place?" she asked him.

"It's orderly. It obviously does a good job of representing some level of normalcy. Everyone seems to be in good health and good spirits. I don't know. Looks can be very deceiving. I haven't been here long enough to make a determination. I don't know what the security is like, I don't know if they have people routinely checking to make sure there aren't any breaches in the perimeter. I don't know what this McCoy guy is like, or how much control he really has here. I know he made it seem like he's more of a manager than a king, but there's more to it than that. I could tell by the way he carried himself and spoke, and how the soldiers acted around him. He's Boss Hog around here, I'm sure of it. He's also definitely not military, which is strange. What sort of respectable Army NCO follows a civilian in a situation like this?"

Vance was apparently very observant. His words had also been genuine, and not laced with sarcasm or indifference. Thomas took that to mean that he was very unsure of the situation, and considered it serious enough to analyze and discuss with the group.

"Yeah, I'm not so sure about that McCoy guy. He seemed really fake, I guess," Mindy added.

"Overfield seemed decent enough," Mark said.

Vance wiped his mouth off with a napkin before saying, "I

think Overfield is a pretty genuine guy, for better or worse. What you see is what you get."

"Agreed," Thomas said, "But there was something strange about McCoy."

"Maybe we're just suspicious of everyone," Mark suggested, "He hasn't really done anything to warrant our distrust of him."

"Yeah, but he hasn't done anything to warrant our trust, either," Vance countered, "That goes for everyone here outside of our group."

So, Thomas thought, *did Vance just indirectly say he trusted all of us?*

"Let's just see how it all plays out and keep our eyes and ears open," Thomas told everyone, looking around the table as he did so, "In the meantime, the next time I talk to McCoy I'm going to offer to help him with any sort of construction or engineering project he might have in mind. As a sign of our good intentions, so to speak."

"So does that mean we're staying for a couple of days?" Mindy asked.

"I think it's a good idea, yes. As long as it's okay with you, of course. I just think it wouldn't hurt to take a couple days off from traveling. Get some good food in us, put our minds toward something else, sleep soundly without having to worry about being eaten." Thomas's plate was clean, and he threw his used napkin on top of it.

"Sounds good to me," Mindy agreed.

"Also, whatever we do here will most likely impact whoever decides to stay, if any of us do. I don't want someone here to have a chip on their shoulder because of something I did, and take it out on the ones who stay behind," Thomas added.

"You're so sweet," Mindy teased as she reached up and squeezed Thomas's cheek.

"Indeed. Very sweet," Vance said, the corner of his mouth raised ever so slightly that no one but Thomas probably noticed it.

The others chuckled a little at Vance's joke, but they weren't aware of the conversation that had occurred between Vance and

Thomas the night before. The comment was slightly more mocking with that information in mind, and also perhaps a little funnier. Thomas raised an eyebrow at him and shot him a glare. Vance revealed a more obvious grin as he stood up and carried his plate away. After Vance returned his plate to the kitchen and was about halfway back to the table, Overfield walked up and started speaking to the group.

"McCoy would like to see all of you," he told them. Vance walked up behind him.

"Do you know why?" Thomas asked.

"I do not. All I know is, he wants to see you as soon as you're done with breakfast." At that, Overfield walked away. Vance gave him a cold stare as he did so.

"Wonder what this is about?" Mindy asked.

"Probably nothing," Vance said as he sat back down.

"Yeah, he probably just wants to get to know us a little better. No reason to be alarmed," Thomas told everyone. But he gave Vance a strange look, one that was given right back to him. The two of them seemed to not believe their own words, and they somehow knew that about each other. The look was one of, *I hope we're right*.

A couple more minutes passed, and the last member of the group had finished their breakfast. After everyone turned their plates in, they made their way to the cafeteria's doors where Overfield was waiting.

"Follow me," he said.

Overfield led the group back up the stairs, but went past the room were they had slept. After going around a corner and past two dark rooms, they finally arrived at their destination. It was a brightly lit conference room, and inside were McCoy and his same two guards who had accompanied him when the group had first met him.

"Please," McCoy said as he stuck out his hand toward the chairs around the table, "Have a seat."

Everyone sat down—even Vance—and turned their attention to McCoy. He was sitting at the end of the long table with his fingers interlaced. His hair was still pulled back into a short ponytail, and he was wearing the same gray thermal as yesterday. But today he had on a black vest, almost like a fisherman's vest. His two associates were still armed—one had his sidearm in a shoulder holster, and the other's sidearm was barely visible on his hip.

McCoy gave the group a slight smile and cleared his throat quietly before speaking.

"First of all, I want to thank you for your cooperation. I understand that it was a stressful situation to put you in, but I have over two hundred people to protect here."

"No, we understand," Thomas said, "There's no problem."

"Good. Now that we have that out of the way, I'd like to get to know all of you a little better," McCoy said as he leaned back in his chair.

"Well, I'm an architect," Thomas said, "Lived and worked in Seattle. I helped the local authorities however I could when things started getting real bad. Fortifying walls, building guard towers, things like that."

"That's a very valuable skill set to have," McCoy said to him.

"My sister—Mindy—you already know that she's a nurse," Thomas continued, "She lived with me in Seattle, and provided medical aid to the survivors in our colony. She also trained others so there would be more nurses around to help."

"Great. So why did you two leave, if you already had the safety of a colony?" McCoy asked.

"We wanted to find our parents in Albuquerque," Thomas replied.

"And this colony in Seattle...was it still standing when you left?"

"Yes," was all Thomas said.

"Interesting," McCoy said quietly.

"I was a farmer," Mark volunteered, "My wife Virginia stayed at home. She's great at sewing, making clothes, cooking, all that stuff. And she used to teach grade school, years ago."

"Excellent. Teachers have much to offer society, especially

now," McCoy said with a grin.

"Go on," Mindy said quietly as she nudged Samantha.

"Well..." the girl began, "My name's Samantha. I'm 15. I guess that's all there is to know."

The girl looked down into her lap, obviously unsure of her surroundings. McCoy made his voice as soft and welcoming as he could.

"What is your story?" he asked gently.

"I was...we were..." Samantha hesitated, glancing up at McCoy briefly before looking back down into her lap, "My family and I were part of a small group. One night, we were overrun by those...*things*. They tore through our tents. I barely made it out."

"Alone?" McCoy asked.

"No. There was a man—one of the guys who had already been in the group when they found us—he made it out with me."

"What about your family?" McCoy's voice was still soft and comforting.

"Both of my parents...they didn't make it. I watched them..." Samantha's voice stopped abruptly, as if it had happened involuntarily, "They were killed. And my younger brother was with them."

"So what happened to this man, the one who escaped with you?" McCoy asked.

"We stayed together for a week or so. He took care of me. Then this other group came along. At first they seemed okay. They were mostly men, and they were armed. Tough-looking. We were with them for a couple of days before the man I was with went out on a supply run with three of the others. They came back, but he wasn't with them. They told me he didn't make it."

McCoy nodded his head slightly before asking, "And then what happened?"

"Well..." Samantha's eyes filled with tears, but she somehow kept her composure, "I stayed with the men for a couple of weeks. They weren't good people. At first they were just mean, but then they..."

Samantha's voice cracked and a single tear ran down her face.

"It's alright honey, you don't have to say anymore," Mindy said, rubbing Samantha's back in a comforting way.

"Then they what?" McCoy pressed. Mindy shot him a piercing glare, but he ignored it.

"Then they started doing...*things*...to me. Every night." More tears ran down Samantha's face. She was shaking slightly, trying to keep herself from exploding into a meltdown of emotion.

"That's enough," Mindy said to McCoy, "It's not important."

"Samantha," McCoy said, completely ignoring Mindy, "You're safe now. No one will ever do that to you again. Ever. I promise."

Mindy looked at McCoy with surprise. So did Thomas. Vance still had a cold look on his face, staring on like the only people in the room were him and McCoy. Thomas wasn't quite sure why.

"Let's go get some fresh air," Mindy suggested, patting Samantha on the back.

"No, I'm..." Samantha sniffled and wiped her face with her sleeve, "I'm fine."

There was a long moment of silence before McCoy turned his attention to Vance.

"And you, what's your story?" he asked with a smile.

"You already know," Vance said softly, although it was hard to ever describe his deep, raspy voice as "soft".

"You were in the special forces, yes. But what did you do when all of this started happening?" McCoy asked him.

"I was working in Nevada as a private security contractor. Everything went to shit and I went out on my own," Vance told him.

"Oh, but it wasn't that simple," McCoy said, a strange grin on his face, "It's never that simple."

"It *is* that simple."

"You don't want to discuss it? That's fine, I'll respect that. I merely wanted to get to know everyone. After locking you away last night, I wanted you people to see that I'm just a normal person. Just like you."

McCoy was still smiling, but Thomas sensed an ulterior motive.

126

"Whatever you say," Vance said. His tone was confrontational and laced with disbelief.

"Alright," Thomas interrupted, before someone lost their cool, "Mr. McCoy..."

"Please, call me Bill," McCoy said kindly.

"Alright, Bill..." Thomas continued, "My sister and I won't be staying. I want to make that known up front. I can't speak for everyone else. But while we are here—while you are being generous enough to let us stay for a couple days—I want to return the kindness by helping you however I can. I can assist you with designing towers, buildings—whatever you need—to help your community here."

"I appreciate that," McCoy said, nodding his head and smiling.

"That being said, I want to make it clear that I won't put my sister in harm's way. She's..." Thomas paused for a moment, "...she's all I have, at the moment."

"That's understandable. I would never require any of you to do anything dangerous. We do have to make frequent supply runs, of course, but going outside the gates is completely voluntary. As is everything else around here." McCoy's voice was still laced with charm and kindness.

"Everything?" Vance quickly asked.

McCoy stared at him for a moment, the same smile on his face.

"Yes. Everything."

There was an uneasy silence in the room for several long moments, before McCoy casually leaned back in his chair and began speaking again.

"There are some rules around here," he began, "First off, we do not tolerate violence of any kind. If you have a problem, you come to me. Second, we deal with thieves in a very harsh manner. That's all I will say about that. Lastly, there are boundaries here. You are not permitted to go all over the base. I simply don't have enough people to make sure it's all safe. We've blocked off what we can, and we still periodically patrol the fences to ensure they're still standing, but that's it. There is no security outside of our immediate area, and if you venture beyond the established perimeter you will be immediately expelled from our community. I cannot tolerate anyone jeopardizing our safety. The airfield is off limits as well, though you'll notice it isn't blocked off. There's simply no way to do it. Everyone understand?"

McCoy spoke in a firm but caring manner. He looked around the room once he was finished, and everyone nodded their heads to show they understood. Everyone except Vance.

7

"And you think we can do this with the scrap materials we come across during our supply runs?" McCoy asked Thomas.

Two hours had passed since they had all met in the conference room, and now Thomas was in McCoy's personal quarters looking over a rough plan on how to build a guard tower.

"For the most part. We will, of course, need some actual lumber for the structural parts, but that shouldn't be too hard to find. The rest of it can be made out of scraps your people find. Plywood, siding, sheet metal, whatever. The important parts are the load-bearing elements."

"Good, good..." McCoy said while nodding, looking over Thomas's quickly-drawn blueprints.

"Even if you don't decide to do it now, at least you have a rough design for if and when you build it," Thomas told him after several long moments of McCoy looking over the blueprints.

"No, no...I'm going to start building it today," McCoy said, finally taking his eyes off the blueprints and turning to Thomas, "This is wonderful Thomas, thank you."

McCoy stuck out his hand and Thomas shook it.

"It's my pleasure," Thomas said with a cordial smile, "Although building a small guard tower that doesn't have to meet certain standards is a simple task. Anyone could do it."

"But not as well as you," McCoy quickly said, "...and not with this level of precision. I imagine we're going to save a lot of building materials doing it your way. You know what works without going through trial and error."

"Well I'm glad you like it," Thomas said, "If there's nothing else..."

"No, nothing else," McCoy told him, then, "Well, there is one more thing you could do for me, if you'd be so kind."

Thomas smiled and pulled his hands away from his sides a few inches, facing his palms outward.

"Please, I'll help you in any way I can."

"Your companion, Vance," McCoy started, "is he a...*trusted*, I suppose is the right word...member of your group?"

"Absolutely," Thomas said without hesitation.

"Good. Do you think he would be willing to help us acquire some of the resources we're going to need for this tower?

"You'd have to ask him," Thomas said, "I'm not in charge of him."

"Well you are the group's leader, are you not?" McCoy asked.

"I suppose I am the de facto leader, yes. I never claimed to be, but everyone just seems to turn to me when a decision needs to be made. Probably because this is my journey and they're just along for the ride, so to speak. I'm not sure how much of a leader I am anymore, since we've found your group of survivors."

"You're their leader because you're smart," McCoy said with a serious expression, "You're the smartest one in the group. And not just book smarts...you have street smarts as well."

"Well I'm certainly not gullible, but I'm not exactly experienced in living life on the edge."

Thomas smiled at him, but it was forced.

"You have common sense, which is one of the most valuable qualities to have in this new world we find ourselves living in." McCoy walked around the table as he spoke and approached Thomas, stopping just a couple feet away and placing his hands on his hips.

"Well thank you," Thomas said to him.

"Would you mind loaning Vance to me for half a day? Just long enough to send him out with my team to gather supplies. All he would be doing is providing security."

"Mr. McCoy..." Thomas began.

"Please, call me Bill," McCoy interrupted.

"Bill..." Thomas started again, "I don't *own* Vance. He isn't under my command, and he's not obligated to even respect my wishes. The only person who can decide if Vance does something is Vance."

"I see," McCoy said, looking down at the floor but keeping his seemingly ever present smile, "Could you just talk to him for me, at least? Ask him to help? Whatever his answer is, just send him my way when you're done, if you wouldn't mind."

Thomas looked at McCoy for a moment, but not long enough for it to be considered awkward or rude.

"I'll speak to him," Thomas replied, and gave a courteous nod before leaving the room.

* * *

Mindy and Samantha were walking around outside, enjoying the calm mood of everyone and the safety that the Air Force base provided. Thomas was in McCoy's personal quarters speaking with him about how to build something.

"I feel like we should be doing something," Samantha said.

"What do you mean?" Mindy asked her.

"Something to help out."

Samantha's features were more striking now that she was cleaned up and some of the swelling on her head had gone down. Her light blonde hair was long—almost to the middle of her back—and her young skin was still soft even with everything going on. Her facial features were rounded, still like a small child's. Her eyes were a deep blue color, but she had dark circles under them from all of the stress and crying and not enough sleep. She was a short and very petite girl, standing somewhere around 4'11" and probably weighing no more than 90lbs. Even Mindy seemed to tower over her.

"I think we've earned at least one day of rest," Mindy said to her, gently patting her on the back and giving her a smile,

"Besides, you need time to heal."

"So what do I do now?" Samantha asked her, catching Mindy off guard.

"What do you mean? You do whatever you want to do. Go with us, stay here...it's up to you."

"There's nothing for me here. And I don't want to be a burden on anyone." Samantha crossed her arms across her chest and looked down at the concrete as they walked.

"You're not a burden. Not at all," Mindy said.

"Thank you," Samantha told her, "for everything you've done. Saving me, taking me in, patching me up. But most of all, for being so nice and caring."

The girl looked over at Mindy and gave her a gentle smile, something she had only done a couple of times thus far.

"You're welcome," Mindy said, giving a smile back, "In case you haven't noticed, I've sort of taken you in under my wing."

Mindy reached a single arm around Samantha's shoulders and gave her a quick hug as they kept walking. She really liked the girl, but she mostly just enjoyed having someone who depended on her. It somehow made everything a little less terrible. Just the fact that she needed to be strong for someone. It also gave her something to do.

"Hopefully we can get to Albuquerque without anything bad happening, and we'll find your parents," Samantha said, smiling again.

Mindy's smile faded from genuine to forced. The girl's words made her realize that all kinds of things could go wrong between here and Albuquerque. Did she really want to expose Samantha to more trauma? Or worse...death?

"I'm sure it will all be fine," Mindy replied.

* * *

"Vance!" Thomas shouted as he came out of the visitor's center.

Vance had been sitting on a bench, staring at the front gate. Thomas jogged slowly over to him and sat down.

"I've been looking for you," he said.

"Oh yeah?"

"Yeah. McCoy asked me to speak to you."

"And what does *unser Führer* want you to speak to me about?" Vance asked sarcastically.

"I drew up some plans for a guard tower. One that can be built with as few supplies as possible. He's going to send out a group on a supply run and wanted to know if you'd go with them and help provide security."

"Now why would I do that?" Vance asked him, still staring over in the general area of the gate.

"Mostly to show that we're willing to help, and so he can trust us. He didn't say anything like that, but I'm assuming that's why." Thomas leaned forward and rested his elbows on his knees.

"Well, you know what they say happens when people assume..." Vance began.

"Yeah, yeah..." Thomas leaned back and smiled, "Look...do it for me, okay? I'm not saying I'll be pissed if you don't, but it would mean a lot to me if you did. I'm fairly certain Mark and Virginia are going to stay here, and I want things to be as easy for them as possible."

"Why can't he ask me himself?" Vance asked.

"Don't know," Thomas told him, "But he said that no matter what your answer was, he wanted you to go talk with him. He should still be in his personal quarters; I just came from there about fifteen minutes ago."

"Thanks," Vance said dryly.

Thomas almost reached over and gave Vance a friendly pat on the shoulder, but quickly remembered that Vance was not your typical person. Thomas guessed that he probably didn't like unnecessary physical contact. Or unnecessary conversation, for that matter. So instead of giving him a friendly pat, Thomas thanked him and got up from the bench.

* * *

Vance followed along behind a soldier who was taking him to McCoy's quarters. Once there, the soldier stepped in for several moments before motioning for Vance to go on in.

"Ah, Vance! Glad you decided to come talk to me," McCoy said joyfully. He stopped what he was doing at his desk and walked over to Vance to shake his hand.

McCoy stuck his hand out, and Vance stared at it briefly before looking back at McCoy's face and giving him his usual cold stare.

"It's quite alright," McCoy said as he let his hand drop down by his side, "We're not friends yet."

"What did you want to see me about?" Vance asked, skipping the unnecessary chatter.

"Did Thomas speak with you?" McCoy asked, although he already knew the answer since Vance was standing in his office.

"Yes," Vance answered.

"Good. So will you help us?" McCoy asked him.

"What were you doing in the conference room earlier? All that stuff with the girl?" Vance asked, catching McCoy off-guard.

"What do you mean?" McCoy asked.

"Come on...you can't bullshit a bullshitter. You don't give a damn about what happened to that girl, or about what has happened to any of us, for that matter. What's your angle?"

Vance's words were quiet but firm. His tone wasn't disrespectful, but it was certainly straight to the point.

"I respect guys like you," McCoy said, "Always able to keep your cool, always separating emotion and reason. Always pushing away from anything you don't agree with and not being shy about making it known. And you have the skill set to back that up, too."

"I asked you about the girl," Vance pressed.

"Vance, people like you and I will never be fully understood by anyone. We always do the right thing—sometimes without giving others our reasons—and we can't be swayed from our predetermined path. No matter what, we have to do what's best.

134

Sometimes that means fooling people, or perhaps being a little deceitful. You understand that of course, don't you?"

"Of course I do," Vance replied.

"Good. Now with that being said, I want you to think about my position. I'm in charge of keeping everyone safe, making sure everyone's fed, making sure everyone comes home alive when they go out on supply runs..."

Vance cut him off.

"In the beginning you said you were *mostly* in charge," he reminded him.

McCoy smiled and leaned against his desk, crossing his arms in front of his chest as he did so.

"Yes I did," he said, "I'm an overseer. I check in with everyone to make sure things are running smoothly. But I don't micromanage. I don't tell Staff Sergeant Overfield how to handle his men, or specific security measures he should take."

"Most commanders don't advise the cooking staff on how to make dinner, but that doesn't mean they aren't in charge of everything." Vance's words were slightly colder this time, less trusting.

"Are you going to help me?" McCoy asked, the same smile on his face.

"Why do you need me to help provide security? You have plenty of security personnel already."

"That's true. But the bottom line is that I want my men to have someone they can look up to and learn from. We don't have anyone here who is quite as...*qualified*...as you are. Now Sergeant Overfield...he's a hell of a leader. But he's not like you. Do this for me—go out with my men a couple of times—and I will make sure you and your friends are well taken care."

McCoy gave a little nod at the end. His arms were still crossed across his chest, and he had the same smile glued to his face. His features often appeared gentle and compassionate, but Vance could see something else beneath the surface.

"Alright, but no one's in charge of me. You understand? *No one* will give me orders, nor will I be in charge. I'll just be along for the ride." Vance's tone became slightly more firm at the end.

Vance turned and started walking out of McCoy's office. As he placed his hand on the door's handle, McCoy's voice sliced through the air enough to give James Vance pause.

"I respect who you are, Vance, and I appreciate you doing as I ask. But if you're going to stay here, you're going to have to realize who's really in charge. I can't afford to tolerate any wild cards on this base."

Vance froze for a brief moment, staring at the door as McCoy spoke. Just a couple seconds after McCoy finished, Vance opened the door and left without saying a word.

* * *

"So what's the good word?" Mark asked Thomas as him and Virginia met him in the hallway of the visitor's center.

"Nothing, really. I was kind of waiting for McCoy to open up and start explaining a few things, but he never did. I'll dig deeper once he feels more comfortable with us. Anyway, I helped him design a simple guard tower as sort of a peace offering."

Thomas ran his fingers through his dark brown hair.

"We just saw Vance a couple minutes ago," Virginia said in her quiet, soft voice, "He looked a little angry."

"Don't mind him. I don't think he likes being here, even though no one's keeping him from leaving. But I think his current problem is that McCoy asked him to go out on some supply runs."

"Supply runs? Why?" Mark asked.

"I'm not sure. That's between McCoy and Vance."

"Hey Thomas," Mindy said as she walked up behind them.

"Oh, hey sis. Hello Samantha," Thomas replied.

"Hi," said the girl in her tiny voice.

"So what's going on?" Mindy asked.

"I was just telling Mark and Virginia that I gave McCoy some simple designs for a guard tower as a token of good faith. If Mark and Virginia decide to stay, I want them to be taken care of."

"I see. Where's Vance?" Mindy asked.

"We just saw him a couple minutes ago behind the visitor's center," Mark told her.

"Okay. Samantha, could you stay here with them for a few minutes? There's something I need to talk to Vance about." Mindy patted the girl on the shoulder and started walking away.

"What about?" Thomas asked her.

"Don't worry..." she answered, her voice trailing off as she briskly walked down the hall and around the corner.

"So there's somethin' that's been botherin' me," Mark said.

"What's that?"

"This is a pretty good sized base. Where are all the people? Where's the damn Air Force?" he asked.

"I don't know. I've been wondering the same thing, and I plan to speak with McCoy about it. But not until after he's more trusting of us," Thomas said.

"And when will that be?" Mark asked.

"Hopefully after Vance helps him out."

* * *

Vance was sitting on a crate behind the visitor's center, smoking a cigarette and looking off at the distant runway. He rarely smoked, but often did when he was thinking deeply or trying to figure out a problem.

"Vance!" Mindy shouted from the building's doorway.

Vance turned and looked at her as she quickly walked toward him.

"Hey," she said once she had gotten closer.

"Hey."

"Listen," Mindy said as she hopped up and sat on the crate as well, just a few inches from Vance, "I never got to thank you. For saving us, I mean."

"You're welcome," Vance replied, still smoking and staring off, his eyes squinting because of the bright sunlight.

"So what do you think about all this?" Mindy asked him, staring at the side of his face.

137

"Not much to think about. We're on an Air Force base with no Air Force personnel, a handful of National Guardsmen, and a shady civilian who's the ringleader." Vance took one last drag off his cigarette before flicking the butt.

"You don't think it's safe?" she asked.

"I didn't say that. I was just stating the obvious."

There was perhaps an entire minute of silence as Mindy chose her words.

"Are you coming with us? With my brother and I?" she finally asked, again looking over at the side of his head because he refused to make eye contact with her.

"I planned on it," he answered.

Mindy smiled and bit her lower lip as she turned her gaze to the pavement beneath her dangling feet.

"Good," she said, "I was hoping you would."

"Oh yeah? And why's that?" Vance asked. His tone was indifferent and devoid of emotion.

"I guess I just like having you around. You *have* saved our asses a few times," Mindy said, giggling slightly at the very end.

Vance didn't say anything. He kept staring out toward the airfield, as if he was lost in thought.

"Vance..." Mindy began, pausing to search for the right words, "...Are you ever going to trust us?"

"What do you mean?" he asked, turning his head toward her for the first time.

"Are you ever going to open up? So far you've been more like a robot. It's just...I can tell you're a good person. Maybe you've been through a lot, but I don't think that changes who you are at heart."

"Heh..." Vance chuckled as he got off of the crate, "If only you knew."

"Well I'd like to. Everyone would, I'm sure. We just want to know who you are, that's all. You saved us, and it looks like you might be with us awhile. Is it too much to ask for you to treat us like your friends?"

Vance halfway turned his head toward her and raised an

eyebrow.

"Friends?" he asked, then said, "Sister, if we hadn't been brought together by a zombie apocalypse, I wouldn't give any of you people a second glance. In case you haven't noticed, I'm not a very sociable guy. I keep to myself, and I like for people to let me be that way."

Mindy was taken aback by his response. She hadn't expected him to be rude. Indifferent, sure. But rude?

"Well, I..." she started. Mindy sighed and then said, "Alright then. That's how it will be."

Mindy hopped off of the crate and walked around Vance, back toward the visitor center.

* * *

"Are you almost ready?" McCoy asked Staff Sergeant Overfield.

"Yep," the NCO replied, "The guys are getting the vehicles pulled around now. Where's Vance?"

"Go find him. Take him to his gear and let him get what he needs. If he needs ammo or anything, get it for him," McCoy said.

"Got it."

Overfield walked down the stairs and went outside. His men were pulling their vehicles around, all fueled up and ready to go. Two Humvees and a deuce-and-a-half. Once parked, his drivers got out and started putting the remainder of their gear on, which was all lined up nice and neat on the side of the road. Overfield looked around his immediate area, but didn't see Vance. He did see Thomas, though, who was in the middle of a conversation with another Hill resident.

"Yo!" Overfield shouted, followed by a loud whistle.

Thomas looked over at him, then said some final words to his new acquaintance before walking toward Overfield.

"Yeah?" he said.

"Where's your SF buddy?" Overfield asked.

"I don't know. Haven't seen him for a bit." Thomas replied.

"Well we're ready to roll out," Overfield said.

"That was short notice."

About that time, Vance was seen walking out of the front doors of the visitor's center.

"Hey!" Overfield called out.

Vance slowly walked over to him and Thomas.

"Boss man said to take you to your gear and let you get what you need. We're ready to move out as soon as possible."

Vance glared at him for a moment before shrugging his shoulders.

"I'll leave you guys to it. Be safe out there," Thomas said as he walked off.

8

"Alright, let's get this over with," Vance said as he threw his M4's combat sling around his torso. He had put on his tactical vest and backpack as well.

"Good deal," Overfield said.

"So what's the mission?" Vance asked as he followed Overfield back around the visitor's center and toward the south gate.

"Routine supply run, but we're supposed to keep our eyes open for anything on this list," Overfield said as he held up a piece of paper, "However, we're not actively looking for any of it. Not today. Today we're just gathering up the normal stuff. Food, water, ammunition, stuff like that."

"And why do you need me?" Vance asked him.

"Well, the truthful answer is that we don't. But we *want* you. You have more training and experience than anyone on this base..."

"Yeah, about that..." Vance began.

"I know, I know. You want to know where everyone else is, right?" Overfield asked him with a smile.

"You got it."

"Apparently they all left once they figured their position here was...'untenable', shall we say? A bunch of them left in aircraft, the others left in both military and personal vehicles. Only a handful of Air Force guys stayed behind."

"Why'd they leave?"

"From what we've heard, a huge horde of those bastards came

through here. The majority of people who were previously here tucked tail and ran, and I don't blame them. Not everyone made it, though. When we got here we found part of the fence on the east side torn down and a couple dozen bodies nearby. What was left of the Air Force survivors were hold up in the barracks a couple roads over. "

"Bodies? Dead, or...dead and walking?" Vance asked.

"Just dead. A bunch of them checked out, if you know what I mean. Not much of them left. I'd guess that the ones who didn't finish themselves off suffered a much worse fate: completely devoured."

"I see."

"Anyhow, we got rid of the bodies—or what was left of them—and fixed the fence. There's a ton of those fuckers out there, but so far they haven't massed together like some of the herds of 'em I've seen." Overfield walked quickly toward the three vehicles waiting to leave.

"How long have you been here?" Vance asked him.

"About five months. A week or so less, maybe."

"And you haven't taken in more survivors?"

"Nope. Not many of them left around here. Most of them hauled ass to more rural areas, which was probably smart. Well, *most* meaning 'most of the survivors', anyway. The vast majority of people are still here, but not exactly in the same state as they were previously."

Vance walked next to Overfield as they approached the first Humvee.

"Alright boys, saddle up!" Overfield barked.

Two soldiers hopped into the cab of the deuce-and-a-half, and four more jumped in the back. Vance and Overfield got in the first Humvee—Overfield sat up front with the driver and Vance sat in the rear driver's side seat—while one more soldier sat in the rear passenger seat. The crew-served turret—an L240B machine gun—remained unmanned. The Humvee directly behind them had a full compliment of five soldiers, one of whom was in the turret manning the .50 caliber machine gun. Two soldiers on guard duty

142

opened the base's south gate—the same one Vance and the rest had entered through the day prior—and the small convoy drove through. A few undead were scattered about along the road leading to the base, but only a couple took an interest in the activity at the gate.

"So, now that we're away from the basilica..." Vance joked, "Tell me about this McCoy guy."

Overfield stared out the passenger side window for a brief moment before asking dryly, "What about him?"

"Well it's obvious the guy isn't military. What's his story?"

"Your guess is as good as mine, friend," Overfield answered.

"Come on...don't be coy," Vance leaned forward a bit and his tone became a little more stern, "Why is he in charge and not you? Or someone else?"

"Wild Bill is a smart man," Overfield said calmly, still looking out of the window, "He's a born leader. Men like him are rare."

"Sergeant Overfield," Vance said, frustrated, "I detest these social games people seem to enjoy so much. So unlike the other survivors, or perhaps even the men under your command, I won't accept something like that as an answer. I require something a little more detailed, or—more specifically—something more to the point."

Overfield let out a heavy sigh before turning in his seat a little bit to look back at Vance.

"McCoy came in with a group of about ten survivors less than a week after we came across Hill Air Force Base. He had already established himself as their leader, and they respected him. For whatever reason, none of them questioned his words or decisions. Honestly, I don't want to be in charge of the community that The Hill has become, and I would have had to go up against McCoy even if I had wanted it. Sure, I have the manpower and firepower to come out on top, but it wasn't worth it. He keeps everyone safe, he makes level-headed decisions, and no one complains. Anything beyond that, you'll have to ask him."

Vance stared into Overfield's eyes, searching for any deceit or dishonesty. He didn't find any.

"Fair enough," he finally said.

"My advice? Fall in line, or get the hell out. Wild Bill doesn't tolerate any troublemakers," Overfield said as he turned back around to face forward.

"He told me as much," Vance said, "Either way, I don't plan to stick around long."

* * *

Thomas walked slowly around the visitor's center with his sister. This was their third lap, and he was beginning to wish that they could move more freely around the rest of the base. But the base was large, and McCoy had blocked off most of it for everyone's safety. He simply didn't have enough personnel to guard it all. Not yet, anyway.

"How long are we staying?" Mindy asked.

"I dunno...until tomorrow, probably. Maybe the next day, if you want," Thomas answered.

"Not really. I'm okay with leaving tomorrow. That McCoy guy creeps me out." Mindy shivered a little to add emphasis to her words.

"Aw, come on. He's okay. You have to understand the pressure he's under," Thomas told her.

"Yeah, I get that, but something about him just isn't right. Samantha feels the same way."

"Well Samantha might have to stay here," Thomas said quickly.

"I thought about that, too. It's certainly safer here. But don't you think we should take her with us if she's going to be miserable here?"

"Heh...this place is unfamiliar to her, that's all. She's like any other kid. She'll get used to it." Thomas ran his fingers through his wavy hair, which was still a little wild, and it bothered him a little that it wasn't parted and neatly combed.

I guess I have some things to get used to as well, he thought to himself.

144

"I like your new look, by the way," Mindy said, as if she could read her brother's mind.

"Thanks," Thomas said with a chuckle, "Vance sort of opened my eyes a little. I can't continue looking like an accountant."

Mindy laughed and covered her mouth with her hand.

"Well you're handsome no matter how you look, but I have to agree with Vance. Without the nicely kept hair and the glasses, you look a little more rugged." Mindy chuckled once more.

The two walked for another minute or so. Their pace was slow, and they were just now getting to the other end of the building. They were on the back side, so the runway and the few planes that were left were easily visible.

"I wonder if anyone here knows how to fly those?" Thomas asked.

"I don't know. Even if they did, what would be the point? Where would they go?" Mindy asked as she stared toward the airfield.

"You wanna go check 'em out?" Thomas asked her with an ornery smile.

Mindy looked at him sharply, but a smile was on her face.

"Yes!" she exclaimed.

They both laughed at each other as they looked around to see who was watching. There were only a couple of Hill residents off in the distance, on the visitor center's east side. They were moving boxes and didn't seem to be paying attention.

Thomas and Mindy slowly jogged away from the visitor's center, toward the very area that McCoy had forbidden them to go earlier that day.

* * *

McCoy looked through his window on the second story of the visitor's center, toward the hangars off in the distance and on the other side of the airfield. Then he noticed the newest additions—the siblings Thomas and Mindy—strolling by behind the visitor's center. He watched them for a moment. Mindy was beautiful, for sure. Her long brown hair and soft features certainly caught the attention of most men, and William McCoy was no exception. But he was a very serious man, and he had other matters on his mind. His gaze returned to the hangars far away. He often looked through this window when he was thinking, off in the distance.

Then McCoy saw the siblings slowly jogging toward the airfield. At first he thought maybe they were just messing around, and expected them to stop before making it to the other side of the grassy median that separated the concrete area behind the visitor's center and the first runway. But they didn't. They both kept jogging, across the first runway, through the second large grassy area, and on across the second runway. A large C-130 Hercules was directly in front of them, and they were headed right for it. McCoy felt his face flush red with anger. He had specifically told them that the airfield was off limits.

"Derek!" McCoy snapped loudly.

One of his two assistants—they were more like consiglieres, really—almost jumped out of his chair, frightened by McCoy's sudden shouting.

"Thomas and Mindy—the two siblings who came in yesterday—they're on the airfield!" McCoy yelled, "Bring them back!"

"On it!" Derek answered, then rushed out of the room.

* * *

Thomas and Mindy approached the large cargo plane with the curiosity of young children. They both had smiles on their faces, captivated by just how large the plane really was.

"Think we can get in?" Mindy asked.

"No idea. I've never seen one of these up close," Thomas said.

Thomas walked around the plane and saw a door in front of the wing. Unfortunately it was far too high to reach, and Thomas didn't see any stairs or ladders anywhere.

"Looks like we're not getting in," he said.

"No, but let's go see what's in the hangar," Mindy replied,

146

already jogging toward the nearest hangar.

Thomas caught up with her and they made their way over to the first door they saw. Now that they were up close, the size of the hangar really blew them away. It was of titanic proportions, and although common sense would dictate that a hangar would have to be massive to house an airplane or helicopter, it didn't detract from its mind-blowing size. The large doors were nearly as tall as the hangar, and each one had to be at least forty or fifty feet wide.

Mindy placed her hand on the small door on the side of the hangar. In actuality, the door was far larger than any common door. But the massive size of the hangar's sliding doors made the door they were about to pass through seem like it was made for an insect. Mindy pushed through the door, which was heavy but swung open surprisingly easy. The inside of the hangar was pitch black, except for the swath of light created by the open door. The air smelled stale, and there was a hint of some sort of foul odor hanging in the air. Neither Thomas nor Mindy knew what sort of odor it was, but they knew their noses did not like it. It wasn't overpowering, nor did it make them recoil back like one would after opening a freezer full of rotting meat. At the edge of the light that the open door provided, Thomas saw what looked like some sort of large tool box on wheels, like what you would find in a mechanic's shop.

"Any light switches by the door?" Thomas asked from about five feet in front of the door. Mindy was still holding the door open.

Mindy reached over and felt several boxes that had switches on them. She flicked all of the switches several times, but nothing happened.

"Damn. Didn't think they would be sending power all the way out here, but it was worth a try," Thomas said before turning and walking back toward the open door.

As Thomas reached the doorway, he heard a noise that sounded like a man coughing. He immediately spun around, back toward the darkness, and froze in place.

"Oh my God," Mindy said, "Did you hear that, too?"

"Was that..."

Thomas's words trailed off as he quietly listened for the noise again. It certainly sounded like a man letting out a single, short cough. Then the sound of a vehicle could be heard outside the hangar. Tires squealed to a halt and several doors opened.

"Thomas!" Mindy said in a loud whisper.

"Hang on."

That *had* to be a person...

"Hey!" an authoritative voice said from outside, "Get out here!"

The man appeared in the doorway, and two soldiers armed with assault rifles were behind him. It was one of McCoy's henchmen, one of the men who always seemed to be following him around.

"Get the hell out of there," the man said forcefully, but calmly.

Thomas turned toward him and pointed at the darkness as he began to speak.

"We thought we heard..."

"NOW!" the man—Derek, although Thomas and Mindy did not know his name—suddenly screamed.

Thomas jumped a little, and so did his sister. They both walked briskly out of the hangar. Outside was a single white Chevy Suburban.

"Get in," Derek told them sternly.

"Thomas..." Mindy began.

"It's alright, just do it," Thomas told his sister. He placed his hand on her shoulder and led her over to the SUV.

After they had both climbed into the SUV and sat down on the bench seat, McCoy's henchman got in the front passenger seat and slammed the door shut. One of the soldiers climbed in the back seat with Thomas and Mindy, and the other hopped in the driver's seat and immediately but the vehicle in gear. The Suburban seemed to be flying across the airfield as they made their way back toward the visitor's center.

"I'm sorry," Thomas said once they were about halfway there, "We were just curious. We weren't going to take anything or do anything bad."

Neither of the soldiers answered, nor did the henchman.

"Look, we heard something that sounded like a man coughing inside there..." Thomas began.

"There's nothing in there," Derek said. Thomas stared at the back of his head for a moment.

"No, seriously. We heard something..."

Derek craned his neck around and looked back at Thomas.

"I said there's nothing in there," he said in an irritated tone, "We use it for storage. Mostly ammunition and hazardous materials."

Thomas looked at Mindy, who seemed terrified. He was confused, and a little worried. Had his mind played a trick on him? Had he heard something completely inanimate, something just settling or perhaps being pushed by the shift in air pressure after the door opened?

The Suburban pulled up behind the visitor's center, and the two soldiers and the henchman got out. Thomas and Mindy climbed out as well, although they did it slowly. None of the three men escorting them said a word as they led them through the back door, and up the set of stairs to the second floor. After turning a corner and passing a couple closed doors, Thomas and Mindy were directed to go in McCoy's private quarters.

Thomas stepped in first. He had just been in this room a couple hours ago, standing over McCoy's desk discussing plans to build a guard tower. McCoy appeared out of his bedroom, shutting the door behind him without giving Thomas and Mindy so much as a glance. The two soldiers and his henchman stood still behind the siblings. McCoy walked over to a long dresser that was against the exterior wall. He grabbed the pitcher and poured water into a glass. After taking a long drink and gently sitting the glass down on the dresser, he walked over to his desk and leaned his backside against it. He delicately dragged his hand across the side of his head, presumably brushing back long strands of hair that had found their way out of his ponytail. Finally, he looked up at Thomas and Mindy with a neutral expression and slowly nodded his head a little. It was barely noticeable, as if he were doing it inadvertently while pondering something.

"You can go now, guys, we can handle this," McCoy said to the two soldiers. The men left the room without saying a word, and Derek closed the door behind them.

"What were they doing, Derek?" McCoy asked, although his eyes were still awkwardly locked onto Thomas.

"They were in the hangar, the one that the C-130 is parked in front of," Derek told him.

"I see," McCoy said before crossing his arms.

"Bill, we didn't do anything bad," Thomas told him, "We didn't take anything, nor did we intend to. We were just bored and wanted to look around. Had we known that the hangar was used for storage, we wouldn't have gone in there."

Thomas's face expressed regret and seemed genuinely apologetic. McCoy nodded his head—this time more noticeably—and then pushed his body away from the desk.

"I explained to you three very basic rules earlier today," he began, now placing his hands on his hips in a very authoritative manner, "Three simple little rules. No violence, no stealing, and no wandering outside of the approved area."

"I know, and we're sorry. We didn't realize that it would be such an issue," Thomas said.

"But you knew it was not allowed. I saw you from up here in my office. You both looked around to see if anyone was watching."

"That is true," Thomas said, "But we..."

"I was very straightforward with you all. I told you that anyone who ventured beyond the established boundaries would be kicked out of here."

"We thought you meant that about the areas that are blocked off. You said the airfield was off limits, but we thought that was more for safety reasons." Thomas threw his hands out from his sides to add emphasis to his words, as if doing so somehow proved his point.

McCoy took in a long breath and exhaled through his nose. He looked very angry, but in the blink of an eye it disappeared. He briefly looked down at the floor before raising his head, a tiny smile on his face, and nodded his head.

"You're both new here," he said, "I understand how a new place can be confusing. It takes time to adapt to new rules. Rules that you may not fully understand the reasoning for."

"We're not saying that what we did wasn't wrong," Thomas told him, "We're just saying that we didn't understand the seriousness of it all. We know that we have to be safe in order to keep everyone else safe. I guess we just didn't think that walking over to the hangars would be a safety issue."

"Of course not," McCoy said, this time in a more understanding tone. He took a couple steps forward and placed his hand on Thomas's shoulder in a friendly way, "And you're right. It wouldn't seem that way. You didn't know that we stored explosives and other potentially hazardous materials in that hangar. How could you? That is my fault for not telling you. But you must realize that we have to protect our resources. I honestly don't have enough manpower to constantly police our colony, let alone the entire base."

McCoy gently patted Thomas on the shoulder before walking back over to his desk and sitting down behind it.

"Let me be clear, though: Very few people here know where we keep supplies like that. It's best not to tell anyone what we're storing over there. We wouldn't want other people getting curious, or perhaps getting hurt, would we?" McCoy spoke calmly, not an ounce of anger present in his voice.

"Of course not," Thomas answered.

"Good. Now, we'll just forget this happened, okay? No harm, no foul."

McCoy leaned back in his chair, and the friendly smile on his face grew.

"Thank you," Thomas said to him, "And again, we're very sorry. We didn't mean to waste anyone's time or put anybody in a bad position."

McCoy gave Thomas a single nod. Derek opened the door and stood beside it, as if that was their cue to leave. Thomas gave

McCoy a quick smile and a nod of his head before following his sister out into the hallway.

"What the hell?" Mindy asked once they were far away from McCoy's office, though she didn't dare raise her voice above a whisper.

"Something's rotten in the state of Denmark," Thomas said as they reached the stairs.

* * *

Vance stood guard in front of the hardware store, scanning his sector just like he had in times of war so many times before. There were a handful of undead down the road, maybe a couple hundred meters, but none of them had taken any interest in Vance or the others. The rest of the immediate area was quiet. Overfield walked out of the store's front door and placed a cigarette in his mouth. His M4 dangled from its sling as he repeatedly flicked his Zippo lighter with no results. Vance reached into his left pants pocket—never taking his eyes off of his sector—and grabbed his own Zippo. He presented it to Overfield, who thanked him and quickly used it to light his cigarette.

"We're gonna have a pretty good haul today," Overfield said as he blew the smoke from his lungs.

"Oh yeah?" Vance answered.

"Yep. Most places are picked over pretty good, but this place still had a bunch of good stuff. Couple chainsaws, tons of nails and screws, plywood, metal piping...we already have a decent stock of common tools and even some materials, but this will do nicely."

Vance nodded his head but gave no other response. Overfield took another drag from his cigarette as he look over his shoulder to check on the progress of his men.

"Can't believe we found all that food at that little mini-mart," Overfield said.

The mini-mart had been one of the first places they had stopped. Inside they found several boxes of ramen noodles, a large box of potato chips, a few stray bottles of alcohol, and a couple cases of water. They had also stopped at a supermarket, but it had been picked almost completely clean. All they got from it were a few bottles of soda, a couple bags of chips, and several cans of wet dog food. Hopefully no one would have to resort to those as a source of nutrients for a very long time.

"Yeah, it'll surely give you a bountiful supply of food in the months to come," Vance said sarcastically.

"Hey, the base already has a good reserve of food," Overfield countered, "This is just a bonus."

"And what happens when all that food runs out? Then what will you feed the couple hundred people you have? All the safety and security in the world won't fill a person's stomach."

"We'll deal with it," Overfield said.

"Right. It's the middle of July, so planting pretty much anything is out of the question. Even if you could find seed, that is."

"We also hunt, from time to time. We'll resort to that on a more regular basis when we need to. Right now we're too well stocked to worry about it, because we've gotta drive several miles out to have any hope of killing wild game." Overfield sounded like he was a little irritated, but not overly so.

"Wouldn't it be better to save the food that you know will keep, and try to hunt and gather as much as you can to feed your people?" Vance asked.

"Look buddy, I'm not the one in charge here," Overfield said, "If I was, we'd be doing some things differently. Right now we're sitting pretty good at the end of the world, so I can't complain."

Vance grunted in reply, and Overfield walked back inside. Several minutes passed before the soldiers started loading everything up into the deuce-and-a-half. Once they were finished, Vance crawled inside the Humvee and enjoyed the wonderful scenery of looted buildings and walking dead on the ride back to the base.

* * *

"Hey sweetie," Mindy said as she walked up behind Samantha in the cafeteria. Several other people were in there as well, but none of them were anywhere near the girl.

"Hey."

"You doin' okay?" Mindy asked her.

"I'm fine," she said, her chin resting on the table.

"You look tired," Mindy said.

"I kind of am. I didn't sleep well last night."

"I don't think any of us did." Mindy sat down next to her.

"So I've been thinking," Mindy began, "When we leave here, what do you want to do?"

"I don't want to stay here," Samantha replied, "I don't like this place at all."

"Why not?"

"I don't know why. Something just isn't right here. That McCoy guy scares me." Samantha lifted her head off of the table and rested it on her hand.

Mindy sat silently for a brief moment.

"He said he wouldn't let anyone hurt you again," she said, "Why does he scare you?"

"He just seems like a creep."

"You know what?" Mindy asked her.

"What?"

"I think he seems like a creep, too," she told the girl, and they both giggled a little.

"Sis," Thomas said as he entered the cafeteria, "Get everyone together."

"What are we doing?" she asked.

"We're leaving. Tonight."

"Tonight? You want to be out *there* when it gets dark?" Mindy got up from the table and looked at her brother, who was fairly calm but seemed a little concerned.

"Out *there* is better than in here. Come on, go find Mark and Virginia."

"What happened, Thomas?" Mindy asked him.

Thomas paused for a moment, looking down at Samantha. He

154

took Mindy by the arm and walked her outside the cafeteria.

"I was just talking to a couple of the people who live here. They heard about us going over to the hangar," he said, looking suspiciously over his shoulder as he spoke, "That sound we heard? That was a fucking *person*."

"How do you know?"

"The guys I spoke to...they said that people go missing sometimes."

"Missing? Wait, slow down..."

"Sis, there was a *human being* in that hangar. I know it."

"Thomas," Mindy said, shaking her head, "What I heard sure sounded like a cough. But you have to explain this to me. What did those people say?"

"They said they heard about us getting caught going over to the hangar. They said a few weeks ago a one of the survivors went missing. Just suddenly vanished. Supposedly one of them went over there at night awhile back and heard a man singing."

"Singing?" Mindy asked.

"Yes! Singing!" Thomas's voice was just above a whisper, and he nervously looked around while they spoke to make sure no one heard them.

"And they think this guy who went missing...they think it was him?" Mindy asked him.

"Yes!" Thomas's voice grew a little more stern.

"So what now?"

"Now you go find Mark and Virginia. I'm meeting those two guys in the east barracks in ten minutes." Thomas let go of his sister and started walking away.

"Where are the east barracks?" Mindy asked.

"Two buildings that way!" Thomas replied as he pointed east.

"What's going on?" Samantha asked as she walked out into the hallway.

"Nothing honey, everything's fine," Mindy said as he stroked Samantha's hair and smiled.

"Mindy..." Samantha said, "I'm not a little girl. I know bad things happen. I've seen plenty of bad stuff since all of this started."

"I'm sorry," Mindy said as she shook her head and briefly buried her hands in her face, "I know you're not a child. I just forget, I guess. I see you and it somehow gives me a light to look at amidst all of this. I shouldn't do that. It's selfish. I'm sorry."

Samantha smiled before wrapping her arms around Mindy and squeezing tightly. Mindy returned the hug, resting her face on top of the girl's head. Mindy was only a couple inches taller than Samantha, and nearly as petite, but that fact didn't seem to deter her from thinking of Samantha as a little girl. Even though they had only been together for less than 48 hours, Mindy had grown extremely fond of the girl. It was fairly obvious that the same was true of Samantha's affection for Mindy.

"Let's go see what Thomas is all worked up about," Mindy said as she pulled away from Samantha and smiled at her.

<u>9</u>

"Where are the others?" Logan—a 27-year-old resident of Hill Air Force Base—asked Thomas.

"They'll be here in just a couple minutes," Thomas said to him.

"We can't make this look suspicious," Logan added, "McCoy looks for shit like this."

Ronnie, a 43-year-old mechanic from Salt Lake City, scratched his bald head as he sat on his bunk and waited. Logan nervously bit his nails and paced. Only a couple of minutes passed before Mindy and Samantha showed up, and Mark and Virginia were right behind them.

"What's this all about?" Mark asked.

"We'll get to that," Thomas said, "Mindy, did you happen to see if Vance was back yet?"

"They're not back," she answered.

"Alright, then we'll do this without him."

Logan cleared his throat, look over his shoulder, and spoke in a soft, quiet tone.

"Okay, so about three weeks ago this guy named Chris went missing. No one—and I mean *no one*—has any clue where he went. He just disappeared. The fucked up part?"

Logan looked over at Samantha, realizing he dropped the F-bomb in front of a kid.

"Sorry," he said, "Anyway, the messed up part is that Chris and McCoy didn't get along at all. McCoy asked him to do something, and Chris told him to..."

Logan stopped abruptly and looked over at Samantha once more.

"...he told him to F-off. Chris just didn't like the guy at all. He's Air Force, and was here with the other Air Force guys before McCoy and his crew got here."

"What makes you think McCoy had anything to do with this guy disappearin'?" Mark asked.

"Right. Well Ronnie and I got a little suspicious, because how in the hell does a person just up and go missing in a place like this? We started thinkin', and we realized how strange it was that no one was allowed to even go over to the airfield. It's not just the hangars that are off limits, but the *whole airfield*. It's like they don't want anyone anywhere near those hangars. So we went out one night and headed over to the hangars. The first one—the one furthest east—it was almost completely empty. Just some tools and stuff, not even any planes or helicopters. But the second one? We went to open the door, and we heard a guy *singing*. Freaked us the hell out. So we opened the door and went to shine our flashlights in there to look around, and the singing got louder. But before we could even go inside, a set of headlights appeared on the runway, coming toward us. We took off toward the back of the hangar. This truck slowed way down and drove past the hangar. We thought they were going to keep going, but they stopped just past the hangar and we heard the truck's doors open and shut, and boots walking around. Ronnie and I took off and barely made it back here without gettin' caught."

"This is a wonderful story," Mark said, "but it's a little outlandish."

"No, Mark, it's not," Thomas told him, "Mindy and I...we went over there just to look around. We both heard what sounded like a guy coughing in that same hangar."

"Holy shit..." Mark said. The old farmer grabbed the straps of his overalls and looked up at the ceiling.

"So," Virginia began in her soft, quiet voice, "McCoy is keeping this man prisoner?"

158

"Gotta be," Ronnie said.

"Yeah, gotta be," Logan added.

"Shit," Thomas said.

"So what now?" Mark asked, turning his attention to Thomas.

"We need to get the hell out of here. I'll explain everything to Vance when he gets back. In the meantime, I want you guys to hang out in the room we stayed in last night."

"So we can get locked in again?" Mark asked, somewhat irritated.

"No. I'll make sure that doesn't happen," Thomas told him.

* * *

Overfield, Vance, and the rest of the troops pulled through the base's gate at around 5pm. They drove around behind the visitor's center, and the deuce-and-a-half backed up to the double-doors to unload their goods.

"It's been fun," Vance said as he got out of the Humvee.

"Whoa, slow down," Overfield laughed, "Aren't you gonna help unload?"

"No, I'm not, but thanks for the offer."

Vance walked away from the Humvee, but Overfield caught up to him.

"Hang on," he said, stepping in front of Vance, "You're going to have to drop off all your gear so it can be secured."

Vance stared at him blankly for a brief moment before answering with a decisive, "No." He then stepped around Staff Sergeant Overfield and continued walking away. Overfield shook his head, but let it go. After all, he had already been permitted to walk around with a sidearm. What difference did it make if he had his M4 and hundreds of rounds of ammunition on his vest?

Vance walked through the other back door of the visitor's center and headed up the stairs. He entered the room they had all stayed in the night before, and he immediately knew something wasn't right. Mark, Virginia, Mindy, and Samantha were there already, and they looked concerned.

"Well..." Vance began as he dropped his backpack on the floor beside his bed, "...who died?"

* * *

Thomas sat in the bathroom of the east barracks, thinking about how they would make a graceful exit without arousing too much suspicion. McCoy would undoubtedly find it strange if they left in the evening, so his original plan to leave that night had to change. They would leave tomorrow morning, after breakfast. Sure, McCoy might still think it's a little strange, but why would he care? They'd be out of his hair, and they had told him they were only staying a couple of days anyway.

Thomas exited the bathroom stall and walked over to the sink. He threw some water on his face, hoping it would give him some clarity. One of the other residents—one of the many who were still strangers to Thomas—entered the restroom and nodded his head at Thomas as he passed him. After he had stepped into a stall, Thomas left the restroom and went up the flight of stairs to find Logan and Ronnie. It didn't take long, but it was right before supper so there were a lot of people in the sleeping area. Thomas looked at Ronnie and sort of flicked his head toward the door, to let them know he wanted to talk. Both Logan and Ronnie followed him out into the stairwell.

"Okay, my group and I are going to leave tomorrow morning after breakfast. You're both more than welcome to come with us," Thomas said.

"What about everyone else?" Ronnie asked.

"Yeah, are we just supposed to leave and say to hell with the rest of the survivors?" Logan asked.

"Look, I don't like it either," Thomas said sternly, "But we can't exactly stand up on a table during dinner and tell everyone that McCoy is keeping this Chris guy as a prisoner."

"Why not?" Ronnie asked.

"Yeah, why not?" Logan added.

"What do you mean? We just...can't. How well do you think that would go over?" Thomas looked at both of them as if they were crazy.

"Well if we tell everyone and they all find out, then what can McCoy do? It's not like he can turn all of us into his prisoners." Ronnie seemed to like the idea of playing the hero.

"Listen," Thomas said, trying to remain calm, "I have to look out for the members of my group. We were never staying here long in the first place."

"But how can you just...*leave*?" Logan asked him.

"Well you two obviously knew about this long before we got here. Why didn't *you* do something about it?"

Ronnie and Logan looked at each other for a moment before Logan answered.

"Well, because now there are more than two of us who know. And you have that mean dude on your side. He'll help, right?"

"No, probably not," Thomas told him, "He's going to say the same thing I'm saying: Get the hell out...now."

"Fuck, man..." Logan said as he threw his hands up.

"We can't just leave this man to rot," Ronnie said a little forcefully.

"You guys do whatever you think you need to do, so long as it doesn't jeopardize the safety of my people."

Thomas was irritated as hell, so he just ran down the stairs to the first floor and exited the building. After breathing a heavy sigh of frustration and desperation, his nerves calmed down a bit and he was able to keep walking over to the visitor's center. Once he reached the front doors, he sat down on the half wall and looked up at the sky. What the hell was he going to do?

"You know we don't take kindly to unions around here," a man said from behind him.

Thomas turned around and saw Derek—one of McCoy's henchmen—standing on the sidewalk.

"Excuse me?" Thomas said.

Derek walked up to him and stopped just a couple feet away.

"Whatever you're plotting, or intending to do...don't. It won't

161

end well for any of you."

"I don't understand..."

"Don't play dumb," Derek said as he stepped closer so that his face was just a couple inches from Thomas's, "What you heard inside that hangar? Whatever it was Ronnie and Logan heard? Forget it. If Wild Bill catches wind that you guys are trying to overthrow him—or take something from him—he will come at you with a vengeance. I've seen how he deals with troublemakers. You don't want to be on the receiving end of his wrath."

Derek gave Thomas a cold glare before walking inside the visitor's center. Thomas felt his heart pounding in his chest. How much did Derek know? And, by default, how much did McCoy know?

****

"Wait, so let me get this straight," Vance said, "McCoy is holding some poor bastard prisoner in one of the hangars?"

Mark and Mindy nodded their heads.

"This does not surprise me," Vance said as he shook his head and walked over to his bunk.

"So what do we do?" Mindy asked.

"We get the hell out of here," Vance told her as he picked up his backpack.

"No, we don't," Thomas said as he appeared in the doorway, "Not yet, at least."

"Why not?" Vance asked.

"After our little incident with McCoy, I seriously doubt he'd allow us to leave right before the sun goes down."

"And why would he give a shit? Even if he knows we know, we'd be long gone and no longer a threat," Vance said.

"A guy like McCoy needs closure. As long as he thinks we're just going to leave and not act weird about it, he'll be fine with it. But he's not going to let all of his people see us doing whatever the hell we want and leaving on a whim." Thomas walked over to his bed and sat down.

"And why the hell are we giving him a choice about it? We just...do it..."

Vance sat down hard on his bed, obviously a little angry about the situation.

"Wait a second..." Thomas said.

"What?" Mindy asked him.

Thomas was staring at the floor, his head cocked to the side. Mindy knew that look.

"Thomas...what?" she repeated.

"What if we don't leave?" he asked, breaking his trance and looking around at everyone.

"Right. And what if we all start shitting gold bricks? It ain't happenin'," Vance said.

"No, no...hang on," Thomas stood up and turned to face everyone, "What if we overthrew McCoy?"

"Thomas!" Mindy exclaimed.

"No, seriously! What if we took him out of power? Vance, you said Overfield is a decent guy, right? We transfer power to him. Think about it. This place could be great. Mindy, you and I would still go get Mom and Dad. But what if we could bring them back up here, if there's nowhere else safe? Mark and Virginia...you guys wouldn't have to worry about staying here. Everything would work out fine."

Thomas seemed excited, almost. His eyes were wide, but his voice was still calm and his words all seemed to be thought through.

"Thomas, I can tell you what we're going to do in seven short words, and since you're having a problem with this concept, I'll say them slowly: We're. Getting. The. Fuck. Out. Of. Here," Vance said sternly.

"Thomas, I can't believe you would even entertain an idea like this. You just said earlier that we needed to leave," Mindy said angrily as she stood up.

"And what about all these people?" Thomas asked.

"No," Vance said as he got up, "Oh no...you're not going to pull this shit. That fucking ridiculous 'We-Have-To-Do-The-Right-

Thing' bullshit. Absolutely not. You know how many good men I've seen die, all because they wanted to, 'do the right thing'? Way too fucking many, and that's exactly what will happen if you attempt this." Vance walked around his bed and placed his hands on his hips.

Thomas thought about what Derek had said to him outside. He hadn't wanted the others to find out because it would cause them a great deal of stress, but it seemed like he had no choice now.

"Derek—one of those guys who follow McCoy around—he knows something's up. Somehow, he knows that Ronnie and Logan were over there and heard or saw something they shouldn't have. He threatened me outside a few minutes ago."

"Shit..." Mark said.

"They have a spy, then," Vance said, as if he wasn't shocked at all.

"Wait...threatened you how?" Mindy asked.

"He said if McCoy finds out that we're plotting against him, he'll come after us," Thomas said, reluctantly.

"Damn it..." Mindy said in a crackly voice. Even from fifteen feet away, Thomas could see tears forming in her eyes.

"Thomas, we need to leave," Vance said in his deep, raspy voice, "We. Need. To. Leave."

Thomas ran his fingers through his hair and turned away from everyone. He took a couple steps before turning around and nodding his head, as if he were answering a question he had asked himself. His face was contorted into an angry, frustrated expression.

"All my life," he began, his voice forceful and laced with rage, "I have backed down from adversity. I was always the one who got bullied and never the bully. I've avoided confrontation whenever possible. I don't know what it feels like to put my foot down and stand up for somebody, not even myself."

Thomas paused briefly, but his mouth hung open while he tried to find the words. His eyes turned glassy and his breathing got heavy.

"I'm not going to be that person anymore," he said, "I'm done

164

letting assholes like William McCoy walk all over me. It's shitty that it took six months of an undead apocalypse to finally make me change. I should have been this way years ago. But no...I always chose to cower in fear and worry about everything. I chose instead to constantly be on the verge of developing an ulcer because I was always so goddamn worried about what everyone around me thinks. Well no more. I am *done* being a coward."

Everyone just stared at Thomas, mostly in shock. His sister was especially surprised. She had never heard her brother talk like that. Hell, she remembered seeing him come home from school on a regular basis with black eyes and a swollen, bloody nose.

"Thomas," Vance said quietly, stepping close to him, "I understand what you're saying, and I agree. I'm glad you've decided to step up to the plate. But now is not the time to take a crash course on how to be a hero. Seriously. Someone's going to get hurt."

"You're right. Someone *is* going to get hurt. But it won't be one of us," Thomas said to him through clinched teeth. Vance shook his head in frustration and walked back over to his bunk.

"Bub," Mindy said shakily as she approached him. She only called Thomas 'bub' when something was really wrong, "Listen to Vance. You don't need to save the day. Not this time."

"I'm doing it," Thomas told her firmly.

"You can't save everybody all the time," Vance said to him, "Sometimes, bad shit happens and you just have to deal with it."

"I know, but this isn't one of those times. We can do something good here. We can make a difference."

"Or we can *die!*" Vance said sternly.

"Look, we're not doing anything about it tonight. Why don't you guys go downstairs and eat supper. I'm going to use the restroom and I'll be down in a few," Thomas said to everyone.

The group got up and headed for the door. Mark gave Thomas a quick pat on the arm as he walked by, and Virginia smiled softly at him. His sister took his face in her hands and gently kissed him on the cheek.

Once everyone had left, Thomas pulled out the screwdriver

from his pocket. He had "acquired" it from a janitor's closet in the east barracks. He scooted the closest bed—it happened to be Vance's—over to the room's door and climbed on top of it. Then he placed the tip of the screwdriver in the first screw of the hydraulic door closer, at the top of the door. Thomas strained as he worked to turn the screw. After a few seconds the first screw loosened, and Thomas smiled a devilish smile.

* * *

"What the hell is he doing?" Vance asked as the group sat in the cafeteria and ate their meal.

"No idea. Maybe he isn't hungry," Mindy said.

Vance and Mark both gave her a dumb look.

"Really?" Mark asked her as a smile formed on his face.

"We're living in the apocalypse, and you think *anyone* is going to pass up food?" Vance asked her.

"It was just a thought..." Mindy said.

"Oh, there he is," Virginia said as she tapped her husband on the arm.

Thomas strolled into the cafeteria and walked right up to the serving line. The guy threw some food on his plate—some sort of beef stroganoff that had undoubtedly been dehydrated—and Thomas poured himself a glass of fruit juice. He calmly sat down at the table with everyone else and began eating. The rest of the group stared at him, exchanging odd looks with each other.

"Thomas?" Mindy said softly, "Thomas, is everything alright?"

Thomas wiped his mouth with a napkin and looked at her with an eyebrow raised.

"Yeah, of course," he said, "Why wouldn't it be?"

Thomas returned to eating, and after a few moments so did everyone else. Vance seemed to have given up trying to figure out what was going to happen next, and kept all of his attention on his food. Mindy, however, continued glancing over at her brother between bites. Samantha kept looking back and forth between

Mindy and Thomas, knowing something was wrong but had no idea what it was. Mark looked over at him a couple of times, but mostly let it go.

The mood in the cafeteria was strangely dark. There was a constant low humming noise of everyone talking quietly to each other, but it was mostly unintelligible murmuring. Overfield and a few of his men were sitting just a couple tables away, and they seemed to be carrying on like nothing out of the ordinary was happening. A few minutes passed and everyone in Thomas's group was almost finished eating when Logan sat down at their table right next to Thomas. He looked around suspiciously before leaning forward and saying quietly, "I think they got Ronnie."

"What?" Thomas asked.

"Ronnie and I always eat together. He's gone. I haven't seen him since right after our conversation in the stairwell." Logan was very obviously frightened. His eyes were about as wide as they could be, his voice was shaky, and he kept looking around like a meth addict who needed his next fix.

"Calm down," Thomas told him, "and stop acting that way. You're going to draw attention to yourself."

"Did you not fucking *hear me!?*" Logan asked him, raising his voice a little, "I've already drawn attention to myself. We all have! If they got Ronnie, then it doesn't matter how I act. They're going to get me, too!"

"Yeah, but if Ronnie's actually just taking a shit and wasn't abducted by the Gestapo, then you're going to create a problem that may have never existed to begin with," Vance said dryly.

"You're not fucking *listening!*" Logan said to him, this time with anger in his tone, "Ronnie and I are best friends! We always walk to the cafeteria together. We *always* tell each other what we're doing. We look out for each other..."

"Stop," Thomas said sternly, "I'm going to handle the situation."

"Well forgive me if that doesn't exactly put my mind at fucking ease!" Logan said.

"I'm going to go look for him again, just in case maybe he

passed out or something. He *is* old, after all."

Logan jumped up from the table and walked off briskly toward the door.

"How old is Ronnie?" Mark asked, his mouth full with the last bite of his food.

"Like forty-two, forty-three. Something like that," Thomas answered.

"Thought so," Mark said, "So that must mean Virginia and I are ancient."

Virginia and Samantha laughed a little at the joke, but Mindy was biting her nails with a terrified look on her face. She only chewed on her nails when she was *really* stressed.

"Hey, thanks for going out with us today, Vance," Overfield said as he walked past the group's table to return his tray.

"Yeah, thanks," another soldier—one whom no one had met—said as he followed behind Overfield.

"Yeah," Vance replied. He didn't even look at them when he said it. Instead, he wiped his mouth off and threw the napkin on his tray.

The group sat around for a couple minutes, but no one really said anything. Mark and Virginia spoke to each other off and on, but other than that there was no conversation. Most of the other Hill citizens were done with their meals as well, but apparently right after suppertime was social hour. Very few got up and left, while the atmosphere perked up a little. Everyone seemed to be talking a little more normally. A few laughs could even be heard here and there. Only another minute or so passed before Logan came back in the cafeteria and sat down beside Thomas again.

"This is bad," he said nervously, "Ronnie is gone for sure. I can't find him anywhere."

"Did you go back to the barracks and look?" Thomas asked him.

"No, because he wouldn't be there. I'm tellin' ya, we both know each others habits like the back of our hands. We don't go anywhere without each other."

"Maybe Ronnie just got tired of you," Vance said rudely.

"Ha-fucking-ha," Logan said to him, "Because yeah...now's a perfect time to be a fuckin' comedian."

"Watch your tone, or Ronnie won't be the only one who disappears tonight," Vance replied, his dark voice cutting into Logan like a sharp blade.

"What the hell do we do?" Logan asked, turning his attention back to Thomas.

"We wait," Thomas told him.

"Wait?"

"Yes, wait. Trust me. I'll take care of everything."

At that, Thomas got up and walked toward the serving area to return his tray. Logan got up just a couple seconds after and disappeared into the crowd of people who were now standing and socializing.

"Your brother's going to get us killed," Vance said to Mindy. She glanced at him, but otherwise ignored the comment.

Another five minutes or so passed, and McCoy entered the cafeteria. Accompanied by his two henchmen, of course—Derek and the other guy whom they had not yet met, but had seen almost constantly following behind McCoy like a pet. The noise in the cafeteria quieted down as McCoy walked to the front of the room. Derek and the other guy stood off to the side. McCoy raised his hands up and politely asked everyone to take a seat. The large group of people fell silent almost immediately, presumably anxious to hear what their fearless leader had to say.

"I don't want to alarm anyone," McCoy said, "but we caught a thief trying to steal supplies."

A roar of whispers erupted from the congregation of people. McCoy raised one hand and waved it up and down to make everyone be quiet, his other hand resting on his hip.

"Rest assured, we caught him before he could take or damage anything, And he's not dangerous, just so you know. At least, we have no reason to believe he is. I'm sure you all know him: Ronnie Summers. I never would have expected Ronnie to do such a thing, but I guess that's what I get for always seeing the best in people."

169

You're good, you fucking snake, Thomas thought. *Well played.*

"I want you all to know that everything is fine. Nothing will happen to Ronnie. We did, however, escort him to his bunk so he could gather his things before leaving. Unfortunately, we can't afford to give anyone second chances when it comes to serious matters like stealing. Ronnie was sent packing about fifteen minutes ago."

More whispers from the crowd, this time quieter.

"I don't want to intimidate anybody—you all know I'm not like that—but I want this to be a reminder to everyone that we take our rules very seriously. We're a small community, so we shouldn't have much of a problem with crime. And we don't, really. But the saying, 'a few bad apples spoil the bunch', is unfortunately all too true. If we allow people to do what they want and get away with wronging others, then that mentality could spread like a wildfire. There must be repercussions for negative actions. I think we can all agree on that."

You're definitely a charismatic son-of-a-bitch, Thomas thought.

"Now, before we kicked Ronnie out, he told us some things with the hope that he would be given amnesty for his crime. Obviously it didn't work out so well for him. But what he told us was quite disturbing, and frankly I'm a little disappointed if it turns out to be true. Ronnie informed us that there are several people here—people in this room—who are plotting to steal a bunch of our supplies and leave the base because they don't like the rules. He even said that someone might be plotting to overthrow me. Or worse—assassinate me. I'm telling you all this to give you fair warning. The soldiers and other security personnel might be a little on edge for the next couple of days or weeks, so I don't want that to scare you."

McCoy looked over at Thomas's table and locked his gaze onto them, "We're currently investigating this matter to narrow down our list of suspects. Don't worry...we'll get to the bottom of this and those who are guilty of planning these things will be held accountable. They *will* pay for threatening the prosperity and security of this community. That's all. I hope you all enjoy the rest of your evening."

McCoy stared at Thomas for one more uneasy moment before turning and casually walking away, his thugs in tow.

"Well now, this complicates things a bit," Thomas said.

Logan spontaneously appeared again and sat down.

"I told you!" he whispered, "We're all fucked! They're going to start picking us off one by one!"

"No," Thomas said calmly, "that's not going to happen."

<u>10</u>

Thomas and the rest of the group walked into their room and sat down on their bunks. Everyone except Thomas, that is. Instead of relaxing, he stood in the middle of the room with his chin resting on his fist in a thoughtful pose.

"What exactly are you planning?" Vance asked him.

"Do you think Overfield would be on our side, if we explained the situation to him?" Thomas asked, completely ignoring Vance's question.

"No. I don't. I think Overfield is going to follow orders for the greater good. For all we know, he could be in on it. Hell, for all we know, this guy in the hangar could be a criminal. How do we know for certain that McCoy is the evil dude you want him to be?"

"You mean besides Logan and Ronnie telling us the real situation? I can feel it in my bones. He's no good. Why not just kick him out? Surely that is a much worse fate than being held prisoner."

"Yeah, well I've had a bad feeling about him since we got here," Vance agreed, "But not liking a guy doesn't mean he is bad, and it doesn't mean he isn't doing a good job of keeping this place safe. He obviously is."

"But at whose expense?" Thomas asked, "Is being in a safe place like this *worth* being lied to and deceived? Being afraid to voice your opinion?"

"Yes," Vance said.

Thomas stared at Vance as a moment of clarity passed over

him. Vance was right. Wasn't he? In a world like this, you had to take what you could get. Thomas hated that fact, but he had to acknowledge it nonetheless.

"Fine," Thomas finally said, "but we're not backing down completely. We're rescuing that Chris guy, the one in the hangar."

"Oh Jesus fucking..." Vance cursed, his words trailing off.

"We don't even *know* if that guy in there is Chris..." Mindy reminded him.

"Well whoever he is, he's getting out tonight. No one deserves to be locked away like that, all alone in the dark. We'll do it tonight—covertly—and then leave first thing in the morning."

"And you think it'll go down like that?" Vance asked him.

"I has to."

Vance wrapped his hands behind his head in frustration.

"Alright," he said as he pointed a finger at Thomas, "but *no one* dies. Got it? Not Overfield, not any of his men, not Wild Bill."

"I didn't plan on killing anyone, Vance," Thomas said, "But I can't guarantee that if someone gets in the way, they won't get hurt."

"So let's hear your plan then..." Vance told him coldly as he sat down on his bunk.

"We do it tonight, around 3AM. I was around the National Guard guys in Seattle long enough to know that's a good time to attempt anything. All the guards who came on at midnight are tired and bored, and not expecting anything to happen that will break the silence..."

* * *

It was now ten o' clock, and Thomas was lying on his bed. Everyone else was washing up or chatting, except for Vance. He, too, was being anti-social. But not because he felt like it. He was actually preparing himself to carry out Thomas's plan, since he would most likely been doing all of the work. He didn't really expect Thomas or even Mark to do any of the heavy lifting. After all, why should they feel the need to when someone like Vance was on their side?

A few minutes passed by, and two of Overfield's men appeared in the open doorway of the group's quarters.

"Time to go to bed," one of them said, "Sorry to do this again, but we have orders to lock you up again until tomorrow night. McCoy always plays it safe."

"No problem," Thomas said to them, "We understand."

The rest of the group put on their best friendly faces as one of the guards grabbed the open door and pushed it closed. Almost. The door stopped closing as soon as it touched the door frame.

"Damn it," the soldier said from the other side, "Damn thing's jammed up."

Loud thumping noises could be heard as one or both of the soldiers pushed and kicked the door, trying to close it all the way so it could be locked from the other side. All attempts failed, and the door was still not closed all of the way.

"Hey, guys," Thomas said as he approached the door, "We're not going anywhere. This place is too good to mess it up. We're good, okay?"

The two soldiers opened the door and stared at Thomas, then at each other.

"Orders are orders," the first one said.

"I get that, but really...it isn't necessary. We've learned our lesson about breaking the rules. Besides, it was only two of us who did something we weren't supposed to. Hell, Vance has his guns and went out with you guys on a run earlier. We're not going to try anything."

The two soldiers looked at each other in an unsure manner, trying to decide if leaving their guests unlocked was acceptable.

"Well...they *do* have weapons," one of them said, referring to Vance's assault rifle, handgun, and sword.

"Yeah...you guys aren't going to try anything. Besides, there will be a guard out here all night," the other said.

The two soldiers told them goodnight and left the door cracked open. Thomas and Vance exchanged glances, feeling fortunate that they didn't have to resort to Plan B, which would have been push through the door and pull the two soldiers inside the room so they could be tied up and thrown in the restroom.

* * *

3AM came quickly, and Thomas, Vance and Mark were all ready to get the show on the road. Vance had taken a short nap between lights out and about 2AM, but neither Thomas nor Mark was able to get any sleep.

The three men quietly approached the door of their room, being careful not to alert the single guard sitting outside. Vance took the lead, since he had firsthand experience conducting these operations. He held his Glock down by his side, gripping it tightly. Mark had been given Vance's M4, in case had to go hands-on with someone. After all, Mark at least knew how to use it, even if he wasn't proficient with it. Thomas had the screwdriver he had taken from the east barracks, and he held it in his hand like he would a knife. Although he wasn't sure what he would do with it if he had to use it. Stabbing someone with a screwdriver? That was personal. It would mean that he was close enough to see their eyes, see if they had shaved that morning, feel their skin against his. He wasn't sure if he could do that. Not yet, anyway.

"Looks clear," Vance said after he peeked through the door.

Thomas and Mark followed Vance as he quietly stepped out into the hallway. The lights were off, except for the two emergency lights at either end of the hallway. Apparently the base's solar panels were providing a surplus of energy, because every building seemed to have power. Except for the hangars, of course.

Thomas felt his heart pounding in his throat as the three men made their way to the stairs. They moved so slowly that Thomas felt like they were only inching forward. Vance kept his handgun raised, and in the dim light that they were approaching, Thomas could see the look on his face. Or rather, the lack of expression. Vance's face was neutral. That was the only way Thomas could think to describe it. And even though there wasn't a hint of emotion on Vance's face, Thomas could still sense his focus, his readiness, his enhanced perception of the world around him.

"No lights on at all downstairs," Vance whispered, "Don't use your flashlights, though. We'll move slow and steady."

And so they did. The three men crept down the stairs, even slower than before. They moved so slowly that Thomas could feel his legs shaking with each step, struggling to remain silent. His heart was pounding even harder now, and Thomas almost felt like it was about to blow up. It couldn't beat any faster.

And then...

"That's far enough..." a booming voice said.

What seemed like a dozen bright lights came on all at once, every one of them focused on the three escapees. Thomas was immediately blinded by the sudden burst of light, so much so that he reeled back and threw his arm up.

"Drop your weapons," another voice said. After just a fraction of a moment, Thomas knew it was William McCoy.

Thomas was barely able to see Mark drop the assault rifle from his hands.

"Pick up your weapon!" Vance's raspy voice roared.

"I'd advise against that," McCoy said, although Thomas still could not see him. Or anyone at the bottom of the stairs, for that matter.

Thomas's eyes adjusted a little more, and he could now see Vance's back, his handgun still raised.

"Vance, I'm going to give you about half a fucking second to drop your gun before I order my men to open fire on all three of you. And then I'm going to go up there and kill everyone else in that room..." McCoy's voice was cold.

"Vance..." Thomas began.

"Fuck!" Vance dropped his Glock and raised his hands above his head.

Thomas, being at the rear of the group, was mostly concealed behind Mark and Vance. He quickly lifted the back of his shirt and stuck the screwdriver in his waistband, making sure that his shirt completely covered it.

"Come on down here," the other voice—Thomas was certain it

176

was Overfield—said.

The three men walked down the stairs with their hands raised. Now that they were closer to their adversaries, Thomas was able to see their faces. The bright lights were actually tall work lights. Three of them, actually, all with two bright lights each.

"Let's go have a chat, shall we?" McCoy began, his hands on his hips and a devilish smile on his face, "It seems we may need to go over the rules once more."

* * *

Mindy sat straight up in bed, startled by an unknown noise.

"What was that?" she asked no one in particular. Then she heard Samantha crying.

"Samantha, honey?" Mindy said as she got out of bed. The girl was in the corner by the door, sitting on the floor with her knees pulled up to her chest.

"What's wrong?" Mindy asked her. Vance, Mark, and Thomas were gone, so it must have been after 3 AM. She assumed that the noise that had woken her up had been Samantha.

"They got them," Samantha cried, "Now what do we do? Who's going to protect us?"

"What do you mean?" Mindy felt her heart speed up.

"Vance! And Thomas and Mark! They caught them!" Samantha sobbed.

Mindy almost felt her heart stop.

"They didn't even make it down the stairs," Samantha explained, "And then I heard McCoy and that Overfield guy."

"Shit..." Mindy jumped up and pushed open the door.

"Back inside!" a mean voice growled.

Mindy recoiled back in fear. She hadn't been expecting someone to be there.

"Where's my brother!?" she asked, her voice raised. Whoever was in front of her turned a flashlight on and shined it directly in her eyes.

"INSIDE! *NOW!*"

Mindy backed up inside the room, terrified and worried and confused.

"What happened to my brother!?" she yelled, "Where's Thomas!?"

She heard the door get kicked shut as far as it would go. It wasn't closed, but it might as well have been. Mindy had no doubt that there was at least one soldier on the other side, and he wouldn't be leaving anytime soon.

* * *

Thomas, Vance and Mark were all escorted at gunpoint to the rear of the visitor's center. There were lights on in a few places, but for the most part the building was dark. Thomas had counted six soldiers, plus Overfield and McCoy. They were all armed to the teeth, and no one was playing nice anymore.

They were forced through the rear entrance, and parked behind the building was one Humvee and a black SUV. Thomas's heart was beating so fast—faster than before, to his amazement—that it felt as if he was going to pass out. He had this sickening empty feeling in his gut. He was absolutely terrified.

"In," Overfield ordered as he looked at Vance.

Vance approached the back door of the Humvee, hands still raised.

"Wait!" McCoy blurted out, "Search him first. Search him *good.*"

Vance was pushed up against the Humvee as two soldiers searched him. One held him at gunpoint while the other—who was smart enough to hand his weapon off to someone else—searched Vance up and down. He wasn't gentle about it, either. Just as he appeared to be done, the soldier reached down and felt around Vance's ankles, lifting up each pant leg as he did so.

"Sneaky bastard," he said as he pulled out a small dagger that had been hidden in Vance's boot.

Thomas was growing more nervous now, if that was possible. They were going to search him and find that screwdriver.

"You two...stand over by the second vehicle!" Overfield ordered.

Thomas and Mark slowly walked over to the SUV. Now that they were separated from Vance, Thomas was even more concerned. He was not able to handle torture, or even a mild beating.

"Got anything on you?" a soldier asked as he approached Thomas. He was still holding his assault rifle, so he apparently wasn't too concerned about Thomas taking it from him.

"No," Thomas answered, and immediately regretted it. Now they were going to find the screwdriver and he had lied to them about it.

The soldier reached out with his left hand and patted both of Thomas's front pockets.

"Turn around," he said. Thomas tried to swallow the knot in his throat as he turned to face away from the soldier.

The soldier patted both of his back pockets, then touched him in the small of his back, just above the screwdriver's handle.

"Move," he barked, and gave Thomas a firm shove.

Thomas stumbled forward as another soldier opened the rear door of the SUV. He climbed inside, his hands still above his head as if they were frozen in place, and breathed a sigh of relief. Relief? How could he be feeling relieved at a time like this?

They did the same thing to Mark before putting him in the SUV beside Thomas. Then the troops—including Overfield and McCoy—loaded up and the two vehicles took off toward the airfield.

Oh no, Thomas thought, *we're going to end up just like that Chris guy. And probably Ronnie.*

The Humvee and SUV drove across the airfield and over to the C-130 that was parked outside of the hangar Thomas and Mindy had ventured into just yesterday. Thomas's breathing quickened, his breaths shallow and forced. His heart was still racing. He was terrified of being thrown in there, in the dark. Who knew what sort of treatment they would receive? The vehicles came to an abrupt stop between the two hangars. The soldiers got out and physically pulled Thomas and Mark out of the back. Thomas saw, however, that they did not treat Vance quite the same way. Two soldiers held him at gunpoint and gave him verbal commands, being careful not to touch him or even get within arm's reach of him. Thomas almost took solace in that, but then he realized that even if Vance had the opportunity and the courage to take a gun away, it would only serve to get them all killed. Sure, he might take down one or two, or even three. But there were simply too many of them, and they were all alert and focused.

Overfield opened the hangar's side door and stepped inside. The three prisoners waited outside with McCoy and the rest of the soldiers. The old NCO disappeared into the dark abyss of the hangar, and it seemed like forever before bright lights suddenly flashed on inside. Overfield reappeared and motioned with his head to bring them in. Thomas and Mark stepped inside, and followed Overfield across the huge, empty expanse of the hangar. Soldiers remained on either side of them, although they didn't seem worried at all about Thomas or Mark trying anything. Thomas glanced over his shoulder and saw a radically different scene with Vance. None of the soldiers walked in front of him, or even directly beside him. They all walked just a couple feet behind, and every single set of eyes were locked onto him. It was obvious that they were terrified of him. Or, perhaps more specifically, they were terrified of what he was *capable* of.

Overfield passed through another door on the other side of the hangar, Thomas and Mark about ten feet behind him. He flicked the lights on, and the room appeared to be more of an office. On the far side of the room—what would be the hangar's exterior wall—was a small set of stairs. The large group walked up them, and once at the top, Thomas saw a large cage about fifteen feet away. It was empty. No prisoners, no cots, no chairs, not even a place to use the restroom. The cage appeared to be made out of thick steel mesh, welded onto steel pipes that made up the cage's shell. But it didn't appear to be made ad hoc. It looked as if it had already been there.

"Inside," Overfield ordered, "Face the far side of the cage and place your hands on the wall."

Thomas and Mark complied. Thomas could feel himself physically shaking now. The two men walked over to the far side of the cage and leaned against it with their hands. Thomas looked over at Mark, who appeared to be quietly sobbing. The sight of the large, older man in tears almost made Thomas lose it. And then he thought about how it was his fault...

"Chris," Thomas heard McCoy say, "Meet your new roommate."

Thomas looked over his shoulder, and noticed an identical cage on the other side of the second floor. A weak-looking man with longer hair and thick beard was already in it, sitting in one of the far corners. He looked emaciated and sick. On the other side of the cage was a bucket, presumably for going to the bathroom in. Vance stepped inside, casual as ever. But Thomas could tell that inside, his blood was boiling.

Both cage doors crashed shut at almost the same time.

"Have a good night," Overfield told them.

Thomas turned around, but Mark stayed facing the cage's wall. McCoy was staring at him, his hands on his hips. That same devilish smile was spread across his face.

"You're just going to leave us in here?" Thomas asked.

"What? You thought I'd let you go again? You had your one 'get out of jail free' card, which is more than what most people get. Now you have to deal with the repercussions of your actions."

McCoy nodded his head at him, still smiling, and disappeared down the stairs along with everyone else.

"Hey!" Thomas yelled through the cage, although he couldn't see anyone, "Hey!"

"Don't do that," a sad, weak voice said from the other cell. Thomas looked over and saw that it was the guy who had already been held here. Chris, presumably.

"We shouldn't have done this," Mark said. Thomas ignored it.

"Chris?" he asked.

"Yes."

"We were actually coming to save you," Thomas told him.

"And what happened?" Vance asked, his voice quiet but still terrifying, "What did I say would happen?"

Thomas turned away to face toward the back of the cage again. He leaned up against the cage's door and placed his hands on top of his head.

"This is your fault..." Mark said, his back still turned to Thomas and the other two.

"Mark, I..."

"This is *YOUR...FAULT!*" he roared as he whirled around to face Thomas. There was maybe five feet separating them.

"Mark..."

"Why couldn't you have just fucking listened to Vance!?" Mark yelled. It was the first time Thomas had seen him angry.

"I..."

"You just had to try to save the fuckin' day! You couldn't live with the fact that you're a weak, pathetic, *boy!*" Mark was breathing heavily now, and beads of sweat rolled down his face.

"Don't yell..." Chris said quietly, as if he didn't have the energy to say it any louder.

Mark took a step toward Thomas, who pressed his back against the cage as much as he could.

"What's going to happen to us now?" Mark asked, his voice a little quieter, "What's going to happen to *MY WIFE!?*"

"Mark, we'll figure this out..."

"What!? We'll 'figure this out'? Are you really that goddamn *stupid!?*"

Thomas's eyes were wide. He was terrified. Now he was locked in this cage with the big, burly man that Mark was. He was enraged and directing it toward Thomas. *And rightfully so,* Thomas told himself.

"I swear, if *anything* happens to Virginia, I will *KILL YOU!!*" Mark screamed as he took another step and pointed his finger in Thomas's face.

"Mark, I'm..." Thomas stuttered, both because of fear and because he was almost at a loss for words, "I'm sorry. I'll get us out of this."

"I was so *stupid* to follow you," Mark said as he turned away, "What the hell was I thinkin'? Some smart kid from Seattle stops by my house one day, and I just decide to follow him. We were perfectly fine in Idaho!"

Mark was mostly speaking to himself. His back was turned and he was throwing his arms up in the air. Thomas remained silent, not wanting to say anything to provoke the older, larger man.

"So what now?" Vance asked calmly after Mark had quieted down. But his question was asked in a mocking manner, and wasn't genuine.

Thomas looked at him for a moment, feeling for all the world like he had gotten every single one of them killed. He knew the grief would hit him soon enough, but for now he was still in shock.

"How the fuck did this happen?" he asked himself, under his breath.

"What?" Mark asked as he turned back around, "Did you just ask how this happened?"

"Mark..." Vance began.

"This *happened* because you convinced us that it would work. This *happened* because you said you were going to do it, with or without us. This *happened* because we didn't want to let you get yourself killed! And now what, huh? Now we're in here to rot, while God knows what they do to the others. To my *wife!*"

Thomas threw his back against the cage and slid straight down to the floor. He felt utterly defeated. He felt ashamed and scared and worried.

"I might know how to get out of here."

Thomas paused before turning around and looking into the other cage. Chris's words were still weak, and it sounded like his mouth was incredibly dry. But they offered hope, nonetheless.

11

Mindy paced back and forth while Virginia sobbed loudly. Samantha was sitting on her own bed, with her knees pulled against her chest and her arms wrapped around them. It was about 6AM now, and they hadn't heard anything from the soldiers.

"What do you think happened to them?" Samantha asked softly.

Mindy stopped pacing and put her hand on her forehead. Tears welled up in eyes for about the hundredth time, but this time she couldn't hold them back. She sat down on the nearest bed and began sobbing as well. Samantha got up and walked over to her. She sat down beside her, and very gently wrapped her arms around her and rested her head on Mindy's shoulder.

"What would I do without him?" Mindy forced through the tears, her voice crackling.

"It'll be alright," Samantha said, "Thomas is smart. And they have Vance with them."

Mindy didn't even answer. She buried her face in her hands and continued crying. Virginia was just a couple beds down, and she, too, couldn't quit crying.

Suddenly, the door flew open. Overfield appeared, and he stared at the three of them blankly for several moments. Mindy wiped her eyes and face and stared back, while Virginia continued her crying fit as if she was completely unaware.

"Boss man wants to see you," Overfield said.

"All of us?" Mindy asked.

"Yep. Now."

Mindy got up and walked over to Virginia. After helping her up and drying her face with a washrag, the three of them made their way to the open door. In the hallway were two soldiers sitting in chairs. They stared at them coldly as they walked past.

"Come on," Overfield said from the stairs.

Mindy, Samantha and Virginia followed him down the stairs and into a nearby room. It appeared to be some sort of large office. McCoy was inside, staring out the window with his hands casually resting in small of his back.

"Have a seat," he said without looking at them.

Overfield shut the door, leaving just the four of them in the room. Mindy and Virginia sat down, but Samantha was hesitant. McCoy turned around, an unfortunate look on his face, and rolled his eyes back and forth between Virginia and Mindy.

"Has the girl suddenly lost her understanding of the English language?" he asked sternly.

"Samantha..." Mindy said as she reached her hand out to her. The girl took Mindy's hand and sat down in the chair next to her.

"I'm sure you're wondering where your three companions are," McCoy began as he sat down at the desk in front of them, "I don't really know how to say this, so I'll just say it. We kicked them out last night, after they were caught wandering through the building with weapons."

"Kicked them out!?" Mindy felt her heart sink.

"Yes. They wanted to take all of you with them, but I couldn't allow that. We loaded them up in the two vehicles you came here with, and sent them on their way."

Mindy's jaw dropped as she stared at McCoy.

"No...you couldn't have," Virginia managed to say, her mouth quivering.

"I did. I can't allow people to break the rules."

"But they were..." Mindy's voice cut out, her mind in disarray, "My brother...Virginia's husband..."

"They knew the rules!" McCoy shouted, startling all three of the females before him, "I gave you and your brother a chance after you blatantly disobeyed me. He apparently couldn't understand the rules I have in place to keep everyone safe."

"Then we'll leave," Mindy said abruptly, "We'll leave and find them. They wouldn't have gone far."

"I assure you, they went plenty far," McCoy told her as he rose to his feet, "We followed them all the way to the edge of town, to make sure they wouldn't hang around and cause problems."

"Then tell us which direction, and we will find them. They wouldn't just leave us!" Mindy broke down and started crying again, but her gaze never left McCoy's face.

"I can't allow that," McCoy said calmly, "The three of you...you'd get yourselves killed within half an hour out there. Especially considering the horde we spotted while escorting them out of the city."

"The horde?" Mindy asked.

"Yes. Don't worry, it's going to miss us. Assuming it doesn't change course, obviously. Probably two hundred or more."

Mindy felt the breath leave her lungs. Her vision blurred and she briefly saw stars. She felt as if she was about to pass out.

"Why did you make them take both vehicles?" she finally asked.

"That was their decision. Didn't ask them why."

Virginia doubled over and buried her face in her hands. She sobbed loudly, and McCoy looked at her while she did so. A slight grin spread across his face, as if he got some sort of satisfaction from her expressing her pain.

"Let us leave," Mindy said once more.

McCoy looked at her sharply.

"No."

* * *

Thomas was sitting on the floor with his knees pulled up and his arms resting on them. It had been nearly eight hours since they had been thrown in the cages, and they hadn't seen any sign of human activity. The single light that dangled between the two cages was dim, and it cast unsettling shadows all around them.

"So are you going to tell us how to get out of here yet?" Thomas asked Chris.

"I didn't say I knew how," Chris said, "I said I *might* know how."

"Alright, well are you going to tell us know?"

"Not yet," Chris replied.

"Goddamn it! Tell us!" Mark snapped.

"Not yet," Chris repeated, "Just wait. They'll be here soon."

Thomas sighed out of exhaustion and frustration.

"So what happened to Ronnie?" Thomas asked.

"Who?"

"Ronnie...he disappeared last night. We assumed McCoy threw him in here with you."

"I think I remember who you're talking about. No, haven't seen him. It's just been me for...I don't even know how long. I have no concept of night and day."

"Logan said it's been about three weeks," Thomas told him.

"That's it?" Chris asked, staring at the ceiling, "Three weeks? It feels like it's been a year."

Thomas thought about that for a moment. Chris had been in here for three weeks, alone, with no concept of time, no way to look outside and see the days come and go. How long would he be kept in here? At least he had other people with him, unlike poor Chris, who had been all alone this whole time. That made Thomas wonder: Why hadn't Chris been more excited to have people to talk to now? He hadn't said hardly anything to them, even though nearly eight hours had passed and Thomas had continuously tried to strike up conversation.

"Aren't you glad to have people to talk to?" Thomas finally asked him.

"I'm still trying to figure out if you all are even real or not," Chris answered, still staring at the ceiling.

"We're real, buddy. And as soon as you tell us how to get out of here, we're *all* leaving," Thomas said.

"And then what?" Mark asked, "We just wander across the airfield, get the girls, and walk out through the gate? Come on..."

"We'll cross that bridge when we come to it," Thomas told him, slightly annoyed with Mark's attitude.

"Oh will we, now? Excuse me if I don't seem to have much faith in you anymore!"

Thomas ignored it, and went back to thinking. If Chris's idea—whatever it was—fell through, he would need some kind of backup plan.

And then they all heard the door open. It echoed throughout the metal and concrete hangar. Chris sat up and quickly crawled on his hands and knees to the front part of the cage. It had been the only time that Thomas had seen him move.

"What's going on?" he asked.

"Feeding time, I think," Chris said, "Time to get out of here."

"What? How? Chris...you need to tell us before whoever just came in gets up here..."

"You'll see," Chris replied quietly.

Thomas could hear boots stomping up the stairs. Three soldiers appeared, but only two of them were carrying a plate of food.

"One plate for each cell," one of them said, "Hope you boys know how to share."

One of the guards pulled out a set of keys and unlocked the door of Thomas and Mark's cage. The other two stood back, obviously ready in case anyone tried anything. The soldier who had opened the door reached over and took a plate from one of the others, then sat it on the floor and slid it inside. It looked like oatmeal, and it slopped over the edge of the plate and onto the floor. The soldier closed the cage's door and turned to face Vance and Chris.

"Hey, can we get a bucket in here like they have?" Thomas asked. He had needed to urinate for the past couple of hours.

"Yeah, I'll get one after we feed you guys," one soldier said, surprisingly politely.

As the soldier fumbled with his keys, Chris latched onto the mesh cage and pulled himself to his feet. He stared at the guard in a strange way, his eyes wide and his mouth hanging open.

As the guard stuck the key in the lock, Chris said softly, "It's the only way."

The door opened, and Chris lunged through it at the guard. He grabbed onto him tightly, and his momentum caused the guard to stumbled backward and slam up against the cage Thomas and Mark were in. Chris was obviously too weak to be a threat, and the strong soldier quickly overpowered him and threw him to the ground at the feet of the other soldiers. Chris reached up and desperately tried to grab the sidearm of one of the soldiers. He almost looked like an animal trying to crawl up the man's leg. Thomas watched as the soldier with the keys pulled out his own sidearm and aimed it at Chris...

And then Vance came rushing out with the force of a truck. He rushed straight toward the soldier holding the gun, but he wasn't quite fast enough. A single shot rang out, its loud *crack* bouncing off of the metal walls and nearly deafening Thomas. Thomas looked on as Vance crashed into the soldier with all his force, less than a second after the gun had been fired. Thomas heard the sound of bones breaking as Vance drilled the man right in the chest with his shoulder, and slammed him so hard against Thomas's cage that it bent the metal mesh. Chris was now lying on the ground, blood seeping out from underneath his body.

Thomas felt frozen as he watched events unfold in front of him. The other two soldiers rushed over and grabbed Vance right after he slammed their friend into the cage. Vance elbowed one in the nose, and the soldier fell to the floor as blood gushed out of his nostrils. The first soldier slid down the cage, a horrible wheezing sound coming from him as he tried desperately to breath air back into his lungs. Thomas was all too familiar with that sound, having been the unfortunate victim of bullies punching him in the chest more than once. But Vance had hit the man so hard that Thomas was surprised his heart was still beating.

Vance turned on the final soldier and wrapped his giant hands around the man's neck. The soldier reached down for his sidearm, but Vance grabbed his wrist and twisted it so he was unable to pull the gun from its holster. The soldier tried to knee Vance in the stomach, but it was futile. Vance tightened his grip and the man's expression turned to one of terror and anxiety. Both of his hands reached up and grabbed Vance's arm. Vance still only had one hand around the man's neck, but it was enough. He forced the man backward and slammed him against the wall at the top of the stairs.

Thomas saw movement out of the corner of his eye. The soldier Vance had smashed was slowly moving now. Moving toward...

"Vance! Gun!" was all Thomas could get out.

Vance turned his head toward his first victim while still maintaining his grip around the soldier's neck. The first soldier reached out and grabbed his handgun that was laying on the floor, and before Vance could react in any way, the soldier pointed it at him and fired.

Thomas's jaw dropped. Everything slowed down. Vance's face tightened into an expression of pain, his gritted teeth exposed. He recoiled from the impact of the bullet, and when he did he inadvertently pushed the soldier in front of him to his right. The soldier tumbled down the stairs, out of sight. Vance fell to the ground, grabbing at his leg.

"Back...in the...cell..." the first soldier managed to spit out.

Vance cringed for a moment as blood oozed through the wound on his leg. The bullet had hit the back of his left thigh, and exited straight through the other side. For all Thomas knew, it might have also hit the soldier Vance had been choking. But he wasn't thinking about that now.

"Move..." the first soldier said, although every word came only through great labor. He was still struggling to breath, and Thomas was certain that he had at least a couple broken bones.

Vance composed himself and stared at the soldier. In his mind's eye, Thomas imagined Vance rising to his feet like a nearly fallen hero, walking over to the soldier, and slapping the gun from his hands. But that didn't happen. A look of defeat spread across Vance's face. He slowly dragged himself over to his cage, crawling over Chris's body and through his pool of blood. Vance finally made it, and the first soldier scooted forward and kicked the door shut. He kept his handgun trained on Vance, just in case.

"Fox!" he yelled, obviously able to breath a little better by this point.

Thomas heard the second soldier—the one with the broken nose—groan in pain as he writhed around on the floor.

"Fox! Get your ass up and check that door!"

The soldier—Fox—slowly got up, his hands covering his nose. He stumbled over to the cage and grabbed the door with one hand. After giving it two hard tugs, he sat back down on the floor and moaned. Blood dripped out between his fingers, covering his shirt and pants and the floor beneath him.

"CQ," the first soldier said into his radio, "This is Peterson. Had a situation in the hangar. Fox and I are injured...bad. Not sure about King's status."

Peterson was obviously in a lot of pain. He leaned his head back against Thomas's cage and breathed heavily. Thomas approached the cage and reached around to the small of his back. He pulled out the phillip's head screwdriver and held it in his hand as if it were some sort of unknown object. He looked up at Vance, who was also breathing heavily from the adrenaline and pain—and possibly blood loss—and stared at him for a moment. Vance stared back, and finally nodded his head the best he could.

Thomas wrapped his fingers through the metal cage so he would have more leverage. With his right hand he pulled the screwdriver back as far as he could, and stared at the base of Peterson's head. It couldn't have been more perfect. The soldier was pressed up against the cage, not paying any attention. The area where his head connected to his neck was perfectly exposed through the metal mesh. With enough force, the screwdriver would penetrate the soft spot around the brain stem and kill him almost instantly. Thomas stood there for another moment, staring with wide eyes and breathing heavily as what he was about to do played out in his mind, as if it had already happened. His breathing increased, his heart was racing, he felt sweat trickling down between his body and his clothing.

"Do it!" Vance told him.

"Shut up!" Peterson yelled back, completely unaware of what Vance was talking about. He was probably so beat up and in pain that he didn't even have the ability to process beyond what was right in front of him.

Thomas was frozen, staring at Peterson's neck. This was it. He would kill his first living, breathing human being. He thought about how it would feel, how much satisfaction he would get from killing one of the men who was holding them captive. The man who had shot Vance, the extent of his injury currently unknown. Thomas looked up at Vance once more, eyes still wide with bloodlust. Vance frowned and nodded his head once more. Thomas's arm had relaxed a little while he had been standing there, so he pulled the screwdriver back once more as far as he could, took aim, and...

He couldn't do it. He simply couldn't kill this man. Peterson—who he had never met before—was injured and completely unaware. He posed no real threat. Thomas didn't have it in him. He just couldn't do it. He backed away from the cage, from Peterson, and put the screwdriver back in his waistband. After briefly looking at Vance, who looked disappointed, Thomas nearly fell to the floor and buried his face in his hands. All of his adrenaline was dumping now. It made him feel weak and woozy. Mark stared at him blankly, as if he didn't care one way or another.

Just a couple of minutes passed before backup arrived. Derek and Overfield both showed up, along with four other soldiers.

"What the fuck happened?" Overfield asked.

"Sergeant..."

"King's dead," Overfield interrupted, "He's laying at the bottom of the goddamn stairs with a broken neck."

"Chris rushed through at us, sir, like he wanted us to kill him. We didn't see it coming. I shot him. Then *he* came out, too." Peterson pointed at Vance with his gun.

"Get him out of here," Overfield barked. Two of the soldiers lifted Peterson to his feet, who cried out in pain, and helped him down the stairs.

"And you," Overfield said as he turned and kicked Fox in the foot, "What the fuck's wrong with you?"

"I think...I think I have a concussion, Sarge," Fox answered.

"And a broken nose," Vance piped up. Overfield shot him a mean glare.

"Don't think you're going to receive any sort of medical attention," Overfield said to Vance, "You can bleed out, for all I care."

"I appreciate the kindness," Vance replied. Defiant until the end, even with a gunshot wound.

"McCoy is *not* going to be happy about this, just so you all know," Overfield said to Thomas.

After Overfield pulled Fox to his feet and everyone left, Thomas looked over at Vance to see just how badly he was hurt. But before he could even ask, Vance pulled himself over to the wall of the cage and sat up.

"Well," Vance said, "I guess Chris's plan to get out of here worked."

* * *

Derek and Staff Sergeant Overfield walked into McCoy's office, both dreading the conversation they were about to have.

"Sir," Overfield said as they both entered the office, "There's been an incident..."

McCoy was furious. It was blatantly obvious by the vein pulsing in his forehead, by his heavy breathing and wide eyes. He stood at the window, bent over with his hands resting on the windowsill, exposing his teeth and clenching his jaw as if he was about to scream in a fit anger. His jet black hair wasn't pulled back into a pony tail, so it hung down over his shoulders and wrapped around his face. It only added to his look of insane rage.

Then, all of a sudden, he pushed himself away from the window and stormed past Overfield and Derek. The two men shot each other a worried look—Overfield more so than Derek—before rushing out of the room to follow their leader. McCoy stormed down the stairs and threw open the doors of the cafeteria. Nearly everyone was in there, still eating breakfast.

"Logan!" McCoy yelled, "Where's Logan!?"

Heads turned toward a table in the back of the cafeteria. Logan was sitting there with food in his mouth, but he wasn't chewing. He was frozen from fear.

Once McCoy had spotted him, he stomped toward him at a very brisk pace. Anyone who was in his way quickly moved, not wanting to see if the rumors were true about Wild Bill's terrifying temper.

"Come here!" McCoy growled as he grabbed Logan by his collar and pulled him to his feet.

"What the..."

"Take him!" McCoy yelled, and threw him toward Derek and Overfield.

The two men caught him and quickly escorted him out, trying to avoid making the ordeal any worse. Once they were gone, McCoy stared at the cafeteria doors and breathed heavily. All eyes were on him. Within moments, he composed himself.

"That man..." McCoy pointed toward the doors, "...that man is a traitor. Because of *him*, one of our soldiers is dead. Two more seriously injured."

That was all the explanation that McCoy felt was necessary. Satisfied, he stormed out of the cafeteria and headed toward the hangar.

"What the hell was that about?" Mindy asked no one in particular.

"I don't like this," Samantha said, "I'm scared."

* * *

Overfield and Derek had just arrived at the hangar with Logan in tow, and were patiently waiting for McCoy to arrive.

"Guys, I don't know what's going on," Logan said anxiously. The two men were standing on either side of him, each tightly holding one of his arms.

"Neither do we," Overfield said calmly.

The hangar's side door flew open, and McCoy stepped inside. He was considerably calmer now, although the same look of fury was all over his face. He didn't speak, instead walking over to the wall of the hangar that had various tools and materials. He briefly looked around before pulling out a small chain from a cubby-hole. Then he walked past Overfield and Derek and toward the stairs. The two men, after a brief moment of uncertainty, followed him. They reached the top of the stairs and saw McCoy throwing the long chain up over a metal rafter. Logan recoiled at the sight.

"Sir?" Overfield asked, but McCoy didn't answer.

McCoy reached over and grabbed Logan, who was terrified. He stuck his feet straight out in front of him, trying to resist. McCoy's patience was nonexistent at this point, and as as result he grabbed Logan by the back of the neck and headbutted him right in the nose. Then, to the shock of everyone watching, he stomped straight down on Logan's knee. Logan let out a horrifying scream as his leg—which had been extended straight out in front of him—snapped and bent so that it looked like the leg of a bird.

"Oh my God!" Thomas cried out.

But McCoy wasn't finished. He had grabbed the chain for a reason. As Logan writhed around in pain—McCoy tightly holding onto his arm—McCoy wrapped the end of the chain around his neck twice before pulling it tight and sticking the hook in one of the links of the chain. Gurgling noises came from Logan's throat as he tried to breath. His eyes seemed to bulge from his head. But it wasn't over.

McCoy grabbed the other end of the chain—the end he had thrown over the rafter—and handed it to Derek and Overfield.

"Hoist him up," he said, calm as ever.

Overfield and Derek stared at him for a moment, mouths open, as if what they had just heard hadn't been real.

"Do it!" McCoy shouted.

Overfield and Derek grabbed the chain tightly and began pulling. Once it became taught, they walked backwards a few feet to lift Logan off of the ground.

"Stop!" Thomas yelled.

Logan was now about two feet off of the ground, kicking and bouncing around. McCoy walked over to the end that Overfield and Derek were pulling on, and grabbed up the extra length of chain from the floor. He wrapped it around the metal railing of the stairs until the length between the two men pulling on it and the railing was nearly taught.

"Let go," McCoy told them.

Derek and Overfield hesitated, staring at the man dangling and choking to death in front of them.

"Every second you waste is one more second *he* gets to spend suffocating!" McCoy reminded them as he pointed at Logan.

They let go. Logan's body fell straight down nearly a foot before coming to an abrupt stop. A horrible snapping noise was heard. Logan's hands—which had been instinctively grabbing at the chain around his neck—fell limp by his sides. His eyes looked as if they were going to pop out of their sockets. His head and face were purple, and his tongue looked too big for his mouth as it poked out between his lips.

"Oh my God..." Mark said as he stumbled back against the cage that was imprisoning him.

"You sick *fucks!*" Thomas screamed.

"This is *your* doing!" McCoy yelled back.

McCoy then took two big steps over to Chris's body, which had not been moved. He grabbed a handful of hair and lifted the body up. A sick—almost suckling—sound could be heard as he pulled the body away from the large pool of blood that had formed beneath it. The bullet appeared to have gone almost directly through the heart. At least the poor soul didn't have to suffer. McCoy dragged him over to the cage that Vance was in.

"Open the door!" he ordered.

Overfield dug the keys out of his pocket and unlocked the door. McCoy threw it open and rolled Chris's body inside with Vance. He then slammed the door shut as hard as he could.

"You'll be in here awhile," McCoy said calmly as he

approached the stairs, "When both of those bodies are fully decomposed, I'll let you out."

And then he was gone. Derek and Overfield looked at each other, still in shock. They had both seen Wild Bill meltdown and demonstrate his wrath before, but never to this extent. Overfield looked over at Thomas and swallowed hard before speaking.

"This..." he began, "...this is. This was..."

Overfield looked around, as if he wasn't sure that it was all real.

"I never meant for anything to go this far..."

Thomas approached the cage door and stared through the mesh.

"Fuck you," he said, "You're just as much to blame as he is."

Overfield looked over at Derek, who had no expression at all. They both walked down the stairs and left without saying another word.

"Horrible..." Mark said before breaking down and sobbing.

"Well," Vance began, seemingly unphazed, "I guess I should have been a fuckin' fortune teller instead of a soldier."

12

It had been an entire day since Thomas, Mark, and Vance had been kicked out of Hill Air Force Base. Mindy was surprisingly calm now, but she knew it was only from shock and denial. She felt very little emotion. Virginia was a mess. She spent most of her time bawling, and refused to eat. Samantha seemed to be feeding off of Mindy's emotions, and was quiet and calm as well.

Mindy and Samantha went down to the cafeteria to eat breakfast. Virginia refused to come down, but Mindy planned on taking up a plate of food to her. The mood in the cafeteria was dark. For whatever reason, everyone was quiet. Not even any murmuring. It was unsettling, only hearing the sounds of utensils scraping against trays, people getting up and sitting down, random coughs and cups hitting the metal tables. Mindy and Samantha both ate slowly. Neither one really felt like eating, especially Mindy, but she knew she had to keep herself going. If they ever managed to get out of The Hill, she needed all her strength to go find Thomas. And Mark and Vance, of course. Meanwhile, she needed to find a way to calm Virginia down. There was no way that she could go out how she was. She was way too hysterical.

"Do you think they'll wait for us?" Samantha asked Mindy, after several minutes of silence.

"Yes, I told you they would. They're not going to just...leave."

"What if..." Samantha stopped herself.

"What if what, honey?"

"Well..." Samantha gave Mindy an uneasy look, "What

if...McCoy didn't make them leave?"

"What do you mean?" Mindy was confused, and it showed on her face.

"What if they're..." Samantha let out a sigh before continuing, "What if he killed them?"

Mindy stared at the girl as if she had two heads. After a moment, she composed herself.

"They're not dead, Samantha," she said.

"But how do we know?"

"They're just...not."

After the two finished breakfast, and Mindy grabbed a tray of food for Virginia (after an argument with the server), the two went back up to their room. Virginia was on her bed, but wasn't noticeably crying at the moment. Samantha sat down and opened a magazine they had found downstairs. Mindy approached Virginia and gently laid the tray on the floor beside her bed.

"Virginia?" she said softly, "I brought you some food. Please eat it, okay?"

Virginia turned her head so that she could see Mindy out of the corner of her eye, but didn't respond. Mindy looked down at the floor—sad and confused and angry—before sitting down on her own bed and staring at the wall across from her.

* * *

"How are you doing?" Thomas asked Vance.

"I'm still alive, aren't I?" Vance replied.

It had been a little over an hour since he had been shot. He seemed a little pale, and a bit weak, but overall he appeared to be doing okay. He hadn't lost that much blood, thankfully.

"Just thought I'd ask," Thomas said.

Vance reached down and adjusted the makeshift bandage he had created with the sleeves of his t-shirt.

"Got any ideas?" Thomas asked.

"Yeah," Vance said, "I'm going to kill every mother fucker I see, every chance I get."

Thomas rubbed his eyes and let out a long sigh.

"There has *got* to be a way out of this," he said.

"No, there doesn't," Mark chimed in. It had been the first thing he had said in over an hour.

"What?"

"There doesn't *got* to be a way out. Every sorry son-of-a-bitch who finds themselves in a situation like this thinks that, and where are they today? Dead."

"Maybe they just weren't able to create a plan that worked," Thomas suggested.

"Goddamn it!" Mark yelled, "Just shut the hell up! We're locked in a steel cage, with nothing more than your stupid screwdriver! Hell, you couldn't even kill that soldier who shot Vance!"

"He didn't need to die. He was just doing his job..."

"He fuckin' *shot* Vance!" Mark shouted. His face was bright red now, almost purple.

"Calm down, Mark. I..."

"*NO!*" he screamed, "How can you tell me to calm down in a situation like this!?"

"Mark..."

"This is *YOUR* fault, dumb ass! We're all in here because of *you*, and no one else! Everyone who's been killed or injured is because of *YOUR* actions!"

"Shut the fuck up, already!" Thomas roared, standing up as he did so.

"Oh, now you're going to stand up to me? Why? Because you know I'm not a real threat to you?"

"Mark, just leave it alone! I never intended for things to go down like this!"

"Vance warned you, Thomas! He fuckin' *warned* you. And you didn't listen. How can you be so goddamn stupid?" Mark's voice had quieted down, but his words pierced through Thomas nonetheless.

"I know that, okay!" Thomas yelled, then lowered his voice, "I should have listened. But I didn't, and now we're here. Pointing the finger of blame won't help anything. Not now. Let's just figure this thing out."

"There is no *figurin' it out*! Don't you see that? McCoy is gonna to kill us. And he's going to kill my wife, and that girl, and *your sister*, if he hasn't already!"

Thomas had had enough. Mark crossed the line. He took two steps toward the big man and grabbed him by one of the straps on his overalls.

"*SHUT UP!*" Thomas growled, "Don't say a single fucking word about my sister begin killed! Do you understand?"

"Thomas..." Vance said, though neither Thomas or Mark heard him over the blood pumping in their ears.

"Don't fuckin' touch me!" Mark barked, and smacked Thomas's hand away.

Mark was several inches taller than Thomas, and certainly larger. He wasn't obese, but he had a naturally large, burly frame, and years of farming contributed to that. But Thomas didn't care. He was so angry and frustrated and ashamed that he couldn't even think straight.

"Smack me like that again, and I'll beat the shit out of you..." Thomas said calmly.

"What!?" Mark asked with a chuckle, "You're gonna beat the shit out of me, huh?"

"I understand...I'm a big fuck up. People have died because of me, I get that. But don't think for one fleeting moment that I don't care. Don't think that I am defeated. I *will* get us out of this."

"Go to hell," Mark said to him, and turned his back to him.

Thomas couldn't take it anymore. He took one more large step toward Mark, formed his hand into a fist, and struck him in the back of the head. The large man staggered forward a couple of feet, but was otherwise unphazed.

"You little *bastard*!" Mark shouted as he turned around to face Thomas, rage burning in his eyes.

"Not a good idea, guys," Vance said, but his words fell on deaf ears once more.

"Do you have any idea what I could do to you?" Mark asked Thomas.

"Try it," Thomas replied.

"I could snap you in half."

"Fuck off or do something, then."

Mark charged forward—faster than Thomas had seen him move thus far—and slammed Thomas up against the cage. It wasn't as forceful as it could have been, but it still hurt like hell.

"Get the fuck off me!" Thomas yelled.

Mark continued pushing him against the cage with one big forearm. His other hand grabbed Thomas by the face and shoved it, too, into the side of the cage.

"Mark!" Vance growled in his deep, raspy voice. Again, no one listened.

Thomas struggled to get out of Mark's grasp, but it was futile. The man continued pinning him up against the cage, putting more and more weight on him. Thomas felt his lungs struggle to provide his body with oxygen. His head felt like it was about to pop. His vision blurred, he saw stars, and a black ring formed around his peripheral vision.

"Do you understand now what I could do to you?" Mark asked him. His voice was quiet, but it was laced with rage.

Thomas swung his right hand and smacked Mark on the left side of his head. Mark chuckled slightly at the fact that another man had just slapped him, and continued pushing.

"That's enough!" Vance yelled.

Thomas swung once more, this time with his hand formed into a fist. He struck Mark directly in his left ear—a lucky shot. The big man recoiled back and let go. His equilibrium was off from the blow to his ear, besides the fact that it had hurt like hell. Thomas was no fighter, and he certainly wasn't all that strong, but he knew human physiology. When Mark leaned over and grabbed his ear, Thomas took the opportunity to strike him as hard as he could in the kidney. Mark dropped down to one knee and let out a growl from the pain. Thomas grabbed him by his neck and toppled him over onto the floor. He then pulled out the screwdriver from his waistband and stood over Mark.

"Thomas! No!" Vance shouted as he jumped to his feet—or foot, to be more accurate—as best he could.

Thomas stared down at Mark, whose eyes were wide with surprise. For just a moment, Thomas thought about how good it would feel to stab him right in the heart with the screwdriver. But then he realized that he was only feeling that way because of other events that Mark had nothing to do with. Mark was just mad and frustrated, and rightfully so. And wouldn't Thomas feel the same way, if someone had gotten them in this situation?

"Don't fuck with me again," Thomas said softly, "We *will* get out of this. But you can't keep challenging me. Get your shit together."

Mark looked up at him, eyes still wide, but said nothing. Then his eyes grew even wider, and a look of terror spread across his face. Thomas looked down at him, utterly confused. Mark let out a grunt as he quickly reached up and grabbed at his chest.

"What's happening?" Thomas said as he backed away.

"My heart...*my heart*..." Mark managed to spit out.

Thomas looked on as the veins in Mark's head seemed to swell up like they were going to explode. The carotid arteries in his neck bulged out as well, and his eyes looked like they were going to shoot out of his head. His mouth hung open, his tongue quivering.

"Mark!" Thomas yelled. His heart was pounding and his breathing became frantic as he began to panic.

The older man writhed around on the floor for a moment, grunting and wheezing. He clawed at his chest with both hands, as if he were trying to dig through it to get to his heart. His face became a dark purple color. Thomas squatted down by his side and grabbed Mark's arm.

"Come on, Mark!" he yelled at him, as if he could cure the man with sheer force of will.

Mark's entire body jolted once more, his back arching and his hands grabbing his overalls so tightly that his knuckles turned white. And then he just...stopped. Everything became quiet as Mark's entire body went limp. No more grunting, or moaning. No more grabbing his chest. His eyelids were stuck open, his gaze directed at the back of the cage.

"Do something!" Vance roared.

Thomas placed his fingers against Mark's neck, searching for a pulse. He didn't find one. Shaking, he placed his hands together on Mark's chest and forcefully pushed down. A cracking sound was heard as cartilage and maybe a bone or two broke from the first chest compression. Again and again, Thomas forced his arms downward into Mark's chest.

"Come on!" he yelled as tears rolled down his face.

Thomas kept going as several minutes passed. His compressions grew harder and harder out of desperation, as if doing so would make the CPR he was performing more effective. He finally became so exhausted that he could no longer continue, and he fell backwards onto the floor. As he coughed and moaned from anguish and grief, tears quickly rolled down his face. What had he done?

"Thomas..." Vance said calmly.

Thomas continued crying, rolling over onto his side and looking like a rag doll.

"Thomas, get up!" Vance yelled.

But Thomas didn't. Instead, he remained on the floor for several long moments while he cried and screamed and smacked himself in the head for causing Mark's heart to give out. How much more damage could he possibly cause? How many more people would he inadvertently harm before this was all over?

* * *

Mindy sat quietly on a bench outside the visitor's center. She was in deep thought, trying to figure out a way to escape or at least convince McCoy to let them leave. She was coming up empty, no matter how hard she tried. She had spent all day trying to conceive some sort of plan, and nothing she could think of seemed rational. It was now almost supper time, and even though she didn't feel like eating, she forced herself to get up and go find Samantha. She was most likely in the room with Virginia—who still had not moved—flipping through a magazine or braiding her hair, or whatever young girls did during a zombie apocalypse these days.

As Mindy walked through the front door, she saw McCoy and Derek talking quietly by the stairwell. She waited by the door, hoping to talk to McCoy about letting them leave. Derek spotted her out of the corner of his eye, and both he and McCoy looked over at her. Their conversation ended, and Derek walked off into the cafeteria. McCoy slowly approached Mindy, a friendly smile on his face.

"Mindy," he said.

"I was hoping I could speak with you for just a moment," she said calmly.

"Of course. I have a minute."

"Look...I know that you have rules here. Rules that need to be followed. And in a way, I understand why you made my brother and the other two leave. I'm not asking you to let them come back. But will you please just let us leave?" Mindy spoke calmly, the desperation ever apparent in her voice.

"I can't allow that, Mindy," McCoy said.

"Why not?"

"How long do you think the three of you would survive out there? Half an hour? Half a day, maybe? I can't let you put yourself in inevitable danger out of good conscience. What kind of man would I be if I allowed that? What kind of *leader* would I be, if I let that happen?"

"I get that, but why can't you let us do what we want? We're adults, and it's our decision..."

"Two of you are adults," McCoy reminded her, "Samantha? She's a child. How could I let you take her out there? She's not old enough to make that decision on her own."

Mindy looked down at the floor. In a twisted way, McCoy was right. Putting Samantha in that situation was foolish. The Hill was safe. There was plenty of food and water. Why would Mindy even entertain the idea of taking Samantha away from a place like that, with just her and Virginia to watch over her?

"Let's talk again in a couple of days once the horde has passed," McCoy said gently and he placed his hand on her shoulder.

"Sure, alright..."

McCoy nodded his head and patted her shoulder before walking off into the cafeteria. Mindy put her hands on her head, completely desperate and frustrated.

* * *

Several hours had passed since Mark's death. Thomas was no longer crying, but he was still stuck in a trance of grief. He sat against the side of the cage, as far away from Mark's body as possible, and stared at the wall. Vance hadn't said much at all since the incident. Thomas was unsure if he would see it as being his fault, but at this moment in time he didn't particularly care.

"So I'm assuming you haven't come up with a plan yet?" Vance asked, forever the smart ass.

"No," Thomas said coldly, without a hint of emotion in his voice.

"What are you going to do? About Virginia, I mean?" Vance asked him.

"Nothing."

"Nothing? That's awful nice of you to do nothing after you killed her husband," Vance said dryly.

Thomas didn't even look at him. Instead, he glanced over at Mark's body and stared at it for a moment. In his mind's eye, he saw Mark still grabbing his chest in pain and writhing around on the floor. He saw his eyes bulging, his mouth gaped open. He saw himself punching him in the side of the head and again in the kidney, and tossing him to the ground. He remembered holding the screwdriver above Mark while he was still living and breathing. He remembered thinking about stabbing him. What sort of a monster was he now?

"One who survives," he said aloud.

"What?" Vance asked, completely taken aback by it.

206

Thomas rose to his feet and approached the cage's door. Through the metal mesh, he stared at Vance with a cold look. He was calm and devoid of emotion.

"I've finally figured it out," he said quietly.

"Figured what out?" Vance asked him.

"You. How you survive."

"What the hell are you talking about?"

Thomas still looked cold, and he even began looking a bit menacing. His head was lowered, his eyes looking up at Vance, his pupils barely visible beneath his brow.

"I think you were born just like everyone else. You are a product of your environment. Through years of turmoil and violence, a new being was forged. And now...here you are. Nearly lifeless and completely lacking in empathy. You've done things that would make most men kill themselves. And that's not a good thing. But in this new world...this World of the Damned...it's the only way to be. We survive...or die. It's a choice, isn't it? A man chooses between doing what is necessary to survive, or letting himself die. And there will always be things that we can't control...things we can't change no matter how hard we want to. But those things are irrelevant, aren't they? You just have to ignore them and focus on the things you *can* affect. And part of doing that is suppressing your conscience. 'Whatever it takes to survive, at any cost.' Right? That's what you told me. So now I fully understand that. We all make bad choices...do bad things...but we just have to keep on going. We can't give a shit about those who we aren't charged with protecting. Not anymore. This world is a much different place now."

Vance looked back at Thomas, speechless. His mind searched for a reply, but he couldn't come up with anything. Instead, he defaulted to something that completely avoided the meaning behind Thomas's words.

"Well...I guess you got it all figured out now, don't you?"

Thomas continued staring coldly, but now his gaze went beyond Vance. As he thought about Mindy, and how he would get out of his cell and find her, he also thought about killing McCoy.

He imagined how good it would feel to wrap a chain around his neck and hang *him*. Or stab a screwdriver through one of his eyes, or both. The feelings no longer felt unnatural or taboo to him. They felt good.

And then he heard what sounded like wheezing coming from behind him. For a moment he froze, until Vance said something to him.

"Uh, Thomas..."

Thomas turned around and saw Mark's body slowly moving. His arms dragged across the floor as he was still lying on his back. One of his legs kicked out to the side. His head began slowly moving back and forth. Was he...reanimating??

"What the fuck..." Thomas said.

"Do it, Thomas!" Vance yelled, "He's coming back! Do it! Or you'll die!"

Thomas pulled out the screwdriver and approached Mark's body. The undead version of Mark sat up sluggishly, and attempted to stand. Thomas kicked it in the chest, and Mark's reanimated corpse fell over. Thomas then took one large step toward him, wrapped his free hand around the back of Undead Mark's head, and drove his screwdriver straight into its eye. The screwdriver made a sick sound as it broke through the back wall of the eye socket and went into the brain. Thomas held it there for a moment, then quickly pulled it out and pushed Undead Mark back to the floor.

After breathing heavily for a moment, he asked, "How in the hell is that possible?"

Vance didn't answer. He rose to his feet and looked on through the wall of his cage.

"Do we all have it?" Thomas asked aloud, although it was only meant to be a thought.

"No."

Thomas looked over at Vance.

"Then how in the hell do you explain *that*? Why did it take so long?"

"Many people have died and never reanimated. Only about one in ten people do. We're all exposed to the infection, but for the most part our bodies are able to fight it off as long as its airborne. For the ones who aren't able to? Usually you'll never know until they die. There's no fever, no pain, no physical symptoms of any kind. Until they die of something else, of course. There is a very unlucky—but small—percentage of the population who can show signs of infection and die just from breathing it into their lungs. However, the saliva of the reanimated entering a human's bloodstream, as you know, is always fatal."

"How do you know all of this?" Thomas asked him as he approached his own cage wall.

"I was a private contractor working at Groom Lake prior to all of this happening."

"Groom Lake? Isn't that..."

"Area 51, yes. Edwards Air Force Base. The government knew about all of this long before any of us did."

"What causes it?" Thomas asked, completely enthralled.

"A strange prion that controls the body once its host is dead. It enters your body and finds its way to the brain. If it enters your bloodstream through an open wound, then the effects are almost immediate. However, breathing it in usually results in it becoming dormant—assuming your body doesn't kill it—until your lungs cease to function. In individuals with a certain gene, it can create pneumonia and flu-like symptoms if it enters the lungs."

"Holy shit..."

"That's why that family we found all died without being bitten. They were apparently unlucky enough that their DNA allowed the prion to make them sick and die, without it initially entering their bloodstream."

"How in the hell...do they know where the prion came from?"

"No. When it went global, it happened so quickly that they didn't have time to continue their research. Edwards Air Force Base became compromised from the inside out—from the test subjects in the levels beneath the base—and the result was catastrophic. Prior to that happening, the scientists believed it was some mutated form of kuru."

"The disease that cannibals can get?"

"That's my understanding, yes."

"So there's no stopping this thing?" Thomas took a step back and looked down at the floor.

"I can't answer that. The two scientists that I escaped with from the base might have been able to, but they're dead now. I was supposed to protect them at all costs, and I failed."

Thomas turned his back against the cage's metal barrier and slid down it to the floor. The realization that *anyone* could suddenly come back after they died—whether from natural causes or human causes—was almost too much for Thomas to bear.

Another hour or so passed, and Thomas was growing increasingly impatient and borderline manic. The fact that the dead body of someone he knew was in the cage with him didn't help matters. Of course, it probably would have bothered him just as much if he hadn't known him. Vance, however, seemed to be doing okay. It was obvious that he was in pain, but he was able to stand and limp around. Chris's dead body didn't seem to bother him much, and he mostly pretended like it wasn't even there. Thomas had been pacing for several minutes. Being locked up really ate away at him. Wondering what was going on outside, where Mindy was, how the hell he was going to get *out*. It seemed like all of those thoughts were rushing through his mind at the same time. He had to urinate again, but was holding it as long as he could. He had already urinated twice through the metal cage, and onto the floor in front of the stairs. It was humiliating and disgusting, but it was better than doing it inside the cell. Vance was lucky enough to have a bucket. Or perhaps he was unlucky. The bucket—according to Vance—was horrid. Thomas could smell it slightly, but Vance told him that it looked like it hadn't been dumped out in a couple days.

Just as Thomas was about to relieve himself again, he heard boots stomping up the steps. He hadn't even heard the hangar door open and shut, so whoever it was must have been intentionally keeping quiet.

"What the fuck..." Overfield said as he appeared at the top of the steps and looked down at the urine on the floor.

"Hey, I asked for a bucket a long time ago," Thomas told him.

"Jesus christ..." Overfield stepped over it and walked over to Thomas's cage.

"Wait...what the hell happened to him?" Overfield asked as he pointed at Mark, "Did you...did you fucking kill him!?"

"Not exactly," Thomas said as he looked down at the floor.

"Poor guy had a heart attack," Vance chimed in.

"That doesn't explain the goddamn hole in his eye," Overfield said.

Thomas and Vance stared at each other for a moment.

"Look, I was comin' up here to be nice and check on you guys, but somebody has to explain this shit to me..."

"He came back," Thomas finally said.

"What? Impossible. He didn't have any bites. And even if he did, he would've turned long before..."

"No...no bites," Vance said.

Overfield turned and stared blankly at Vance for a moment. Logan's dead body still hung by the chain, swaying ever so gently to the point that you could only see it if you were paying close attention.

"It's airborne. Most everybody has contracted it at some point in time. Some people's bodies fight it off, others don't and then it lies dormant in the lungs until..." Thomas abruptly stopped talking and looked over his shoulder at Mark.

"Until you die from somethin' else?" Overfield asked.

"Yeah," Thomas replied.

"Shit..."

"Look...sorry about the mess. If you give me a mop I'll clean it up," Thomas offered.

"Sure. Come on out," Overfield said as he dug the keys out of his pocket and unlocked the cell door, "Follow me."

Thomas followed Overfield down the steps and into a supply closet next to the office. He pulled out a mop bucket and pushed it over to the faucet. As he reached up to turn the handle, he looked over at Overfield.

"Go ahead. The hangar has a small reservoir of water attached to it. McCoy had it installed."

Thomas turned the knob, and water poured out into the bucket. Without even thinking, he dropped to his knees and caught the stream of water with his mouth. It tasted amazing.

"That water isn't potable...hasn't been boiled or treated or anything..."

Thomas didn't care. His mouth was so dry and his lips were chapped. Once he had filled his belly with water, he let the mop bucket fill up and then squirted some disinfectant solution in it. After grabbing the mop and wheeling it over to the stairs, Overfield helped him carry it up to the cages.

"Work on cleaning that up. I'll go get you guys some water," Overfield said, and then walked back down the stairs.

Thomas slowly squeezed the water out of the mop and then dragged the mop head across the floor.

"Apparently he feels bad," Vance said as he clung to the metal cage with his fingers and watched Thomas clean.

"I'm going to kill him," Thomas said coldly as he mopped.

"What? No, you're not," Vance said to him in a whisper, "At this point he's the only one who has even expressed any sympathy for us. Or for you, at least. He might be our ticket out of here."

"You're right. I'm going to kill him, and then you're going to take his gun," Thomas's words were so devoid of emotion that they almost seemed empty, "I'm betting he has at least one more firearm in the vehicle he drove over here."

"Yeah, and maybe a couple of soldiers standing around outside..."

"He wouldn't have been quiet if anyone was with him," Thomas said, "We didn't hear a car door shut, and we didn't hear the hangar door open and close. He's not supposed to be here."

"All the more reason to leave him alone!" Vance said in a loud whisper.

"Alright..." Overfield's voice echoed as he walked up the stairs, "Brought a few bottles of water with me."

"Thank you," Thomas said to him.

"Not sure how I'm going to give you yours," Overfield said as he stared at Vance, "To be honest, I'm not sure I want to do anything for you."

Thomas looked past Overfield's head and stared at Vance as he dipped his mop back in the bucket.

"I was just doing what I had to," Vance told him, "You can't expect anyone to just resign themselves to this place. Especially someone like me."

"Yeah...I know..."

Overfield opened his own bottle of water and took a drink.

"I know you didn't want to do that," Vance said as he nodded his head toward Logan.

"You're right. I didn't." Overfield turned his back to Thomas and leaned up against Vance's cage with his shoulder.

"You can change things, you know," Vance said to him. Overfield looked down at the floor and sighed heavily.

"And then what, huh?" Overfield asked, "I take over? Derek takes over? And then one or the other of us turn into the next McCoy?"

Vance looked at him, but didn't speak.

"I think that no matter who is in charge, they'll develop a hunger for power and a thirst for blood. It's human nature. At least this way I'm not a target."

"Sergeant..." Vance began, sighing as well, "I know you're a good man. And you're a good soldier. Hell, you seem to be a damn fine NCO. But you can't let this guy walk all over you. You can't allow him to make you do things that you don't think are right."

"And you never have?" Overfield asked him. Vance stared back at him coldly.

"Of course I have."

"You know exactly what it's like to follow orders that you don't agree with. Hell, you've probably felt like shit for the things you've done at the behest of your superiors. But you do them anyway."

Vance turned his gaze away from Overfield and stared into the cage across from him.

"Yeah, but that doesn't make it right."

Overfield shook his head and rubbed his eyes.

"How would you guys do it? If you were to get out of here, I mean?"

Vance snapped his gaze back to Overfield. Thomas continued slowly mopping, but watched Overfield out of the corner of his eye. They were maybe three feet from each other.

"We'd do as little damage as possible, and we'd make you the new leader. Hopefully with a different attitude," Vance said.

"Damn..." Overfield shook his head again, "Look, I know McCoy isn't a great guy. I've always known that. But shit...I never saw something like this happening."

Overfield looked up at Logan's body. Thomas continued pushing the mop with one hand, but reached around to the small of his back with his right hand. Vance was looking past Overfield and saw him. His eyes grew wide and he shook his head ever so slightly.

Overfield's eyes moved down from Logan and into Thomas's cell. He appeared to be staring at Mark. After a few brief moments, his eyebrows turned downward into a frown.

"Hey..." he said, "...what the hell did you stab him with?"

Thomas lunged forward and drove the tip of the screwdriver into Overfield's neck.

"No!" Vance yelled.

Thomas pushed Overfield up against Vance's cage, maintaining his grip on the screwdriver's handle and pushing it even further into the right side of Overfield's throat. Overfield's eyes were wide as he gurgled and coughed. He fought as hard as he could, trying to push Thomas away. But Thomas had the upper hand. He had used the element of surprise to land a serious blow, and now Overfield was helpless. Thomas wiggled the screwdriver back and forth, making the puncture site even larger. Blood sprayed out, coating both of Thomas's arms, the top half of his shirt, and his own chin and neck. Within seconds, Overfield's body stopped fighting and started falling to the ground. He still gurgled and twitched a little, but he was no longer able to put up a fight. Soon his eyelids relaxed, and his eyes weren't quite so bulged out anymore. His face was white as a ghost, and his lips were blue.

Thomas stood over Overfield's body, still holding onto the screwdriver that was buried in his foe's neck. He was breathing heavily, and the blood that coated him was now dripping down onto the floor, as well as onto Overfield's body. Thomas slowly pulled the screwdriver out of Overfield's neck and took a step back. He was still breathing heavily. His mouth hung open, and his lower jaw was jutted out as if he had an under-bite. His own eyes were bulging now, filled with rage. But his bloodlust was not yet satisfied. Thomas gripped the screwdriver so tight that his knuckles turned white, and he continued staring at Overfield's body as if it held the secrets to every question he had ever asked.

"He was going to help us, Thomas!" Vance finally yelled after the shock and surprise had worn off a little.

"He needed to die," Thomas said.

"He was our *way out!*" Vance screamed, this time even louder.

"No. *We* are our way out," Thomas told him, and then reached into Overfield's pocket to dig out the keys.

After unlocking Vance's cage, the veteran hobbled out and struggled to bend over and remove Overfield's handgun from its holster. It was a standard Army-issue Beretta M9. The old 9mm did not have a good reputation among service members, but Vance had absolutely no complaints with having it at the moment. Thomas watched Vance intently as the former special forces operator checked the Beretta's magazine, ensured there was a round in the chamber, and flipped the safety off.

"Let's see if we can find something in here to get you bandaged up a bit better," Thomas said to him.

"I'm fine. Let's go."

Vance limped over to the stairs, not showing a bit of pain or emotion as he did so, and slowly made his way down the steps. Thomas stared at him for a moment as he hopped down each step, until only Vance's head was visible. Then he walked over to the stairs and descended them himself.

"Let's look around for weapons," Vance said dryly as he began walking to the back half of the hangar.

Thomas stayed in the office and searched around. Surely there was something that would prove more deadly than the phillip's head screwdriver he was currently carrying. As he opened drawers and cabinets, he finally caught something very obvious out of the corner of his eye. How had he missed it? Sitting at the end of the desk was a large paper cutter. Thomas felt a warm feeling spread over his buddy as he approached the paper cutter and grabbed the handle. As if he was testing the blade's efficiency, he raised it up and brought it down decisively. The iconic sound of the paper cutter's blade grinding across the base echoed throughout the mostly empty hangar. Thomas grabbed the single nut that was holding the blade on, and with one forceful turn he loosened it. Once he had removed the blade, he held it in front of his face and stared at it.

"Thomas..." Vance said as he stepped inside the office. In his left hand he had what looked like some sort of long crowbar.

Thomas turned to face him, still holding the paper cutter turned machete vertically in front of him.

"Glad to see you've found something gruesome," Vance said, "I didn't find anything worth taking. Let's go."

A muffled noise that seemed to come from above them startled both the men.

"Radio..." Vance said. He had been so shocked by Thomas's brutal murder that he hadn't even thought to grab Overfield's radio.

Thomas ran upstairs, and in just a few seconds he came back down with the radio in hand.

"CQ to Sergeant Overfield..."

"Well?" Thomas asked.

"Let me have it," Vance said.

Thomas handed Vance the radio. Vance stared at the wall while he waited for the soldier to call for Overfield again.

"CQ to Sergeant Overfield, come in..."

"Go," was all Vance said.

"Sergeant, McCoy is asking where you're at. He's requesting to see you. Over."

"Copy."

Vance turned and walked toward the hangar's side door.

"Wait..." Thomas said, "McCoy can see this hangar from his room, and it's not dark yet."

"So what do you have in mind?"

"That C-130—the one right out front—it's parked directly in front of the hangar. The side of the building that the door is on is easily visible from the visitor's center, but it's unlikely that anyone would see the large hangar doors open just enough for a person to squeeze out."

"Well then, let's move," Vance said, his eyebrows raised but his voice the same as always.

"Don't these things use a motor to open?" Thomas asked as they approached the huge doors.

"I think so, but I don't know. I was a grunt, not Air Force," Vance answered rather rudely.

Thomas walked over to what appeared to be a manual lock on the left hangar door, and disengaged it. He then walked to the center where the two sliding doors met and grabbed the left door. After getting his footing, he pulled as hard as he could. The door didn't move at all.

"Come on, Archimedes," Vance said as he approached the door, "Use your head."

Vance stuck the end of his newly acquired tool between the two doors and used all of his body weight to pull on the crowbar like it was a lever. The doors opened a couple of inches, and Thomas grabbed the left door and strained to open it while Vance pulled on the crowbar. The door opened another few inches—just barely enough for an average adult male to squeeze through sideways. But while Thomas was of average size, Vance was not. His large chest would have no hope of making it through.

"One more time," Vance said as he leaned the crowbar up against the right door, and then put both hands against the left door to push.

Thomas and Vance grunted as they forced the door open another three inches. When they were finished, Vance leaned up against the door and put all of his weight on his good leg. His left hand fell down and grabbed at his thigh. Thomas genuinely felt bad for his injury, but there was nothing he could do about it.

"Well..." Vance began, breathing heavily from the pain, "...I guess let's go kill McCoy."

* * *

Mindy and Samantha sat on the steps that led up to their quarters and also McCoy's room. When it wasn't meal time, there was actually very little activity in the visitor's center. Most Hill citizens were out doing their chores. Mindy and Samantha, however, had no chores. Not yet, anyway, but Mindy didn't intend on sticking around that long. In her mind, she almost felt like McCoy's trophy. The reminder that he had absolute power and control. He had separated her from her brother—and Virginia from her husband—and most likely enjoyed the idea of hurting Thomas in retaliation for his disobedience.

"Wanna go for a walk?" Mindy asked Samantha.

"Nah. I just feel like sittin' here," the girl answered.

"Okay, well then we'll just sit here," Mindy said.

"Go ahead. I don't need to be by your side every minute," Samantha told her.

"No, that's okay honey..."

"I..." Samantha stopped and looked down at her feet, "...I sort of want to have some time alone, anyway. If that's alright, I mean."

Mindy looked at her and smiled gently.

"Of course it is," she said as she patted Samantha on the back, "I'll just be walking around the building, so if you need me I won't be far. Why don't you go check on Virginia for me real quick while I'm gone? Just pop in there and make sure she's doing okay."

"Alright."

Mindy got up and walked through the front door. The air was dry today, and the hot July sun was beating down relentlessly. Mindy had to squint to keep the bright light bouncing off the pavement from blinding her. As she headed for the side of the building, her eyes adjusted a little. It was funny, really. Before everything went to hell, she never walked or ran outside just for the fun of it. She had had a gym membership, and spent a lot of time on a treadmill, but never even really considered the option of walking or running around outside just to be outside. So many things to look at, so many people meandering about while they carried out their tasks for the day. In a way she felt a little guilty for not doing so. She had chosen to cut herself off from the outside world—from her fellow human beings—and instead run in an artificial, temperature controlled environment, on a machine that simulated running from point A to point B. Why couldn't she have just ran or walked outside? Why did she take so much for granted? And it wasn't just her exercise choice that was bothering her. She also thought about all the times she didn't feel like going out to eat, and instead ordered delivery. Or all the times when she told her friends she didn't feel well so she wouldn't have to leave her apartment, simply because she was worn out and tired. She regretted not eating that half a box of chocolates before she was forced to move in with her brother inside the quarantine zone. All of the petty arguments she had had with her friends, or her parents, or her coworkers...she regretted those, too. Most of all, she regretted falling in line and being a robot. A being more machine than human, automatically waking up and carrying out its assigned tasks before recharging its batteries for the next day. She hadn't done anything extraordinary. Sure, she helped people on a daily basis. She always remained kind and courteous, even on days when she felt like crying. But it wasn't like she saved lives everyday. She had started out as an ER nurse, where she did indeed save a lot of people, but she only did that for a year before getting a job at a private practice. The practice was a large one, and the money was certainly good. Monday through Friday, eight to five, all weekends and holidays off, a nice little bonus at the end of every year... There were people who would kill for something like that. But here she was, stumbling through the end of the world, and suddenly all she could think about was how much none of that mattered. Human beings live for their freedom. They live for love and happiness and intrigue. How much of those things had she experienced? Not much, in the broad scheme of things. She was—like every other human being—always left wanting more. More money, more freedom, more recognition and importance. And now those things were so much more valuable than they had been before. The 'human condition' was fundamentally different now. Previously it had existed within the realm of an orderly, functioning world that seemed chaotic. Now she didn't know what it was, exactly. Now it had changed from finding oneself to protecting oneself. Always fearful, always expecting the worst. The universal questions, *'Where do we come from, why are we here, and where are we going?'* hadn't crossed her mind in months. Now it was all about eating and staying clean and keeping yourself from going mad. Pondering those philosophical questions almost seemed arrogant and selfish now, like you were foolishly pretending that the world around you wasn't falling to pieces. Like you had the luxury of ignoring the never-ending threat around you. But perhaps there would come a time when those questions became normal again? Perhaps—once all of this became the accepted norm and people felt more comfortable with the world around them—those same inherent questions would come back to terrorize the mind...

* * *

"Virginia? Is everything okay?" Samantha asked as she poked her head inside the group's quarters.

Virginia was sitting on her bed, but was not crying. She was simply staring at the floor and nervously wringing her hands.

"Virginia?" Samantha asked once again.

"I'm fine, dear," Virginia finally answered, without even looking at Samantha.

"Is there anything I can get you?" Samantha asked.

"No thank you," Virginia replied.

Samantha thought about walking into the room and sitting down beside Virginia, but then decided it would be better to leave the woman alone for awhile. After all, her husband had been forced to leave her behind, and no one knew when they would see the others again...if at all.

Samantha left the room and slowly made her way back down the steps. As the staircase turned, she nearly ran into Wild Bill McCoy as he was walking up the stairs.

"Oh...hi..." she said uneasily.

"Samantha," McCoy said, friendly as ever, "How are you."

"I'm...fine, I guess," the girl said nervously.

McCoy grinned at her and nodded his head.

"I know you think I'm some terrible monster," he said, "but I'm really just a guy who has the safety of his people foremost in his mind."

"Okay, well I'm going to go now..."

"Hold on..." McCoy said as he turned his head a little and looked at Samantha out of the corner of his eye.

"Do you want to see something really neat?" he asked her.

"Not really," she said, "I'm going to go find Mindy now."

"Oh, Mindy's running a little errand for me," McCoy's smile grew bigger, "She'll be busy for an hour or so. I want to show you something."

"Really, it's alright..."

"Come on," McCoy said, with a grin still frozen on his face.

Samantha was terrified of William McCoy, and although he was smiling, he still made her feel suspicious.

"Where are we going?" Samantha asked as the two of them walked through the back door of the visitor's center.

McCoy approached his SUV and opened the passenger door to let Samantha in, before walking around the front of the vehicle and hopping up into the driver's seat.

"See that plane over there?" McCoy asked her as he started the engine.

"Yeah."

"I'm taking you to see that."

"I don't think Mindy would want me..."

"Well Mindy's not in charge," McCoy said in a calm, quiet voice, "I am. She's not going to be mad at you for doing what I tell you to."

McCoy drove across the airfield and stopped right below the rear door of the huge C-130. The two of them got out, and McCoy climbed up on the roof of the SUV.

"Come on," he said with a smile and a hand stretched out.

Samantha took his hand and he pulled her up.

"Only a handful of people have seen inside here," McCoy said as he turned the handle on the rear hatch and opened it. The door creaked loudly on its hinges.

"What's it for?" Samantha asked.

"A bunch of things. Sometimes they're just cargo planes...sometimes they're equipped to drop bombs and stuff. Go ahead...have a look inside."

Samantha stepped up through the airplane's doorway and looked around.

"It's so dark..."

"Yes it is, but luckily I always keep a flashlight on my belt. Here...you do the honors."

McCoy pulled a small flashlight from his belt and held it out in front of Samantha. Samantha took it from him and turned it on, looking around at the dusty innards of the plane.

"We're going to have a lot a lot of fun, you and I..."

McCoy wrapped his burly arm around Samantha's neck, and placed his other hand over her mouth. He wasn't squeezing hard enough to prevent her from breathing; not even hard enough to cause any pain. Samantha struggled and kicked her feet up in the air while her attacker dragged her backwards.

"Settle down, now..."

Samantha moaned and grunted as she flailed about. Her incredibly small frame made it impossible to do anything to a man like William McCoy. McCoy dragged her over to a bench seat and held her there for a moment.

"If you scream," he said, "I'll kill you."

McCoy forced her down onto the bench. Already beside it was a pair of handcuffs—as if he had used the spot before. One of them was hooked around the metal support that helped hold the bench up. The other one went around Samantha's right wrist tightly, and it was covered with dried blood. The girl was quiet now, but she was terrified and tears were streaming down her face. She was still coughing and moaning.

"Quiet now. I'll be right back."

McCoy pulled a large roll of duct tape off of a crate and used it to attach Samantha's free hand to her leg. He then placed a piece over his mouth.

"No jackin' around," he said, "I'll be back before you know it."

McCoy walked out of the C-130 and hopped down onto the roof of his SUV. He felt such excitement building inside him, as he imagined all of the things he would do to the girl...in front of Thomas and Vance. And then he realized...what's that other SUV doing here? Directly after that he noticed the partially open hangar door. He walked over to his own SUV and pulled out a handheld radio.

"Overfield, this is McCoy," he said into the mic. Silence.

"Sir, this is CQ. We just spoke with Overfield about ten minutes ago to inform him that you wanted to speak with him. He copied."

"Well where the hell is he?" McCoy asked.

"Unsure, sir. Want me to send some guys out to look for him?"

"No. He'll turn up."

McCoy casually pulled out his sidearm and cautiously stepped between the two hangar doors. Almost every light was on, which was unusual. After several minutes of looking and listening, he went inside to check on his prisoners. After all, everything he was about to do was part of their punishment.

As he crept slowly across the hangar, he started running through scenarios in his head. Was it possible that Vance and Thomas had escaped, or at least pulled another stunt like they had with Peterson, Fox, and King? Vance had a pretty bad bullet wound to his leg, and Thomas was a weakling incapable of harming anyone. Or at least, that's how he appeared. Vance had been the only one in their group capable of causing any serious damage. Maybe the old redneck, Mark, if he had been younger.

"CQ, has anyone checked in at the hangar?" McCoy asked quietly into his radio.

"No sir. No one."

"Send a few guys to the hangar. I'm inside checking out some suspicious activity."

"Yes sir, I'll notify the QRF."

QRF stood for *Quick Reaction Force*, which was separate from the soldiers and guards on duty. Normally, if there was some sort of incident or security concern, the QRF would be mobilized so that the soldiers already working weren't left weak and vulnerable in other areas.

McCoy shoved the radio in his back pocket and continued into the office. He scanned the room, seeing nothing out of place. He then turned around quickly and looked behind him, just in case it was a trap and someone was lying in wait. Seeing no one, he slowly stepped up the stairs, his handgun raised. And then...

The paper cutter. It was missing its blade. McCoy stopped advancing up the stairs and stepped back down into the office. He looked around the room once more, as if someone was somehow hiding in the open room.

Something wet and lukewarm hit his head. McCoy instinctively reached up and touched the spot where it hit. As he pulled back his hand, he saw bright red blood on his fingers. And then another drop hit him on the shoulder, but this time it was larger. McCoy's stepped back and looked up. He was standing at the very bottom of the steps, next to the paper cutter. Straight above him was the opening in the ceiling of the office for the stairs. Blood was running over its edge and dripping down onto the last step of the stairs and the floor of the office. McCoy stared in horror as the steady trickle of blood ran over the edge and down onto the floor beneath it.

"CQ!" he shouted into the radio, "I need men here *now!*"

"They're on their way, sir. What's your status?"

McCoy ignored the question, and instead ran up the stairs with his gun pushed out in front of him. Laying on the floor, with the right half of his body leaning against the cage Vance had been on, was Staff Sergeant Overfield. His eyelids almost looked like they were peeled back, his pupils blown and completely lacking any sign of life. A large pool of blood surrounded his body. Through the massive amount of blood smeared all over his upper-body, McCoy could see a puncture wound in his neck. It was a perfect shot. This had to be the work of Vance. Thomas would never be able to do something so up close and personal as stabbing a man in the neck and letting him bleed to death. As McCoy looked over Overfield's body from the top of the stairs, he noticed that his radio was missing from his belt. Both cage doors were open, and inside Thomas's cage was Mark's body, laying on the floor. McCoy saw a small pool of blood beneath his head, but didn't even care to go investigate. Instead, he ran back down the stairs and pulled out his radio. As he walked through the office, six soldiers—plus Derek— were running into the hangar.

"CQ! Prisoners have escaped! Overfield is dead!"

There was a long, uneasy silence.

"Sir, did you advise that the prisoners have escaped and..." the soldier on the other end paused, *"...and that Sergeant Overfield is dead?"*

"Affirmative!" McCoy shouted, "Two have escaped. The special forces guy and the architect are both missing!"

"Sir, what the hell..." a soldier began as he approached McCoy.

"Find them!" McCoy barked, his eyes wide with anger.

McCoy walked briskly out of the hangar and climbed on top of his SUV. As he wrenched open the C-130's door, he felt his heart pounding with rage in his chest. Adrenaline and wrath coursed through his veins, so much that he almost couldn't hear anything. It was like he was underwater. He approached a terrified Samantha, who was bawling and moaning through the duct tape over her mouth. McCoy removed the handcuff that was keeping her from getting up. He wrapped her arm behind her back and clicked the handcuff around her left forearm, but left her hand duct taped to her leg. He then literally dragged her across the floor of the C-130, and aggressively pulled her out through the door and onto the roof of the SUV. McCoy grabbed her long, blonde hair and threw her body over on its side before pointing his handgun right at her head and raising his handheld radio to his mouth.

"Wherever you are," he growled, "You have thirty seconds to make yourselves known before I kill the girl!"

There was a brief pause as McCoy looked at either side of the hangar, half expecting Vance and Thomas to emerge. They couldn't have gotten too far, especially with Vance's injury.

"30...29...28...27...26..."

* * *

Thomas and Vance looked on as the chaos unfolded a couple hundred meters away. McCoy had just dragged Samantha out of the C-130 and onto the top of his SUV.

"This might end badly..." Vance said. Thomas could feel the genuine concern in his voice.

"Admittedly, I was not expecting him to show up with the girl," Thomas said, "That was a completely random act that was in no way predictable."

"But it doesn't change the fact that it happened..."

"Wherever you are..." McCoy's voice growled through the radio, *"You have thirty seconds to make yourselves known..."*

Thomas felt his heart speed up as he listened to McCoy speak. This was it. The end. It had to be. There was no other way.

"30...29...28..."

"Can you do it?" Thomas asked Vance.

"Mother fucker..."

"Vance! Can you pull this off?"

Vance pulled the MRAD rifle tight against his shoulder and adjusted the location of his cheek on the rifle's stock. They had found the sniper rifle in Overfield's SUV, and it was possibly the first real stroke of luck any of them had had thus far.

"Looks like we're about to find out..."

* * *

McCoy grew increasingly impatient and furious as he continued counting, and it was showing in his voice. His handgun shook as he held it out in front of him, keeping it trained directly on Samantha's head as she remained lying on the roof of the SUV. The girl was moaning loudly, absolutely terrified.

"10...9...8...7...6..."

And then something caught his eye. McCoy stopped counting and looked a couple hundred meters away at a shrub that was just off of the runway. Something looked unnatural about it. And then...

"At the end of the runway!" he shouted, "They're at the..."

McCoy's head jolted back as the .338 Lapua round penetrated his skull, followed immediately by the loud and iconic *crack* of a sniper rifle. The bullet had hit him less than half an inch above his right eye, and exploded out the back of his head where the skull was more porous. Skull fragments shot out like the pellets from a shotgun shell, sending bone and blood and brain matter scattered out across the hood of the SUV, as well as all over Samantha.

The soldiers who had arrived at the request of McCoy stood in shock as several of them saw nearly half of their leader's head explode into a pink mist. A few of them—the ones who had experienced combat—instinctively ducked down and raised their rifles to their shoulders, searching for the threat.

"The end of the runway!" one shouted, "He said they were at the end of the runway!"

"Fucking *WHERE!?*" another asked.

* * *

"Direct fucking hit!" Thomas said loudly, an odd and almost worrisome smile on his face.

"We're not out of the woods yet," Vance reminded him.

"This is over," Thomas said into the radio, "We have that hangar locked down with a very effective sniper, as we have already demonstrated. Do not come after us, do not return fire, and do not harm the girl. If those commands are obeyed, we will not fire on you."

A long silence followed, and it made Thomas increasingly nervous. Vance was still looking down the scope of the powerful MRAD, ready to engage the others if necessary.

"We will not fire," a shaky voice came across the radio, *"I repeat...we will not fire."*

"I got ya' covered," Vance said in his disciplined, soldier tone, without taking his eye away from the scope.

Thomas looked down at the end of the runway, and every soldier he could see was raising his weapon above his head.

"Sit them down," Thomas ordered into the radio, "We have no reason to kill any of you. This is over. There doesn't need to be anymore violence."

After a brief moment, Vance confirmed that he could see weapons being placed on the ground through his scope. Thomas stood—the blade from the paper cutter still in his hand—and began walking toward the large group of soldiers. For a moment he felt scared. How hard would it be for one of the soldiers—or all of them—to reach down and grab their weapons as Thomas neared, and shoot him dead? Sure, Vance was providing overwatch with the sniper rifle, but he could only aim and squeeze the trigger so fast. But what purpose would it serve, for them to do such a thing? Revenge? They surely felt some sort of bond with Overfield, but Thomas doubted that any of them felt any committed loyalty to their fallen leader, outside of being afraid of his ruthlessness. But they had just witnessed a whole new form of wrath.

"We're done?" Derek asked Thomas, once they were close enough to talk without yelling.

Thomas got closer, but stopped when he was about fifteen feet away from the first soldier. Derek stepped between two soldiers and approached Thomas, seemingly unperturbed by McCoy's death, or by the fact that Vance probably had the crosshairs of the sniper rifle directly on his head. The former henchman stopped about two or three feet from Thomas and stared at him. After a long, uneasy moment, he asked his question once more.

"So...are we done?" he asked again.

"Yeah..." Thomas said, his piercing glare aimed right at Derek's eyes, "We're done."

Thomas suddenly jolted forward, swinging his machete-looking weapon above his head and bringing it down as hard and fast as he could. Derek had only had enough time for a terrified and shocked expression to spread across his face before the blade split through his forehead and stuck in his skull. His face held that same expression as he slumped down to his knees and fell over, Thomas still maintaining his firm grasp on the paper cutter's handle. After pulling on his weapon once and finding that it was lodged in Derek's head like King Arthur's Excalibur, he placed his foot on Derek's face and jerked upward as hard as he could. A terrible grinding noise came from Derek's skull as the blade was forced out. A surprisingly small pool of blood was starting to form beneath his head.

Thomas walked over to McCoy's SUV and grabbed the fallen leader by the arm. After one forceful tug, McCoy's body rolled off of the SUV's roof and hit the pavement hard. Thomas reached around and pulled the screwdriver from the small of his back, and in one quick motion, jabbed it directly in McCoy's left eye. The act was pointless, and even Thomas wasn't sure why he had done it. But it had felt damn good.

Thomas sighed heavily and looked around at the soldiers, who were staring at him in disbelief. None of them said a word, and none of them reached for a weapon of any kind. Thomas took two steps forward, the same look of rage and bloodlust on his face. When he did so, several soldiers quickly took a step back, even though he was at least ten feet away from them. The blood of Staff Sergeant Overfield coated Thomas's shirt and arms, undoubtedly making him look like a ruthless barbarian. Thomas then looked over at Samantha, who was still crying loudly on top of the SUV. Her muffled groans were unsettling. Thomas approached the passenger side of the SUV and reached up to remove the duct tape. He pulled it quickly, and Samantha let out a roaring scream as he did so. But it wasn't from the duct tape being removed. It was from

229

the horror of the situation. Thomas then turned to the soldiers and glared at them.

"Get her down from there and remove her restraints," he ordered.

Two of the soldiers literally ran to the front of the SUV and climbed on top. They gently removed the duct tape that was around her left arm and leg, and another dug the handcuff keys out of McCoy's pocket. Once she was free, she nearly rolled off of the SUV's roof. Thomas caught her and helped her to the ground. She buried her face in Thomas's chest—either not noticing the blood-soaked shirt or not caring—and continued bawling.

"This is over," Thomas said, tears abruptly filling his eyes, "No one else dies."

<u>13</u>

Thomas and Vance drove Overfield's SUV back to the visitor's center, Samantha still crying in the backseat. The soldiers who had responded to the hangar were behind them, but kept their distance. As Vance pulled the vehicle around to the front of the building, Thomas felt extremely uneasy. His initial excitement and bloodlust was gone, and now he actually felt nervous. The anxiety associated with telling Virginia that her husband was dead was eating away at him. He no longer felt like the cold, emotionless individual that had been in the hangar and on the runway. Just a few short hours ago, he had never killed a human being. Hell, he had never intentionally killed a living thing of any kind. Now he had killed two men. Three, if he counted McCoy. Thomas hadn't pulled the trigger, but it was his plan and the assassination was carried out at his behest. Granted, it was entirely necessary to ensure Samantha's safety, but Thomas had created the plan and instructed Vance to shoot McCoy before he ever knew that Samantha was in danger.

Vance put the Suburban in park and slowly crawled out of the driver's seat. He limped to the rear door of the SUV and opened it so Samantha could get out. Thomas reluctantly got out, glad that he was going to see his sister but dreading the conversation he was about to have with Virginia.

"Vance?" a shocked Mindy said as she walked outside, "Samantha? What's going on?"

Thomas walked around the front of the Suburban, and him and his sister made eye contact. The two stared at each other for a short moment, before Mindy rushed over and threw her arms around his neck. Tears of joy and relief streamed down her face. She held her brother tightly, and almost started sobbing.

"What happened? I heard gunshots..."

And then she realized that her brother was covered in blood. She let go and took an uneasy step back. His light gray t-shirt was now dark red, all except for a small strip of gray at the very bottom. Thomas's arms were also covered in blood, as well as his neck.

"What..." Mindy frowned, looking into her brother's eyes for an explanation.

"Mindy..." Samantha said, still crying.

Mindy stepped away from her brother—who was staring down at her blankly—and wrapped herself around Samantha. The poor girl was bawling now, burying her face in Mindy's comforting embrace.

"It's over," Thomas said to her, "No one here has to worry about McCoy ever again. Or Derek."

"What about that other guy...McCoy's other henchman?" Vance asked.

"He didn't seem to participate in McCoy's affairs much. Maybe he was just an assistant?" Thomas guessed.

"Where's Mark?" Mindy finally asked, looking around the SUV to see if the older man was simply standing out of view.

Vance and Thomas exchanged uneasy looks. Thomas placed his blood-covered hand on Mindy's shoulder, and a look of sadness and regret spread across his face.

"I...I tried, Mindy..." Thomas began.

"You tried? What does that mean?"

"I tried to save him. I just...couldn't." Tears filled Thomas's eyes, but his voice remained calm.

"Oh, no..." Mindy said as she pulled herself away from Samantha and placed a hand over her mouth.

"McCoy...that son-of-a-bitch..." Thomas looked up at the sky, as if searching for the words.

Vance squinted at Thomas and cocked his head to the side.

"He's dead, sis," Thomas finally said, "McCoy killed him."

Vance took an involuntary step back.

"We need to tell Virginia," Thomas finally said.

Mindy nodded her head as she looked toward the back of the SUV, finally noticing the other vehicles full of soldiers.

"Are they..." Mindy tried to speak, but found that she couldn't.

Thomas glanced back at the soldiers.

"They're not going to be a problem. Let's go get our things together so we can leave."

Thomas gently took Mindy by the arm, and the two started walking to the front door of the visitor's center. As Thomas passed by Vance, the veteran's menacing stare locked onto him.

The group stepped into the room they had been staying in and went to work getting their things together. Virginia abruptly sat up in bed after hearing Thomas's voice as he spoke softly to his sister.

"Virginia..." Mindy began.

"Where...where is Mark?" Virginia asked as she stood and walked to the center of the room.

Thomas looked back at Vance, who had a look of disgust on his face as he grabbed his two bags.

"Virginia, I'm sorry," Thomas said, the words feeling hollow as they left his mouth, "Mark is dead."

Virginia dropped to the floor, throwing her hands up to her face in grief. After a moment of absolute silence, she let out a horrifying scream. Mindy knelt down beside her to offer some level of comfort, but Virginia pushed her away and screamed once more. Mindy looked over at her brother, as if she wanted him to magically make everything better. Thomas turned away from the scene and walked over to the door. He didn't leave, but he stopped in the doorway and placed a firm hand against the wall as if he was simply waiting.

"I need to go get my weapons back from those guys," Vance said as he stepped past Thomas.

Thomas followed him down the hallway. He wanted to be by Vance's side in case the soldiers tried anything, especially since

Vance was wounded.

"Hopefully they don't try anything," Thomas said to Vance as they passed through the front doors of the visitor's center.

"What the fuck is the matter with you?" Vance asked as he abruptly stopped and turned toward Thomas.

"Vance..."

"How far down this hole are you going to go, Thomas?" Vance asked him, "Just how much like that McCoy bastard are you going to become?"

The words pierced through Thomas like sabers.

"I have to keep my sister safe. I have to shield her from the horrors of this new world..."

"No, you have to shield *yourself*," Vance countered, "You're afraid of telling her the truth because you don't want her to know you're changing."

"I'm not changing, Vance. I'm merely adapting my tactics. I'm still the same person."

"Right. Give it time. You don't think I've seen this sort of transformation before? You're going to end up no different from McCoy, or any of those other ruthless, self-serving bastards."

"Hey, didn't you tell me to survive at any cost?" Thomas's voice got a little louder, and he took a step closer to Vance.

"Absolutely, and I meant that. But I didn't say to kill people who didn't need to die. I didn't say to lie and make those around you think you're a fuckin' saint when you're really nothing more than a murderer." Vance turned and limped away, toward the soldiers.

"It was *you* who said you were going to kill every mother fucker you saw!"

"I had just been shot!" Vance countered, "And shit changed when Overfield was going to help us!"

"We had no guarantee that he would..."

"He would have!" Vance yelled, almost loud enough for the others to hear, "And then no one else would have died! With the help of his men, McCoy would have had no choice but to relinquish control!"

234

"Vance..."

"And Mark..." Vance turned away from Thomas and put his hands on his hips, "...Mark didn't need to die."

Thomas was at a loss for words, but his jaw hung open while he searched for something to say.

"We're done," Vance said over his shoulder as he started walking, "I'm going off on my own again."

Thomas didn't follow. He felt empty now, like his insides had just been ripped out of him. Was Vance right? Overfield and Derek both *deserved* to die after what they did to Logan. McCoy certainly needed to die, without question. Thomas felt a little angry, like Vance had somehow accused him of things that weren't true. But he knew that wasn't right. He knew he was changing inside, regardless of whether or not his actions were justified. But he was willing to accept that, if it meant keeping his sister alive. And Samantha, and whoever else was part of their group. Thomas also didn't have any qualms with lying to them about the harsh reality of certain situations. What purpose did it serve, for them to know the truth? What possible difference did it make?

* * *

Thomas, Samantha, Mindy, and a brokenhearted Virginia pushed through the front doors of the visitor's center. They headed toward the building directly to the west so they could retrieve their original vehicles. They found Vance leaning up against the side of Overfield's Suburban, the one he had driven over from the hangar. Soldiers were gathered in small groups, scattered all over, but none of them showed any signs of hostility.

"Uh, Thomas..." a shaky voice said from behind them.

Thomas turned and saw a soldier walking out of the visitor's center.

"Daniel wants a word with you, before you go," he said.

"Daniel?" Thomas asked.

"Yes, sir. Daniel. You probably haven't met him, but I'm sure you've seen him. Do you mind?"

Thomas looked at Mindy, then at Vance, and finally sat his bag down.

"You guys get everything ready to go. I'll be out in a minute."

Thomas looked at Vance once more, halfway expecting him to go inside with him. It didn't happen. The rough man just stared at him coldly and stayed leaning against the Suburban.

Thomas walked inside and followed the soldier upstairs. As they made their way to McCoy's old quarters, Thomas felt a little anxious. Who was Daniel?

"He's waiting," the soldier said as he opened the door to McCoy's room and motioned for Thomas to go inside.

Thomas stepped in, and saw McCoy's other 'henchman' sitting behind the desk. He was the one Vance was asking about earlier, and the one they had seen with McCoy when they first arrived and a couple times after that.

"I understand that Bill is no longer with us?" Daniel asked.

Thomas said nothing, and instead stared at Daniel with an uneasy glare.

"My name is Daniel," he said, "and Bill was my brother."

Thomas felt the blood drain from his face, and his legs became weak. Had Daniel called him up here to exact revenge?

"Sorry for your loss," Thomas managed to say, but it was little more than a whisper.

"When I first heard the news, I wanted to kill you," Daniel said as he got up from behind the desk. He was not a tall man, but was fairly stout. He appeared to be in his late forties, maybe, with a stern face and rough features.

"I know he wasn't a good person," Daniel said, "and I know he did some pretty awful things. Him and I...we often disagreed. But at the end of the day, Bill kept everybody safe."

"Unless they disagreed with him," Thomas interrupted.

"Do you have any *fucking* idea what it takes to keep an entire community safe in the middle of all this?" Daniel asked, although he didn't raise his voice.

Thomas stared at him.

"No, of course you don't. I saw what Bill went through every

236

single day. I saw how he was forced to change, how he made himself do things that he didn't want to do. It was all part of leading a functioning group. A tiny civilization amidst the gnashing teeth beyond the fences, the blood-sick people out *there*." Daniel pointed out the window.

"Your brother was a psychopath who enjoyed making others suffer when they didn't agree with him," Thomas told him matter-of-factly.

"This is pointless," Daniel said, "I didn't call you up here to argue and discuss my brother's ethics. I called you up here to tell you to stay the hell away from The Hill, from the whole goddamn area. If I so much as hear about you being within twenty miles of this place, I will order my men to wipe you off the map. Do you understand?"

Thomas stared at Daniel coldly, thinking about whether or not he should kill him. After all, the man just threatened him. But then he remembered that they were planning on heading to Albuquerque anyway. He remembered that he had said no one else needed to die.

"We won't be anywhere near here. We're heading south."

"Good. Now, with all that being said..." Daniel let out a heavy sigh, tears filling his eyes, "I understand that shit is never simple in this world. We all do things we later regret. That was true even before all of this. Now it defines every single day of our lives. My brother was not an easy man to get along with. All emotion aside...I have no personal grievance against you."

"Wouldn't matter to me if you did," Thomas said to him. Daniel shook his head and chuckled slightly, but it was not a humorous chuckle.

"I don't know what transpired between the two of you," he began, his voice shaky and filled with sadness, "I don't know what Bill did, I don't know who he hurt, and I don't care. I know he was often a wild card. Regardless...it's all over. You've proven to be capable and ruthless, and not worth the fight to kill. That is the one and only reason why I am letting this go. Do you understand that? I'm letting you leave this place without answering for your crimes because I don't want the headache. Too much has happened already today. I need my soldiers, and I need my people in as good of spirits as possible. Making you an enemy would be more trouble than it's worth. Now get out and don't come back. Ever."

Thomas turned without saying a word and left the room. As he walked down the stairs, he thought about what Daniel had said. *You've proven to be capable and ruthless, and not worth the fight to kill.* Hadn't that been what Vance told him to be like? To appear like someone who isn't worth testing?

Thomas suddenly heard a single muffled gunshot as he reached the bottom of the steps. He briefly froze, but as soon as his brain processed the sound, Thomas bolted for the front doors.

* * *

"Thank you," Mindy said, "for making sure my brother and Samantha made it back."

Vance stared down at the ground as he lit his cigarette.

"It wasn't me," Vance told her, "Your brother is the one to thank."

Mindy looked at him with a frown, confused.

"You mean...my brother killed McCoy? And Derek?"

"Derek, yes. Rather gruesomely, I might add. I killed McCoy, but it was only because of the plan Thomas came up with, and at his direction."

"Wow," Mindy said, "I know I shouldn't feel happy about any of this, but...I guess I kind of am. It makes me feel better knowing that he stepped up to the plate. But poor Mark..."

"Listen," Vance said as he blew smoke through his nose, "just promise me that you guys will always keep your wits about you, okay? Don't...don't get tangled up in anything bad. Just stay alive."

"What do you mean? Aren't you..."

"I have somewhere else to go," Vance interrupted, before Mindy could say anything else.

Vance looked past Mindy and saw Samantha sitting in the backseat of the Durango with the door open.

238

"Just look out for the girl, okay? And yourself? Don't let your brother do anything stupid."

"We'll be okay, but I wish you were..."

"Don't wish for anything," Vance said, cutting her off again, "Just keep your mind on doing what you need to survive."

Mindy nodded before turning and walking back over to Samantha. On her way she saw Virginia, walking away from the Durango and over toward Mark's pickup. Mindy slowed down and stared at her, trying to figure out what she was doing. She was on the passenger side, so she wasn't getting in to drive.

And then she saw Virginia pull out a handgun from the truck's cab. The older woman, in her pale blue dress and old-fashioned white blouse, looked as if the firearm in her hand was an alien device. Some sort of instrument which she had never seen before, nor knew the purpose of. But then Mindy realized what she was doing.

"Virginia, NO!" she screamed.

Virginia placed the muzzle of the handgun beneath her chin, almost against her throat.

"Vance!" Mindy shouted, turning back to glance at Vance before looking at Virginia again and rushing toward her. Perhaps the weapon wasn't loaded, and she would be able to reach her and take it from her?

"Virginia! Don't!" Mindy yelled as she ran as fast as she could. She was nearly halfway to her.

Virginia looked up at the sky, tears running from the corners of her eyes and down to her ears. Mindy felt everything slow down. It was almost like she was stuck in some sort of dream. Her mind was racing, but she couldn't really think. Her legs and arms were moving, but they didn't feel fast enough.

BANG!

The handgun fired a single shot, and the top of Virginia's head opened up. Mindy skidded to a stop as the handgun flew back out of Virginia's hands and toward the truck, and Virginia's body went limp and fell to the ground. Mindy's eyes were locked on as blood and tissue and skull fragments flew backwards away from Virginia,

239

landing on the pavement. Mindy fell to her knees, inadvertently smacking them hard against the concrete. She threw her hands up over her face and screamed. She suddenly felt a hand on her shoulder, but didn't know who it belonged to and she didn't care to look.

* * *

Thomas blew through the front doors, his own handgun in his hand, and ran as fast as he could toward where the Durango was parked. He ran past Overfield's suburban, around the building, and saw a handful of soldiers running in front of him in the same direction. As he neared he saw his sister on her knees, weeping, and Vance standing behind her and bent over at the waist, his hand on her shoulder. He could see Mark's truck, and....

A body. The truck sat high enough that he could see Virginia's body laying on the other side. Thomas stopped in his tracks when he was about twenty feet away. A look of shock spread across his face, and somehow he knew immediately what had happened. He didn't even think about what had happened; he just somehow knew. Virginia—stricken with grief and shock and pain—had shot herself.

"Oh my God..." a soldier said as he ran around the front of the truck and saw the scene up close.

Thomas felt the muscles in his face twitch, his mouth widen, his forehead wrinkle and his eyebrows raise. There were no tears, yet he felt so stricken with grief himself that he couldn't even move. He stared on, forcing his gaze from Virginia's body and toward Mindy and Vance. As if in some horrible dream, he saw his sister sobbing and moaning with despair. He saw Vance offering comfort for the first time ever. He saw Samantha, standing next to the Durango with the door open, hands up over her mouth and nose in shock and disbelief. Then he felt his own legs weaken, and he fell to the pavement. There were still no tears, but as Thomas sat there, he felt utterly defeated and lost. More than anything, he felt guilty.

Finally, Mindy rose to her feet and turned to Vance. The much larger man wrapped his arms around her as she buried her face in his chest. Now there were only muffled cries as Vance placed a big hand on the back of Mindy's head and laid his head on hers. Thomas forced himself to get up, and even though his legs still felt weak, he pushed on toward his sister.

"How..." Thomas tried to suppress the knot in his throat, "...how did..."

Vance looked over as Thomas walked up to them, but didn't say anything. Tears finally filled Thomas's eyes, and through his blurry vision he could have sworn that he saw Vance's own eyes glazing over. Mindy pulled away from Vance and wiped her mouth, nose, and eyes on her sleeve. A wet spot ordained Vance's shirt where Mindy had been crying into his chest.

"How could we have..." Mindy's voice cut out, and she coughed, "How did I let this happen?"

"Mindy..." Thomas began.

"We should have done something," Mindy said as she looked over at Virginia's body once more.

"It's no one's fault, sis," Thomas said as he reached out to her.

Vance shot him a mean glare as Thomas and Mindy hugged. Thomas could see Vance's mouth quivering—whether from rage or sadness, he wasn't sure—and he actually felt afraid of what he might do.

"This..." Vance growled, "...this is *yours* to live with."

Vance pointed a finger at Thomas as he spoke. Mindy pushed herself away from her brother and looked back at Vance.

"What do you mean?" she asked. Then to Thomas, "What does he mean?"

"This is it for me," Vance said, shaking his head, "Good luck out there."

The tough man limped over to his own belongings without saying another word. Thomas watched him, almost expecting Vance to raise his assault rifle and shoot him dead. Thomas knew he felt like doing it, but he surely wouldn't in front of Mindy and Samantha. Especially with both of them so close. Instead of doing anything drastic, Vance threw his things in the back of the Suburban and crawled into the driver's seat. Without hesitation, he pulled away and drove toward the nearby gate. The soldiers pushed it open, and Vance drove through it. Once he was clear, Vance mashed the gas and the SUV sped up at an alarming rate. He quickly got further and further away before turning onto the first cross street, the Suburban's tires screeching as he did so.

"What was he talking about?" Mindy asked, her tone quickly changing from sad to mad, "Why did he say that? Why did he leave us?"

"Mindy, I..."

"Tell me, Thomas!" his sister yelled.

Thomas looked around himself and saw nearly a dozen soldiers staring back at him. Samantha was now sitting on the ground, still staring in the direction of Mark's truck, and Thomas could actually see her shoulders bouncing up and down as she sobbed.

"Vance thought it was my fault that Mark died. He thought I could have done something to prevent it. Maybe he was right."

Inside, Thomas felt guilty as hell. Guilty for fighting with Mark and working him up so much that he had a heart attack. Guilty for killing Overfield, and even Derek. Guilty for deceiving his sister.

"What do you mean?" Mindy asked him, her tone back to normal.

"I'll explain later, Mindy. Let's just get the hell out of this place."

Thomas gently took his distraught sister by the arm and walked her over to the Durango. As he passed by the soldiers, he felt as if he was walking through a gauntlet. A dozen pairs of eyes were locked on him, and somehow he felt like they were all screaming, *This is your fault! You did this!*

242

14

Thomas stared through the Durango's windshield, though he was barely even paying attention to the road they were traveling down. He felt utterly disgusted with himself. In his mind's eye he kept replaying the tragic events that transpired just within the last few hours. Mark's death, and then killing him after he reanimated. Murdering Overfield in cold blood. Vance blowing open McCoy's head with the sniper rifle. Sticking the paper cutter's blade in Derek's head. Shoving the screwdriver into McCoy's lifeless eye. Seeing Virginia's body on the pavement. He felt broken and defeated, but he knew that he couldn't remain that way. Mindy and Samantha would still need him to protect them. Thomas couldn't let his past decisions endanger those who still relied on him.

"So...are you going to explain everything to me?" Mindy finally asked, breaking the long silence that had existed since leaving The Hill.

"I said I'd explain it," Thomas said, taking a deep breath, "and I will. What do you want to know?"

"Everything that happened."

"Well, you already know about our plan. The three of us sneaking out and rescuing that guy McCoy was holding prisoner. It didn't go as planned, obviously. Apparently those two guards had told McCoy about the door not working correctly, and he anticipated our plan. So he threw us in these cages in the hangar. Chris—McCoy's prisoner—was there. He was in Vance's cage. Apparently he had lost his mind, and charged the guards when they opened the door to feed him and Vance. They were forced to shoot him after he tried grabbing one of their guns. Vance saw an opportunity to escape—or try to, at least—and ended up killing one of them. He got shot in the leg, and his escape attempt was over. Overfield and Derek brought Logan up, after McCoy found out about our escape attempt. McCoy had him hanged by a chain from the rafters, between our cages. And then Mark...he started having trouble breathing. Stress, I guess. And then all of a sudden he fell to the floor, grabbing his chest. I tried to do CPR...I did it for a long time. And then Overfield...he came up to get us, so McCoy could 'punish' us. I had a screwdriver hidden in my waistband, and when I saw an opportunity, I..."

Thomas paused and swallowed the knot in his throat. Out of the corner of his eye, he could see his sister sitting quietly and staring out toward the road. He felt a strange tingling sensation pass over his body, and a hollow feeling in his gut.

"...I had to kill him. It was our only way out. Vance and I got out of the hangar and found a sniper rifle in Overfield's SUV. When we saw McCoy show up with Samantha—which was completely unexpected—we were already set up so that we could attempt the rest of my plan. McCoy discovered we were gone, and called more soldiers over. Knowing we had to be nearby, and had Overfield's radio because it was missing, he held a gun to Samantha's head and threatened to shoot her. Vance shot him. The soldiers put down their weapons, and I confronted Derek. He tried to tackle me, so I killed him. He deserved to die for what he had done to Logan, anyway. And that's...that's it."

Thomas heard Mindy take in a deep breath. He glanced over at his sister, who had a stern look on her face, almost as if she was trying to suppress more tears.

"And that guy—Daniel—who was he? Why did he want to speak with you?" she asked without even looking at her brother.

"He was..." Thomas let out a sigh, "...he was Wild Bill's brother. The other 'henchman' we saw wandering around by McCoy's side from time to time. He wanted to make sure we were leaving and never coming back."

Thomas saw Mindy's lips curl up before she quickly looked

through the passenger window. He knew his sister's body language enough that he could tell she was quietly crying.

"Mindy..." Thomas began as he reached over and took his sister's hand, "...this is how the world is, now. We have to survive..."

"At what cost?" she snapped as she pulled her hand away and turned her tear-filled eyes to her brother, "How many people do we have to get rid of, to make sure *we* live?"

"Sis..."

"No, Thomas," she said softly, her voice little more than a whisper, "I don't want you to justify it, or tell me it's okay. I don't want to accept that we have to be ruthless and mean and inhuman in order to survive. I understand that you have to be tough, and keep pushing forward. But I don't want to lose you. The *real* you. I don't want you to be like Vance, or McCoy, or even Overfield. I want my gentle, loving, compassionate brother. My brother who couldn't even swat flies when we were children because he couldn't see how their lives had any less value than that of our own. We need someone like Vance—someone who doesn't care and can kill anyone who threatens us—but I don't want that someone to be *you*. Promise me you won't be that person."

Tears filled Thomas's own eyes as he looked at his sister's face. He had never seen her this distraught and confused, even when their aunt had died from cancer. Mindy looked utterly lost and lonely, like she was the only one left in a world gone mad. Strangely, Thomas saw guilt in her eyes. Nothing had been her fault, yet her eyes conveyed regret and failed responsibility.

"I promise," he finally said, "I'm sorry."

"For what?" Samantha asked from the backseat. The girl appeared fine now, although on the inside she had to be feeling just as bad as Mindy.

"I...I just...am," Thomas answered.

"You did what you had to do," she said, looking out the window, "We can't be the same people we were before all this. Maybe if my mom and dad had realized that, them and my brother would still be alive. Maybe if I had realized that, I wouldn't have been beaten and raped by those men at the camp. Maybe if Craig had realized that, *he* would still be here, too."

"Craig?" Thomas asked her.

"The man I escaped with—the one who took care of me—after our camp was overrun."

Thomas didn't say anything. He couldn't say anything. The girl was right, but he didn't know how to talk to her about everything. He couldn't imagine the confusion and psychological trauma that this plague had caused her. It had to be immense. The weight upon her shoulders—just the weight of looking around every corner, striving to stay alive, carefully choosing who to trust and who to stay away from—had to be more than any young girl should ever have to deal with. And losing her parents *and* little brother...that had to be horrific. It was undoubtedly ten times worse because it happened in the middle of the world getting flipped upside down.

Thomas continued driving down I-15. They were only a couple minutes away from Salt Lake City, and the huge buildings filled the landscape before them. They passed by countless vehicles—some left in the middle of the road—as well as more and more walking dead. The reanimated corpses wandered about, and their numbers were increasing in frequency as they got closer to Salt Lake City. Suddenly, Thomas hit the brakes on the Durango and brought it to a halt. There was a Culligan truck parked halfway off the interstate, and Thomas couldn't pass up the opportunity to get a few jugs of fresh water.

Thomas left the Durango in the middle of the road, and cautiously checked their surroundings. There were no zombies in the immediate area, although he could see dozens of them stumbling around further down the road and also on either side of the interstate. The closest ones were about a hundred feet away, which gave Thomas plenty of time. Thomas reached into the backseat floorboard and grabbed the tire iron. After double-checking his Beretta to ensure it was fully loaded and had one in the chamber, Thomas opened the door.

"Don't get out under any circumstances. Crack the window and yell out if you see any of those things getting close," he told his sister.

"Are you sure it's worth it?" Mindy asked.

"We can't afford to pass up easy water."

Thomas stepped out of the SUV and looked around once more. Only a couple of zombies had taken notice, and were slowly making their way toward him. They were still pretty far off, so Thomas was unconcerned. He walked briskly toward the Culligan truck, continuously scanning the area in front of him just in case any undead were lying in wait. Within just a few short seconds he had made it to the side of the truck, and grabbed the strap to lift up the sliding door. With one quick motion, the door slid open and revealed dozens of large water jugs. Thomas grabbed three of them and sat them down gently on the ground. He decided to leave the door open just in case any other survivors passed by, so they could surely spot the invaluable water.

As Thomas bent over to pick up one of the jugs and take it to the Durango, he heard a quiet, raspy groan that sounded like it was coming from the other side of the truck. He silently pulled out the tire iron from his belt loop, and placed his free hand on the handle of the Beretta shoved in his waistband. Slowly, he crept around the back of the truck, toward the side of the road. He slowly poked his head around the side of the truck, his heart racing and his hands shaking. What he saw relieved him. On the ground before him was a zombie, its legs crushed beneath the Culligan truck's front passenger side tire. It was completely out of view of the Durango, so Thomas had no way of spotting it when he had scanned for potential threats. Thomas stared at the struggling zombie as it scratched at the pavement, instinctively trying to escape. It hadn't yet noticed Thomas. Its groans were quiet and almost sounded labored, although it had no need for air and it obviously didn't feel tired from repeatedly trying to crawl away. Thomas had no idea how long it had been there. For reasons unknown to him, Thomas stepped around from behind the truck and approached the moving corpse. It noticed him as he neared, and immediately switched from trying to crawl away, to trying to grab Thomas. Thomas stopped just beyond its reach, and looked down at it with an expressionless look on his face. The zombie growled and reached both of its hands toward Thomas. Its hungry sneers and moans did not perturb Thomas, who continued staring down at it. He looked over at its legs, both of which were smashed beneath the truck's tire. They were no longer firmly attached, and just barely holding on by a few strands of decaying muscles and tendons. Thomas was unsure how long the zombie had been trapped here, but it was obvious that it had been quite awhile and that the zombie was making progress at escaping. He looked at the undead creature's outstretched hands, and noticed that all of its fingers were mangled and torn to shreds. Every fingertip was worn down, the bones exposed. Thomas looked at the pavement directly in front of the zombie, and saw white scratch marks covering the ground. It had been there so long that it was grinding its exposed bone against the asphalt, leaving behind dust that closely resembled what was created from filing one's nails.

The thing almost looked weak, like it was wasting away. Its skin was thin and stretched over its frame, and the outline of nearly every bone was clearly visible. It almost looked like a thin rubber suit stretched tightly over a skeleton. Its mouth was torn and rotting away, and there was absolutely no sign of the iconic black, viscous fluid that almost always ran from the mouths of the undead. Thomas saw no sign of humanity in its eyes, which were light gray and covered in a thick film. It was doubtful that the creature could even see anymore. There was absolutely no hair on the thing's head. But why did it look worse than all the others Thomas had seen? Or did it? Thomas thought back to the zombie he had found inside the Durango, and remembered how pathetic it looked. At the time he hadn't thought anything of it, but now something clicked in his mind and made him compare the two. Were they capable of dying? Starving? Or perhaps it had something to do with the heat?

"This world is yours now," Thomas finally said to the undead creature lying before him, "We're just visitors. Travelers. Constantly reacting to the actions of others like you. Making decisions based on the things *you* do. Who would have thought that the dead would inherit the earth? This is the end for us, isn't it? Our extinction event, just like the dinosaurs? Except the dinosaurs didn't get wiped out from their own kind rising from the dead and eating them. Or perhaps they did."

Thomas took one more small step toward it, and was now close enough that the thing's fingers were scraping against his loafers.

"I need new ones anyway," he said, and raised the tire iron above his head.

Thomas brought down the tire iron, smacking the socket wrench end against the top of the creature's head. The zombie let out one more weak groan as its skull split open and its face smacked against the pavement. It slowly raised its head a couple inches off the pavement, but made no noise or attempt to attack the food source in front of it. Thomas brought his weapon above his head once more, and again struck the zombie on the back of the head. This time, instead of a dull *thud*, the wrench end broke through the skull and crashed into the brain. The sound it made was reminiscent of tenderizing meat. The creature was now motionless, face-down on the pavement with black and gray goo oozing from the open spot on its skull. Thomas found himself raising the tire iron again, and brought it down hard against the zombie's head. Again he brought up the tire iron, this time striking the zombie with more force. Thomas felt anger flood into his mind, and his face contorted into a vicious, ruthless expression. His nose wrinkled and he bared his teeth as he swung the tire iron again. And then again, and again, and once more. Breathing heavily, Thomas took half a step back before raising his melee weapon and bringing it down with all his might against the zombie's skull. The creature's head now more closely resembled the unused scraps in a butcher's shop, instead of the head and face of a human being. Or even that of a zombie, for that matter.

Thomas nearly stumbled backward as he inhaled and exhaled deeply, quickly. His eyes were still locked onto what was left of the zombie, his tire iron still firmly in his hand. The look of rage and bloodlust disappeared from Thomas's face as his heart slowed down and the adrenaline subsided. In his mind, the zombie he just brutally beat to a pulp symbolized everything going on around him. It was a lifeless being, with no fear or hate or emotion of any kind. It was completely incapable of committing a morally wrong action, constantly defaulting to finding food as if it was a robot with only one objective programmed into it. It felt no pain—physical or emotional—and it passed no judgment. It didn't feel loss or companionship or depression, or any feelings at all for that matter. It simply...was. A being—no, *creature*—with no thoughts or goals, no regret or anger. Just hunger.

Thomas left the zombie and walked back around to the other side of the truck. As he picked up the first jug, he noticed the zombies that had previously been far away were now closing in. He quickly walked to the back of the Durango, and Mindy popped the hatch. He placed the jug inside, but quickly noticed something was missing.

"Mindy," he said from the back, "where the hell are our rations?"

"What?"

"Our food. Our bag of food. There's nothing back here."

"It's not here, either," Samantha said as she glanced down at the backseat's floorboard.

"Son-of-a-bitch!" Thomas cursed as he ran over to the remaining two jugs.

After loading both up both jugs of water—and just in time, as the first zombies were now a mere twenty feet away—Thomas hopped in the driver's seat and put the vehicle into gear. He quickly but carefully pulled away from the scene, driving around a couple zombies who had been slowly but steadily making their way toward him while he was grabbing the water.

"Those assholes must have taken our food," Thomas said angrily.

"We'll find more," Mindy said, though her words sounded hollow.

"Son-of-a-*bitch!*" Thomas cursed loudly and slapped his hand against the steering wheel.

"What are we going to do?" Samantha asked, worry in her voice.

"I can't believe those bastards took it! What the hell do they need it for, huh? They have their own stockpile of food. Greedy fucks..."

"Calm down," Mindy said.

"I can't calm down, we..." Thomas stopped himself and took a deep breath. After a second or two, he managed to calm himself, "We'll find something. Soon. No big deal. Nothing to worry about."

"I'm already hungry," Samantha immediately said.

"So am I." Thomas shook his head in anger and frustration, but kept it inside.

"Surely there's something in Salt Lake?" Mindy said hopefully, this time with a little emotion in her voice.

"Surely," Thomas agreed, though it was more to offer assurance than it was an honest belief.

* * *

The three stared on at the scene in front of them. They were stopped on the interstate, just inside Salt Lake City. Before them was a veritable sea of undead, packed so tightly that they were bumping into each other and occasionally knocking one another over. The large city looked like a nightmare, with no signs of human life or any sort of refuge whatsoever. If the interstate was this bad, of all places, then the city itself had to be flooded with zombies. To make matters worse, there were cars left haphazardly all over the road. Most of them were on the other side of the median, going north, but there were still quite a few in the southbound lanes. Some were facing the right direction, others were facing north.

"Now what?" Mindy asked.

"Shit..." Thomas said under his breath.

"According to the map, we can go back a few miles and get on I-215. It at least doesn't go through the heart of the city," Mindy

251

suggested, looking at the map that they kept in the glove box.

"But doesn't that join with I-15 again further down?" Thomas asked.

"Yeah, but it's on the south side of town. We would be bypassing the major part. Or we could get on I-80 and go west a little ways. Take back roads south from there when we get the chance."

"Goddamn it!" Thomas cursed, although he didn't do it loudly.

"We better make a decision," Mindy said, "Before we're boxed in."

The huge crowd of undead was making its way toward the Durango, albeit at a very slow pace. They were about three hundred feet away, so it would take the horde quite awhile to get to them. Especially with how tightly packed they were. Touching elbows and shoulders and stepping on each other made them move much slower.

Thomas put the Durango in reverse and navigated through the abandoned vehicles. Once he had enough room, he flipped the SUV around and headed back north as fast as he could. Within just a couple of minutes they reached I-80. Thomas pulled the Durango around to get on the on-ramp. I-80 was also littered with vehicles, and there were undead scattered here and there, but it was nothing like what they had just encountered.

"I suppose it was foolish to think that it would look any different," Thomas said as he pulled the SUV onto the interstate.

"We were told that it wasn't as bad in the South," Mindy replied.

"Yeah, well apparently that information was wrong."

"Unless we're just not far enough south yet," Mindy said.

"I think it's time to stop being hopeful, and instead accept the fact that the whole world looks like this. Or at least the whole country." Thomas let out a frustrated sigh.

"I can't do that," Mindy told him, "And we shouldn't do that. We have to keep hoping and praying..."

"Praying?" Thomas interrupted, "Just how much do we have to see before people finally realize that there is no God? No salvation, no miracles, no divine intervention. We're in this alone, and on top of all that, we can't overlook the fact that the world around us is *dead*. Literally. If there is some sort of god, then he's an asshole. He has killed off *billions* of people around the globe, and then brought them back to wander the earth like automatons. Then he left a small percentage of us to somehow coexist with them, or fight them, or be *eaten* by them. No...if there is indeed a god, then I have no interest in trusting him or asking for his help."

There was an uneasy silence, and Thomas's words seemed to hang in the air. They drove past the airport, which actually had very few planes left, and could see hundreds of walking dead meandering about.

"My father was a preacher," Samantha finally said, staring at the airport as they went by it.

Mindy shot Thomas a piercing glare, and although Thomas meant every word he had said, he still felt inconsiderate and mean. In all honesty, he hadn't even thought about Samantha when he spoke.

"I, for one, believe," Mindy said as she turned her head toward the backseat.

After driving a couple more miles, weaving in and out of parked vehicles, the tiny group came upon *The Great Saltaire*. It was some sort of concert hall, possibly an amphitheater, but looked more like a mosque. It was a rather large building, and had golden teardrop-shaped domes on each of its four corners and also on either side of the entrance. It might have been a nice place to visit, once. Now it was little more than a landmark.

"So what's coming up?" Thomas asked his sister.

"Highway 36 is coming up shortly. It will take us south to a few small towns. Looks like the first one is Stansbury Park."

"How small?" Thomas asked.

"Pretty small."

"Good. Small is good."

As they continued on, the exit for Highway 36 came into view quicker than Thomas had anticipated. He exited carefully, navigating through the four vehicles haphazardly parked closely together on the side of the interstate. He was relieved to see that Highway 36 looked completely normal, besides the lack of traffic. But even out here, one might only encounter a vehicle every couple miles. There wasn't much south of I-80, not yet anyway. It was a welcomed break from the constant chaos and destruction and death. It oddly reminded Thomas of the drive through Idaho, when they drove for miles and miles and saw nothing but beautiful landscape. The landscape in this area, however, was not nearly as pleasant to look at.

They soon came upon Stansbury Park, but the highway passed alongside it instead of through it. They were close enough to the town that they could see its layout and undead activity. There wasn't much, which was a good sign. Thomas actually felt like maybe there might be survivors in that town. He continued on, however, determined to make up lost time and reassured by Mindy telling him there were even smaller towns further south.

"Coming up in just a minute is the road that goes to a tiny town called Erda," Mindy said, "Might be a good place to stop and scavenge."

Thomas almost smiled at how his sister's mind was changing. He knew she was still in shock from recent events, and that was completely understandable, but now she seemed to have more of a survivalist mindset. Planning ahead, carefully looking at the map, the hunt for resources at the front of her mind.

"Here?" Thomas asked as they came upon a sign for 'E Church Rd', even though there was another sign that had 'Erda' on it with an arrow pointing to the right.

"Yep. Want to check it?" his sister asked.

"Why not?"

Thomas was interested in more than just finding supplies. Yes, they desperately needed food, but he was also concerned about the capabilities of their group. If it could even be called a group. An architect and his sister nurse, with a tag-along 15-year-old girl was hardly a 'group'. They needed more people to ensure their safety. People who were capable, and hopefully had a vested interest in reaching Albuquerque. People who wouldn't abandon them or betray them. But Thomas didn't mention this to his sister. It would serve no purpose, and he didn't want her to know that he was actively looking for more survivors to join them.

Erda was indeed tiny. The city limit sign they passed said, "Welcome to Erda – Population 4,642". But the town itself didn't even look like it could support that many people. It appeared completely rural, with vast open land between houses. But then they came upon another road that turned south, and down that way looked like the town proper. There were buildings that were actually side-by-side, although overall the town still looked like something out of a 1950s TV show. Beautiful old buildings— which only someone like Thomas could truly appreciate the architecture of—and small streets with tiny trees and old streetlights. But then in the center of the city blocks—if they could even be called that—were small fields. It was certainly a rural area, which could be both bad and good. The residents would most likely have the typical Southern hospitality, but they would also inevitably be armed and suspicious of strangers.

"Look!" Samantha said as she pointed out the window.

Thomas slowed the Durango to a crawl, and down a small side street he saw something very comforting and reassuring—people. A handful of locals were standing outside of what looked like an old grocery store. A few children were playing nearby, tossing a ball around. Thomas turned the SUV down the street and very slowly made his way toward them. It didn't take long for the people to see him. After all, there weren't many vehicles on the road these days. Even if Thomas had been driving down this road six months ago, before the outbreak, the locals would probably take notice and stare at the unfamiliar vehicle as it approached them.

Two of the adults walked over to the kids and interrupted their playing. They gathered them up and moved them further away from the road. Now that they were much closer, Thomas saw four men and three women standing in the group. One of the men had a pistol on his hip, and another quickly walked over to his truck and opened the door. He presumably had some sort of firearm in there, but he didn't brandish it. Instead, he simply stood beside his truck with the door open. Thomas rolled down the window, moving at little more than a crawl now so as not to alarm them, and stopped about fifteen feet away.

"Hello," he said.

Two of the men—the ones who had reacted defensively while he had been approaching them—exchanged suspicious glances before walking up to Thomas's vehicle. The man who had been standing with his truck door open pulled out a shotgun from the seat, and followed the man who had a pistol on his side. Thomas pulled his shirt up over the Beretta in his waistband, exposing the gun's grip, in case he needed to use it. He didn't want to appear to be a threat, but he also didn't want to look like a defenseless person just asking to be robbed. He was, however, in *their* territory and encroaching on *their* loved ones and resources.

"Strange to see an outsider passing through," the man with the pistol said.

"Strange to see a town that isn't full of dead people walking around," Thomas replied, a slight smile on his face, "My name's Thomas."

"Paul," the one with the pistol said as he looked inside the Durango to see its occupants. After only seeing the woman and girl, he seemed to relax a little.

"We're not exactly prepared to assault the town," Thomas said jokingly.

"I see that," Paul replied, "You can come on out and talk, if you want."

"Sure."

Thomas opened the door and nodded his head at Mindy, motioning for her to get out as well. He wanted to seem open and friendly to these people.

"Where'd ya'll come from?" Paul asked.

"Seattle, originally."

"Seattle? Washington?"

"Yeah. We spent some time at Hill Air Force Base. There was a sizable survivor colony there. We're trying to get to Albuquerque, to find our parents," Thomas turned to his sister, "This is Mindy, my sister. And that's Samantha."

"She your daughter or something?" Paul asked with a smile. Thomas almost chuckled at the thought of himself looking old enough to be Samantha's father. He was indeed old enough, of course, although it would be slightly unlikely since she would have been conceived when he was 16. Certainly not unheard of nowadays, but still a little humorous.

"No, she's my niece," he said.

"So she's yours?" Paul asked Mindy, "You don't look old enough, honey."

"No, not hers. A good friend of mine's daughter. No blood relation, but I've always been like an uncle to her."

"I see. Well that's good of you to do that." Paul looked a little sad as he stared at Samantha, undoubtedly thinking about the hellish fate of her parents.

"I'm Robert," the man with the shotgun said. He was no longer defensive with his body language, and the firearm hung by his side casually.

"Nice to meet you," Thomas replied.

"You folks need somewhere to stay?" Paul asked him.

"Not necessarily, but we're looking for food. Our stash got stolen at Hill, and we didn't realize it until we left. We're not looking for handouts, of course. We'll work or trade for whatever you can offer."

Paul and Robert exchanged smiles, apparently relieved to hear honest words from a stranger.

"Let's see what we can get for you," Paul said as he waved his hand for them to follow him.

As Thomas and the other two followed Paul and Robert into the store, Thomas took the opportunity to look around at their immediate surroundings. It looked just like a normal small town. Perhaps with less activity, but there were no burned out cars or undead walking around. No bodies in the streets, no smoke rising in the distance. It was oddly peaceful and quiet.

The grocery store was larger than Thomas had thought from

the outside. It was also apparently the town's warehouse, now. There were neatly stacked piles of food and other resources scattered about in an organized fashion. Several people were inside marking things down on clipboards, presumably keeping a close eye on their inventory.

"We have a ration system," Paul explained, "No one goes hungry, but we don't let people take whatever they want, either. We hand out rations every other day, and try to have a large communal supper a couple times a week in the community building down the way. No one is required to contribute, although we keep tabs on who does and who doesn't. If someone isn't contributing in some way, it's awfully hard for them to get rations. We don't let them starve, of course, but their bellies don't stay as full. The exception are the sick and elderly. We take care of them just like they were contributing."

"Sounds like a wonderful system," Thomas said.

"It is. It's funny, really. Since the outbreak, we've had virtually no crime and no social problems. No stealing or fighting, not even any big arguments. It's like we all just came together and put everything to the side."

"That's great," Thomas said. They walked down a long aisle, toward the back of the store.

"I just wish it hadn't taken a horrible plague to make everyone join together."

"Right. So how have you guys handled that? The plague, I mean?"

"Well, we're a surprisingly closed community. We're only thirty minutes away from Salt Lake City, and ten minutes from Tooele. But we have a great local economy so most of our residents stay close. A lot of them used to commute, but other than that they stayed around home. Long story short, whatever that plague is hasn't affected us too much. We still have the occasional isolated outbreak in town, one or two people turn up dead and walking around, but they're handled swiftly and disposed of safely."

"Interesting. You don't know how good that makes me feel, to hear about a place like this. It gives me hope." Thomas smiled to himself as he walked behind the two men.

"Here we are," Paul said as he pushed through a door and led them into the back room.

"These are our reserves," Robert told them.

"We can give you some of what we have stashed back here. It's not as good as the stuff in the front of the store, but it's food. We'll set you up with a bundle, and anything more than that you'll have to trade or work for." Paul placed his hands on his hips and smiled as he spoke. Thomas briefly imagined McCoy standing before him, with his permanent friendly smile and authoritative stance.

"Thank you," he said, "this is more than generous. We will purchase some of the stuff in the front, but I'd also like to give you what we can for the food you were going to give us for free."

"What did you have in mind?" Paul asked.

"I have an extra handgun in our car, as well as some ammunition, batteries, magazines, a flashlight or two, some tools...we can take a look and you guys can let me know what you're interested in."

"Sounds good."

The group made their way back through the store and out to Thomas's Durango. He unlocked it and popped the hatch. In the back was a plethora of goods, although it wasn't immediately apparent. Since Thomas had a hand in it, everything was of course organized and packed away neatly. Thomas grabbed two of the bags on the right of the cargo area and pulled them over to him.

"Mindy, can you get the handgun out of the glove box, please?" he asked. His sister hesitantly walked around to the passenger side, still never having touched a firearm before.

Thomas unzipped the first bag. Inside was a random assortment of batteries and several flashlights. Paul and Robert leaned in, looking over the contents.

"I'm only willing to give up two flashlights, and maybe a quarter of my batteries," Thomas said.

"Batteries are valuable," Paul said, "Let's head back inside and we'll check out some of the food we have."

"Here you go," Mindy said as she appeared and carefully handed the handgun to Thomas. She handled it like it was going to explode.

"Haven't used this one," Thomas told them as he checked to make sure it wasn't loaded, "but an Army guy told me it was probably decent."

"Taurus," Paul said as he took it, "They've gotten better over the years. Hell, can't be picky anymore. We really don't have a short supply of firearms, so they aren't worth a whole lot to us, but it will get you something."

After haggling a little and settling on ten extra cans of food (in addition to the free food they were nice enough to give him), a carton of fresh eggs, and a case of ramen noodles, Thomas felt satisfied. One of Paul's friends showed Thomas how to preserve the eggs, and helped him do it. Thomas was amazed at just how easy it was to do. Using a little bit of heated olive oil, they coated the eggs and placed them back in the carton. Simple as that. He explained to Thomas that you would ideally use mineral oil because it doesn't go rancid and can preserve the eggs for as long as a year, but such preservation was rather unnecessary. Thomas and the other two would consume the eggs long before they went bad, probably even without the oil coating. However, the bloom had been washed off of the eggs (the man explained that the "bloom" was the natural coating on the egg), so it needed some sort of layer to keep the oxygen out, since refrigeration wasn't an option.

Thomas actually felt a little anxious to learn more techniques like this. Rugged survival had its perks, especially with the world how it presently was. Thomas was completely unaccustomed to survival techniques, and desperately wanted to know more. After all, the very survival of him, his sister, and his "niece" would inevitably depend on it. Their parents, too, assuming they made it to Albuquerque—and assuming his parents were alive.

"Hey Thomas," Paul said as he appeared in the back room of

the grocery store, "A few of us were talking, and...why don't you guys stay the night? We're having one of those community dinners tonight, and you're welcome to it."

"Thank you," Thomas said to him, a smile on his face, "We'd like that very much."

* * *

Thomas, Mindy, and Samantha walked into the Erda community building at about six o' clock. Heads turned, and looks of both suspicion and disdain were on many faces. Thomas ignored them, but he could tell that it bothered Mindy and Samantha. He had watched the young girl long enough that he knew when she crossed her arms across her chest, she was feeling uncomfortable.

"It's okay," Thomas said to her as he placed a reassuring hand on her shoulder.

"Hey guys," Paul said as he appeared from the crowd, "Follow me."

Paul was in his early forties, maybe, with tan skin and a solid, stout build. He was maybe an inch shorter than Thomas, but his forearms were large and his chest was broad. On his hip was some sort of old revolver. He dressed plainly, in blue jeans, work boots, and a gray t-shirt. He had salt and pepper hair that was thick but short, and a rough face. Thomas suspected that he had been a smoker, based on the deep lines on his face. Paul carried himself in a confident way, and Thomas had already figured out that he was some sort of leader here. Probably not *the* leader—if there was one—but one of the people in charge. Although, it didn't seem like they had any amount of oppression here. No one barking orders or demanding reports. Just normal people, making due with what they had. Keeping it simple and as close to normal as possible.

Paul sat them down at a table that only had three seats open. The community building was packed full of people, and Thomas wondered if every resident of Erda was here. He also wondered how in the world a tiny town could feed this many people in a communal meal. There had to be almost 300 citizens inside the building. Everyone seemed average enough. No one looked like a soldier or criminal, no one too rough and tough. Then he saw one—someone who fit the description of a rugged, tough, bad ass individual. At the end of the table they were sitting at was an older man—probably in his fifties, maybe older—with longer, silver hair and a full bear. His beard appeared trimmed, although it was still thick. His mustache was the thickest and longest part of his facial hair. He had a long scar on the left side of his face, stretching from the corner of his eye almost to the corner of his mouth. It was an old scar, obviously from an injury many years ago.

"Here you are," a woman said as she appeared beside Thomas, a plate in each hand. Paul was behind her with a third plate.

"Oh, thank you very much," Thomas said, "You didn't have to serve us our food, though."

"It's no trouble," the woman said with a smile. Paul also smiled as he sat the last plate down and patted Thomas on the shoulder before walking away.

Thomas felt sadness spread over him as the woman's appearance stuck in his mind. She had reminded him a lot of Virginia, although she wasn't as old and wasn't dressed quite the same way. For whatever reason, his mind had immediately made him think of the kind, sweet woman who had shown him and Mindy so much generosity back in Idaho. Her quiet personality, her gentle features. And Mark...

"Thomas?" Mindy asked.

"Yeah?"

"You okay?"

Thomas stared at his sister for a moment, completely aware that a look of sadness was still stuck on his face.

"Yeah sis, I'm fine," he finally answered, a forced smile spreading across his face.

After the three of them ate, Thomas made it a point to find out about the older man that was sitting at the end of his table. He told Mindy and Samantha that he needed to use the restroom and would be right back, and then went in search of Paul. He found him standing by the front entrance, talking to another older man who was also in normal clothes but had a badge and gun on. Thomas slowed his approach, not wanting to interrupt them, but Paul spotted him and invited him over with a smile on his face.

"Hey Thomas, this is Henry Clemmons. He's the local police chief."

"Nice to meet you," Henry said as he grabbed Thomas's hand and shook it.

"Nice to meet you as well," Thomas replied.

"Henry is in charge of security, now that we don't have much of a crime problem," Paul said, "Don't let the badge scare you, he just wears it to make people feel safe."

Paul chuckled a little, as did Henry.

"I mainly jus' patrol 'n keep an eye out for creepers," Henry said in his much thicker accent.

"Creepers?" Thomas asked.

"Yeah, that's what Henry calls them. Don't worry, it hasn't caught on." Paul laughed and nudged Henry with his elbow.

"What does everyone else call them?" Thomas asked him.

"I just call them zombies, or undead," Paul said, "but *lurkers* seems to be the name most people around here use. Fitting, I guess."

"Lurkers..." Thomas repeated to himself, testing the word with his own voice, "Yeah, it's very fitting."

"Did you enjoy the meal?" Paul asked, changing the subject.

"Absolutely. Thank you so much for that."

"Not a problem. You seem like good people, and I can't imagine what you've been though. Traveling all the way from Seattle? Damn...I just can't imagine. And that poor girl—your niece—she must be beside herself."

"She's a pretty tough girl," Thomas told him, "But yes, she's been through a lot. Both of her parents and brother were killed."

"Damned shame," Henry chimed in.

"Hey Paul, who's that guy sitting at the end of our table? The older man with the silver hair, mustache..."

"The Cowboy?" Paul said, "His name's Lee, but he's not a

local. Rolled in about a week ago, said he was just passing through. Keeps saying he's going to leave, but hasn't yet."

"Is he good guy?"

"Seems to be. We were sort of wary of him at first, just because he looks mean and is real quiet. But he actually turned out to be a gentle, helpful man. Caught him kicking a ball back over to the kids a couple days ago, and could have sworn I saw a smile on his face. He puts up a pretty strong front, though."

"Why do you call him The Cowboy?" Thomas asked.

"Because he looks like something out of the Wild West," Paul laughed, "Always wears a cowboy hat and boots, and an old duster. Took off the coat and hat for supper, of course, because he's old school. But when he's not sitting at a dinner table, he almost always has them on. Carries a revolver of some kind, too. Fancier than mine."

"Interesting."

"He helps out around here however he can. I don't really get it, though...he said he was passing through, and keeps telling us that he's leaving, but obviously hasn't. It's like he can't work himself up to do it. Or maybe he's taken a liking to the place. Hell, I dunno."

"Thanks, Paul," Thomas said with a smile, and walked back over to his table.

Mindy and Samantha were chatting, although they could barely hear one another over all the commotion in the building. Most everyone had finished eating, but now it was social time. Thomas didn't mind the atmosphere at all. It reminded him of normal life.

"Hey," Mindy said.

"Hey." Thomas sat down and looked at Lee out of the corner of his eye. The old man wasn't talking to anyone, although he was constantly looking around the room as if he was waiting for something bad to happen. Thomas was anxious to meet him, but he had to figure out how to do it.

"What's the plan?" Mindy asked him, breaking his concentration.

"Well, I guess we'll stay here and head out in the morning,"

Thomas said.

"Well duh," Mindy laughed, "I mean...where are we staying?"

"I don't know yet. I'm sure they'll accommodate us somehow."

Thomas turned to Samantha and looked thoughtfully at the girl. As softly as he could with all the noise, he asked, "How are you doing, kiddo?"

"Fine," she quickly said, giving him a forced smile.

"We've been through a lot today," Thomas said to her, "I just want to make sure you're doing alright."

"I'm fine," she said, and looked away.

Thomas stared at her for another brief moment, wanting to talk things over with her but knowing now wasn't the appropriate time.

* * *

Another two hours passed, and the community building was beginning to clear out. Thomas and Mindy had spent most of their time talking to random citizens, most of whom were beginning to warm up to them. Thomas knew that having Samantha along undoubtedly made people more trusting of them. When just about everyone was gone, and only a few people were left behind, Paul and Robert approached them.

"Hey guys," Paul said, that same genuine smile on his face, "we have some cots in the back. I know it isn't ideal, but..."

"No, it's perfect," Thomas said to him.

"Sorry we can't put you up in a hotel," Paul joked, "If you were staying for a few days, we'd have no problem letting you stay with one of us. But...you understand."

"Absolutely," Thomas replied, "What you're doing for us is more than generous. Trust me, we aren't offended in any way."

"Good. I want you people to feel welcome to stay here, if you need to. We'll get the cots for you and you can crash in here tonight."

"Thank you so much," Mindy said.

"Yes, we greatly appreciate all of this," Thomas said as well, genuinely feeling fortunate and appreciative.

Thomas stepped outside to get some fresh air while Mindy and Samantha washed up. The community building was still hot from all of the people who had been in there. The Sun was just barely peeking over the horizon still, and Thomas found comfort in the quiet serenity that the small town provided. The sky was a deep red, fading up into the clouds above. Thomas lost himself in it, realizing that this was the very first time since leaving Seattle that he was actually admiring something.

"Gorgeous, ain't it?" a raspy voice said from his right. It sounded oddly similar to Vance's voice, but with an added country twang.

Thomas turned and saw Lee—The Cowboy—leaning up against the side of the community building, smoking a cigarette. He was certainly tough-looking. Everything about him screamed, *Don't mess with me*, which was exactly what Thomas wanted. Lee wore black cowboy boots and black jeans. His shirt was a dark charcoal button-up, and he even had a vest on. The duster he wore was dark brown, and had probably been an expensive coat at one time. Now it was worn and tattered at the bottom. The man's cowboy hat looked in pretty good shape, although Thomas could tell that it was old as well by the apparent texture of its material. Lee had an old leather gun belt around his waist, complete with extra ammunition lining it, although the revolver he was supposed to be carrying was covered up by his duster. He even had black gloves on. Thomas was taken aback by his appearance. He truly looked like someone who would be wandering through Dodge City in 1905.

"Yes, very," Thomas replied, his eyes still locked on Lee.

"No matter what's going on in life, I have a rule to always stop what I'm doing and admire the sunset if I'm able," Lee told him, staring out at the horizon.

"Good rule," Thomas said, "Where are you from?"

"Here, for now," Lee vaguely replied, "What about you?"

"Seattle, Washington."

"Long way from home, pardner." Lee threw his cigarette butt

on the ground and stepped on it.

"That I am."

"Aren't we all..." Lee looked back up and stared out at the sunset once more.

Lee enunciated his words very clearly, and he spoke like an educated man. His accent was an old one, like what one might have found fifty years ago on a ranch in Montana, but didn't make him sound less intelligent or unintelligible. It was obviously not the typical Southern Utah accent, like what was common in rural Utah. Thomas sometimes struggled to understand country folk, especially the further south he went. In rural areas of Utah, syllables were often dropped and a lot of words typically ran together. Sometimes the letter "T" was dropped off of the end of words, and words like "and," and, "in," were often replaced with a short, flat "N" sound and tacked onto the end of words instead of forming a separate word altogether. Neither Paul nor Robert displayed this speech, despite their slight twang, but Thomas had noticed it among many of the townsfolk. The Chief of Police, Henry Clemmons, spoke this way slightly, but it wasn't too bad.

"We're on our way to Albuquerque," Thomas said, taking advantage of his opportunity to speak with Lee, "We've had it pretty rough along the way. I wish we could just stay here."

"So do I," Lee said quietly.

"Why can't you?"

"Oh...I'm just a wanderer, now. Haven't stayed in one place for more than a couple weeks since the outbreak. I've always liked my solitude, anyway." Lee took a few slow steps toward Thomas, still looking at the sunset as he did so.

"I understand that."

"What are you goin' down to Albuquerque for?" Lee asked him.

"Our parents are there. We want to be with them."

"That's awful noble of you, traveling all that way just to be with them."

"I guess. I'm just afraid of what I might find there." Thomas looked away from the sunset and down at the grass across the road.

"Albuquerque's a big place," Lee said, "Do they live in the city, or outside of it?"

"In the city, but not in the heart of it. North Valley, actually."

"Nice place. Hope it still is," Lee said softly.

"Yeah, me too..."

"Thomas," Mindy said as she appeared behind him. The doors to the community building were still propped open.

"Yeah?"

"What are you out here doin'?" his sister asked, a slight smile on her face. Thomas figured she was bored.

"Just talking, watching the sunset with..." Thomas pretended to not know Lee's name.

"Lee Granger, ma'am," he said politely, touching his finger to his cowboy hat in greeting.

"Nice to meet you, Mr. Granger. My name's Mindy. I'm Thomas's sister."

"Just call me Lee, thank you. Nice to meet you, pardner," Lee said as he reached out and took Thomas's hand. His handshake was firm but not overly so.

"Nice to meet you as well," Thomas replied.

"Mind if I join you?" Mindy asked.

"Of course not," Thomas told her.

Mindy stood on the other side of Thomas, her arms crossed across her chest and her eyes staring out at the beautiful sunset.

"I'm worried about Samantha," Thomas said.

"Yeah."

"Yeah? That's it?"

"Well what do you want me to say? Who shouldn't be worried about these days?" Mindy looked over at her brother.

"You're right, of course. I just feel...obligated to make sure she's okay. The same way I do with you."

"Let me worry about Samantha," his sister said.

"That girl who came with you...she your niece or something?" Lee asked.

"Yes. Well, she was the daughter of a good friend of mine. Her parents are dead, so now we're taking care of her."

"What happened to them?" Lee's voice became even softer, but still possessed the same deep, raspy tone.

"The plague happened," was all Thomas said.

"Have you lost anyone?" Mindy asked Lee, leaning forward and looking around Thomas.

"Mindy..." Thomas began.

"Gotta have somebody to lose for that to happen," Lee said.

Thomas looked over at him. The old cowboy was still looking out at the sunset, his eyelids still pushed together almost to the point that they were closed. He had looked this way nearly the whole time, and that was when Thomas realized that Lee Granger looked almost identical to the actor Sam Elliott.

"I'm sorry," Mindy said.

"For what?" Lee asked her.

"For not having anyone."

"Looks like it finally paid off. I don't have to go through the things you people do."

"So where are you planning to go next?" Thomas asked him, changing the discussion.

"Don't know for sure. Maybe south. Maybe west. Hell, I don't know."

"Want to come with us?" Thomas asked. It was a risk this early on, but oh well.

Lee slowly turned his head toward him.

"I don't think you'd want an old salty bastard like me with you," he said, breaking his stoic expression for the first time and smirking while he chuckled.

"It's just the three of us. I'd honestly like someone who can handle themselves by our side."

Lee's expression turned serious again, and he cocked his jaw over to the side as if he was thinking.

"Hell, I dunno. I like bein' on my own."

"I understand that. Listen, if you decide you want some company for awhile, let me know before we leave tomorrow. We'd be happy to have you along." Thomas grinned softly at Lee, conveying trust and potential friendship.

"I appreciate it," was all Lee said.

"We've got an early day tomorrow," Mindy said as the last sliver of Sun poked out above the horizon.

"Yes we do. Lee, it was very nice meeting you. Come find us in the morning if you change your mind. We're going to try to get out of here about an hour or so after sunrise." Thomas turned and stuck out his hand for Lee to shake once more.

"Thank you. If I don't see ya', you folks take care. And take care of that little girl."

Lee gave Thomas a half-grin as he shook his hand. For some reason, Thomas felt a strong connection with this man. Something about him made Thomas desperate for him to travel with them. He seemed honest, and capable, and *good*. Of course, Thomas knew he could be completely wrong about him. Just like he was with McCoy. This time, however, Thomas had previous experiences to warn him. He felt no suspicion or uneasiness about Lee Granger. In fact, he felt almost completely open and comfortable with him. It was crazy...he barely knew the man. Yet here he was, thinking about him deeply as they walked back inside, hoping the man changed his mind and came looking for them in the morning...

<u>15</u>

Thomas looked around at the vast, white room he was standing in. It seemed to have no end. No walls, or ceilings, or even floors. Just...white. Everything had a slight glow to it, and his movement seemed slow and exaggerated. Around him were people...people he didn't know. A whole crowd of them, everyone just walking around in various directions like on a busy city street. As he walked through them, politely turning to the side to avoid bumping into anyone, he saw Mindy appear directly in front of him. She looked lost, and hadn't seen him yet.

"Mindy?" Thomas said, but she didn't hear his voice.

"Mindy!" Thomas yelled, "Over here!"

"Thomas?" his sister said as she looked around, although not in his direction.

"Mindy!" he let out once more.

Mindy finally turned and made eye contact with her brother. She had a look of despair, not relief. Thomas smiled at her, still pushing on through the people, but his smile faded as he saw her expression. He finally made it just a few feet from her, and all of the noise from people's feet hitting the ground and brushing against one another faded.

"Thomas..." Mindy said quietly, desperately.

"Hey..."

And then Thomas looked down. Mindy was holding her hand over her wrist, as if she were covering something.

"What's wrong?" he asked her.

271

Mindy stared at him, tears forming in her eyes. She continued to clasp her right wrist, but left it hanging down by her side.

"Mindy?" Thomas said as he reached out.

His sister removed her hand from her wrist, revealing a red spot.

"What happened?" Thomas asked her, taking her hand in his and bringing her wrist up for closer inspection.

"I tried," she said, her voice quiet and hollow, "There was nothing I could do."

As Thomas brought his sister's petite wrist up to his face, he realized what the mark was. It was a bite mark. Blood oozed from the wound. Although it was not a terrible injury on its own, it was fatal nonetheless.

"I'm sorry," she said to him, tears rolling down her face.

"No..." Thomas said, tears forming in his own eyes, "No...no, no, NO!"

The people around them stopped moving, and then they all turned to face Thomas and Mindy. To Thomas's horror, all of the previously normal looking people were now terrifying and horrid. Their faces seemed to be rotting away, although their body language and stature still appeared human. Then they moved in on them, and their bodies took on the iconic, slow stagger of the undead. Before Thomas could do anything—before he could react in any way—they all pounced on Mindy quicker than what was possible for any lurker. Ignoring Thomas, they rushed past him and focused all of their attention on his sister. Mindy screamed, and Thomas found that he was unable to move. His feet felt glued to a floor that wasn't there. Before his very eyes, the only blood relative he had was being torn apart and devoured.

Thomas screamed as he abruptly sat up. After a few seconds of heavy breathing, he realized that it was all just a dream. He was in the community building, on a cot. On the next cot over was his sister, perfectly fine. It didn't appear that his shout had woken Mindy or Samantha. As irrational as it was, Thomas felt compelled to lift up her arm and check her wrist. He didn't, though, and instead got up and walked over to the window. It was tiny, and didn't provide much light for the extremely large, mostly empty, room. On the other side of the room was a large garage door, which had two small windows as well. There was just enough light to keep from stumbling over things.

Thomas was completely freaked out. Even though he based his life on logic and reason, he couldn't help but feel like his dream was very real on some level. Staring through the window, he saw absolutely no activity. That was a good thing. No people with assault rifles patrolling the streets, no zombies—or lurkers, as he had decided to call them from now on—wandering around in search of food. Just...peace. Thomas looked down at his watch. It was 3 o' clock in the morning. The middle of the night. This time last night, he was locked in a cage at Hill Air Force Base. Both his body and mind were totally exhausted, which was probably why he had had such a vivid dream. After rubbing the sleep from his eyes and determining it would be awhile before he was able to relax again, Thomas walked back over to his cot and put on his jeans and shoes. He needed some fresh, relaxing night air. The Moon was providing some light, and the sky was incredibly clear.

Thomas pushed through the front door and walked over to a bench that was pushed up against the side of the community building. He nearly fell down on it, completely rundown and tired of everything, and looked up at the night sky. It was absolutely breathtaking. He couldn't even remember the last time he had looked up at the stars, even before the plague. The sky was exceptionally clear, especially without the massive amount of light pollution from all the large cities. Thomas had never seen a night so clear, not even when he went camping out in the middle of nowhere with his dad so many years ago. There wasn't a cloud to be seen, and each star seemed to pop out of the sky. Thomas was overwhelmed by visual stimuli, and for a short time, he smiled just to smile. He wondered how many of those stars he was looking at had planets around them, and how many of those planets harbored life. How many had *intelligent* life? Were they dealing with something just as bad, or worse? Or were they living peacefully without a care in the world? No money, no disease, no crime...no lurkers. Just happy existence. Was it even possible? Thomas couldn't imagine a world so wonderful.

Movement, at the bottom of his vision. Thomas barely saw it. Had he been looking straight up anymore than he was, he surely wouldn't have. Thomas turned his attention to whatever it was. Across the road, in the empty grassy field, was some sort of...thing...moving. Through the dark night, Thomas couldn't make out what it was at this distance. It could have been anything, really. He didn't even see a silhouette...just movement. Thomas patiently waited, his eyes still straining to see, and as it slowly got closer he could have sworn it was humanoid. What was he supposed to do, if it was a lurker? He didn't know the protocol—if there was such a thing here—or who lived where.

As the movement turned into a distinct silhouette in the moonlight, Thomas became certain that it was a person. Or a lurker. What would a person be doing out this late? And then he saw more movement, behind the person or lurker or whatever it was. A lot of movement. Thomas's eyes grew large as he rose to his feet and held his breath, almost certain that what he was looking at was a horde of zombies but hoping that it somehow wasn't. The movement turned into more silhouettes, and the original one he had seen was now more clear. Its slow, uncoordinated movement was undeniable.

"Shit!" he said to himself as he rushed inside, almost falling down as he did so.

"Wake up!" he yelled, "Now! Lurkers!"

And then he realized that the new term would probably only confuse Mindy and Samantha.

"Undead! Heading this way! Get up! *Get up!*"

Mindy sat up in bed, eyes wide. Thomas had scared her. Samantha was on the cot next to her, but was only lifting her head off of the pillow and looking around through half-open eyes.

"Move!" Thomas roared, "Get up!"

Mindy literally jumped to her feet and put on her clothes over her nightwear. Samantha was slower, but she was getting up now and her eyes were wide with surprise and fear. Thomas grabbed his small bag of clothes and miscellaneous items, as well as his Beretta. He didn't have his tire iron, or an extra magazine. Both were in the Durango, which was just parked not even half a block away.

"What do we do?" Mindy asked nervously.

As his sister spoke, Thomas's brain forced images from his dream to the front of his mind. Mindy being eaten alive flashed through his thoughts.

"We stay alive," he said, and grabbed her by the hand.

The three of them rushed through the front doors of the community center, and the sounds of the undead echoed through the night as they grew closer. Thomas was still tightly holding onto his sister's hand, and she Samantha's, as they ran around the building and took off down the sidewalk.

"What about everyone else?" Mindy struggled to ask as they ran.

Thomas didn't even answer. He just kept running as fast as he could. The Durango was just ahead, and as they raced toward it Thomas thought about his options. What was he going to do? When they were just a few feet away, Thomas unlocked the SUV remotely and jerked the door open. He started the vehicle just as Mindy and Samantha hopped in.

"Thomas...what about everybody else?" Mindy asked once more.

"I don't know! I don't know what to do!" he yelled at her.

"Do *something!*" she yelled back.

Thomas placed his hand on the Durango's gearshift, staring out ahead while thoughts raced through his mind.

"Thomas!" Mindy yelled once more.

Thomas looked in the rear-view mirror, and although the horde had not yet made it to the town proper, he was still able to see a wall of lurkers stumbling closer and closer.

Thomas put the Durango in drive and took off. He immediately slapped his hand against the center of the steering wheel and held it there, setting off the car's horn. The horn blared as Thomas held it down and drove. He stopped momentarily to roll down the two front windows, and then laid into the horn once more.

"HEY!" he screamed through the windows, "WAKE UP! LURKERS!"

After a brief moment, Mindy and Samantha joined in. It really didn't matter what sort of noise they made, as long as it woke people up and alerted them that something was wrong. Within just a few moments, they came upon a couple houses with scared, tired-looking individuals standing on the porches.

"Lurkers!" Thomas yelled to them, "A whole horde of them!"

Thomas leaned out and pointed behind them, toward the direction of the horde. The people standing on their porches briefly looked back east—where Thomas had been pointing—and some of them ran down their stairs to get a better look. Then they rushed back inside to do whatever they were going to do to keep their families safe. Thomas continued driving slowly through the town, blaring his horn and yelling. There was more activity now, as more people were waking up to the noise and realizing they were in danger. Thomas made a big loop through town, and after coming back around he saw flashlights and headlights coming on all over the place. It looked disorganized and chaotic.

"I hope they have some sort of contingency," he said to Mindy.

"We're not leaving, are we? We can't leave," his sister said, even though Thomas wasn't heading out of town.

"Well what are we going to do against *that?*" Thomas asked her.

"I don't know, but we can't just leave these people behind!"

"There's nothing anyone can do except run!" Thomas argued, "Look! That's what everyone is doing!"

But that's not what everyone was doing. Although there were numerous headlights turning on and vehicles starting to move, the people of Erda were not prepared to abandon their town. Thomas quickly realized that they were executing some sort of plan, taking defensive positions. Most of the people he saw were men, but there were quite a few women out there, too.

"See! We have to help them!" Mindy said to him.

"I want to leave!" Samantha cried out, her breathing quickening as she began to panic, "I want to get out of here!"

"Honey, it's..." Mindy began.

"No! This is how my parents and brother died! We need to go!"

"Shit..." Thomas said to himself as he stopped the Durango.

"What are we doing?" Mindy asked.

"Get in the driver's seat and go," he told her as he reached in the center console and got out his extra magazine for the Beretta. He then reached in the backseat and retrieved his tire iron.

"Thomas, no! We can't split up!" Mindy screamed.

"Just drive outside of town, wherever it's safe. We'll find each other when it's over."

"No!" his sister yelled, panic filling her eyes.

"Mindy..." Thomas said, grabbing her by the arm and locking his eyes with hers, "I'll be fine. This town is so small...it won't be hard to get out if I need to. You'll be able to see when it's over, I'm sure."

"Thomas..." Mindy said quietly, tears now filling her eyes.

Thomas got out of the Durango and slammed the door shut. Mindy climbed into the driver's seat, but it almost seemed like she only did so to get closer to her brother instead of to drive.

"Go, now!" Thomas barked, and then turned away and ran toward several vehicles that were lined up about forty feet or so down the road.

Thomas looked back over his shoulder just long enough to make sure that his sister was doing as he had instructed. She was. The Durango's taillights were growing smaller as she drove away. Thomas hoped—and almost prayed—that it wouldn't be the last time he saw his sister.

"Thomas!" Paul shouted as Thomas rushed over to the vehicles.

"Was that you who woke everybody up?" Paul asked him. He was standing beside his truck, rifle in hand.

"Yeah. I just happened to be outside and saw them coming."

"A whole shit ton of 'em, too," Paul said, "God, I'm glad your ass couldn't sleep."

"What's the plan?" Thomas asked.

"You're lookin' at it. Hold our ground for as long as we can."

"This isn't going to work," Thomas said to him anxiously, "We need to do something better than this."

"Like what? Run them over with our vehicles? We'd get bogged down before we even killed half of them!"

"Get the ones who have rifles up on the roofs!" Thomas suggested, "Spread your people out! Doing so will spread out the horde as well."

"Son-of-a-bitch," Paul said, reluctant to try Thomas's suggestions even though they made perfect sense.

Thomas looked down the road. The horde had made it to the community building, which was a mere two blocks away. Maybe three dozen people and a line of vehicles stood between the lurkers and the rest of the town.

"Listen up!" Paul roared, "Those of you who have scoped rifles and are good with them at a distance, get somewhere high! On the roof of a house or building, whatever! Something that the lurkers can't tear down!"

Paul looked over at Thomas, who nodded his head at him.

Paul turned away once more and said, "Half of you get in your vehicles and move over to another street! Spread out!"

The citizens looked at Paul with confusion and apprehension, but followed his orders anyway.

"Give me a vehicle," Thomas said.

"What? Why?" Paul asked him with a frown.

"Trust me. I'm going to provide a distraction."

"Crazy son-of-a-bitch..." Paul said as he opened the door of his truck and stepped away.

"Just tell your people to be careful and not shoot me," Thomas told him, and hopped in the driver's seat, "If anyone has heavy machinery—a dump truck, big tractor, whatever—that'd be helpful, too. Something heavy enough that it can smash the bastards and not get bogged down."

"Good idea. Good luck."

Thomas slammed the door shut on the old Ford and took off toward the horde. He wasn't sure if he had finally lost his mind, or was just stupid, but he certainly didn't feel courageous. He had always imagined that all those heroes who did selfless and dangerous things for the good of others felt awfully good about themselves while they were doing them. But he only felt fear and doubt. Perhaps his idea was just a very poor one.

He raced toward the horde, and as his headlights shined brightly on them, he fully realized just how much of a mess he was in. The horde was larger than the one that had almost taken them out back at the house several days ago. But that didn't matter. Regardless of a horde's size, it was made up of individuals. The lurkers didn't work as one unit. They were selfish, hungry beasts of prey. They couldn't reason, or weigh options. Instinct drove them to go after the closest food source.

At the last moment, Thomas did something that was unexpected even for him. Instead of stopping in front and luring them away, or turning onto the cross street, Thomas sped the truck up. He flew toward the horde and slammed on the breaks just before hitting them. The truck slid through the lurkers, maybe ten rows deep, and the impact had created a kinetic shock-wave that no one could have foreseen. Thomas didn't just take out the ones in his path. The impact had thrown lurkers in all directions, causing them to hit the ones behind them, and the ones behind those. Thomas looked out and realized that nearly every lurker within fifteen feet of his truck was now on the ground. Better than that, they were having problems standing back up. Since they were all individuals, and didn't do anything with each other in mind, they didn't wait their turn, or help each other. Rising back to their feet was another obstacle for them on its own. A few would manage to stand, but then a few more would try to rise as well and bump into them, which would cause the ones already standing to trip over the ones still on the ground. Some were more dextrous than others, and were perfectly capable of stepping over simple obstacles, but not moving ones. Not obstacles that were writhing around and

279

crawling over each other. Thomas put the truck in reverse and spun the tires as he backed up, leaving smoke in his wake. The lifted truck bounced up and down as he ran over the fallen lurkers, as well as a few that were managing to stay standing.

Once he was clear of the horde, Thomas turned down the next street and slowly drove away. The truck was barely crawling, but the moderately loud exhaust and lights were enough to draw the attention of most of the horde. They probably weren't close enough yet to really make out the humans standing down the road, but the lights probably attracted them. Thomas honked the horn, which caused more of them to change their course and follow him instead of continuing on into the town. He felt like St. Patrick banishing the snakes from Ireland—if the legend was actually real instead of just a legend.

Not all of the lurkers followed him, though. Not even half of the horde, actually. The ones in the back—the ones who couldn't see his truck and weren't close enough to care about the sound it was making—continued on their present path. The townsfolk opened fire as the other part of the horde grew closer. Thomas could hear a barrage of gunfire behind him, and in his rear-view mirror he saw lurkers getting hit with bullets left and right. Most of the bullets were hitting them everywhere but in the head, but here and there one's head would blow open and the lurker would drop to the ground. Thomas continued his crawl down the road, determined to draw as many of them away as possible. To where, he wasn't sure yet. But his current technique seemed more effective than trying to kill them all. There were simply too many, and the townspeople would surely run out of ammunition before the last lurker fell.

And then a very helpful thing happened. About thirty seconds after Thomas passed through the previous intersection—and only about twenty-five feet away from it—a giant yellow vehicle appeared and tore through the intersection. The huge bulldozer literally decimated every lurker in its path. It actually scared Thomas, because he hadn't been expecting it. With the dozer's bucket down and almost touching the ground, it scooped up a dozen lurkers and took them with it. The rest got smashed and were either dead for good, or completely helpless. Thomas continued on, hoping the driver of the bulldozer would make another pass. It did. Swiftly going back through the intersection again, it took out the next wave of lurkers. There were maybe two or three dozen still directly behind Thomas, faithfully following him as if he were some sort of savior.

The driver of the bulldozer tore through the intersection again, but this time it turned down the same street Thomas was driving down and quickly made its way toward him. Thomas floored it, ensuring he was well out of the dozer's way. He watched as the bucket lifted and picked up a handful of zombies, raising all the way up and then dumping them as it drove. Lurkers fell to the pavement, their heads smacking against the road and cracking open like eggs. The ones that hadn't been picked up by the bucket were effectively smashed by the bulldozer's giant tires. A few lurkers survived, crawling along the street still in pursuit of a potential food source. Fewer managed to get up, but were even slower then before. Broken legs and backs made it quite difficult for them to walk.

The bulldozer came to a stop, and no lurkers remained between it and Thomas. Thomas turned the truck around and drove toward it. Once there, he rolled down his window and looked up into the cab that sat so very high off of the ground. A few lurkers were still making their way down the road toward him, but they were about half a block away.

"Need a lift?" the driver of the bulldozer yelled as he opened the cab's door. It was Robert.

Thomas turned off the truck and quickly hopped out. The bulldozer was extremely loud, which was a slight disadvantage, but its advantages surely made up for it. Thomas climbed the short ladder, and the driver stuck out a helping hand. Thomas took it and pulled himself up. The cab only had one seat, and wasn't big enough for two people to stay in (unless Thomas wanted to sit on Robert's lap, which he did not). However, there was plenty of room to stand beside the cab and plenty of things to hold onto.

281

"Don't fall off," Robert said as he turned the giant dozer around, inadvertently—or perhaps he didn't care—running over a stop sign. It didn't serve much of a purpose now, anyway.

Robert and Thomas tore down the street—running over several lurkers along the way—and back toward the main drag that the lurkers had originally been traveling down.

"Shit..." Robert said as they made it to the street.

A large portion of the horde was now dangerously close to Paul and his line of townsfolk. Robert honked the bulldozer's loud horn, hoping it would alert Paul and the rest so they wouldn't accidentally shoot them. But how could they not see a giant, yellow bulldozer?

"Better lean in here as much as you can, just in case," Robert said.

Thomas took his advice, and placed one leg inside the dozer's cab. Most of his body was now leaning inside. It certainly wouldn't keep him from getting shot, but the glass would at least slow the bullets down.

"Watch this," Robert said as he lifted the dozer's bucket.

The bucket raised until it was directly in front of the cab, completely shielding both him and Thomas from any stray gunfire.

"How do you know where you're going?" Thomas asked him.

"I know the town. It's easy. Plus I can see about ten feet or so in front of us, beneath the bucket."

Thomas watched as lurkers abruptly appeared beneath the dozer's bucket. His sense of distance was not as good as Robert's, since he didn't know the layout of the town. The bulldozer ran over the lurkers, and Robert slowed it down to a crawl. Almost all of the gunfire stopped, except for the sound of a couple rifles, but they weren't directly in front of them. Before long, a row of headlights came into view beneath them and Robert stopped the dozer completely. He let the bucket down, and Thomas could see Paul and a handful of others standing wide-eyed. Multiple dead lurkers were directly in front of the vehicles, and a few were even beyond the wall of headlights and had almost made it to the people. Paul ran over to them.

"Awesome idea!" he shouted as he climbed the ladder almost all the way up, but he stopped once he reached the top.

"I always knew this hunk of junk would be handy someday!" Robert said with a laugh.

"No shit. We're not out of the woods yet, though. A good chunk of them broke off and wandered north between the houses. I sent someone over to the next street to hopefully alert the others before it's too late."

"I'll make my way over there, then," Robert said, then to Thomas, "You sticking with me or getting off?"

"Let's go," Thomas said. He almost felt giddy inside. The safety that the dozer provided and the power he felt by riding on it overwhelmed him and made him feel unstoppable.

Robert moved the dozer as fast as he could, running over the occasional stray zombie. Thomas looked around carefully as they went, in case anyone needed any help. They came around the corner, and Thomas saw two sets of headlights down the street a little ways. Through the light he could see countless lurker silhouettes.

"Stop!" Thomas shouted.

Robert brought the bulldozer to an abrupt stop, much quicker than Thomas would have thought possible.

"What is it?" he asked.

"There!" Thomas pointed toward a house, "We have to help them!"

A man and woman were between two houses, and five lurkers were surrounding them. The man was the only one with a weapon, but it was just a baseball bat and didn't offer much protection against multiple zombies.

"But the others..." Robert began.

"Just go!" Thomas yelled as he climbed down and hopped off. The bulldozer roared as it sped away.

Thomas ran over to the yard between the two houses, tire iron in his left hand and 9mm Beretta in his right.

"Run!" he shouted to the couple, but they really couldn't.

The man repeatedly swung the baseball bat in almost a

complete circle, doing his best to protect himself and his female companion. He was certainly hitting the lurkers approaching them, but they just kept getting back up and advancing again. As Thomas got closer, he noticed that the man was becoming fatigued. It looked like it was all he could do to maintain his grip on the baseball bat.

"Hey!" Thomas yelled, trying to get the attention of at least a few lurkers, "Over here!"

Thomas was maybe ten feet away, and the closest two turned toward him and decided he was an easier target. They advanced toward him, and once the first one was dangerously close, Thomas dispatched him with a single point-blank shot to the head. He forcefully swung the tire iron at the other, hitting it in the face and causing it to fall down. He was well aware that it wasn't dead, but it was certainly less of a threat than the other three lurkers still going after the man and the woman.

"NO!" the man screamed as one of the lurkers latched onto him from behind.

The woman screamed in horror and stumbled backward, tripping over a bush and falling down to the ground. Thomas rushed over, hoping to get there in time. A lurker fell down on top of the woman, but Thomas got to her and kicked the zombie off. With one quick shot—without even aiming, it seemed like— Thomas put a bullet through the zombie's head.

"AHHH....!" the man roared as the lurker that was latched onto him bit into his neck, ripping a chunk of it out.

Thomas hesitated at the sight, realizing that he had not yet seen someone get bitten up close until now. But his hesitation only lasted for a brief moment, and he quickly bashed the tire iron into the head of the other lurker, which was just now realizing that Thomas was a viable source of food.

The man fell to the ground, the zombie still firmly attached to him and repeatedly biting him. Thomas turned sideways and swung the tire iron low, almost like a golf club, and caught the lurker in the temple. It flipped off of the man and landed beside him. The man was crying now, gripping his neck and moaning loudly. The bite was deep, and he was losing a lot of blood. Before Thomas could do anything at all—not that there was anything he could really do—the man stopped moving and making noise all together, and went completely limp. Even in the dim moonlight, Thomas could see him turn pale.

"No!" the woman cried weakly as she crawled over to him.

"Get back!" Thomas warned her, "Get away from him!"

"John..." she cried, and threw herself on top of him.

"You need to go find the others..." Thomas said as he grabbed her by the arm.

But the woman forcefully pushed him off of her, and again fell down on top of the man.

"He'll come back!" Thomas warned once more.

A guttural growl came from behind Thomas, and he turned around just in time to deflect the attack of a stealthy lurker by throwing up the tire iron in front of his face. The lurker's blood-covered mouth inadvertently latched onto the tire iron. A one in a million shot. Thomas pushed it away with all his might, causing it to trip and fall backwards. He then jumped up in the air like some sort of samurai, and brought the socket wrench end of the tire iron crashing down on the zombie's face. The lurker's head literally exploded. Its face caved in and brain matter shot out of its ears.

Thomas turned to go back for the woman once more, but he was too late. Another zombie—coming from behind the houses—had already made it to her. Thomas watched as it completely surprised her and fell on top of her, sinking its teeth into her shoulder blade. Just as Thomas was about to rush over to it and take it out, he noticed three more lurkers coming from the same direction. Although every bone in his body hated doing it, he retreated and ran back toward the dozer. Those lurkers would be taken care of after they had solved the much larger problem.

The bulldozer was making short work of the lurkers, repeatedly pulling forward and then back, and occasionally lifting up the bucket and smashing it down on them. Thomas raced over to it, but was sure to stay clear of it. Robert would not be able to see him very well in the low light and with all of the activity around him. Thomas ran around the heavy machinery and over to the handful of survivors taking refuge behind the vehicles.

"We're winning this!" he told them, "Kill all of them you see! We can do this!"

* * *

Mindy sat nervously in the Durango. Although she could see most of the town from where she was at, it did nothing to reassure her. She had seen the horde of zombies split up and spread out, and in her mind that was bad.

"It's been too long," she said, mostly to herself, "We have to go back in."

"No!" Samantha told her. She was now sitting in the front seat.

"Samantha, we have to! Thomas might be in trouble! We've been sitting here forever."

They were parked in an empty lot, just outside of the town proper.

"Please, Mindy...don't!"

"I'm sorry, Samantha. I have to."

Mindy put the Durango in gear and quickly sped toward the town's center. The half of town that she was on was mostly deserted, and there weren't any zombies in the immediate vicinity. Samantha dropped her head down and threw her hands behind her neck, as if she were trying to think of a happier place to be. Mindy didn't care at this point. She felt terrible for putting the girl through this, but she couldn't sit back while her brother was in danger and she couldn't very well leave Samantha by herself, exposed with no protection.

Mindy drove toward the lights and gunfire. As she neared, the number of zombies increased. It scared her, but she pushed on ahead. Even though she was desperate to find Thomas and scared for his safety, she kept a level head as best she could and refrained from mashing on the gas. She carefully navigated around the zombies that they came across, and before long she was behind the first line of cars. This area wasn't bad at all, although it was littered with corpses. About a dozen townsfolk were holding firmly, shooting all of the zombies that they saw as they came within range. Beyond them was another handful of survivors, standing behind two parked vehicles, and...

...a giant bulldozer. Someone had gotten smart and utilized the heaviest piece of equipment in town. It was ripping the zombies to shreds, and the stragglers were being taken down by the handful of townsfolk.

"Thomas!" Mindy shouted when she saw her brother, who was standing with the line of people and firing his handgun.

Thomas looked like someone else—someone who wasn't her brother. He seemed calm and focused, and was shooting his handgun with great precision. Or at least it appeared that way to Mindy, since she couldn't exactly see if he was hitting anything. Knowing her brother, though, he had to have been. He wouldn't continue to waste a valuable resource like ammunition if he wasn't.

"Thomas!" Mindy shouted once again as she rolled down her window, bringing the Durango to a halt a mere fifteen feet or so away from the line of people.

Thomas whipped around and stared at his sister with wide eyes. A look of both surprise and annoyance spread across his face, and he rushed over to her.

"What the hell are you doing?" he asked angrily, "I told you to drive outside of town and stay put!"

Just as Mindy was about to answer, she saw a zombie appear in the street behind her brother. Before she could even say anything—and as if Thomas just somehow *knew*—her brother turned and swiftly swung the tire iron in his hand. It caught the zombie right above the eye, caving in its skull. Thomas turned back to her and continued chastising her, like the near miss was no big deal.

"Get out of here! We're handling this!" he said.

"But..."

"GO!"

Glass shattered, and for a moment Mindy was completely frozen. It had scared her, and her brain hadn't yet processed where

287

it came from. And then she realized that a zombie had thrown its head through the rear passenger window. It reached in and grabbed Samantha by the shoulder of her shirt.

Samantha screamed as she pulled away. The zombie maintained its tight grip, although it had no way of actually tearing into her with its teeth. She was in the front passenger seat, and from the back passenger window it could only grab at her. If it had broken through the front passenger window, however, she could have already been bitten.

* * *

"How are we doing?" Thomas asked one of the townsfolk, "I saw a couple people go down. Have we seen anyone else?"

"I heard some screams that were far away, but I have no idea where they were," one of the women said, briefly taking a break from pulling the trigger on her assault rifle.

Thomas continued pumping rounds into lurkers as they came close enough. Some of his shots were missing, but more were hitting their intended targets. He was surprised with his own ability, especially since he had never really used a firearm. Admittedly, he was waiting until they were within six or seven feet.

"Thomas!"

His sister's familiar voice broke his focus, and he turned around quickly to find her. About fifteen feet behind him, his sister and Samantha were sitting in the Durango. Thomas ran over to them.

"What the hell are you doing?"

Thomas began to scold her, and then told her to get the hell out. Just then, he heard the sound of nearby glass breaking. It sounded like it was just on the other side of the Durango. And it was. Through the cab he could see a lurker reaching in from the rear passenger window. It had managed to grab Samantha by her shirt. Thomas took off around the front of the vehicle. Just as he was about to make it to the passenger side, a loud shot rang out. It was closer than the gunfire from the townsfolk he had previously been standing next to. The lurker that had been grabbing at Samantha fell to the ground like a ton of bricks, a large hole in its skull.

About ten feet behind the Durango, standing on the sidewalk, was Lee Granger. He stood sideways, his large revolver stuck straight out in front of him and gripped firmly in one hand. His other hand hung down casually by his side. The old duster was pulled back behind his gun holster, and now more than ever he looked like a gunslinger straight out of the Wild West.

The old man let his gun hand hang down by his side and briskly walked over to the passenger side of the Durango.

"You okay, miss?" he asked through the broken window, polite as ever.

"Thank you," Samantha said to him, eyes still full of fear.

Lee walked to the front of the Durango, where Thomas was standing, and touched his fingers to his cowboy hat to greet him.

"Thanks," Thomas said.

"No problem. Looks like we have quite a fight on our hands."

"Not as bad as it was," Thomas told him, "Mind giving us a hand?"

"My pleasure."

Thomas and Lee walked back up to the firing line and took their positions. Lee was still holding his revolver with one hand, and turned to the side so he had to turn his head almost all the way to the right to see down his sights. It was effective, nonetheless, for all of his shots found their targets. When his pistol was out of ammunition, he quickly rolled the cylinder out and dumped the empty casings. From his gun belt, he pulled the individual bullets from out of their leather holders and smoothly threw them in the revolver's cylinder. With one quick flick of his wrist, the cylinder snapped back in position and he continued firing.

Thomas was certain that he wanted Lee on his side, now. The man not only looked mean and proficient with a gun, but he had now proven that he was. Thomas wasn't sure what sort of revolver Lee had, but it was large, shiny, and loud. Deafening, almost.

Although, Thomas's ears had been ringing beforehand from all of the gunfire.

"Thomas! Look out!" he heard Mindy say from behind him.

Thomas quickly whirled around and saw three lurkers quickly approaching. They were walking right past the Durango. Lee had apparently not heard Mindy's warning, or possibly trusted that Thomas could handle whatever it was.

"Behind us!" Thomas yelled.

Thomas brought up his Beretta and fired at the closest lurker, who was probably less than ten feet away. His shot missed, so he pulled the trigger again. And then he realized that the slide on his Beretta was locked open, indicating that the weapon's magazine was empty. Thomas pressed the magazine release and reached into his pocket for his spare.

"Behind us! Behind us!" he yelled again.

This time one of the townsfolk heard him, and turned around to deal with the threat as well. But either Thomas had not been quick enough, or the lurkers had been much faster than he had anticipated. The undead creature reached out and accidentally smacked Thomas's Beretta from his hands. Now all he had was a loaded magazine in his other hand. He reached down and grabbed the tire iron from his belt loop, quickly stumbling backward as he did so.

Now the lurker was almost directly next to Lee Granger as it lurched forward to pursue Thomas. It realized this, too, and quickly turned its attention to the closer source of food. Thomas watched as the survivor who had turned around pumped one shotgun shell into the head of one of the other two lurkers. Thomas fumbled with the tire iron, and swung it as quickly as he could.

His reaction time was poor, and the lurker latched onto Lee's arm as Thomas swung his melee weapon through the air. The old cowboy instinctively jerked away and jumped back. Thomas's tire iron connected with the lurker's back, but it didn't even phase it. Lee had been lucky, and the lurker missed its first two attempts to sink its teeth into him. It did, however, have both of its hands wrapped tightly around Lee's left arm. Lee pointed his revolver directly at the lurker, but didn't fire. In the middle of it all, he stopped himself from shooting it because if he did, he would be firing directly at two of the other survivors who were off to his left.

Thomas brought the tire iron above his head and swung it straight down, connecting with the very top of the lurker's head. It forced the creature to fall to the ground, and a large crack formed on its skull, but the blow had not been enough to kill it. Thomas kicked it in the ribs to get it away from Lee's feet, and then struck it once more in the face. His attack hadn't landed well, and it caught the lurker in the mouth. Its teeth shatter and there was a horrible crunching noise, but it still continued on its mission to get on its feet and eat something.

"Die already!" Thomas yelled at it, and smacked it in the head once more.

This time it was much more forceful, and Thomas actually grunted while attacking. The socket wrench broke through the lurker's skull and killed it instantly.

"Much obliged," Lee said to him with a smirk.

Thomas nodded, put the fresh magazine in his Beretta, and continued firing at the advancing lurkers. He was being much more careful now, since he was almost out of ammunition. Carefully picking his targets and allowing the lurkers to get too close for comfort, he slowly squeezed the trigger on his handgun over and over. Out of five shots, he hadn't missed yet. Ten shots remained in the magazine, and Thomas was beginning to get a little nervous as he looked beyond the first scattered line of lurkers and saw another small group behind them. Although they were incredibly slow and dumb, they were relentless. They felt no fear or panic, and they didn't hesitate or seek cover. They just kept coming, no matter what opposition they were up against. No weapons were needed, besides their teeth and fingernails. Both were capable of inflicting a large amount of damage, especially the teeth. All it took was their saliva entering the bloodstream, and it didn't matter if the injury was severe or superficial.

"This ain't lookin' good," Lee said, still standing beside Thomas.

"I'm out!" one of the other survivor's yelled, throwing down his shotgun and picking up the baseball bat leaning against his truck.

"I'm getting close!" another shouted out.

"Shit..." Thomas said under his breath.

Thomas still had seven shots left in his Beretta, but he turned away from the line and jogged away.

"Where are you going?" Lee asked as he watched Thomas leave.

"I told you to leave!" Thomas yelled at Mindy as he ran by.

Looking over his shoulder as he ran down the street, toward the group of survivors fighting on the next street over, Thomas saw the Durango backing up to leave. As he turned his gaze back to the road in front of him, he saw several lurkers stumble out onto the street from the small park that sat in the middle of town.

"Shit!"

Thomas jumped to his left and ran around them, knowing full well that he couldn't take on the five or six on his own. Especially since they were all focused on him. He picked up his pace and reached the end of the block. As he rounded the corner, he saw one of the survivor's who was on the firing line get mauled by two lurkers. They took him to the ground and ripped away at his flesh with their teeth. The firing line was getting overrun. Robert and his bulldozer were down the street, cleaning up the stragglers in the rear. Two of the survivors who had witnessed their friend get attacked turned and fired at the two lurkers. Only one of the lurkers fell over as a round went through its head. The other had been shot twice, but both were in its torso. One of the survivors who had fired at them fell to the ground, grabbing at her leg. Thomas rushed over, unsure of what had happened.

"Oh my god! I'm sorry!" the man on the right said, his eyes locked on the woman lying on the ground.

"You shot me!" she screamed, grabbing at her thigh.

Thomas skidded to a halt right next to her, and knelt down to see if there was anything he could do.

"It's just in the leg," the man said, a look of shock still on his face, "It was an accident..."

"Accident or not, she needs to get away from here," Thomas said to him.

Blood gushed from the woman's leg, creating a growing pool of blood on the street beneath her. The bullet had most likely nicked an artery. Thomas quickly pulled off his shirt and wrapped it around the woman's thigh. She groaned with pain as he tightened the shirt around her leg.

"My sister...she's a nurse..." Thomas said, almost overwhelmed with the situation.

Thomas took the woman in his arms and picked her up. As fast as he could, he made his way back over to where Mindy had been parked. But he had told her to leave, hadn't he? What would he do? He knew very little about providing medical aid, especially for trauma injuries. Mindy, however, had been an ER nurse.

"Damn it!" Thomas growled through clenched teeth. The Durango was nowhere to be seen.

"Please..." the woman cried, her arms around Thomas's neck, "...please help me..."

The woman's face was pale now, and her grip around Thomas's neck was weak. Her eyelids fluttered, and her mouth was no longer contorted into an expression of pain and fear.

"Hold on," Thomas said to her, "You're going to be alright. Just hold on."

Thomas ran over to the nearest building—a small barber shop—and kicked the door in an attempt to open it. After two attempts he realized that the door didn't swing in, and instead opened toward him.

"Just hold on!" he told the woman once more. His brain couldn't think of anything else to say.

Thomas pulled out his tire iron and swung it at the door's glass. It shattered, and Thomas reached in and turned the lock on the door. After slipping the tire iron back through his belt loop, he quickly picked the woman up once more and pulled the door open with his foot.

"You're going to be okay," he said, "You're fine."

293

Thomas ran to the back of the shop and stepped into the small bathroom. He gently placed the woman on the floor in front of the sink and looked her over once more.

"Please..." she mumbled quietly. Thomas was barely able to understand her.

"Just hold on. Hold on."

Thomas tightened the shirt around her thigh a little more, and reluctantly stood up and backed away from her.

"I'll be back. I promise. Just hold on..."

Thomas closed the bathroom door and ran back outside. The situation out on the street had changed rapidly. The lurkers were no longer packed together, but were now scattered out and seemed to be everywhere he looked. There weren't any in his immediate vicinity, but that did little to comfort him. Just then he saw a couple of men running down the middle of the street. It didn't take him long to recognize one of them as Paul.

"Thomas!" Paul shouted as he got closer, "We can't do this! There's too many!"

Thomas stared at Paul as he rushed toward him, and then noticed the small horde of lurkers come around the corner. They were pursuing Paul and the other man as fast as they could. The two men were half a block ahead of them, but that didn't mean they had the advantage. Human beings tire...lurkers don't.

"Don't draw them this way!" Thomas finally yelled, "The other group...they're on the next street! You'll lead them right to them!"

"Come on!" Paul barked as he quickly changed his course. Him and the other man ran between two buildings, just a few feet away from Thomas and the barber shop.

Thomas began to follow them, but then saw another way to help the situation. Instead of following the two men through the small parking lot between the buildings, he stayed in the street and let the lurkers get closer.

"Hey!" he yelled at them, waving his arms, "Come on, you sons-a-bitches!"

Thomas took off through the park—toward where the lurkers

had originally been coming from—and made sure to jog at a slow pace. Once again, he was leading the zombies like they were faithful followers. He just hoped he wouldn't run into a bunch more, and could outrun the ones pursuing him.

Two more lurkers appeared from behind a tree in the park. Thomas jumped to his right, narrowly missing them, but stumbled when he landed. He fell to the grass and rolled, and when he got his bearings he saw the two lurkers stepping toward him with their arms outstretched. Thomas pulled out the Beretta from his waistband and quickly fired without aiming. The shot had hit the lurker on the right side of the stomach, and didn't even slow him down. Thomas fired once more, hitting it in its left shoulder. This time the kinetic energy of the bullet caused the lurker's shoulder to recoil back, forcing the undead creature to pause. Once more he fired, this time hitting it right in the head. A lucky shot. But what happened next was not so lucky.

The second lurker had made it the short distance to Thomas and literally fell on top of him. Thomas threw up his forearm, connecting with the lurker's neck and preventing its teeth from gnawing his face off. This was the closest he had been to one, and it was absolutely terrifying. The lurker gnashed its teeth only an inch or so from Thomas's face. Its black bile oozed from its mouth and dripped down onto Thomas's face and neck. Its arms flailed about, grabbing at Thomas wherever it could and trying to pull him closer to it. Thomas finally placed the muzzle of his Beretta against the creature's head and pulled the trigger. The flash blinded him, gunpowder burned his face, but he felt the lurker stop moving and go limp. Thomas pushed the lurker off of him, just in time to look to his left and see the original group that he had been leading away from Paul. They were now only a few feet from him, and their groans and chomping teeth made them look both excited and desperate to tear into him.

This is it, Thomas thought, *I'm going to die.*

But Thomas didn't die. Much to his surprise, a vehicle appeared from his left and slammed into the front portion of the group of lurkers. Thomas turned his head away and threw up his arms as blood and fluids were hurled in all directions. Once the vehicle had passed, Thomas looked up and saw that it was his black Dodge Durango, complete with the shattered window. Its front end was banged up from slamming into the lurkers.

"Mindy..." Thomas said to himself as he got up and put some distance between him and the remaining lurkers.

The Durango circled back around, its tires throwing up grass and dirt as it turned, and drove toward Thomas.

"Get in!" Mindy shouted before the vehicle had even came to a stop.

"Go! Go!" Thomas said frantically as he hopped into the backseat, directly behind Samantha.

Mindy took off, sliding the back end of the Durango a bit as she did so. Thomas shifted in his seat, realizing he was on the side that had the broken window.

"That way!" he yelled as he pointed in the direction that Paul and the other man had gone.

Mindy turned the vehicle back onto the road and navigated around the straggling lurkers on her way to the small parking lot.

"It's a dead end!" Mindy shouted as they entered the parking lot.

"There's a woman in the barber shop, in the bathroom! She's injured!" Thomas yelled as he opened the door and jumped out, "Come on!"

Mindy also got out, grabbing her medical bag, and ran behind her brother. There were no lurkers around them, although they could still see quite a few wandering about at a distance.

"In here!" Thomas threw open the door of the barber shop and sprinted to the back.

Thomas carefully opened the bathroom door, not wanting to hit the woman in case she had moved. She did not look well. Her skin seemed even more pale, she was shivering, and her breathing was shallow and slow.

"What happened?" Mindy asked as she dropped to her knees and opened her bag.

"She was shot, on accident," Thomas told her, staring at the woman, "Can you help her?"

"Thomas..." Mindy began, giving him a worried look.

"Can you help her?" he asked once more.

"I'll do what I can," Mindy said to him.

Thomas bent over and gently placed his hand on the woman's face.

"Just hold on," he said softly, "You're in good hands. Just hold on."

Thomas pulled out the Beretta and handed it to his sister.

"What?" she asked.

"I have to go. Samantha's still out there. She's probably terrified. Take this in case something bad happens. Remember: aim for the head."

Mindy carefully took the handgun and sat it on the floor beside her, then got to work trying to stop the bleeding and properly dress the woman's wound. Thomas closed the door and ran back outside. Before he had even rounded the corner, he heard Samantha screaming.

"Samantha!" he yelled.

As Thomas ran into the small parking lot, he saw a single lurker latched onto the driver's side window. It was gnashing its teeth at the glass, completely oblivious to what was separating it from a potential food source. Thomas rushed around the Durango and grabbed the lurker by the collar, pulling it away from the vehicle and tossing it to the ground. Its skull made a *thud* as it hit the pavement, but the lurker immediately rolled and attempted to stand up. Before it could even get halfway off the ground, Thomas grabbed the tire iron with both hands and swung it with all his might. The socket wrench connected with the lurker's temple, and hit so hard that the creature spun and fell back to the ground.

Thomas opened the car door and jumped in. Samantha was mashed against the passenger side window and breathing heavily.

"You're okay," Thomas told her as he grabbed her hand, "Everything's okay."

"Where's Mindy?" Samantha asked, her voice quiet and full of fear.

"She's helping someone who's hurt. Now I need to help other people so they *don't* get hurt."

"I want to leave, but we can't leave Mindy."

"We're not leaving Mindy," Thomas said as he put the Durango in reverse, "and I have to do what I can to help these people."

Thomas backed out onto the street and headed back to the last group of survivors he had seen. Their line was on the verge of being overrun when he had left, so he was hoping the tables had turned. He was also concerned about the others who had been with Paul. What had happened to them? And Lee...where was he at now? Thomas forced these questions from his mind and tried to maintain his focus on the immediate problem.

As he came upon the next street, he saw three survivors still fighting the zombie horde. They had fallen back about twenty feet or so, away from their vehicles. Two of them were now using melee weapons—an axe and a baseball bat—and the other was still pumping rounds into the lurkers with his handgun.

"Hold on," Thomas told Samantha as he turned onto the street and drove past the survivors.

As Thomas drove by the lurkers, ahead of the survivors, he opened the car door and kicked it out with his foot. He took out several of them this way, and wasn't concerned about damaging the Durango. There were plenty of vehicles sitting around, and this one was already missing a window.

"We can't do this," he finally said, turning around to make another pass, "There are just too many of them."

And then something unexpected happened. Thomas saw three sets of headlights turning onto the street he was driving down. They were about two blocks away, so all he could see were headlights. The vehicles were moving fast, though. Were these townsfolk, regrouping and launching a more aggressive attack? As the vehicles got closer, Thomas pulled up onto the sidewalk. Two Chevy Tahoes and a Ford Crown Vic flew past him, running off of the road and through the front lawns of people's houses. Thomas noticed some sort of writing on them, and was definitely able to catch the badges on their doors. The Crown Vic had a light bar on top. These were law enforcement vehicles.

The vehicles came to an abrupt halt, and several armed men jumped out of them and began laying waste to the remaining lurkers. Some of the men had assault rifles, a couple had shotguns, and the rest had sidearms. These men were definitely law enforcement.

"Who are those guys?" Samantha asked.

"Friends, apparently."

The cops made short work of the lurkers, effectively eliminating every threat in sight. Thomas could still see a few townsfolk here and there, finishing off the occasional lurker that had broken away from the horde. Thomas told Samantha to stay in the car and then got out.

"Holy shit...just when I thought all was lost..." Thomas said as he approached the group of police officers.

"You're lucky we still have enough ammunition left," one of them said, "We just had this same problem in Tooele. More of 'em though, of course."

Thomas nodded his head at the man, looking all of them up and down. Some were wearing tactical gear, some were in uniform, some were wearing civilian clothes with a badge on their belt, like Henry Clemmons.

"Thomas!"

Thomas turned around and saw Paul walking out of the park and onto the street.

"Glad to see you made it out," Thomas said to him.

"Are we done? Is it over?" he asked.

"Looks like we have some cleaning up to do, but the main threat is over."

"Who are our friends?" Paul asked.

"Tooele County Sheriff's Department," a voice said, although where it came from wasn't obvious. Somewhere around one of the Tahoes.

The man appeared from around the SUV, and held up his hand in greeting. He was a short, portly man—probably 50 or so—and was dressed in civilian clothes. His hair was almost silver, and it was combed straight back against his head.

"Sheriff Kenneth Alanbrooke," he said as he approached Paul and Thomas.

"Well Sheriff, I'm awfully glad you showed up," Paul said to him, still breathing heavily.

"Let's take care of everything, then we can do the meet and greet," Thomas suggested, "Still some lurkers to take care of."

Occasional screams filled the night, and it was a stark reminder that townsfolk were still fighting for their lives and possibly dying.

* * *

After Thomas checked on Mindy and left Samantha with her, he quickly went to work assisting the remaining townsfolk with the cleanup. There were lurkers here and there, but most of them were wandering alone or crawling around with some debilitating injury. It didn't take long to take care of them, but Thomas was dreading the next part of the cleanup process. They would need to gather up all of the dead townspeople and burn the bodies. Worse than that, they would have to stab them all in the head so that none of them would come back while they were cleaning up. It would be a horrible experience, but Thomas was prepared to do it. After all, he owed it to the town since they had shown him such kindness and generosity.

The sun was starting to come up, and Thomas was getting ready to destroy the head of the very first dead person he had come across. He looked at his tire iron, and was perturbed by how gruesome and inhumane this was going to be.

"Hey," Robert said from behind Thomas, "Want to use something else?"

Thomas turned and nodded his head. Robert opened the tool box in the back of his truck and dug around for a moment before pulling out a very brutal looking tool.

"Claw bar," he said, "Not quite as messy."

Thomas took the claw bar and held it in his hands. It was stainless steel, and only about twelve inches long. It was also very light, and felt right in his hands. The handle had numerous triangular holes cut out of it, presumably to reduce its weight. One end was flat with a v-shape cut out of it, for pulling nails. The other end was pointed, jutting out away from the tool at a right angle. It looked like something used for demolition. Something that would be able to pry up boards and nails, and also stab through materials and create a hole.

"Thanks," Thomas said to him, although he wasn't sure why.

Although this new tool was just as brutal as the tire iron, it had a pointed end that allowed Thomas to stab the bodies in the head instead of bash them in. It would be cleaner, and seemingly more respectful.

"How many have you seen come back?" Robert asked as he hopped out of the bed of his truck.

"Just one," Thomas quietly replied.

"How long?"

"Several hours, but he hadn't been bitten."

"Yeah...we've had a couple of those, too. Seems like most people don't come back though, unless they're bitten. We haven't figured it out yet."

Thomas raised the claw bar and swung it down, piercing the skull of the dead citizen. When he tried to pull the tool back out, he found it was lodged in the person's head. Thomas reluctantly placed his foot on the person's head and jerked upward, dislodging the claw bar. He was, however, relieved that there was very little mess. Blood seeped out through the hole in the person's forehead, but that was it. Thomas moved on to the next person, taking time to look at their face and think about who they had once been. Rinse and repeat.

"Have you seen Lee?" Paul asked as he approached Thomas, who was on his fourth body.

"No. I hope he's okay."

"He is." The voice was not Paul's.

301

Thomas turned around and saw Lee limping over to them. His leg was locked out straight, and it was obvious that he had sustained some sort of injury.

"Holy shit. You okay?" Thomas asked him.

"Sure. Tweaked my knee a little, but other than that I'm fine." The old cowboy sat down on the curb and rubbed his leg.

"Where were you?" Thomas asked.

"Had to run when shit went bad over there," Lee said, pointing to the next street over, "Came upon the old folks and the sick ones. They keep them in a larger house over on the edge of town. No one was with them, so I stayed. Had some lurkers try to get in, but I managed to take care of them."

Thomas smiled and nodded his head, relieved that Lee was okay and had injured himself doing something noble.

"Lee..." Paul began, "...it ain't that I don't trust you, but..."

"I didn't get bit," the older man said, raising up his pant leg.

Lee's left knee was slightly swollen, but other than that it was fine. No bite, no blood.

"Thanks," Paul said.

"Mindy and Samantha are over at the barber shop," Thomas said, "There's a lady in there who accidentally got shot. You can take my car over there if you want."

"I'm fine." Lee carefully stood. It was apparent that he was well aware of what a worse injury meant for him, and seemed to be doing his best to avoid aggravating the one he had. People didn't last long in this new world when they had injured legs or feet. Surviving at one's full potential was hard enough.

"Hey Paul, I'm going to go check on Mindy and the other lady..."

"Tracy," a man said from behind him. Thomas turned around and saw the man who had accidentally shot the woman.

"Tracy," Thomas said, "I'm going to go check on Tracy."

"Let me know, okay? I...I didn't mean to shoot her. I just freaked out when I saw Bill go down, and..."

"It's fine," Thomas told him, "No one thinks you did it on purpose."

302

Thomas walked over to the Durango and climbed in. He took a deep breath, and all of a sudden felt a strong urge to weep come over him. His eyes filled with tears, and his shoulders began bouncing as he started uncontrollably sobbing. All of the recent events came crashing down on him like a boulder. So much turmoil, so much death and sorrow. After a few moments, Thomas regained his composure and buried his sadness deep inside. He wiped his eyes and nose and put the car in drive.

"Mind if I tag along?" Lee asked through the broken rear passenger window.

"No, of course not," Thomas said, wiping his eyes once more so that Lee couldn't tell he had been crying.

Lee opened the door and slowly crawled in. His knee was really bothering him, but the salty old man didn't let it discourage him. Thomas watched his movements, how everything he did was deliberate and thought out. He was never antsy or unsure...he always knew exactly what he was doing. Lee looked over at Thomas once he was completely inside, and Thomas quickly turned his gaze to the windshield and took off down the road.

"Shitty night, huh?" Lee said to him, looking away as well.

"Yeah."

"Could have been worse."

"Could have."

"Those deputies showin' up really helped us," Lee pulled a pack of cigarettes out of his duster and put one in his mouth, "Mind?"

"No."

"You doin' okay, kid?"

Thomas continued staring through the windshield, driving around the block to get back to the barber shop.

"Are any of us?" he replied.

"Guess not."

Thomas parked the Durango in front of the barber shop and walked through the front door. Lee limped along behind him, but managed to keep up. Samantha was sitting in one of the barber chairs, flipping through a magazine to distract herself. They reached the bathroom door, which wasn't closed all the way anymore but nearly was, and Thomas slowly pushed it open. Mindy was sitting against the wall, and the woman—Tracy—was lying on the floor in front of her. She appeared lifeless.

"She lost too much blood," Mindy said, tears in her eyes. It was obvious that she had been crying.

"I'm sure you did everything you could," Thomas told her, but his voice was only a whisper. He stared on at Tracy, and his eyes began filling up with tears again. Seeing her lying there seemed to speak volumes to Thomas. It symbolized the constant struggle, how everyone was always tempting fate and narrowly avoiding death. Or...not. In the middle of all this mess, who wanted to die from an accidental gunshot wound from a fellow survivor? Sure, it was arguably a better fate than turning into a lurker, but it was horribly unfortunate. An incident that, in hindsight, seemed so easily avoidable.

"Let's go, kid. We've got things to do," Lee said from behind Thomas.

Thomas knelt down and gingerly took Tracy's petite body in his arms. As if she were still alive and made of glass, he slowly lifted her up and carried her out of the bathroom, being careful not to bump her into the door frame or walls. He walked right past Samantha, who looked up and stared in surprise.

"Pop the hatch," Thomas said to Lee once he had made it outside.

Thomas placed the woman in the back of the Durango, then climbed into the driver's seat. Lee got in as well, and they drove off back toward Paul and Robert. It was less than a minute drive, and once they had arrived Thomas carried Tracy's body over to Robert's truck and gently placed her on the tailgate.

"Damn shame," Paul said, shaking his head.

"Sure is," Robert agreed.

Thomas stared at her for a moment longer, then swallowed the lump in his throat and coldly said, "Someone should tell that guy she's dead. He might want to know he killed her."

And then something inside Thomas called out to him. A little voice inside saying, *Just like you killed Mark.* Thomas stared at Tracy's lifeless body once more, clearly remembering the previous day's events. He had killed Mark. It hadn't been on purpose, but he was responsible nonetheless. Just like the guy who accidentally shot Tracy. It was so easily avoidable, yet it hadn't been avoided. Part of Thomas broke during that moment. Something fundamentally important to what made him a civilized human being. Ruthless survival, full of unfortunate twists and turns, defined every aspect of life now. Both good decisions and bad had repercussions, but that was no different than life before all of this. It just seemed easier to make bad decisions, now.

"It wasn't his fault," Thomas whispered softly, just barely loud enough for the others to hear, "He didn't mean to."

16

After a late breakfast, Thomas went off and found a quiet, secluded place on the other side of town to sit and think. Or mourn, or grieve, or yell...whatever feeling came over him. As he sat in the Durango and looked out over the vast field outside of town, he thought back to how everything was before the outbreak. It was really just as chaotic, possibly even just as dangerous. This was just a different kind of danger. A kind that no one was used to, at least not yet. But everyone had to change, or they would find themselves dead. Sometimes, however, people died just *because*. There wasn't always a reason or a mistake that caused it. Sometimes, no matter what precautions are taken, people die. Thomas didn't like that, but he had to accept it. Then he thought back to something Vance had told him not long ago: *You can't save everybody all the time. Sometimes, bad shit happens and you just have to deal with it.* And Vance had been right. It had always been true, plague or no plague. It was just much more apparent now, and the stakes were higher. If you died in this new world, it might very well mean that someone else would die. One strand of the spider's web removed, and the whole thing might come down. Thomas took a deep breath and rubbed his eyes. Would he ever get over all of this? Would he ever be able to ignore these feelings of despair? And if he did, what would that mean? Would he still be a human being?

Thomas caught movement in his rear-view mirror, and immediately realized that it was one of the Sheriff Department's

SUVs slowly creeping down the road. He looked at the two occupants—or at least the only two he could see—and saw them pointing at buildings. The passenger was writing things down on a notepad or something. Thomas thought it was a little strange, but decided it wasn't his problem. He pulled the Durango onto the road and drove back to the town proper.

* * *

"Look, with all due respect, this is our town. We've been doing okay so far," Paul said to Sheriff Alanbrooke.

"Yeah, that's very apparent by all of your dead citizens," Alanbrooke told him.

"Hey, those were our friends and family..."

"And now they're dead. You obviously can't protect your people." Alanbrooke shoved both of his hands in his pockets, an authoritative look spreading across his face as he lifted his chin in a pompous manner.

"What's it matter to you, anyway? This is *our* town. You're just passing through."

"Well, we haven't decided what we're doing for sure just yet," Alanbrooke said, turning away from Paul and scanning his surroundings. His deputies were huddled together, talking.

"What does that mean?" Paul asked.

"Tooele was overrun. That's why we headed north and came across your town. As Sheriff of Tooele County, I am obligated to set up my command center and continue to serve the people of this county however I can. This town is small, out of the way, and with some changes we can make it safe. That's why we might end up staying."

"Look Sheriff," Paul began, "we don't have a problem with you and your deputies staying here. Not at all. In fact, we welcome it. But we can't allow you to take over our affairs. We have a system here...a system that *works*. No one is going to be okay with you muscling your way in and changing things around."

"No one is saying anything about pushing anybody around,"

Alanbrooke said with an awkward laugh, "But we might have to make some changes if we're going to coexist, that's all. Let's cross that bridge if and when we come to it."

"Yeah...*if* we come to it..." Paul replied.

* * *

"So have you heard how many the town lost?" Thomas asked Lee as he got out of the Durango in front of the community building.

"Not sure. A few dozen, maybe, but that's about a quarter of the town." Lee slowly stood, using the arm of the bench to help himself up.

"Damn..." Thomas ran his fingers through his hair.

"Could have been a lot worse, pardner," Lee said to him.

"Yeah, I guess."

"Chief Clemmons is dead, from what I hear." Lee hobbled over to Thomas.

"He was in charge of security, too. That's unfortunate," Thomas replied.

"Sounds like there's a new sheriff in town," Lee told him, "I overheard that Alanbrooke fellow and Paul arguing about some things. Might not hurt to go stick our noses in it...see if the townsfolk could use some help. After all, it wasn't us who lost people last night."

"Alright, let's go."

Thomas walked off around the community building, slowing his pace so that Lee wouldn't have a problem keeping up with him. There was a group of survivors about half a block down, and Sheriff Alanbrooke and some of his men were gathered there as well. Thomas didn't know a thing about any of these people, really, but he already felt some tension before he even reached his destination.

"Thomas," Paul said, breaking away from a small group of townsfolk, "thanks again. God knows it would have been worse without you."

"No thanks needed," Thomas said, "It's the least I could do."

"So what's goin' on with that sheriff guy?" Lee asked, squinting his eyes as he looked over Paul's shoulder.

"He was talking about establishing his command post—or whatever—here in Erda. I don't have a problem with that, but if he does then he said there will need to be 'changes' made."

"Well, they *did* save our asses," Thomas told him.

"Yeah, but that doesn't mean they can just come in here and take over."

"I'll let that stay between you guys. My little group needs to get out of here today," Thomas said.

"Hate to see you go, but I understand."

Thomas looked beyond Paul and saw an older man shut the door on one of the Tahoes. He was most likely too old to be a patrol deputy, and the way he carried himself indicated he held a position of power. Or used to, anyway, before the outbreak. Sheriff Alanbrooke walked over to him, and the two men spoke quietly off to the side.

"When are you leaving?" Paul asked Thomas.

"Well, I'm not sure. It's already almost midday. We might wait until tomorrow if we can't get out of here soon. I'd like to find another vehicle to take, since one of the windows on mine got shattered last night."

"You're welcome to take whatever you need." Paul patted Thomas on the shoulder and walked past him.

"Don't like the look of some of these guys," Lee growled in his deep, raspy voice.

"Yeah, maybe. Not our problem, though."

"It'll be somebody's problem, sooner or later," Lee replied.

Thomas turned away from the gathering of people and headed back toward the community building. Mindy rounded the corner and sighed heavily at the sight of her brother.

"What's up?" Thomas asked her.

"Just exhausted, that's all," Mindy said as she hugged her brother briefly.

"How's Samantha?"

"Okay, I guess."

"We can't keep exposing her to things like this," Thomas said.
"Do we really have a choice?"

Thomas shook his head and looked down at the ground. That
poor girl was going to be scarred beyond repair, if she wasn't
already.

"Hey!" someone yelled from down the street.

Thomas turned around in time to see two deputies squaring off
with two townsfolk. Both sides were arguing and their voices were
raised.

"What the hell's goin' on now?" Lee asked.

"Wait your fuckin' turn!" one of the deputies yelled, pointing
his finger in the face of the man in front of him.

"This ain't for you anyway!" the man yelled back, "We've
been out here bustin' our asses, cleaning up the bodies of our
friends and family! This water is for *us!*"

"Yeah? Well I have a gun, and you don't. So get outta my
way!"

"This will not end well," Thomas said, and took off walking in
that direction. Lee was limping along behind him as fast as he
could.

"You're not going to come in here and push us around! Not
after everything we've been through!" the citizen shouted. The
other civilian was standing next to him, fists clenched.

"Hold on," Thomas said as he approached them, "What the
hell's going on?"

"These bastards are trying to take all our water!" one of the
men said.

"Well that's the benefit of being armed to the teeth, ain't it?"
the deputy said with a devilish smile.

"Fuck that!" the other Erda citizen said, and stormed off.

"That's right! You'll wait your turn!" the deputy shouted at
him.

"This ain't right," the other man said, "It ain't right at all."

"Look," Thomas began, "We're all on edge. But that doesn't
give anyone the right to push people and take what isn't there's to

take. I'm sure they wouldn't have had a problem letting you have some water if you had waited your turn."

"I was thirsty," the deputy said.

Thomas looked behind him and saw Sheriff Alanbrooke and the other older man watching the scene, not intervening at all. Thomas shook his head in disgust and turned back around to the two deputies.

"After everything we've been through, we deserve whatever water we want," the same deputy said. The other one chuckled slightly as he filled up his own bottle.

Thomas looked beyond the single citizen, who was still shooting off to the deputies, and saw the other citizen walking back over. This time, however, he had a shotgun in his hands.

"What the..." Thomas began.

The deputies saw it too. They saw the man holding the shotgun in both hands, marching toward them with a purpose. An angry look was still present on his face, and although the shotgun was not pointed at them, it was up and at the ready. The first deputy—the one who had cut in line and was shouting—dropped his bottle of water and brought his MP5 submachine gun to his shoulder. The other deputy pulled his sidearm from its holster and pushed it out in front of him.

"No!" Thomas yelled, "Don't!"

Both deputies opened fire. The angry citizen immediately dropped to his knees, involuntarily throwing the shotgun out in front of him as he did so. His body fell over and hit the ground hard, and it was almost in slow motion. Several bullets had torn through his torso, and there was no hope of saving him. He was probably already dead before he hit the ground.

Thomas found himself instinctively backpedaling away from the deputies. Lee pulled out his revolver and held it to the back of the first deputy's head. Several other townsfolk pulled out their firearms as well, and Thomas noticed his own hand pulling the Beretta from his waistband.

"Drop 'em," Lee said calmly.

Lee's revolver was maybe four inches from the deputy's head.

That same deputy was still facing away, and had his weapon trained on another armed citizen. His partner was doing the same thing. Thomas had his gun aimed at the same deputy Lee was aiming at. It was a chaotic setup...everyone was pointing guns in every direction, and no one knew exactly how many muzzles were aimed at them.

"Drop your weapons or we will open fire!" the second deputy shouted.

"Drop 'your weapons! Fuckin' drop 'em!" the first one yelled.

"You shot that guy," a citizen shouted out, "You fuckin' shot him!"

"Put 'em down!" another deputy barked from behind Thomas.

"Now!" yet another deputy roared, "We will fucking shoot you!"

Thomas took a moment to look around him. If a single bullet was fired, this would quickly turn into a bloodbath. The deputies outnumbered the armed civilians (the ones who were present) 2 to 1, and they were trained to operate under these conditions. Thomas saw Sheriff Alanbrooke and the older deputy peeking out from behind one of the SUVs. Mindy and Samantha were nearby, huddled down behind a bench. It would do little to protect them is shit went south.

"Wait!" Thomas shouted, before he even had time to think, "Everyone wait! We're putting our weapons down!"

"The hell we are," Lee growled.

"Lee! Do it! We can't win this!" Thomas knelt down and placed his handgun on the asphalt.

"They'll have to kill me before I'll drop my gun."

"Lee! Please don't do this! It's a misunderstanding! We can't..." Thomas paused, adrenaline pumping through his veins, "No one else needs to die..."

Lee hesitated for a single moment, then placed his revolver back in its leather holster and halfway held his hands up.

"Now the rest of you! Put down your weapons!" the same overaggressive deputy ordered.

A single gunshot rang out, and that same deputy's head

recoiled back as it opened up and sent blood spraying all over Thomas, who was just a few feet behind him. Thomas stood in shock as the deputy fell to the pavement, completely lifeless. He had no clue where the shot had come from.

More gunshots now, and it took a brief second for Thomas's brain to figure out what was going on. In fact, it wasn't his brain that saved him. Thomas felt a strong hand wrap around his bicep and pull him away, down to the ground. It was Lee.

"We need to get the hell out of here!" the old cowboy shouted over the gunfire.

Thomas finally realized what was happening. Citizens and deputies were exchanging gunfire in all directions. Everyone was spread out, mixed in with each other, and it was a bloody mess. Thomas managed to look over in Mindy and Samantha's direction as he crawled away, following Lee. The two girls were still knelt down behind the bench, mostly out of the way of the bullets flying through the air. Thomas and Lee made it to the sidewalk, crawling directly past a deputy who was returning fire at an unseen threat.

"Ah!" the deputy cried out as he fell over onto Thomas.

Thomas felt the air forced out of his lungs as the deputy's body landed on him. It was dead weight, literally, and Thomas wheezed as he tried to draw breath. He panicked, and rolled over onto his back to try and push the body off of him. The deputy was barely alive, his arm slowly and haphazardly moving across his chest. The bullet had struck him in the center of his torso, and it was certainly a fatal wound. Thomas managed to crawl out from underneath of him and up onto the sidewalk.

"Come on!" Lee shouted back to him.

Thomas kept his eyes on Mindy and Samantha, focusing on their bodies. That's all he needed to do...just focus and get out of this mess. It had only been a few moments—maybe 10 seconds—since all of this went down, but it felt like an hour to Thomas.

And then the inconceivable happened. Mindy suddenly jolted and fell over onto the pavement, rolling from side to side. Thomas felt his heart stop, and without even thinking he rose to his feet.

"Mindy!" he screamed, running as fast as he could over to her.

Thomas thought he heard Lee shouting at him, but he wasn't sure. He didn't care. Strange noises were going past him, and Thomas assumed they were bullets flying dangerously close to his head. Buzzing noises, almost like some sort of small, fast firecracker. Samantha was on top of Mindy, completely covering her face from Thomas's view.

"Mindy!" Thomas shouted once more, and skidded to his knees once he reached her.

"Thomas...oh my god...what do we..." Samantha began.

"Mindy! Mindy! Talk to me!"

"Ah, shit!" his sister said, clutching her left arm.

"Let me see it!" Thomas said to her.

Mindy peeled her hand off of the wound, and Thomas was relieved to find only a small laceration on the outside of her bicep. There was hardly any blood.

"Mindy, you're okay," he said to her, "It just barely hit you. You're fine!"

"Are you...are you sure?" his sister asked, looking down to see for herself.

"We need to get off the street!" Thomas yelled.

And then everything suddenly died down. Thomas looked behind him and saw Lee scrambling to his feet, jogging over to them with a strange skipping motion so he didn't hurt his knee ay further. No more gunshots, no yelling. In the middle of the street, there was no more fighting of any kind. Several townsfolk were laid out in the street, some of them dead and some of them moaning or yelling in pain. A couple had surrendered, lying flat on their stomachs with their arms outstretched. A couple deputies were injured, and two were dead. Thomas's eyes were wide with fear and shock. How did something so bad happen so incredibly fast?

"Everything secure?" Alanbrooke asked from behind the SUV.

"Believe so, Sheriff," a deputy responded.

Alanbrooke and the other man came out from cover and approached a couple of the deputies. Thomas didn't even pay attention to what happened after that.

"Come on, sis," he said, and grabbed Mindy.

After getting Mindy to her feet, Thomas threw her arm around his neck and helped her walk toward the community building. Honestly, the shock of the situation was probably affecting her more than anything. Thomas looked over his shoulder and saw Lee leading Samantha along behind them. The girl was turned to their rear, her eyes locked on the scene behind them.

* * *

"What the fuck..." Paul cursed as he walked into the community building. A few townsfolk were already there, and Thomas was comforting Mindy the best he could.

"Paul, I don't really know what happened..." Robert said when he noticed Paul had entered the building.

"A fuckin' mess happened, that's what!"

"It was a fight over the water," Lee explained, "Then one of your guys came down with a shotgun. Didn't point it at them, but he sure looked like he might use it. Guess the deputies didn't want to find out. Two of 'em shot him dead, and then it was on after that."

"Goddamn it..." Paul rubbed his temples, "How's your sister?"

"She's fine," Thomas told him, "The bullet barely nicked her arm. Shook up pretty bad, but I'll take that over a worse injury."

"Sorry she's hurt. You know you're welcome to whatever you need."

"So what now?" Lee asked.

"Hell, I dunno. The Sheriff and his men have regrouped and moved into the police station. Guess they're coming up with a game plan just like we are." Paul sat down beside Thomas and Mindy.

"Or getting ready to launch an assault on the town," Lee said.

"There aren't enough of them to do something that overt. But I'm afraid of where this might take us."

"So let's hit 'em before they have a chance to come up with a plan!" Robert yelled.

315

"A few farmers armed with their daddy's shotguns, against trained law enforcement with automatic weapons and body armor? No thanks." Paul shook his head in frustration.

"Who said we had to use conventional techniques?" Thomas asked.

"What?" Paul looked over at him, not expecting Thomas to have anything to add to the discussion.

"Man to man, gun to gun, they would win. Probably even if they're outnumbered. So why don't we use guerrilla warfare?" Thomas stood up and walked around Paul to be in front of him.

"What the hell do any of us know about that?" Paul asked.

"It's common sense," Thomas said.

"Before we go doing anything too stupid, we have to try diplomacy," another citizen—unknown to Thomas—said from another group.

"I agree," Paul said as he jumped to his feet, "We need to go talk to them. Unarmed."

"So who will go?" Robert asked.

"I will," Paul replied, "and I'd like to take Thomas with me." Thomas stared at him for a brief moment.

"You're unbiased, you're smart...and you aren't part of this town. It makes sense," Paul told him.

"It does," Robert agreed.

* * *

"Nervous?" Paul asked.

The two men were walking down the street, alone, and Paul was carrying a white flag made out of a broom handle and a t-shirt.

"Kind of," Thomas told him, "Never done anything like this before."

"I'm not gonna lie, I'm about to piss myself," Paul said with a chuckle.

"What do we do if they take us hostage?"

"Why the hell would they do that?" Paul asked him, "What would be their motive?"

"No idea. Just a thought," Thomas said.

"If that happens, I guess I stop holding it and let my pants get soaked."

The two men laughed a little, though neither felt like it was genuine. So much blood, so much violence and loss. When would it all end? It seemed like no matter where a person went, death and destruction would eventually surface. No one was excluded from the turmoil that accompanied this horrible plague.

"Thank you," Paul said, "for everything you've done."

"Why thank me? You're the one who helped me before we even knew each other."

"Yeah, but you could have taken advantage of that. And you could have tucked tail and ran when that horde started going through. I probably would have, if I was just passing through a town that wasn't mine. But you didn't. You stayed and you fought for us. This town is as much yours as it is ours."

Thomas felt a knot form in his throat, and he almost felt tears in his eyes. After everything he had done, was he still a good person?

The police station came into view, and on top of the roof Thomas and Paul could see two deputies standing guard. Both of them now had their weapons pointed at Thomas and Paul, even though the two of them had no exposed weapons. They didn't even have any concealed weapons, but in all fairness the deputies didn't know that.

"Hold it right there!" one of them shouted from the roof.

Thomas and Paul stopped about twenty feet from the doorway, and they held their hands up over their heads. Almost a full minute passed by before two more deputies came out through the front door of the tiny police station. Yet another deputy stood in the doorway, watching over the two who were walking out into the street to meet their visitors.

"Can't be many more left," Paul whispered.

"You armed?" one of the approaching deputies asked.

"No," Paul replied.

The two deputies motioned for them to advance, and kept their firearms trained on them as they did so. Once they got within just a few feet, they stopped them and quickly patted them down.

"They're clean, L.T.," one of the deputies said to the man standing in the doorway.

"Bring them in," the deputy—'L.T.'—said to them.

Thomas and Paul were led through the waiting room of the small police station, and into one of the conference rooms. It was probably the only conference room, actually. In a town this small, they couldn't have a budget that would support a police station any larger than this. It probably only had a couple of jail cells, if any at all.

"So what did you boys come over here for?" Sheriff Alanbrooke asked loudly as he entered the room. He spoke fast and to the point, and it was obvious that his goal was to bum rush whoever he was talking to and overwhelm them before they could come up with an adequate reply.

"We came to negotiate," Paul replied.

"What is there to negotiate?" Alanbrooke quickly asked, "Two of my deputies are dead and two are wounded. One of them probably won't make it."

Thomas looked around the room. It was just "L.T.", The Sheriff, and that same older man Thomas had seen earlier.

"Only after you killed one of our citizens in cold blood..." Paul shot back.

"He was carrying a shotgun toward my deputies, like he was going to use it on them..." Alanbrooke argued.

"In case you haven't noticed, everyone is armed these days," Paul said.

"Deputy Rhodes said he saw the man point the shotgun at him and Deputy Strauff. That's the first deputy who got killed, by the way—Tim Strauff." Alanbrooke tucked his hands into his pockets, and shifted his weight from side to side as he spoke.

"Again, only after he murdered one of my people," Paul replied through clenched teeth.

"So what now? We obviously can't coexist after what happened," Alanbrooke asked as he sat down at the table.

"You're right. We can't. I think it would be a good idea if you all move on down the road. You have my word that no one will harm any of you." Paul leaned back in his chair, and Thomas could tell it was all he could do to not jump up and strangle The Sheriff or one of the other two.

"No, I don't think so," Alanbrooke said, a smile spreading across his face as he also leaned back in his chair, "I think we'd like to stay."

"To what end?" Thomas jumped in.

"It's a small town. I like it. The people here need some good leadership, someone to restore order."

"They don't need order restored. There was order before you and your deputies got here," Thomas quickly replied.

"I think Deputy Strauff would disagree with you," Alanbrooke said.

"So what now? We can't agree, so now what happens?" Paul asked.

"We can agree, and we *will* agree. You boys go on now, and tell the rest of the town what is going to happen," Alanbrooke told him.

"And what exactly is going to happen?" Paul leaned forward and gave The Sheriff a mean stare.

"We're in charge now. Have everyone drop their weapons a block north of the police station, out in the middle of the road so we can see it. We'll sort through this mess and designate some competent townsfolk to help us provide security. This whole thing will work itself out." Alanbrooke stood and pushed his chair in before quickly walking to the room's exit.

"The town won't stand for this! I won't stand for this!" Paul objected firmly, and stood up.

Alanbrooke stopped and slowly turned around to look Paul in the eye. The Sheriff was a good four inches shorter than Paul, but by the look on his face he didn't know it.

"You sure you wanna go that route?" Alanbrooke asked him. Paul hesitated, staring at Alanbrooke coldly.

"That's the only route there is to go, Sheriff. No one is going to be okay with this."

Alanbrooke turned around once more before simply saying, "Okay," and leaving the room.

"I don't think there's anything else to discuss," the older deputy said. It was the first time Thomas had really heard his voice.

"And who are you?" Paul asked.

"I'm Captain Danny Hathaway, the Undersheriff of Tooele County," the man replied.

Captain Hathaway had a sinister look about him. His face was ugly and wrinkled, and now that Thomas was closer to him, the man looked like he was at least 60 years old. His eyes were constantly narrowed, and he seemed to continuously nod his head slightly when he was speaking or intently listening to someone else speak. Liver spots dotted his hands and arms here and there, and his skin had a very unhealthy color that almost resembled spoiled meat.

"Let's go," L.T. said, after Thomas and Paul had a moment to shoot Hathaway a few menacing stares.

"And what's your name, since we're all getting to know each other?" Paul asked sarcastically.

"Lieutenant Darren Blythe. Now let's go."

Lieutenant Blythe had an athletic build, and was taller than average height. He was most likely in his late thirties, but his face still had very soft and kind features. His voice was quiet and perhaps even friendly, had they been spoken in another setting. His hair was kept trimmed up, but it was obvious that it hadn't been tended to in a few weeks, much like Captain Hathaway's.

Thomas and Paul were quickly escorted to the front door of the Erda Police Station by Lieutenant Blythe and Captain Hathaway. Thomas felt some of his anxiety fade as they got closer to the door. He was no longer concerned with being held hostage, and frankly didn't really know why he thought it was a possibility to begin with. They certainly wouldn't gain anything from doing something so overtly hostile.

"Fuck them," Paul cursed as they walked outside.

"We'll figure something out. Something that doesn't involve violence, preferably," Thomas told him.

"Just a little while ago you were talking about going all guerrilla warfare on their asses."

"That's still an option, but let's exhaust all peaceful measures before going any further." Thomas had to walk faster than normal to keep up with Paul's brisk pace.

"It's not your concern, anyway," Paul reminded him, "You and your people get out of here while you can. This is our fight."

"I wouldn't feel right walking away from this. Not after how much kindness you people showed us."

"And you're willing to die for us?" Paul asked, stopping in the middle of the street and turning to face Thomas, "You're willing to put your sister in harm's way? Or your niece?"

"They shot my sister," Thomas finally admitted. Or rather, he was finally admitting why he cared so much. He was angry and out for blood, no matter how good he hid the fact.

* * *

"Shoot him," Sheriff Alanbrooke said coldly after the front door shut.

"Which one?" Captain Hathaway asked him.

"The one in charge...Paul. Let them get a little ways down the street, and shoot him. We can't waste time with those who oppose us. We don't live in a democracy anymore."

"And the other one?" Hathaway asked.

"Let him go back to the others and tell them what was said."

Alanbrooke walked away, his hands still in his pockets. Hathaway turned to Lieutenant Blythe and nodded his head once, as if he was giving him permission. Blythe disappeared, quickly going up the roof access to pass on the order to the deputies keeping watch up there.

"Sheriff gave the order to kill the stocky one," Blythe said, popping his head up through the hatch on top of the roof.

"The tan farmer guy?" one of the deputies asked.

"That's the one. Shoot to kill."

And at that, Lieutenant Blythe disappeared back down the ladder.

"So much for diplomacy," the deputy with the scoped rifle said.

That deputy was Eli Rhodes, and he was deadly accurate with his rifle. The rifle was a civilian AR-15 .308, and had a large scope on top that Rhodes kept sighted in with an unhealthy obsession. Deputy Rhodes placed the rifle's bi-pod on the edge of the building's roof, got himself situated, and took aim.

"You gonna back me up, Spiers?" he asked, still looking down his scope.

Deputy Simon Spiers stared out into the street, watching the two unarmed civilians walk away. His own assault rifle—this one didn't have a scope—hung from his shoulder in a casual manner. Spiers took a deep breath before stepping away from the edge so that he couldn't see the two strangers.

"I can't do that," he finally said, "I can't kill an unarmed man."

"Well you ain't gonna have to," Rhodes told him, "Cause I ain't gonna miss."

"Come on, Rhodes. Can you really do this? You can shoot that man in the back?" Spiers asked his partner. Rhodes was silent, still looking down the scope of his rifle.

A loud, sharp *crack* rang out, and Rhodes' rifle recoiled back against his shoulder. Spiers jumped a little, his eyes wide.

"Nope!" Rhodes said, pulling his eye away from the scope, "But I can shoot him in the head!"

Rhodes let out a devilish laugh, as if he had just heard a humorous joke. Spiers felt his heart stop as he inched forward closer and closer to the edge. It didn't take long for the man's body to come into view about fifty yards or so down the road.

* * *

Thomas stared at Paul's lifeless body. It had happened so fast, and his brain hadn't yet processed what it had witnessed. Thomas felt something wet on his exposed skin, on his arms and hands and even on his face. What was it? It wasn't raining, was it? Paul...why had he fallen? What had that noise been?

Thomas instinctively jumped backwards and turned sharply to run away. In his mind's eye, he replayed Paul's head suddenly jerking to the side and his body falling limply to the pavement. His head had opened up and red mist sprayed out in all directions. Paul had been shot. *Paul had been shot!*

Thomas ran through the park, expecting a barrage of gunfire to be sent toward him as he fled. But it didn't happen. Nevertheless, Thomas continued running as fast as he could, making a large circle around a couple of blocks to get back to the community building. When he finally arrived, his legs felt like they could go no more. But they did. They carried him through the front doors and finally gave out in the large, mostly empty room. He slid down onto the slick concrete floor and looked up at the ceiling. His fingers shook violently as they worked to wipe his eyes. Was it blood? Did he have blood in his eyes?

"Thomas!" his sister shouted, "Thomas, are you hurt?"

"Holy shit! Where's Paul!? Thomas, where the hell is Paul!? Is he still out there?" Robert rushed over to Thomas's side, lifting him up.

"I'm...I'm fine..." Thomas said, catching his breath.

"You're bleeding..." Robert said to him.

"No...no, it's not mine..."

Thomas spontaneously jumped to his feet and ran into the kitchen. The small group of citizens who were gathered there quickly moved out of his way. Thomas nervously turned both faucets of the sink on and put his arms under the water. The blood was thick and partially dried already, but Thomas continued his attempt to remove the foreign substance from his skin. He breathed quickly and shallowly, and felt like he was about to hyperventilate. Why had they shot Paul? Why the hell would they do such a thing? How did the community building have running water? There must be a reservoir on the roof, something the townsfolk had installed after the plague broke out. Why the hell was his mind thinking

323

about the *water?*

"Thomas, where's Paul?" Robert asked once more through the kitchen door.

"They...they shot him," Thomas responded.

Robert didn't say a word, and Thomas didn't turn to look at him. He was obsessed with cleaning off the blood that covered his body. The blood of an innocent. The blood of a man only concerned with doing the right thing. And even though he had only known the man a day, it was still the blood of a friend.

After Thomas had cleaned himself and calmed down a bit, he explained to the townspeople what had happened. He told them exactly what was said at the meeting, and how Paul's slaying had been so unexpected. Who the hell were these people? They were okay with brutally killing another human being in cold blood, for no other reason than the fact that he disagreed with them? Thomas felt like curling up in a ball and crying, but he was beyond that. His bloodlust had only been fueled even further. Like a fire being stoked and fed more logs, Thomas felt his bloodthirstiness evolve into a ruthless *need* that screamed to be satisfied. *And it will be*, he said to himself, *They will pay for what they've done.* Not only had these people wounded and almost killed his sister, but they had shot and killed several citizens over a disagreement with the water. And then they killed yet another in cold blood when he refused to cooperate. These people could not be allowed to continue on their present course.

"So what are you going to do?" Mindy asked. Most of the townsfolk had quieted down, and some of them had gone back home. It was almost dusk now, and many of them were scared of being out at night (and understandably so).

"I'm going to make this right," Thomas told her. He stared through the front doors of the building, standing completely alone until his sister had approached him.

"I'm scared, Thomas. I don't want you to end up like Paul."

"And if I do nothing, then we can say with absolute certainty that someone *will* end up like Paul. Somebody's brother, or sister, or father..."

"But those people aren't *my* brother, or sister, or father. They're not *you*." Mindy looked deeply into her brother's eyes, feeling her own glaze over.

"But they are someone's. How many of them have they killed? Five? Six? How many will most likely die because of their wounds? You were injured because of their actions, and it could have been a lot worse. And now they've killed the town's leader, the one everyone turned to for help."

"Thomas, please..."

"No, Mindy," Thomas cut her off with a firm tone, "I'm not walking away from this. I'm *fixing* this."

Mindy stared into her brother's eyes for a few moments more before hugging him and walking away. She knew there was no talking him out of this, and deep down she knew that she shouldn't try. Just like with what happened at The Hell.

"Have you decided?" Robert asked, appearing from around the side of the building.

"Yes, I have. We need to act quickly. They won't be expecting it so soon." Thomas stared out toward the sunset, thinking over his plan and quickly patching any holes.

"Good. Give me that list whenever you're ready, and I'll see what I can find." Robert walked inside the building and started asking everyone to head home. Everyone except those who would participate, of course.

Lee walked up beside Thomas and leaned against the doorway. He slowly pulled a pack of cigarettes out of his duster and stuck one in his mouth.

"You know I'm going with you, right?" Lee asked Thomas as he flicked his lighter and held the flame to the end of his cigarette.

"How's your knee?" Thomas asked him.

"Feels better. I just tweaked it. I can put weight on it now without much problem."

"It's not sprained or anything?"

"It's just old, pardner," Lee replied, then, "Is this plan of yours gonna work?"

"I sure hope so."

Thomas pushed the doubt from his mind and focused on the elements of his plan that hadn't been worked out yet. Would it go as horribly as his plan to save Chris, back at The Hill? He hoped not, and if he had been a religious man, he would've sent a few prayers up above asking for help.

<u>17</u>

"Everything's all set," Robert said from behind Thomas.

Thomas looked out through the night, his eyes locked on the police station. From behind the park's bushes, he could see the front of the building entirely. There were no deputies in sight, but he knew that there were at least a couple of them still keeping watch from the roof. He also knew that there were about nine of them left. By The Sheriff's own admission, two had been killed and another two were wounded. The Sheriff himself probably wouldn't fight. He didn't look much like a fighter, nor had he participated in cleansing the town of lurkers when they first arrived. Neither had Captain Hathaway, although Thomas was certain that he would be more inclined to enter a gun battle than The Sheriff. Hathaway had a cruel look, and he would almost certainly have no qualms with personally dispatching a threat.

"Tell them to go ahead," Thomas finally said, his words quiet and monotone.

"Alright guys, it's showtime," Robert said into his two-way radio.

Lee and three other townsfolk were squatted down behind Thomas and Robert. All were armed with sidearms and either rifles or shotguns, besides Thomas and Lee, who both just had their handguns. Thomas also still had the claw bar Robert had given him, and Lee had his fixed-blade knife hidden beneath his duster.

"Sure hope this works," Robert mumbled.

"It'll work," Thomas told him reassuringly, although he was

327

not quite as confident as he led on. He quickly rubbed his face, tired from the long day and lack of sleep. It was nearly 2am, which he had predicted would be a perfect time to act.

Joe and David—possibly the two most important participants in Thomas's plan—stumbled out into the street from the alley across from the police station. Thomas could hear them faintly arguing, pushing each other. Their voices got louder, and their altercation intensified.

"Fuck you!" Joe yelled, pushing David in the chest.

"Don't fuckin' touch me!" David roared back, slurring his words slightly.

Joe finally punched David in the side of the head, and David staggered back before tackling Joe and taking him to the ground. Thomas noticed his breathing increase as he impatiently waited. Everything hinged on what happened next.

And then it happened, maybe ten seconds after David and Joe's staged altercation began. One of the deputies—presumably one on the roof—started yelling into the street. He was ordering David and Joe to break it up and go home, but they pretended to either not hear him or not care. Then the front doors on the police station flew open, and two deputies briskly walked down the steps. One had a shotgun, and was in tan BDU pants and a t-shirt. The other was wearing a green BDU uniform with a tactical vest and an assault rifle.

"Hey!" the one with the assault rifle yelled, *"Break it up!"*

"Now?" Robert asked, his voice a little shaky.

"Not yet," Thomas replied.

The two deputies shouted a bit more before moving in and physically separating David and Joe, who were wrestling around on the ground. The deputies quickly dropped down, putting their knees in the backs of the two men and taking control of their arms. As soon as one of the deputies pulled out his handcuffs, Thomas gave the order.

"Do it."

Multiple shots rang out, but not from Thomas's location. Three Erda citizens were posted up on one of the buildings across the

328

street from the PD. Both of the deputies who had responded to the fake fight keeled over, and one let out a terrifying scream. Thomas saw a flash from the top of the police station, but it only happened once. He assumed—and hoped—that one of the three citizens had eliminated the threat that was on the PD's roof.

David and Joe immediately broke out of their drunken characters and quickly stood up, pulling out their concealed handguns from their waistbands. They moved up to the PD, and knelt down at the base of the stairs leading up to the front door. Thomas saw the door fly open, and another deputy appeared. He was immediately put down, and Thomas was impressed with the efficiency of his small and untrained force.

"Move in," Thomas said to Robert, his eyes still locked on the PD.

Thomas stood as Robert talked through the two-way radio. Lee and the other three citizens stood as well, quickly stepping past Thomas and hurriedly making their way toward the station. Robert stood as well after he put his radio away, and walked beside Thomas with his shotgun raised. Closer to the police station, two more citizens moved in from the left to support David and Joe, who were still closely guarding the front entrance.

"Enter the building," Thomas said coldly. Robert parroted the order through the radio.

"It's locked!" Joe yelled after turning the handle.

"Shoot it open," Thomas said to him directly, now that he was close enough to be heard.

Another citizen armed with a shotgun ran up the stairs and placed the muzzle of his weapon against the building's old, wooden double-doors. He fired the shotgun, and the mechanism of one of the doors gave way to the blast. The door flew open halfway, and all of the nearby citizens rushed through it.

"You sure they're not going to stay and fight?" Robert asked as him and Thomas were now within spitting distance of the front door.

"I'm sure. They haven't been here long enough to establish anything important. There's nothing for them to defend." Thomas's words seemed devoid of emotion, and it almost gave Robert chills.

Lee brought up the rear of the citizen assault team, barking out the occasional order here and there. Thomas appreciated the old cowboy's cool mindset under pressure, and his ability to command the respect of those tasked with following his orders.

Several shots were fired inside the building, and Thomas saw Robert flinch out of the corner of his eye. The shots were very close together, and no more came after that. Only silence followed.

"Damn...hope one of ours didn't go down..." Robert said to himself.

Thomas walked up the steps—his Beretta firmly in his hand—and entered the building. Two men were standing in the entryway, guarding the front door. The rest—including Lee—were clearing the building as instructed.

"Hear that?" Robert asked as he stood in the doorway.

Thomas looked out to the street, and soon he could hear it, too. The remaining deputies were making a quick getaway. Thomas heard tires screech as he stepped outside, and when he did he saw a single Tahoe going around the block and driving deeper into town.

"Shit...you called it," Robert said, adding a chuckle at the end.

"Any casualties?" Thomas asked, forcing himself to hide his satisfaction and remain serious.

"We're all good," Lee said as he walked back up front, "Building's clear, and we have three prisoners. Two of 'em are wounded."

"Good," Thomas said, although the word had slipped from his mouth before he even had time to think. Then, "Get them mobile so we can get out of here."

Thomas walked down the stairs and back out onto the street. The two deputies who had been shot were both dead. One had most likely been dead before he hit the ground, and the other had bled out as Thomas had been walking up to the station.

"And then there were four..." he said under his breath.

"What's that?" Robert asked from behind him.

"Should only be four left. Two wounded and two dead in the incident earlier, three dead here, one prisoner. I'm guessing the two wounded prisoners we have are the two from earlier."

"Let's find out," Robert said as he ran up the steps.

"No," Thomas quickly replied, "Get them out and get the rest of it done."

Robert stopped and turned to look at Thomas as he spoke, although the de facto leader was still staring out into the night with his back to him.

"Right. Got it," Robert said quietly, and headed inside.

Thomas stared down the dark street. It was extremely quiet now, and he could hear crickets and other ambient noises echo through the night. Not even 24 hours ago, they had all been fighting for their lives against an undead enemy. Now they were fighting against a very much alive one.

"Here's the uninjured one." Robert appeared once more behind Lee, who was leading the handcuffed deputy.

"He surrendered peacefully," Lee told him.

Thomas turned and looked over the deputy. He was about six feet tall, towering over Thomas. His stocky frame made him look uncomfortable with his hands bound behind his back. He had kind features, with eyes too dark to tell the color of in the low light. His expression conveyed no fear, no malice.

"What's your name?" Thomas finally asked him.

"Simon Spiers," the man answered.

"Why did you surrender?"

Spiers looked down at the pavement for a moment before pulling his head up high and looking Thomas dead in the eyes.

"Those guys...they used to be friends. I had a lot of respect for them. After all that happened..." Spiers paused briefly, "...they were like family. The only family I had left. But I can't follow people like them. I've seen some of them do terrible things. I was always able to reconcile their reasons in my head, but not this. Not killing an unarmed man who only wanted to talk. After that, I was just looking for the right time to leave. You guys chose the time for me."

Thomas stared back at Spiers, finding a great deal of empathy for him. He glanced over at Lee, who was still holding onto Spiers

331

by the arm.

"He was on his knees with his hands behind his head when we found him," Lee said to Thomas.

"So you had planned on surrendering before you even knew what kind of opposition you faced?" Thomas asked.

"Yes. I didn't care. I wasn't going to fight for them anymore." Spiers clinched his teeth, causing his jaw muscles to tighten.

"And what if we had decided to not take prisoners? What if we were just going to kill anyone we came across?"

"I was prepared for that, but I saw it as unlikely," Spiers replied.

"Take him back to the community building after you're done here," Thomas ordered, then turned and walked away.

"And the other two? The wounded ones?" Lee asked.

Thomas stopped and thought briefly before turning back around.

"We'll figure out what to do with them eventually," he said, "For now, just take them to the location we talked about."

* * *

"Everything's done," said Lee as he walked through the front doors of the community building.

"Good. No problems?" Thomas asked softly. He was sitting in the corner of the room, behind a folding table. It was dark, and only a few candles were lit for the entire room. Their flames flickered, casting shadows that danced around the room. Through the darkness, Lee could see Thomas's silhouette but nothing else.

"None," Lee replied, "Nobody got bit, so that's always a plus."

The cowboy chuckled at the end, but Thomas remained silent. Robert walked in behind Lee just a few moments later, followed by all of the citizens who participated.

"Everything's in place. Any last minute additions?" Robert asked as he walked across the room.

Thomas leaned forward, placing his forearms on the table and interlacing his fingers. A sliver of moonlight from the window illuminated part of his face as he did so, and the scene seemed almost eery.

"No additions," he said coldly, "We continue as planned."

"The prisoner—Spiers—he's outside. Want us to bring him in?" Lee asked.

"Yes, please," Thomas replied quietly.

Lee turned and motioned to one of the citizens, who disappeared outside. A short moment later, three citizens entered the building with Spiers in tow. They brought him up to Thomas's table, cautiously maintaining their control over him by holding onto both his arms.

"Remove his handcuffs," Thomas ordered as he leaned back in his seat, disappearing once again into the shadows, "and get him a chair."

The citizens quickly worked to do the things asked of them, and Spiers thanked them after his restraints were removed. He rubbed his wrists, which had red marks around them from the handcuffs. A folding chair was brought over and he slowly sat down.

"You're not like them," Thomas said.

"I was," Spiers told him, taking a deep breath, "back when they were human beings."

"And what are they now?"

"Animals."

Thomas tapped his fingers against the plastic table, and they were the only things illuminated by the moonlight. The light cast by the candles stopped just short of the table, and they flickered ominously against the wall.

"You haven't done any bad things?" Thomas asked him.

"No, I haven't. I agreed to go with them, to continue helping people. But over time most of them changed. They became aggressive and controlling, as you saw. I should have left them a long time ago, but..." Spiers' voice trailed off, and he took another deep breath.

"But...?"

"...but they can be very persuasive. And where would I go?

333

They were all I had left. I constantly tricked myself into believing that the things they did were justified, but I can't do that anymore."

"You said *most* of them changed," Thomas said softly, "Not all of them are bad people?"

Spiers looked down at the floor, rubbing his hands together and thinking of an appropriate response.

"Well..." he began, "I guess none of the good ones are left. Besides Fields, but he's wounded."

Spiers looked up and his eyes grew wide. He worriedly looked around the room at his captors.

"You're not going to...*kill* them, are you?" he finally asked.

"The two wounded ones?" Thomas asked him.

"Yeah...Fields and Williams."

"Don't worry about them," Thomas said, "Two wounded deputies are the least of our concerns."

Spiers relaxed a little and sat back in his chair.

"Who was the one who shot Paul?" Thomas asked, his voice suddenly becoming stern.

"Rhodes. God...he's turned into quite the sadistic bastard over the past few months. He was always a little...*off*...but I never would have expected him to become this bad."

"And is Rhodes still alive?" Thomas asked.

"As far as I know. He went out the back with the others."

"And who are 'the others'?"

"Sheriff Alanbrooke, Captain Hathaway, and L.T."

"I see." Thomas started tapping his fingers against the table again.

"So what happens now?" Spiers asked.

"Now you do whatever you want. When this is all over, you're free to go," Thomas told him.

"Just like that?"

"Just like that."

"Why the kindness?" Spiers had trouble believing there wasn't a catch.

"I have no reason to kill you. You've done nothing wrong."

Spiers looked down at his hands, and tears began filling his eyes.

"That's...that's not entirely true," he finally said.

"Oh?"

"This morning—when we had that firefight—I was part of that. I think...I think I shot one of the citizens. I- I don't know if he died or not, or if it was even me. But I aimed at him and...and I pulled the trigger." Spiers' eyes were still glazed over, but his voice remained the same and no tears fell. Thomas could see his eyes shine in the moonlight, and it only added to Thomas's belief that Spiers was a good man caught in a horrible world.

"That's different," Thomas said, and Spiers looked up in shock.

"Why are you defending me?" he asked.

"Why are you telling me things that could lead to a very different fate for yourself?" Thomas countered.

"Because I...because I feel obligated. I feel guilty. I was part of that, and it was wrong."

Spiers brought a single hand up and covered his eyes. If he was crying, he was doing an incredibly good job at hiding it.

"Give us a moment," Thomas said to Lee and the others.

"You sure?" Lee asked him.

"I'm sure," Thomas told him as he pulled out his Beretta and sat it on the table in front of him.

Lee, Robert, and the others stepped outside, and Thomas leaned forward over the table far enough that Spiers could just barely see his eyes.

"None of us are innocent anymore," Thomas said calmly, "Not in this new world, this World of the Damned. If we're alive, it's because we have done something bad. Whether it's hurting someone who may not have deserved it, or denying someone food, or water, or safety...we're all guilty of 'bad' things. But intention is everything. Who we are *inside* is everything. I'm sure you were only doing what you thought was right. What's important is that you saw them for what they were, and you did what you thought was necessary to avoid contributing to their crimes any further."

Spiers nodded his head and looked down at the floor once

more.

"Thank you," he said, "for understanding. For not blaming me. I'm not a killer."

"I can see that," Thomas said, "Don't blame yourself."

"This sounds crazy, but..." Spiers rubbed his temples and leaned forward, "...can I help you? To stop them, I mean. I don't...I really don't want to hurt any of them if I don't have to. But I need to make this right. I need to atone for the things I have done, to feel vindicated."

"I'm not sure I can allow that," Thomas told him, "How can I trust you? I mean, my heart tells me you won't betray me. I can see that you're a good person. But can I give you a gun and rely on you to use it against your friends if necessary?"

Spiers swallowed the knot in his throat and quickly nodded his head.

"Like I said, I don't want to hurt any of them if I don't have to. But if it comes to that—if I feel justified in doing it—I will do what's necessary. They have done *horrible* things, and they've dragged me through it all. And I did it out of fear, out of a misguided sense of loyalty. But when I saw that man go down—when Rhodes killed him in cold blood—something inside of me broke. I couldn't bear to be part of it anymore. I knew that they would do something terrible to me if I made that known, so I didn't act immediately. But as soon as I saw an opportunity, I took it. Now all that's left is to stop them from hurting anyone else. I couldn't live with myself if I didn't prevent them from doing that."

"You know what that means, don't you?" Thomas asked him.

"What?"

"Stopping them from hurting anyone else. You know what that requires?"

"I...I'm not following..."

"It's not enough to drive them out, Simon."

Thomas stood and slowly walked around the table. As he came into the candlelight, Spiers saw a look on his face that conveyed determination, disgust, and vengeance.

"If we force them to leave, they'll only go on to hurt more

336

people. It has to end here."

"But I...can't we..."

"There's no other way, Simon. You know that. Have we really done something good, if we make them leave here and allow them to go on to the next town and hurt others? Would that be a victory? Sure, the people of this town would be safe from them, and they would be grateful. But then we would only be pushing the problem off on the next unsuspecting community. Because that's what they'll do, Simon. They'll leave here, defeated, and find somewhere else to build themselves back up. Somewhere else to be tyrants and hurt innocent people. I can't let that happen in good conscience."

"I have a lot of history with those people. I don't want to harm them if it isn't absolutely necessary..."

"You said it yourself, Simon. Just a moment ago you said you couldn't live with yourself if you let them go off and hurt others." Thomas approached Spiers and stopped just a couple feet away. His hands were on his hips in an authoritative manner, and his voice was mostly monotone and stern.

"Christ..." Spiers ran his fingers through his short brown hair and sighed.

"I don't like this anymore than you do," Thomas said, "But this is the world, now. There's no jail. There's no public humiliation, no phones or internet to spread the word. The next town they go to will most likely welcome them with open arms, and they will pay the price for it. And that price will be paid because you and I didn't do everything we could to prevent it."

"May I stand?" Spiers asked. Thomas nodded his head.

Spiers slowly rose to his feet, being careful not to move even an inch toward the handgun laying on the table. Instead he walked around the chair he had been sitting in and peered through the window.

"I said it myself. I couldn't live knowing I let them continue on to hurt others. And you're right, that's what will happen. Tooele...Tooele was terrible. In the weeks leading up to the city being overrun, Alanbrooke was becoming more and more desperate. He could see what was going to happen, and he wanted to retain some level of power no matter what. Needless to say, it didn't go well. Inside I know that he is responsible for what happened there, with it being overrun by the undead. He always said we had to restore order, but it seemed like our methods only caused more *disorder*."

"So are you going to join me, in these things I have to do?" Thomas asked after a brief moment of silence.

"I'll help you," Spiers said, "But please...give me your word that we won't become just like them. We can't be cruel or treat anyone inhumanely. I won't participate in anything like that."

"You have my word that everything we do will be completely justified and right."

* * *

The morning came quick, and Thomas awoke to find himself slumped over in a chair sitting next to Mindy's cot. His sister was still asleep, and for the first time in awhile, Thomas saw genuine happiness on her face. She must have been having a good dream, and that thought alone made him smile. Samantha was on her own cot across the room. Thomas stood and stretched, finding that he felt sore and tight despite the fact that he hadn't done anything too strenuous the day before. He attributed it to extreme stress, and changed into a fresh pair of clothes. Although his attire was simple—a pair of blue jeans, a blue short-sleeve shirt, and work boots—Thomas felt like he was somehow more confident now. A change was occurring inside of him, and he noticed that the way he spoke and carried himself was beginning to convey a certain sense of authority. It had been several days since he had shaved, and much to his dissatisfaction, his facial hair was the thickest and longest it had been since his college days so many years ago. It was almost long enough to consider a beard.

After gently kissing his sister on the forehead while she slept, Thomas made his way into the large open room of the community building. Lee had setup a cot right outside the room Thomas, Mindy, and Samantha had claimed as their temporary home. The older man was already awake, fully clothed, smoking a cigarette, and leaning against the wall like he was standing guard. Thomas nodded his head in greeting and forced a smile, and continued on through the building. Lee fell in behind him.

"Where's Spiers?" Thomas asked him.

"Outside. Don't worry, I got a couple guys watching over him," Lee said as he caught up and walked beside Thomas.

"Your leg still doing okay?"

"Feels great."

"Good. We're bound to have an interesting day ahead of us." Thomas continued walking, but Lee fell behind. He noticed that the iconic rhythm of cowboy boots hitting a hard floor had stopped.

"How far are we going to go with this?" Lee asked.

Thomas stopped and looked down at the floor before turning around and looking his loyal new companion in the eyes.

"What do you mean?"

"With these sheriff guys. There are only four of them left. How much harm can they do?"

Thomas gritted his teeth and looked down at the floor as he slowly approached Lee.

"These men...they killed six citizens of this town in an incident that I can only compare to the Boston Massacre. They wounded my sister," he said, his voice calm and quiet, "Then they murdered Paul in cold blood, blowing his head off right in front of me. I was covered in his blood and brain matter. We'll take this as far as needed to ensure they never do anything evil ever again."

"And how far is that?" Lee asked him, squinting as he always did.

"I guess we'll find out," Thomas replied after a brief pause.

Thomas turned away and walked outside. Spiers was sitting on one of the benches with two men standing guard over him. As soon as he saw Thomas, he quickly stood and slightly nodded his head in his direction.

"Morning," Spiers said.

"Good morning. Are you still wanting to help?" Thomas

asked.

"Yes. My decision won't change."

"Are you committed to this?"

"Yes, I am."

"Good," Thomas touched Spiers on the shoulder and led him over to the sidewalk, "You can be of great help. If you went to them and told them you escaped, they would have no idea that you are working against them."

"You want me to be a double agent?" Spiers asked.

"In a sense, yes. Not for long, of course. I was going to do this another way, but you wanting to help is going to make this a lot easier."

"What exactly are you planning?"

"That's not important, for now. It will all come to pass soon enough. Right now I want you to focus on what you're about to do." Thomas spoke with authority, without even realizing it.

"And what am I about to do?" Spiers seemed a little unsure, no matter how committed he said he was, which was why Thomas wouldn't tell him exactly what the plan was. In fact, no one knew the whole plan. Not even Lee.

"Once we find where they are, you're going to stumble across them. They will take you in, and you will tell them that we took you prisoner. You had to attack me to make it out, and barely escaped."

"And what purpose will this serve?"

"You will be my insurance policy, so to speak. My ace in the hole. It is much easier and safer to strike when your opponent isn't expecting it. More so when they expect you *not* to." Thomas smiled a little, and Spiers nodded his head in understanding.

"If a standoff occurs, you will tip the scales in our favor. Don't worry, all of my men will know you're on our side. No harm will come to you."

"Okay. Let me know when you need me to help."

"Will do. Until then, enjoy the scenery." Thomas shook Spiers' hand and gave him a quick pat on the shoulder before walking over to Lee.

"Everything squared away?" Lee asked him.

"Yes. Where's Robert?"

"Doing some recon. Trying to find where our sheriff friends are hiding," Lee said.

"Not alone, I hope?" Thomas asked.

"Of course not. He has a couple guys with him."

"And we're sure they didn't leave?" Even though Thomas was absolutely certain that Sheriff Alanbrooke wouldn't accept defeat and tuck tail—at least not while he had men to follow his orders— he was worried about being wrong. After all, he didn't even know The Sheriff.

"Well we're not positive, but I agree with you. I don't think they'd do that. They most likely expect us to think they left town, but they're still here. I'm sure of it."

"Okay, well let me know when Robert comes back," Thomas said.

About that time, both Thomas and Lee heard several pairs of boots smacking against concrete from around the corner. Robert and three other men quickly appeared. They were slowly jogging, but didn't look like anything was wrong.

"We got 'em," Robert said before he even stopped running, "They're over on the north side of town, holed up in the old Burns Insurance office."

"Good job, Robert," Thomas said, "Let's get to work."

"What about me?" Spiers asked.

"Come with me," Thomas told him.

Thomas, Lee, and Spiers walked around to the back of the community building. It was a mostly open gravel parking lot, save a couple of cars and a 5 gallon bucket.

"God...smells awful," Spiers said as he buried his mouth and nose in the crook of his arm.

"It has to look legitimate," Thomas said as he stopped in front of the bucket.

"What are you talking about?" Spiers asked.

"Your story will be that you attacked me, right? You're bound to get some of my blood on yourself."

"Aw, shit..." Spiers cursed.

"Don't worry, it won't be much. Too much won't look real. It's lurker blood, after all. Fresh, but it still looks different. Just on your hands and a little on your shirt. It will look like dried blood, and they're unlikely to give it much scrutiny anyway."

"Okay, well let's get this over with," Spiers said.

Thomas nodded his head to Lee, who already knew about this part of the plan. The two of them had discussed it the night before and got the barrel ready. Granted, they weren't relying on Spiers' help, but the original plan had still involved Thomas playing possum.

Lee pulled a large rubber glove out of his pocket and reached into the bucket. From it he pulled a handful of dark red goop, and he walked over to Spiers with it.

"Wait...I'm not going to get infected, am I?" Spiers asked.

"No. We know for certain that won't happen. To prove it, I'll go first," Thomas said as he reached out and wiped his hand across the blood and flesh in Lee's hand.

"Why do you need it?" Spiers asked.

"You injured me, right? I have to play the part as well."

Thomas rubbed his hands in it, then took a little more from Lee and dabbed it on a single spot on his abdomen.

"The story is that you stabbed me in the police station, and the rest of the townsfolk are out looking for you. Some of them decided they didn't have the stomach for this sort of thing after all, and they were scared, so they went back home. It's believable that most of them won't see your old friends as a threat after last night, and won't want to continue anymore violent behavior."

Thomas grabbed a handful of blood from Lee and spread it on Spiers' hands, then wiped his own hand across Spiers' chest.

"That'll do," Thomas said, "Now it's showtime. Repeat the story back to me."

"You guys took me prisoner, early this morning I escaped and stabbed you in the process. Since then I've been wandering around looking for my guys. The townsfolk are out looking for me, but most of them didn't want to participate anymore. They got scared.

You're at the police station, alone."

"Good. Robert will point you in the direction of the office your friends are supposed to be in."

Thomas stuck out his hand to shake, and after Spiers' stared at it for a moment, he took it. It was a gruesome sight: two men with blood-covered hands, shaking hands in a civil manner.

<u>18</u>

Spiers made his way down the street, replaying Robert's directions over in his head. The town was small, and the directions had been simple, but Spiers was a little rattled and nervous. Would Thomas's story work? Surely it would. His sheriff 'friends' had no reason to believe any different.

Spiers turned onto W Erda Way. There were very few buildings in Erda, and as such it was no problem at all to spot the two buildings standing beside each other. One was Burns Insurance, and the other looked like an old bank that hadn't been in business for several years. Spiers looked behind him, as if he was looking to see if he was being followed. He heard shouting on the next street over. The townsfolk were certainly doing a good job at making this look legitimate. Spiers even felt a little like he was really being pursued, like he had really just escaped from custody. In a way, he sort of had.

Right outside Burns Insurance, Spiers stopped in the street and placed his hands on his knees. He gasped for air, as if he had been running for a long time and was winded. He briefly and anxiously looked around. He hoped that he looked lost, desperate. Out of the corner of his eye, Spiers saw movement inside the Burns Insurance building. He pretended not to see it, and started jogging very slowly.

"Spiers!" a voice said.

Spiers stopped and stood straight up, trying to look genuinely surprised.

"Rhodes?" Spiers asked as he looked over at the building. Eli Rhodes was poking his head out of the glass door.

"Get in here!" Rhodes said quietly.

Spiers quickly ran over, rushing through the door and once more resting his hands on his knees.

"Fuck, man! I thought you guys left!" Spiers said. Lieutenant Blythe was standing in the lobby area with Rhodes.

Sheriff Alanbrooke and Captain Hathaway appeared from the back. The Sheriff stared at Spiers for a moment, like he was trying to process what was going on. Hathaway walked right up to Spiers and looked him up and down.

"Whose blood is that?" Hathaway asked.

"That guy who was with the local...Thomas. Had to stab him to escape. Didn't have a choice." Spiers sat down in one of the chairs like he was exhausted.

"So he's dead?" The Sheriff asked.

"I don't know. I got him pretty good, but I think it was in his side or something. I didn't stick around long enough to find out."

"Where is he? What sort of manpower does he have?" Hathaway asked, immediately switching over to tactician mode.

"He's at the police station. Alone, when I left. A handful of locals went out looking for me. I heard them yelling and driving around. Most of them went home, though. Before I escaped, I heard a few of them say they didn't want to fight anymore. They think you guys left town, so I doubt they give a shit about me. There are a few who are still loyal to Thomas, though."

"Is he their leader, now?" The Sheriff asked.

"Guess so, Sheriff. They follow his every word. God, am I glad to have found you guys..." Spiers tilted his head back against the wall and let out a long sigh.

"Let's go get that fucker, Sheriff. End this shit," Rhodes said eagerly.

"Don't worry. You'll get your chance to take some of them out," Alanbrooke told him. Rhodes smiled and nodded his head.

"I can't believe they did that shit last night," Spiers said, "Civilians, for fuck's sake! How many did we lose? I saw O'Doyle

345

and Hood dead in the street on my way out. They just...left them there. Disrespectful bastards."

"Foster was on the roof. They got him, too," Lieutenant Blythe said.

"Shit..." Spiers shook his head and stared down at the floor.

"What's the plan, boss?" Rhodes asked, obviously impatient.

"Well, we know where he is," Hathaway said, "And he's the leader, so if we take him out then we can almost guarantee no one else will step up to the plate. Especially after Spiers said most of them don't want a part in it anymore. Not to mention the fact that it will be the second leader of theirs that we've killed in the last 24 hours."

Hathaway let out a quiet, devilish chuckle. It gave Spiers chills, and it reminded him of what these people had turned into. People he once respected and looked up to. People who had relied on him to do his job and do it well. People who he had devoted a large portion of his life to. He had fought and bled for them more than once, and he had believed in the cause. But there was no cause anymore. Law didn't exist. There were no more courts, or jails, or attorneys. Just people trying to survive any way they could.

"You feel up to going after them with us?" The Sheriff asked Spiers.

"Absolutely, Sheriff," Spiers replied, putting on his best angry and determined face.

"Well, then...let's get this shit over with," Rhodes said with a smile.

* * *

"They're on their way," Lee said as he quickly walked into the small office area of the Erda Police Station.

Thomas got up from behind the desk and took his position on the floor, just outside the booking area and offices.

"Remember, don't come out until I give the order," Thomas reminded Lee.

"Don't worry. We're not gonna jack this up," Lee said with a nod, "I'll make sure of it."

"Remind the guys outside how this is going to go down," Thomas added.

"I will." Lee briskly walked out back, leaving Thomas completely alone inside the police station.

Thomas scooted up against the wall, increasing his breathing to make his injured state look convincing. He placed his right hand over the spot where his wound was supposed to be, on his abdomen close to his right side. He just hoped that his plan wouldn't lead to him sustaining a real injury. Or getting killed. Thus far his plan had worked exactly as intended, and they had really caught a break with Spiers. If it hadn't been for him, they would have had to risk letting one of their people get captured and leading The Sheriff and his men back to the PD.

"Doesn't look like anyone's around," Thomas heard a voice say from the other side of the front door.

"I told you...most of those cowards tucked tail. The ones who didn't are out looking for me." That was definitely Spiers' voice.

The front door opened, and a strong beam of sunlight shone through and hit Thomas right in the face. Thomas held up a shaky hand in front of his eyes, breathing heavily and groaning a little.

"My, my," Alanbrooke began as he walked through the door and looked around, "Looks like somebody bit off more than they could chew."

"Fuck you," Thomas spit out with some effort.

"Good job, Spiers. You got him pretty bad," Hathaway said with a chuckle. His features were just as ugly today as they had been the day before.

"Looks like you're not going to last much longer," Rhodes said with a laugh as he approached Thomas.

"I got nothin' left to live for," Thomas told him, "You bastards killed my sister. I'll welcome death."

"Good to hear," Rhodes said as he raised his assault rifle.

"No!" Spiers let out. All eyes turned toward him, "Let that mother fucker suffer. He's as good as dead."

Rhodes stared at Spiers, and for a moment Spiers thought that

347

Rhodes and the others might be seeing through his bullshit.

"Damn, you're right," Rhodes said to him, then turned back to Thomas, "As much as I'd like putting a bullet in your head, I think I like the idea of you bleeding out much better."

Rhodes bent over at the waist, and reached down to pat Thomas on the head like he was a child. A disgusting, smug grin spread across his face. But Thomas was done acting. In one quick motion, he grabbed the knife he was sitting on with his left hand and forced it straight into Rhodes' right side.

"Checkmate, mother fucker," Thomas growled as he twisted the knife and yanked it out.

That was the codeword, "Checkmate". Lee Granger, in typical gunslinger style, threw open the door leading back to the offices and aimed his Smith & Wesson revolver right at Sheriff Alanbrooke's head. In his other hand was a two-way radio. As four more Erda citizens rushed through the door and stood shoulder-to-shoulder with Lee, the old cowboy held down the transmit button on the radio and repeated the word, "Checkmate". Three more citizens appeared behind Alanbrooke and his men, rushing up the steps and into the lobby. The Sheriff and his four deputies—three, really, since Rhodes took a knife to the ribcage—were surrounded and outgunned.

Rhodes fell over, and as he did so Thomas grabbed the assault rifle from his hands. The Sheriff's eyes were wide with surprise and fear. Captain Hathaway's face was contorted into an angry and disgusted expression now more than ever. Lieutenant Blythe—the more pragmatic one—had already thrown down his weapon and raised his hands in surrender. Spiers pulled out his handgun, as if he was going to fight, but instead turned it on his former comrades.

"What the hell are you doing!?" Sheriff Alanbrooke shouted at Spiers.

"You disloyal, ungrateful, mother *fucker*," Hathaway scowled.

"Don't act like I'm the bad guy here," Spiers said calmly, "You're the bad ones. You're the ones who have earned a ticket on the express lane to Hell."

"I'm bleedin' out over here..." Rhodes said loudly, sprawled out on the floor. His face was white as snow, and a large pool of blood was forming beneath him.

"So what now?" Hathaway growled, "You gonna kill us or what?"

Sheriff Alanbrooke kept looking around the room, as if he couldn't believe he had been outsmarted and ultimately defeated. Most of all, he had been betrayed by his own man.

"I think I dislike you the most," Thomas said to Captain Hathaway, "You and your boss both come off as pompous pricks, but I think you're the one who's responsible for most of this. Your level of narcissism is so extreme that it bleeds through your pores and ends up on those beneath you. There's no room in this world for people like you. Never was, and definitely not now."

"So put a fuckin' bullet in my head," Hathaway roared, "You'd be doing me a favor."

Thomas noticed Sheriff Alanbrooke eying the door that led back to the booking room. The man looked like he would bolt at any moment. Well, "bolt" as fast as any short, overweight, middle-aged man could.

Sure enough, he did. Thomas could have easily grabbed him and thrown him across the room, but he let him go. It was part of the plan, after all. Granted, he hadn't planned on The Sheriff taking *himself* back there, but hey...Thomas accepted any luck he could find.

"Oh, no...don't run..." Thomas said quietly and facetiously as Alanbrooke pushed open the door and ran as fast as he could.

Once Alanbrooke was through the door, there was only one place to go: the booking area. Thomas looked at Lee and nodded his head toward the front door. Lee immediately understood, and told his men to take the other deputies outside. Thomas, on the other hand, walked calmly toward the booking area where Sheriff Alanbrooke had ran. The heavy steel door had been shut, which meant it automatically locked. As he approached the security door that separated the short hallway from the booking room, he saw Alanbrooke on the other side of the glass. The man looked very distraught. He did, however, appear to be experiencing some amount of relief. And why shouldn't he? He was now locked in a secure room, behind bulletproof glass, completely safe from Thomas for the time being.

"All I ever wanted to do was restore order!" Alanbrooke yelled through the glass, his voice muffled, "I have an obligation to the citizens of Tooele County to do that however I must! But you wouldn't understand that!"

Thomas simply stared through the glass, watching intently.

"What do you think's gonna to happen to everyone, huh? What's going to happen when this thing gets worse and there's nobody like me around to coordinate defensive measures, save people, ensure a working community continues to exist!?"

Still, Thomas just stared. There was no expression on his face whatsoever.

"Let me leave here alive, and I'll give you my word that I won't come back around here..."

The Sheriff's words finally made Thomas break his silence.

"You propose now to negotiate? You think I'm going to compromise with you? Show you mercy?" Thomas asked loudly so he could be heard through the glass.

Sheriff Alanbrooke stared at him, breathing heavily.

"All Paul and I wanted to do was negotiate. We wanted to agree to some sort of compromise. But that wasn't good enough for you, was it? It was all or nothing. And now a good man is *dead* because of your evil deeds. Along with six other Erda citizens, and all your deputies. Their blood is on *your* hands."

Just like me, with Mark, and Virginia, and the others, Thomas thought. He banished it from his mind.

"That wasn't me!" Alanbrooke shouted, throwing himself toward the glass and slapping his hands against it, "That was Danny! Captain Hathaway ordered Paul's murder!"

"You're a fucking coward," Thomas told him. Then, "I do hope you enjoy your company, Sheriff. I think you'll find that you have a lot in common with them."

"What? In common? Company? What the hell are you talking about?"

"You're both dead inside," Thomas replied, his cold eyes piercing through Alanbrooke like knives.

Sheriff Alanbrooke heard the moans and groans before he even turned his head. He froze for a brief moment, then looked over his shoulder and saw several lurkers entering the booking room from the changing area. Had Alanbrooke known Thomas's plan, he wouldn't have ran to the booking room for refuge. He would have known that Thomas placed almost a dozen zombies in the back room, and created a simple obstacle so they wouldn't make their debut prematurely. The empty filing cabinet he had placed in the doorway only served to slow them down once they heard and smelled a living human nearby.

"NO!" Alanbrooke screamed, "Let me out!"

"You locked yourself in," Thomas said, holding up the keys to the door, "There's no getting out."

Alanbrooke pulled out his sidearm and began shooting at the lurkers. He hit the first one in the chest, but his second shot hit it square in the head. He was frantic, and backed up as far as he could until he hit the wall. The lurkers were closing the distance across the tiny booking room extremely quickly, and even if Alanbrooke had been able to dispatch them with amazing efficiency, he wouldn't have been able to get them all before they made it to him.

Just before the lurkers were within arm's reach, Alanbrooke stopped firing and held the gun to his head. Thomas felt his heart pounding, but it wasn't from adrenaline. It was from excitement. The extreme fascination of the whole thing satisfied him greatly. His plan had worked, and now the unknown element of the whole thing was about to make itself known. Would Alanbrooke shoot himself before the lurkers got to him, or would he be too cowardly to even do that?

It was the latter. Thomas could see Alanbrooke's hand shaking as he held the gun to his head. The lurkers lunged forward and grabbed at Alanbrooke, who dropped his firearm and tried to push away his undead attackers. The lurkers forced themselves on him and quickly overpowered The Sheriff's small, overweight frame.

Lee appeared. Thomas heard the door open and could just barely see him out of the corner of his eye. But he didn't divert his attention from the scene in front of him. He continued staring, with no expression, and deep down he felt almost giddy. As the lurkers proceeded to rip Sheriff Alanbrooke to shreds, Thomas felt a warm sensation pass over him. Blood squirted in several directions, flesh was ripped from The Sheriff's body by the gnashing teeth of the undead, dying screams filled the booking room and hallway.

"Thomas...let's go," Lee said.

But Thomas didn't answer. He continued staring, fascinated by the scene before him. It was gruesome and horrible and terrifying...but in Thomas's mind, it was the ultimate form of justice. A fitting end for the man who ordered Paul's death. The man who was indirectly responsible for his sister's injury, no matter how superficial it may have been.

"Thomas. He's done. Let's go deal with the others," Lee said, once more trying to break Thomas from his trance. The sight was too much for even Lee to witness, and he turned his back to the scene.

"Just a little longer," Thomas said coldly. Lee stared at him, and his eyes grew a little larger. A growing feeling of concern passed over him, but the cowboy didn't say another word. He simply walked down the short hallway and left.

As the lurkers consumed what was left of Sheriff Kenneth Alanbrooke, Thomas felt his bloodlust continue to grow. That wasn't supposed to happen, was it? Wasn't this supposed to satisfy his thirst for vigilante justice? Wasn't he supposed gain closure from all this? Thomas watched for another moment, until there was no longer a single shred of flesh that resembled the man that The Sheriff once was. Then he nodded his head for no reason in particular and walked off down the hallway.

"They're all outside, just like you asked," Lee said. He was standing in the lobby, waiting for Thomas to finish watching his gruesome show.

"Good."

Thomas walked past Lee and down the front steps. Captain

Hathaway, Lieutenant Blythe, and even Deputy Rhodes, were all lined up in the street. Rhodes was half laying down, using his elbow for support as best he could. His face was still white as a ghost, and Thomas was surprised that he was still drawing breath. Hathaway and Blythe were on their knees.

"Help me," Rhodes let out, although it seemed like he was saying it to no one in particular. Had Mindy been there, she probably would have said that the man was starting to go into shock. Realizing this as a possibility, Thomas approached him first.

"Please," Rhodes whimpered, "Save me. I just need...I just need it stitched up. Please..."

Thomas stared at the man, remaining silent without even a hint of remorse or mercy on his face.

"I...I was just following orders. I never liked those mother fuckers," Rhodes mumbled, but it only came through great effort, "I just had nowhere else...to go. What was I supposed to do? I had no...had no...choice."

Without saying a word, Thomas pulled out his Beretta and pointed it at Rhodes' head. At point blank range, he pulled the trigger. The back of Rhodes' head blew apart, throwing blood, brain matter, and skull fragments all over the road behind him. His lifeless body slumped over.

"Jesus Christ!" Lieutenant Blythe yelled. He was sitting right next to Rhodes.

"Thomas! What the fuck?" Spiers shouted. Thomas shot him a piercing glare.

"Please! Please don't!" Blythe begged, "I'm a good person! I'm a Christian! I never meant to do anything bad!"

"Yet, you did," Thomas said calmly, "You're just as guilty."

"No...*please*," Blythe was crying now, "*Please* don't do this! I'm..."

Thomas abruptly raised his Beretta and aimed it at Blythe's head. The lieutenant fell back on his haunches and threw his hands up in front of his face. Thomas almost pulled the trigger, but stopped himself. He slid the handgun back into his waistband, and Blythe lowered his hands. A look of relief spread across his face,

353

even though his crying continued. But as Thomas reached for the claw bar hanging from his belt, it became clear that he was now offering a far darker fate than being shot in the head. In one swift motion, Thomas pulled the tool from it's leather strap, raised it above his head, and drove it straight into the top of Lieutenant Darren Blythe's skull. Blythe's mouth fell open, the muscles in his face went limp. His arms jerked violently a couple of times, and one brief gurgling noise emitted from his throat. His eyes rolled back in his head, and Thomas forcefully yanked the pointed end of the nail puller out of his skull. Blood poured out of the hole as Blythe's body fell limply to the pavement.

Thomas moved onto Hathaway, whose eyes were wide and locked onto his lieutenant's body. His mouth hung open, shocked at the gruesome execution. After a moment, he forced himself to regain his composure.

"I'm not going to beg," Hathaway said quietly as Thomas stepped in front of him, "Put a fucking bullet in my head."

"Defiant until the end..." Thomas said.

"My family's dead. Fuck it. I've been waiting for a bullet with my name on it." Hathaway sat on the pavement casually, not on his knees or with his hands behind his head.

Thomas looked over at the Tahoe that the deputies had driven to the PD.

"Does that have a can of gas in the back?" Thomas asked him.

"Go fuck yourself," was all Hathaway said.

"Don't worry, I brought my own," Thomas said.

Thomas looked over at Robert and motioned toward the truck with his head. Robert quickly walked over to it and reached into the bed. From it he pulled out a full can of gasoline.

"Anybody live in that house over there?" Thomas asked as he pointed to the little house on the corner. Beside it was a small tool shed.

"Not anymore. Used to belong to one of the aldermen, but he skipped town not too long after all this happened." Robert brought the can of gas over to Thomas.

"Perfect. That's very convenient. Take him inside the shed."

Robert and Joe—one of the participants in the staged altercation—grabbed Hathaway by the arms and dragged him across the street to the small shed. It was very apparent that they were out for blood just as much as Thomas was.

"Thomas, what are you doing?" Spiers asked. Thomas ignored it as he followed the two men to the shed.

Robert kicked open the locked door of the shed and helped drag Hathaway inside. Thomas entered behind them, and started looking around the tiny shed. He finally came across a roll of twine.

"This will do nicely. Tie up his hands and feet," Thomas said as he handed the twine to Robert.

Robert and Joe quickly wrapped up Captain Hathaway's hands and feet. Hathaway put up no fight whatsoever.

"You think you're better?" Hathaway asked from the ground, "If you do this, then you're just a fucking hypocrite."

"No, because the person I'm killing deserves it. He's not some innocent civilian just trying to survive," Thomas replied.

"You're right. He's just an old deputy sheriff trying to survive..." Hathaway countered.

Thomas stared at him for a moment, then popped the top on the gas can and began pouring it all over Hathaway's body and the floor around him.

"Just put a fucking bullet in my head!" Hathaway screamed as gasoline ran down his face.

Thomas and the others stepped outside, and he handed the gas can back to Robert.

"We've all done horrible things!" Hathaway continued to yell, his voice gravelly and roaring, "We're all going to Hell! No one's innocent anymore!"

"Got a light?" Thomas asked. Robert dug around in his pocket and handed Thomas a Zippo.

"Nobody's innocent!" Hathaway continued to yell, "Nobody's innocent! This doesn't make you better!"

Thomas stared into the shed for a moment. He looked down at the lighter in his hand, and flipped the top. This was going to be very satisfying for him. Thomas flicked the lighter with his thumb, and a small flame appeared. But then he thought back to what his sister had told him just a couple of days ago: *We need someone like Vance—someone who doesn't care and can kill anyone who threatens us—but I don't want that someone to be* you.

"Spiers," Thomas said.

"God, Thomas, what the hell..." Spiers said as he walked up to him.

"You do the honors," Thomas said to him.

"I can't do that," Spiers quickly replied.

"This won't change the things you've done to survive!" Hathaway roared, "It doesn't change anything that any of us have done!"

"Have you forgotten why we're here?" Thomas asked, keeping his attention on Spiers, "Why we're doing this? You of all people should know this piece of shit deserves it. You've witnessed more than I have. You said yourself that they had done horrible things. You don't think this death is justified?"

"Thomas..."

"There's no room in this world for people like him. He's worthless. Putting a bullet in his head is too good for him. He needs to suffer before he dies. Do it."

Thomas held out the lighter. Spiers stared at it for a moment before slowly taking it and switching his gaze to the gasoline coating the ground.

"Spiers! You fuckin' traitor! Don't let them do this! Just put a *fuckin'* bullet in my head!" Hathaway screamed.

"Do it, Simon. Light that son-of-a-bitch on fire," Thomas encouraged, taking another step closer to Spiers.

"Thomas, this isn't..."

"Make him pay for all of the things he's done," Thomas interrupted, "Make that bastard suffer."

Spiers looked down at the lighter's flame, his mouth hanging open and his eyes wide.

"Better hurry, before all that gasoline evaporates," Thomas told him.

"You're going to be right there next to me in Hell, Spiers! Right *fucking* next to me!" Hathaway's screams grew more desperate.

Spiers took a deep breath and tossed the Zippo inside the shed. Flames immediately erupted, and Hathaway's terrifying screams filled the air. Through the orange glow, both Spiers and Thomas stared at Hathaway's body writhing around. Spiers quickly turned away and walked off, unable to watch any longer. Thomas continued staring, taking in the sight of Hathaway burning to death and hearing him let out blood-curdling screams. He finally turned away, satisfied with the outcome. And although this whole situation was unfortunate, Thomas could barely hide the fact that he was overjoyed. Not only had he discovered the part of him that was capable of keeping his loved ones alive, but he had formulated and executed a plan that had worked perfectly. Most of all, though, he succeeded in making those bastards suffer. For just a brief moment, he thought back to when he was younger. All of the bullying he had to go through. The tormenting and physical abuse and ridicule. Now *he* was the one who had the power, and no one would ever push him around again.

As Thomas walked back toward the small group of citizens who had made all of this possible, he heard Lee curse behind him.

"Holy shit..." was all the old man said.

Thomas turned around and saw a ghastly sight. The man that used to be Captain Danny Hathaway was now crawling out of the burning shed. Slowly, shakily, the charred body dragged itself along, until it was completely out of the flames. Nearly every inch of Hathaway's body was burnt. Parts of him were burned so bad they were black, and all of the hair on his head was gone. A terrible wheezing sound was coming from him, and it was obvious that only one of his arms was working right. Thomas walked back over to him, stopping just short of his reach. Hathaway, obviously in shock, reached up and grabbed his own face. Nearly the entire left half peeled away in his hand, exposing just flesh and muscle and even a little bone.

"Shoot...me..." Hathaway wheezed.

Thomas pulled out his Beretta and pointed it at Hathaway's head. His finger bounced against the trigger. Hathaway was crying out in pain, and each attempted scream only resulted in a terrible wheezing noise. Parts of his clothes had been completely burned off, while other spots seemed to be melded to his skin. The twine that had held his wrists and ankles together was long gone, completely incinerated by the intense flames. Hathaway's head didn't have a single hair on it, and his entire body really looked like something that crawled out of the depths of Hell. There wasn't a thing about him that resembled the Danny Hathaway from just a minute ago.

"Do it," Hathaway strained to say, "Shoot...me..."

Hathaway reached up and weakly grabbed the end of Thomas's handgun. He attempted to pull it closer to his head, but was obviously unable to. After a few terrifying moments, Thomas stuck the Beretta back in his waistband and turned away.

"Let the mother fucker die a slow death," he said, and walked away.

"Spiers..." Hathaway moaned, "Kill...me...!"

Spiers walked up to his former captain and pointed his own handgun at his head.

"Do it!" Hathaway groaned.

Spiers felt his hand shaking violently. He touched the trigger with his fingertip, but just as he was about to grant Hathaway's request, he stopped himself. This same man had ordered so many ruthless, cruel things. Spiers had once witnessed him push a man off a bridge because he was defending his supplies from the deputies. Thomas was right: How could Spiers justify showing him any mercy now? Not to mention the fact that Thomas had told everyone to leave him be. Spiers didn't want to make any enemies now that he was finally free of his superior's control. As horrifying as it was to watch, and as cruel it was to let Hathaway die from blood loss, or gangrene, or infection, or shock, Spiers somehow felt okay with leaving him that way. The man was inconsiderate, narcissistic, cruel, crooked...evil. He always had been. Something about it still didn't feel right, but Spiers accepted it for what it was.

He put his handgun back in its holster and stepped away from his former captain. Hathaway's outstretched hand fell to the ground, and his wheezing slowed...

<u>19</u>

Thomas walked through the open doors of the Erda community building. He slumped down into the first chair he came across, completely exhausted. It felt as if a huge weight had been lifted from his shoulders. He looked down at his hands, still stained with the blood of the lurker and also covered in the fresh blood of Eli Rhodes. Thomas closed his eyes and replayed the events in his head. In his mind's eye, he could see Alanbrooke getting torn apart by lurkers. He saw himself stabbing Rhodes, and then shooting him. Brutally piercing Blythe's skull with his claw bar. Pouring gas on Hathaway. Had it all been too much? No, of course not.

"Glad to see you're okay," Mindy said as she appeared from the back room, breaking Thomas from his trance, "I've been so damn worried. Wasn't sure how it would all turn out."

Thomas looked up at her, and he extended a hand as his sister approached him. Mindy looked down at it, noticing the dried blood, but took it anyway. The two hugged, and for just a moment, they both felt like everything was okay.

"It's all over, sis," Thomas told her, "The town's safe."

"Good."

"My plan worked. Those guys will never hurt anyone again."

"That's good, bub. What happened?"

Thomas pulled away from Mindy a little and looked down at the floor.

"They're all dead. Except for the one who surrendered. He helped us."

Mindy looked away from Thomas, her gaze focused on the wall behind him. After a brief moment, she stepped away and gave him an awkward smile.

"I'm glad you're okay," she said once more, then turned and walked away.

"Sis," Thomas said when she was about halfway across the room.

"Yeah?"

"I didn't forget my promise to you."

Mindy smiled once more, although she looked sad. When Mindy didn't respond, Thomas said something that he knew she could never ignore.

"Love you, sis."

"Love you too, bub."

Thomas watched as his sister—the only blood relative that he knew for sure was alive—quietly walked away to their room. He wondered what was going on inside her head. He wondered if she somehow knew the horrible things he had done, if she was starting to see him as a monster. He wondered if she somehow knew that he had lied to her about keeping his promise.

"You doin' okay?" Lee's voice startled Thomas as he was deep in thought. The old cowboy was nonchalantly walking into the building, his duster pulled back behind his holster and his hand resting on the grip of his revolver.

"Doing fine, thanks. What about you?"

Lee stepped in front of Thomas and pulled a chair up. As he sat down, he pulled out his pack of cigarettes.

"Want one?" he offered.

"Sure."

Lee pulled out two smokes and handed one to Thomas.

"There's somethin' I don't get, pardner," Lee began as he held out his lighter.

"What's that?" Thomas asked as he took the lighter from Lee's hand.

"Why the cruelty? Don't get me wrong...those bastards deserved everything they got and then some. But the things you

361

did..." Lee paused and took a drag off his cigarette, "That's somethin' only a man with a long-held grudge would do."

"Guess I'm just tired of people taking advantage of other people."

"It's more than that," Lee said.

"Hey, you said they deserved it..."

"Yeah, and I mean that. But feeding a man to lurkers? Lighting a guy on fire? A man out for a little vigilante justice doesn't do things like that. Why not just put a bullet in their heads and be done?"

Thomas coughed slightly as he exhaled his first drag of cigarette smoke.

"It served a purpose," he answered quietly.

"Just you and me here, pardner. What purpose did it serve?"

"Would you cross someone who burned a man alive?" Thomas casually asked him.

"Probably not," Lee replied.

"And would you learn that crimes against your fellow man are no longer tolerated by that person anymore?"

"Yes."

"Then it served its purpose. Yes, it was extreme. But I've had a life of watching the strong lord over the weak, the cruel and unworthy pushing around good people who deserve more than they have. I'm done with that. Wherever I go, I want to make it known that I have no tolerance for people like Alanbrooke, Hathaway, Rhodes...the rest of those guys. People will be afraid to cross me."

"Well, you've succeeded." Lee stood up and put the chair back. As he walked past Thomas, he paused and gave him a quick pat on the shoulder.

"Lee?" Thomas said before the cowboy could make it to the door.

"Yeah?" Lee asked from over his shoulder, stopping halfway to the door.

"The things that happened today...my sister doesn't need to know."

Lee faced forward and slowly started walking again.

"I know, pardner," he said, "I know."

Thomas smoked the rest of his cigarette like a robot, staring wide-eyed at the floor in front of him. He only hoped that he could separate the two parts of him. The cruel, ruthless man he was becoming could not carry over into the sympathetic, caring brother that his sister wanted him to be.

After smoking the cigarette down to the butt, Thomas got up and walked outside. He flicked the cigarette into the street, and felt the cool breeze against his hot forehead. Spiers walked around the corner of the building just a moment later, and he approached Thomas in a cautious manner.

"Thomas..." he said, stopping beside him, "What do we do now? Where do we go?"

"You're coming with me?" Thomas asked.

"Where else am I going to go? I don't want to stay here, staring into the faces of the citizens everyday, knowing that most of them probably despise me."

"I think you've made your peace with them."

"Even so, I don't want to be here. The whole place just feels...*wrong*. The shit that happened yesterday morning—the massacre I was apart of—then killing people who I once called friends and mentors. I can't stay here."

Thomas turned and looked at Spiers' face. As hard as it was, Thomas saw a gentle and honest person.

"My sister and I are going to Albuquerque. Our parents live there. Hopefully they still do. We have to find them."

"Well, I'd like to go with you," Spiers said.

"I'd be happy to have you along," Thomas replied, and shook Spiers' hand, "And thanks again for helping us. You did a good thing."

"Yeah," Spiers said quietly. Deep down he felt just as guilty now as he had for shooting at the citizens of Erda. He still felt wrong, ashamed...*bad*. But he didn't say anything about that. He told himself that it would pass in time, and eventually he would see that what he did was right. After all, he had just been following orders. And what had happened to Sheriff Alanbrooke? Spiers had

363

heard talk about him being torn to shreds by zombies. Was that true? How would that have happened? And what about Fields and Williams, the two deputies who were injured in the shootout with the townsfolk? Thomas had told that cowboy guy—Lee—to take them to the 'location'. Where the hell was that? What had come of them?

It had all happened so *fast*. If he had been given time to think about it, would he have tossed the lighter? Would he have set Captain Hathaway ablaze and then left him for dead? Probably not. Why had Thomas done that? Why had he made *Spiers* do that? Deep within the dark recesses of his heart, Spiers felt a small spark of satisfaction with what he had done. He knew it was inherently wrong. It was inhumane and cruel and terrible...but Captain Danny Hathaway was such a horrible person. How many people had he killed, either directly or indirectly? How many fathers had he taken away from sons, and vice versa? Spiers looked into himself for a moment, and found that spark of satisfaction once more. He took it and fueled it even further, telling himself that Hathaway fully deserved what he got and that what he had done had not only been acceptable, but *just*. Thomas was right...there was no room in this world for people like Hathaway. Never had been.

* * *

Thomas helped Mindy and Lee load up their supplies in their new vehicle. Thomas had found it across town in a gravel parking lot. An older Chevy Blazer, ripe for the taking. Thomas was a little sad to leave the Durango behind, but with a shattered window it was too risky to continue using it as their form of transportation.

"Think this is the last of it," he said to Lee as he handed him a cardboard box full of canned goods.

"Hey Thomas..."

Thomas turned and saw Robert walking down the sidewalk. His shotgun was hanging from his shoulder by a strap, and his pants were still tucked into his boots.

"Hey," Thomas said.

"Look, uh..." Robert's voice got quiet and a look of disappointment spread across his face, "Turns out that a lot of people left here while we were dealing with The Sheriff and his deputies. Guess they didn't want to get caught in the crossfire, or maybe they didn't agree with what we were doing. I dunno. Thing is...I don't want to stay here anymore."

"Why not?" Thomas asked.

"It's my town and all, but I just feel like I need to move on. With Paul being dead and a lot of people leaving and all that...it just doesn't feel right sticking around. Not to mention all of the changes people are wanting to make."

"The other citizens will need you. Someone needs to lead them."

"Yeah, well that someone isn't gonna to be me." Robert took a deep breath and sighed, "There aren't many left to lead, anyway."

"How many are left?"

"Between all the people we lost when that horde passed through, the handful who were killed by the deputies, and the folks who left...not many. A few dozen, maybe."

"What about the elderly? The sick?"

"They're being taken care of. The whole town didn't pack up and leave, but...a lot of folks did. Maybe it's for the better. Less mouths to feed," Robert let out an awkward chuckle, "People are shook up over what's happened the past couple days. They don't want to do anything to spark violence. A bunch of them are talking about making it a law that no one can carry guns, except for an 'approved' security team. Some of 'em want to stop doing the community supply thing and switch to everyone fending for themselves. It's like they want to close themselves off from everyone except their own households."

Thomas looked down at the ground, thinking about what Robert had said. Did the man secretly feel a little guilty, like this was all somehow his fault? Did he regret what Thomas had done?

"I'm sorry, Robert. For everything."

"Not your fault, buddy." Robert shrugged his shoulders and sighed again.

"What about the people who helped us?" Thomas asked.

"Hell, some of them have already left. To be honest, a lot of them are horrified with..." Robert paused and looked at Thomas awkwardly, "...they just didn't like how things went down. They were thankful that you stepped up to the plate and took care of business, but...they're all just simple people. Farmers, mostly. They don't want to be involved in stuff like what we did."

"What we *had* to do," Thomas added.

"Yeah, with what we *had* to do," Robert nodded his head in agreement, "I think a lot of them are a little traumatized. They just weren't expecting it to get that messy, ya know?"

"What about you?"

"I'm okay," Robert said, "I mean, it's a shame things had to go down like that. But it is what it is, right? Honestly, some of those people blamed me. Doesn't matter. I know what we did, and I know it was right."

Thomas wanted to ask, *What about burning a man alive? Was that right?*

"We're going to Albuquerque. Sure you want to go with us?" Thomas asked him, deciding instead to leave the discussion where it was.

"Yeah, doesn't matter where we go," Robert shook his head, "Look, I respect you for what you did. You saved this town, and I'm sure everybody is grateful for that. You're a good person."

"So are you, Robert," Thomas said, "I'd be honored to have you along."

The two shook hands, and Thomas gave Robert a friendly, welcoming smile.

"You'll have to find a ride, though," Thomas told him, "We've already got five in our group. It'll be better this way, anyway. Not so cramped. And it's good to have an extra vehicle around, just in case."

"Sure thing. I got my truck."

"Good. Be sure to stock up on as much gas and other supplies as you can. We're going to head out by two o' clock, if we can," Thomas said.

"Got it. I'll be ready."

Robert nodded his head at Thomas before turning and walking away at a fast pace down the street. Thomas smiled to himself, happy to finally have a capable group. But that also meant more people who he would be responsible for. More mouths to feed, more tempers to control, more lives in his hands. Was he ready for that? Thomas wasn't sure, but he knew he would find out soon enough. And what about the remaining citizens of Erda? For some reason, Thomas had imagined them picking him up and carrying him through the streets like a hero. He hadn't heard any praise, not that he really needed it. But if he were to stay, hypothetically, would the citizens allow it? Or would they tell him to leave? Or perhaps they would be so scared of him that they wouldn't say a word about it? Thomas decided that it was better to be feared and alive, than revered and dead.

"Still carrying around that claw bar?" Lee's voice startled Thomas a little.

"Yeah, it's better than that old tire iron," Thomas replied. He looked down at the claw bar hanging from his belt. He had made a makeshift hangar for it out of an old leather strap he had found. It was simply a small loop tied to his belt, and the claw bar hung from it by its hook and handle.

"I suppose it is," Lee said.

"No one wants to get killed by a nail puller," Thomas joked, though there was a coldness in his eyes when he said it.

"Didn't know lurkers were afraid of death," Lee said.

"No, but people are. If I've learned anything on my journey thus far, it's that *people* are the biggest threat. Lurkers don't betray you, or have some ulterior motive. We know exactly what to expect from them."

"True. It's unfortunate that it has to be that way." Lee closed the short distance between him and Thomas and stopped just a little more than a foot away.

"It doesn't have to be that way," Thomas said, "I will make sure that we take care of anyone who proves to be a threat to us."

Lee smiled slightly and tipped his hat to Thomas before slowly walking away.

* * *

Thomas and his new group finished eating lunch around noon.
They were all ready to go and ahead of schedule, which made
Thomas feel good for some reason. Mostly because the people he
had with him were efficient and quick to accomplish their goals. It
assured him that they would be able to handle future situations that
demanded such qualities.

Thomas got up from the picnic table and walked outside of the
community building. It was a hot, dry day. He wiped the sweat
from his brow and headed over to his new vehicle. The Blazer was
packed full of supplies. Everything from the Durango, plus Lee's
belongings (which wasn't much), and a few other things they had
found around town. Simon Spiers was leaning against the Blazer,
his arms crossed and his gaze directed at the ground.

"You ready to go?" Thomas asked him.

"Yep."

"Good. Everyone is done eating, so I figure we'll head out
within the hour."

"Sounds good."

Spiers smiled softly, although it didn't seem genuine. Thomas
slowly stepped closer to him and put a hand on his shoulder.

"I know you don't like what happened yesterday," Thomas
began, "But I want to assure you that what you did was right. You
know better than I do that those men were horrible creatures. They
deserved more torturous deaths than what they got."

"I know," was all Spiers said.

"And at the end of the day, everything that happened is on me.
You were just following my orders."

Spiers' eyes locked onto Thomas. *You were just following my
orders.*

Thomas patted Spiers on the shoulder once more and then
walked away. As he did, he began thinking about what he had just
said. Spiers had only done what Thomas told him to do. Yet

Thomas had killed Rhodes and Blythe for following the orders of their superiors. What did that make Thomas? He banished the thought from his mind, not wanting to contemplate the potential hypocrisy any longer.

Thomas pushed through the doors of the community building and saw his group sitting around chatting with each other. They all quieted when they noticed he had entered, and all eyes were upon him.

"Is everybody ready to go? If so, let's work on getting out of this place," Thomas said.

Everyone stood and made their way outside, except for Mindy. She stopped just a couple of feet in front of Thomas and waited for the others to leave.

"Thomas..." she said.

"Hey, how's your arm?"

Thomas stepped forward to give his sister a hug, but she backed away and placed a hand on his chest.

"My arm is fine," she said.

"Mindy..."

"Promise me..." Mindy paused and looked down at the floor.

"What, sis?"

"Promise me you won't change. Promise me you'll always be my brother."

Thomas stared into his sisters eyes for a moment with a blank stare.

"Mindy, I'm still your brother. I'll always be here for you."

Mindy gave her brother a forced smile before stepping forward into his embrace. But her hug was weak and empty, and after just a couple of seconds she pulled away and stepped past him. Thomas watched her walk through the front doors of the building before following her out.

Lee was putting the last box of supplies in the back of the Blazer, while Robert was topping off his truck's gas tank. Samantha was already sitting in the backseat of the Blazer, the door hanging open to let the breeze in. Mindy was sitting down on the curb, staring at the ground and gripping her hurt arm.

"We're all ready to go," Lee said as he slammed the hatch shut on the Blazer.

"Good deal. Anyone have anything they want to do before leaving?" Thomas asked.

Robert looked around, his hands resting on his hips. Lee waited patiently, looking for all the world like a gunslinger from the Old West. His face wasn't visible, hiding behind his cowboy hat with his head tilted down. His duster was thrown back around his holstered revolver, and his hand rested on the gun's handle.

"Yeah, I'm ready. There's nothin' else here," Robert finally said. Then, after a pause, he added, "Nothin' but old memories of happier times, anyway."

<u>20</u>

The group had been on the road for just over five hours, and everyone was starting to get restless. Thomas's lower back was hurting pretty bad, and Mindy had already said that she was getting a headache. The group had only stopped once during the journey to stretch their legs. Samantha looked tired as hell, but she hadn't taken a nap. She just continued staring out the window, watching the landscape pass by at 70 miles per hour.

Just as Thomas was about to pull over in the desolate area that was southern Utah, they passed a sign for the next town. It was called *Blanding*, and it was only five miles ahead. Thomas decided to wait until they got there, and hopefully there would be some sort of refuge.

Blanding was a small town of only 3,000 or so people. Or at least, that's how many inhabitants it had *before* the plague. Now it looked like a ghost town. There wasn't a soul to be seen, and only the occasional abandoned vehicle marked the streets. Dried blood was periodically seen on the sidewalks, in the road, and on the side of buildings. Down a side street, a stray dog was chewing on half of a human carcass. All Thomas could think was, *At least it isn't moving.*

Thomas turned into the parking lot of a sporting goods store and brought the Blazer to a halt. He pushed open his door and slowly got out, feeling as stiff as an old man. Mindy and Samantha quickly hopped out, while Lee moved just as slowly as Thomas had. Behind them, Robert pulled his old Dodge truck in and parked it several yards behind the Blazer. He and Simon crawled out and stretched.

"Grab a couple of those guns from the back of the Blazer," Thomas said as he looked over at Robert.

The group had confiscated two M4 assault rifles and one MP5 submachine gun from the deputies back in Erda. Robert walked over to the Blazer's hatch and grabbed two of the M4s. He had his own hunting rifle, so he tossed one of the assault rifles to Spiers. The deputy instinctively checked the magazine and chamber. Robert tried to hand the other to Lee, who shook his head and turned away.

"I'll take it," Thomas said.

Robert handed it to him, and Thomas looked over the weapon. He had inspected one of the M4s earlier that morning to familiarize himself with it. It still felt alien in his hands.

"It's coming up on supper time," Robert said, "Want to eat here?"

Thomas looked around them. There was nothing moving, which was a good sign. No sounds of death and terror could be heard.

"Yeah, let's go ahead and eat."

The group tore into the first box of food, grabbing an assortment of canned goods and bags of chips. Thomas wasn't feeling very hungry, but he made himself eat a stick of jerky.

"Those rations aren't going to get us very far," Lee said quietly as he walked up behind Thomas.

"I know. Not as much as it looks, is it?"

"Nope. We need to scavenge for supplies at every opportunity." Lee pulled out a cigarette and lit it.

"You're right. That's who we are now...scavengers."

"Yep. Our whole world revolves around it."

"I guess I didn't really know what it would be like," Thomas began, "Mindy and I have been in Seattle all this time, in a safe area of the city guarded by Army guys. Jesus...it seems like so long ago. What has it been? Not even two weeks? I've lost count of the days."

Lee took a long drag from his cigarette and continued scanning their surrounding area.

"Days like these will make ya' old," the cowboy said.

Thomas chuckled.

"They'll make ya' somethin', that's for damn sure."

"Guess I'll grab a bite to eat," Lee said, "You should, too. More than just a stick of jerky, anyway."

"Yeah, I'll try. Thanks."

Thomas continued looking around while everyone else ate. The town was eerily quiet. Surely there was *someone* still around, whether alive or dead. Instead the streets were completely silent. Not even the wind was blowing. The only sign of life had been that dog, but he was nowhere around anymore. Thomas threw the last bite of jerky in his mouth and tossed the M4's strap over his shoulder.

And then a disturbing realization hit him. Blood stains...but no bodies. Not a single sign of death, save the dried blood. If lurkers had been responsible for cleaning the streets of corpses, then wouldn't they still be around? That only left one logical conclusion...

"Guys," Thomas began, "Get up!"

"What is it?" Robert asked, immediately jumping to his feet and gripping his hunting rifle with both hands. Spiers was right behind him.

"I don't think we're alone here," Thomas said as he looked around.

"What do you mean?" Lee asked him.

"Bodies...there aren't any bodies..."

"Yeah?" Spiers said, obviously confused.

"No lurkers, and no bodies. But there's blood. What does that tell you?"

"We're not the only ones alive in this town," Lee chimed in.

"Exactly," Thomas said, a hint of worry on his face.

"Well that's not necessarily a bad thing," Robert suggested, "More people means safety."

"Not if those people want to kill you and take your supplies," Thomas said.

After The Hill, after Erda...Thomas had grown so distrusting of other human beings that he could only think about bad outcomes when faced with the prospect of meeting someone new. He realized that not everyone was bad, but it was the *possibility* that worried him. Unnecessary risks could not be taken, not now. Not when they were so close. Not after all of the death that had been left in his wake. Not after Mark and Virginia, and Logan. Not after Overfield, and Derek, and McCoy. Most certainly not after Sheriff Alanbrooke and his crooked deputies.

"So what do we do?" Lee asked as he walked up beside Thomas.

"We only have a couple of hours before we start losing daylight," Thomas told him, "We can't afford to leave, not when there are empty buildings to stay in."

"What about our friends who are probably still around?" Lee asked.

"We'll find somewhere to go. Now. We'll post a guard and take shifts. If they find our vehicles, then hopefully they won't be able to find *us*."

"Alright. Where do you want to go?" Lee had become the de facto *consigliere*, and as such was doing everything he could to carry out Thomas's requests.

"There," Thomas said, and he pointed.

Not very far down the road—back the way they came—and on the other side of the street was a dollar store. It was a small building, but it had two garage doors on the side of it and the area around it was open and flat. The back half of it appeared to be older than the front half, suggesting that the part with the garage doors used to be some sort of shop.

The group immediately loaded up and drove to the dollar store. They parked their vehicles directly in front of the garage doors, so that they could pull inside once they cleared the building. Assuming the inside of the old shop wasn't packed full of junk, of course.

Spiers and Lee walked around to the front of the building shoulder-to-shoulder, Thomas and Robert following close behind them. Thomas still had the M4, while Robert had his handgun out and his rifle slung over his shoulder. Samantha and Mindy stayed in the Blazer with the doors locked.

Through the store's windows, the four men could see merchandise still on the shelves. It looked like it had barely been touched. Securing the front doors, however, was a logging chain and a big padlock.

"Doesn't do much good when the doors are made of glass," Spiers said with a grin.

"Or when the owners are most likely dead." That came from Lee, but he did not grin. His face was as stoic as ever.

Both Spiers and Lee turned to look at Thomas, as if asking for his approval to break in. Thomas gave them a nod, and Spiers forcefully shoved the muzzle of his M4 through the front door's glass. The window exploded, sending a pile of tiny glass shards to the ground in front of them. Spiers went in first, ducking down to squeeze beneath the horizontal handle going all the way across the inside of the door. Once inside he quickly stood and brought the assault rifle to his shoulder, scanning the store for potential threats. Lee crawled inside right behind him, also bringing up his revolver and scanning.

After Thomas and Robert made their way in, the group slowly and quietly made their way down the main part of the store. They checked every isle as they went by, and so far it looked completely abandoned. As they made their way further in, the ambient light from outside grew dimmer. Spiers turned on the flashlight that was attached to the rail of his rifle, as did Thomas. Robert pulled out his own flashlight, shining it around them quickly. Lee did not have a light, but he didn't seem to be too perturbed by this fact.

No noises, no movement. The men cleared the whole store without incident. The shelves were still mostly stocked, although the store didn't have much in the way of food. There was an assortment of junk food, as well as bottled water and sports drinks, but not much more. They didn't care, though. Food was food, good or bad, and water was always a blessing. And while the store lacked a plethora of nutrition, it did, however, offer an abundance of miscellaneous supplies. Toothpaste, soap, over the counter medication, cheap clothing, gardening tools, silverware...things that were not absolutely necessary to survival but had great value nonetheless.

"Hopefully the back is the same way," Thomas said once they had determined that the store was safe.

"Yeah...hopefully. I've come to always assume that my luck is going to be shit..."

Thomas chuckled at Lee's response as the cowboy opened the door in the very back of the store. They stepped through the threshold, and were immediately greeted with an even bigger surprise than before. In front of them sat numerous boxes and crates of supplies. Except these did not appear to be items normally stocked in a dollar store. One crate contained an assortment of ammunition, while another had several machetes, hatchets, and pry bars.

"Holy shit..." Robert whispered as he looked around.

"No signs of life," Lee said.

"Let's assume there is," Thomas told them.

The shop was mostly one big room, except for a small bathroom and an office. There wasn't a body to be found—living or dead—and there were still no signs of anyone currently living there.

"Guess we hit the jackpot," Spiers said once they were through clearing the building.

"No room for the vehicles," Thomas said, "Let's get the girls in here and then we can go through all this stuff."

"What about our supplies? Want to bring them in?" Robert asked.

"No, I think we have enough to fall back on if the vehicles get broken into during the night..."

* * *

An hour had passed since they had brought Mindy and Samantha inside, and the group had been spending all of their time sorting through supplies and making sure the building was secure. If a door didn't have a lock, then they reinforced it with a shelf or piece of cord tied around the handle and attached to something heavy. Even though there hadn't been any sign of lurkers in town, Thomas feared a horde might pass through. He had unfortunately seen the horrifying effects of hordes before, and was utterly terrified of them. He was, however, more afraid of a living threat.

"You think whoever put this stuff here is dead?" Robert asked after moving a box of bottled water to the main area of the old shop.

"Hope so," Thomas said.

"I'm betting the owners did this. Probably put a big lock on the front door to keep looters out. Maybe they didn't want to stay where all their supplies were? Or maybe they went out and got killed?"

"No, I don't think so," Spiers said as he approached them, "The lock obviously didn't do much to secure the place. It doesn't make any sense that it would be put there to prevent a break in. It would be more of a deterrent, I would think."

"Well, whoever they were and whatever their reasons, they sure left us with a nice gift," Lee said.

"Let's focus on consolidating some of this stuff and getting it ready to take with us in the morning," Thomas began, "Obviously food and water come first, but ammunition for our current weapons comes second. Get as much of it as you can. We'll go through the hygiene stuff after that, and then start on all the other useful items. Tools, medicine, stuff like that."

Spiers and Robert took off to carry out Thomas's orders. Lee appeared from the shadowy corner of the shop and walked up beside Thomas. The two of them stared at the floor for a moment, as if neither one knew the other was there.

"Thank you," Thomas said, "For everything."

Lee looked up at him and gave him a soft smile.

"No thanks needed, pardner," he replied, "You saved my life."

Thomas nodded his head and returned the smile, then he walked over to a nearby crate and sat down on it. Lee followed him, taking off his cowboy hat as he took a seat. It was a rare occurrence; the older man almost never removed his hat.

"Ya know..." Thomas began, and after a sigh and a brief pause he continued, "I envy you. You have nothing to lose. You just have to look out for yourself. But me..."

Thomas stopped and looked down at the floor. He sighed again and then lifted his head up.

"...Me? I have everything to lose. My parents might already be dead, and if they're not there's a good chance they will be. My sister is the only family I know for certain isn't dead, and she resents me. I pretend to not realize it, but I do. She started thinking differently of me after The Hill..."

"The Hill?"

"Long story..." Thomas shook his head, "...and then after Erda, after the things that happened there, I'm not sure she will ever look at me the same. She doesn't know everything. Not specifically, anyway. But we're close. We *were* close. We can look into the other one's eyes and know exactly what is going on. She thinks I'm not the same person because of what I've done since leaving Seattle. Hell, *I'm* not even sure I'm the same person. But everything I did was for her. She's what matters most to me. Without her, I might as well be a lurker. What kind of hell is this? This is my existence now: keeping my sister and myself alive so we can grow more distant. I don't know if you believe in God or not, but I can tell you that I certainly do not. If God exists, then he's one hell of a sadistic bastard."

Lee squinted his eyes as he stared on at Thomas. There was a wisdom in his eyes, ever present to the mindful observer. There was also a deep pain...a hidden sorrow. After a long and almost awkward silence, the old cowboy's crackly voice cut through the air.

"I had a wife, and two daughters," he said, "Had myself a nice ranch in Wyoming. I inherited it from my father, but back then it

378

was small. Had less than thirty head of cattle. But I worked my ass off, and ended up owning over a thousand acres, had more than a hundred head of cattle, and twenty horses. Everything I worked for is gone now, lost to those things you call *lurkers*. So is my wife, and both of my daughters. All three of them were taken from me in one evening. Didn't even have time to mourn. If it hadn't been for one of my ranch hands, I would have died there with them. He pulled me out of there, risked his neck to save my old ass. And now he's dead too."

Thomas stared at Lee, all at once realizing just how wrong he had been.

"You're wrong about me," Lee continued, "I still got somethin' to lose. I have the memory of my family to lose, because when I'm dead—when my luck runs out and those undead *things* finally tear me to shreds—there won't be any memory of them left. No, I don't believe a god exists. And if he does, to hell with 'em."

"I'm- I'm sorry, Lee," was all Thomas said.

"Don't be sorry. But you do whatever the hell you have to do to keep you and yours alive. No matter what. No matter how sick it makes you—no matter how ruthless you have to be—you do what's needed. This is a very different world now. Some folks will never realize that, or just refuse to. But that doesn't change it any. There aren't any expectations anymore, no checks and balances. We can't rely on anyone else to make sure those around us are playing by the rules."

"You said you never had anybody to lose," Thomas said after a moment of silence.

"Yeah, I know."

"I understand why. I'm sorry I assumed."

"No reason to be sorry, pardner."

Lee got up, and Thomas could have sworn there were tears forming in his eyes. Thomas felt like crying himself. His wife *and* two daughters? How the hell does a person keep going on after something like that? Thomas didn't know, and he never, *ever* wanted to find out.

* * *

Morning came quicker than Thomas would have liked. He had taken first watch, and then it took him several hours to finally fall asleep. Now it was 6:30 in the morning, and his back was so stiff he could hardly stand up straight. He tried to ignore it, however, and set his focus on getting ready to leave.

Everyone else seemed to be moving just as slowly. Lee's age seemed abundantly apparent as he got ready. Thomas was expecting his knees to start making creaking noises at any moment. Spiers and Robert were both very quiet, but they moved swiftly to load up the supplies. Samantha barely seemed awake, and the girl had not spoken more than a couple of words since yesterday morning. Mindy seemed to be doing okay, but her arm was obviously giving her problems. The wound itself had been superficial, but now it was sore and Thomas feared infection.

"How's the arm, sis?" Thomas asked her as he gave her a gentle pat on the back.

"Fine."

"Let me see it."

"It's fine, Thomas."

"Mindy, let me see it."

"I'm a nurse!" Mindy shouted.

The others immediately stopped what they were doing and looked over at the siblings. Thomas froze in place, shocked that his sister had just yelled at him.

"I know, sis," he said softly, "but I want to make sure it's okay."

Mindy looked around at the eyes staring at her. She let out an exhausted sigh as she reached up and peeled back the gauze from the wound on her arm. Thomas leaned in and inspected it closely.

"It looks like it might be infected," he told her. The wound was slightly puffy and red.

"Is that your professional opinion?"

Thomas looked at his sister and gave her a forced smile, trying to keep her mood as calm as possible.

380

"We didn't find any antibiotics here, did we?" he asked the others.

"Nothing I saw," Spiers said.

"Damn."

"It's fine, Thomas. There's no need to worry yet." Mindy's tone was much more relaxed now.

"Just keep taking care of it," Thomas said to her.

The group finished loading up their newly acquired supplies, packing the back of the Blazer as well as the bed of Robert's truck. They didn't have room for all of it, but it would have to do. Spiers was keeping watch while they did this, scanning the southern side of the building. The town still looked completely empty. Still no sounds, still no activity.

And then the all-too comfortable silence was broken. The sound of a vehicle's engine could be heard from deeper within the small town.

"Heads-up!" Spiers said loudly, although everyone else had heard the noise as well.

"Inside!" Thomas shouted, pushing Samantha and Mindy through the open garage door.

"Robert! Go in there with them and shut the door!"

Robert slung his rifle over his shoulder and grabbed the MP5 from the back of the blazer before following the girls inside.

Thomas, Lee, and Spiers took cover behind Robert's truck, staring down the road and waiting for whatever was coming their way. Thomas's heart was pounding, and it felt as if it were in his throat. He could feel his whole body shaking with adrenaline. A deafening ring filled his ears, and his visioned narrowed. His entire focus was on the road.

"Sounds like more than one," Lee said, his voice calm.

"Yeah, definitely at least two cars," Spiers added.

"We're just going to hide and hope they pass," Thomas said. His voice was slightly shaky, but he wasn't afraid. There was no sense of fear inside of him, only uneasy anticipation.

A red Chevrolet Impala appeared from around the bend in the

road. Only seconds behind it was another vehicle, an older model Jeep Wrangler. Thomas pulled his head down behind the bed of Robert's truck, so that his eyes were barely looking over. Lee and Spiers did the same.

The Impala sped up, growing closer and closer to the dollar store. Thomas felt his grip tighten on the M4 in his hands. The two vehicles were now less than a block away, and just when Thomas was convinced that they were going to drive on past, the Impala hit its breaks and pulled into the large dirt lot beside the dollar store. The Jeep did the same, and the two vehicles now sat less than fifty yards away from Thomas and his two cohorts.

A tall, slender man exited the Impala. He had long, black hair, and his skin had an olive complexion. He was followed by another man from the passenger side, and yet another from the backseat. Two more men got out of the Jeep. All five of them were armed; two with assault rifles, one with a shotgun, and another with a scoped hunting rifle. The first man had a handgun held firmly in his right hand. The group of men slowly and cautiously approached the side of the dollar store, and various scenarios flashed through Thomas's mind. They were seconds away from being discovered.

"That's close enough!" Thomas shouted as he stood and raised his assault rifle. Most of his body was still behind the cover of the truck bed. Spiers and Lee followed his lead, surprised by Thomas's sudden decision.

The group of men jolted and raised their weapons as well. They all froze in place, their sights trained on Thomas and his two comrades.

"What are you doing here?" the first man—the one with long, black hair—asked forcefully.

"Just passing through!" Thomas answered, "We were just leaving!"

"With some of our property, I assume?" the man asked.

Thomas hesitated, searching for the right combination of words that would grant them safe passage.

"We found some things inside...yes," he said, "But we didn't take much. Just what we needed. We didn't know anyone still claimed it."

"Well someone does," the man replied, this time more calmly, "So return what you've taken and leave."

The group had acquired at least a week's worth of food from the dollar store, in addition to a plethora of miscellaneous supplies. It was too valuable to let go of. Thomas wasn't about to let his sister starve, or any of his other group members, for that matter.

"I can't do that," Thomas said, "We had hardly any food left."

"Understandable," the man answered, lowering his handgun, "So let us come look at what you have, and we'll let you go. We'll make sure you don't starve."

"What the fuck?" one of the other men said, shooting a mean glare at the first man.

"How do we know you won't kill us as soon as we lower our weapons?" Thomas asked.

"You don't."

"Doesn't sound like a risk I want to take!"

"It's a better risk than an inevitable gunfight, isn't it?"

Thomas thought about his options. He looked over at Lee, who was coldly staring down the sights of his revolver.

"I don't think we have much of a choice," the old cowboy said quietly.

"Okay!" Thomas yelled, "We're lowering our weapons! But move slowly!"

The first man holstered his handgun and started walking forward. His other men followed him, although a couple looked displeased with the situation. Both groups stared each other down, and the tension was thick.

"Don't worry," the first man said as they got closer, "I'm not an unreasonable man. I don't want good people to die."

"How do you know we're good?" Thomas asked.

"I don't, but I'm guessing you're just trying to survive like the rest of us."

Both groups were now only about fifteen feet away from each other.

"I'm Hector Castillio," the first man said.

"Thomas Briggs."

"Nice to meet you, Thomas."

Hector and his men stopped only a feet away from Thomas, Lee, and Spiers.

"We didn't take much," Thomas began.

Hector looked into the bed of the truck. There were several boxes and crates.

"Looks like a lot to me," he said.

"There's plenty left inside," Thomas replied.

"You're right. We have accumulated quite a collection of supplies. But I can't let you take this much. And no ammunition."

"Fuck that," one of Hector's men said, "Don't let them take a fuckin' thing."

The man who spoke was rough-looking. His head was completely shaved, he had a thick goatee, and he wore a biker's vest with blue jeans and black boots.

"What has the world come to, if we can't help our fellow man?" Hector asked him.

"I'm with Voss. We worked hard for this shit."

The other man looked just as rough, with long, scraggly hair, a full beard, and a sleeveless shirt. His muscles were large, and he was well over six feet tall.

"They have guns," Hector told them, very matter-of-factly, "It's not worth someone dying over."

"No one needs to die," Thomas agreed, "We'll take whatever you're willing to give us."

"Voss, Luke..." Hector said over his shoulder, "Unload the ammunition and take a look inside. Make sure our new friends are being honest with us. Let them keep the food, so long as they haven't taken too much from us."

"This is bullshit..." the man with the full beard—presumably Luke—said under his breath.

"It might be bullshit, but at least it's not death," Hector told him.

Luke stepped passed Thomas—coming awkwardly close to him—and dropped the tailgate on the truck. Lee still had his revolver in his hand, hanging by his side, and he took a step back so he could watch Luke closely. Voss, however, didn't do as Hector had told him to.

"Voss?" Hector said.

"Fuck that," Voss said once more.

"Alright. Bill, help Luke."

The man named Bill—who looked much less terrifying—stepped between Hector and Voss and started helping Luke unload the truck.

"I'll go inside and take a look around," Voss said, "Make sure they didn't take too much."

Thomas stepped in front of the larger man and stared at him coldly.

"I can't let you do that. We have more people in there."

"Oh really?" Voss grimaced and stepped a couple inches closer to Thomas, "Any pretty ladies for me in there?"

Thomas didn't think his heart could pound any harder, but he had been wrong. Every muscle in his body tensed up, and it was everything he could do to not hit Voss with the butt of his rifle.

"There's nobody in there for you," he said through clenched teeth.

The frown on Voss's face disappeared and was replaced with a smile. It was as if he knew from Thomas's answer that there were people inside who he wouldn't mind meeting.

"Voss!" Hector snapped, "Back off!"

Voss held his smile and hesitated for a few moments before finally stepping away from Thomas.

"Let me check the Blazer," Luke said as he pulled another box from the bed of the truck.

Thomas nodded his head at Spiers, who popped the hatch and stepped out of the way. Luke and Bill walked over to it and started digging through everything. Thomas's blood was still boiling because of Voss, and he was more on edge than he had been when they first made contact.

"You understand, I'm sure," Hector said, "We can't let people steal our supplies."

"No, I understand," Thomas answered, his eyes still locked on Voss.

Hector seemed like a normal guy. He had a friendly demeanor, and Thomas sensed no ulterior motive. His eyes were soft, his features firm yet compassionate. His jet black hair was pulled back in a ponytail, and Thomas had to force himself to not associated it with Wild Bill. At first glance Hector seemed like a competent leader. And yet, there was a look of uncertainty in his eyes. Almost like he was just as lost as Thomas, with more responsibility than he was accustomed to.

"So are you guys wanderers, or are you really just passing through?" Hector asked.

"Just passing through. We're on our way to New Mexico."

"Not much further to go, then," Hector said with a smile.

"No, not at all."

"Whereabouts in New Mexico are you going?" It seemed as if the situation was just as uncomfortable for Hector as it was for Thomas, and he was making conversation to smooth the mood.

"Albuquerque," Thomas told him.

Hector's friendly smile disappeared, and his face turned sour.

"We have a survivor from Albuquerque," he said, "I wouldn't advise going there."

Thomas felt his heart stop. All at once, the pounding in his chest disappeared and his knees felt a little weak.

"What..." he paused to swallow the knot in his throat, "What's it like?"

"Gone."

Thomas let go of his M4 with his left hand, and his right arm fell down by his side. The muzzle of the rifle almost touched the ground.

"Family?" was all Hector asked.

"Yeah...family."

"That's all of it, Castillio," Luke said as he shut the hatch on the Blazer. Thomas barely heard him.

"You look a little sad," Voss said provokingly, "Somebody close to you probably got eaten, didn't they?"

The words broke Thomas from his trance, and he looked up at Voss. The man was laughing now, staring back at Thomas.

"Voss! This is the last time I'm going to tell you: Back off!" Hector raised his voice.

"You're letting them take our shit!" Voss fired back, his face contorting into an angry look, "You expect me to just be okay with all this? Treat them like they're our fuckin' friends!?"

Voss took a step closer to Hector, who didn't even flinch from the outburst.

"If you were in their shoes, you'd appreciate a little generosity," Hector told him, his voice firm but calm.

"Yeah, except I'm not in their shoes, am I?"

"We'll discuss this later," Hector told him, much as a parent would tell their child.

"Don't worry Voss, I'm sure some good Samaritan will come by and replenish what's been taken from us," Luke said sarcastically, taking a jab at Hector's timid demeanor.

"That's enough!" Hector roared. Voss's laughter disappeared, and his angry expression returned.

"Who the fuck do you think you are, talkin' to me that way?" Voss asked him.

"Hey Voss, I see some pretty eyes lookin' at us," Luke said, quickly turning Voss's attention away from Hector.

Thomas turned around and saw Samantha peeking through the garage door's window. He looked back at Voss and Luke, who were already trying to make their way past him.

"No!" Thomas yelled

Thomas brought up his assault rifle, but before he could even aim it at one of the two men, Voss grabbed the barrel and tossed it to the side. Luke pushed Thomas with both hands, sending the much smaller man to the ground. Spiers and Lee automatically brought up their weapons, aiming them at Luke and Voss. Thomas jumped to his feet and did the same, but the two men kept walking toward the garage door.

"Stop!" Thomas yelled.

"Luke! Voss!" Hector shouted over Thomas's shoulder. The

other two men in Hector's group were just standing there, as if they were bystanders. Luke and Voss were both laughing at each other as they got closer to the garage.

Crack!

Thomas fired a single round into the dirt behind Voss and Luke. Both men whirled around, instinctively throwing their arms over their heads.

"You're not stepping inside that building," Thomas told them, his voice deeper and more gravelly than it had ever been. His eyes were wide and his jaw was clinched. Voss and Luke stared at him, but neither one raised their weapons.

"You think you fuckin' scare me?" Voss asked him.

"No," Thomas replied, "But I should."

"I don't think you'll shoot me," Voss said, a smile spreading across his face.

"You'd be wrong," Thomas told him.

"I think you should listen to him, Voss," Hector added.

"Alright, maybe you will. But I don't think you'll shoot an unarmed man in the back. You look too *good* to do something like that. You're a pussy, just like Hector. If you weren't, you would have shot at us as soon as we pulled up."

Voss chuckled as he threw his assault rifle to the ground. He stared at Thomas for a little longer before turning and continuing his progress toward the garage door. Luke, however, did not follow him.

Thomas felt his true self fading away, his primal instincts taking over. His whole body shook with anger, and his eyes grew wide with bloodlust. He let the M4 fall from his hands, and the whole world around him disappeared. All he could see was Voss's back. Thomas walked toward him briskly, pulling the claw bar from his belt as he did so. He stepped past Luke, who seemed to be frozen. Voss had made it to the garage door, and he bent down to grab the handle and open it up.

Thomas drove the pointed end of the claw bar into Voss's back while he was bent over. The man fell to the ground and both of his arms became rigid. His left hand was still tightly gripping the handle of the garage door, and his right hand was sticking straight out in front of him.

Voss screamed in agony. Thomas placed his foot on the man's back and used it as leverage to yank out the claw bar. He swiftly brought it down again, stabbing him in almost the same place. Voss let out another painful cry. Again, Thomas pulled the claw bar from Voss's back and immediately struck him once more. Voss rolled over, and his wide eyes locked onto Thomas. But Thomas wasn't done. He couldn't be done. Over and over, he drove the spike into Voss's body. Even after Voss had stopped moving, Thomas continued. Blood splattered onto the garage door every time Thomas pulled his instrument of death from Voss's body. He growled for several seconds as he quickly and repeatedly hit Voss's lifeless body with the claw bar. Finally he stopped, and staggered back a couple of feet. Voss's blood adorned his own body, and he wiped it from his face. Thomas's eyes were still wide, his teeth still clinched. He breathed heavily as he stared at Voss's corpse.

Thomas turned and walked away, back toward Lee and Spiers. He once again walked past Luke, who was still frozen in fear and surprise. Thomas abruptly stopped walking, and in one swift motion he whirled around and struck Luke in the side of the face with the claw bar. Luke screamed and fell to the ground, clutching his horribly wounded face. The pointed end of the claw bar had caught his cheek, ripping it all the way to his mouth. Thomas pulled back his foot and forcefully kicked Luke in the stomach with his boot. Luke coughed and screamed, and it sounded almost like he was choking on his own blood. Thomas kicked him in the gut once more, this time harder. Luke's cries ceased momentarily as he took a huge gulp of air. Thomas raised the claw bar above his head, brought it down swiftly, and lodged its tip in the side of Luke's head. He struggled to remove his weapon from Luke's skull for several seconds before finally dislodging it. Thomas was out of breath, his mouth hanging wide open and his hair dangling down over his eyes. After a moment he turned and looked at his spectators, all of whom were speechless.

"There's no room in this world for men like them," Thomas

finally said, "Never was."

<u>21</u>

Hector Castillio stared at Thomas, who was still breathing heavily from his rampage. The two men behind him looked even more shocked, their armed hands hanging out in front of them as if they had forgotten what they were holding. They weren't soldiers. They were just regular people, trying to survive. Both sides stared at each other for what seemed like an eternity. Spiers and Lee seemed just as shocked, and their weapons were still raised as if their arms were frozen in place. Finally, Hector took half a step forward and spoke.

"I didn't like them," he said, "they were bad people. Criminals. But I don't want anyone else to die. Take what you want."

Thomas took several more fatigued breaths before replying. His temper cooled and his heart stopped pounding quite as hard.

"You're not like them," he finally said, "I won't steal from you."

Hector didn't say a word, curling his lips in and nodding his head instead. Thomas slowly walked over to his M4 and casually picked it up. He turned around to look back at his two victims, but instead caught Mindy staring at him through the window. Her hand was over her mouth, as if she were horrified. Had she seen what Thomas had done?

"Are you still going to go to Albuquerque?" Hector asked.

"I have to. I have to see it for myself."

Despite what Hector's two comrades might have been feeling, Hector himself was not afraid of Thomas. Sure, he was in shock because of what he had just witnessed. But it had been far from the worst thing he had ever seen. He had been surviving for months with no real refuge, going from group to group until finally settling down in Blanding just a few weeks back. In that time he had seen many killings, some justified, some not. Hell, he had killed a few people himself. The death of his two most hardened group members was certainly a loss, but he told himself that he probably would have done the same thing. He didn't know who was inside that building, but whoever it was, Thomas was extremely protective of them.

"As I said before, we have someone who came from there. You could speak to him, if you'd like. Maybe what he has to say will help you."

"Thank you. I appreciate that. Are your other group members nearby?"

"Yes, although there aren't many. We just have eight, in total. Well...six, now."

Thomas nodded his head. Hector almost expected him to apologize in some way, but it didn't happen.

"Take me to this man."

Thomas and the rest of his group followed Hector through Blanding. Spiers was driving the Blazer now, with Thomas in the passenger seat. Neither Samantha nor Mindy said a word. In fact, no one said anything. Thomas felt no remorse, however. He had seen an evil inside Voss, and he wasn't about to let someone like that anywhere near his family. Luke...perhaps he hadn't been as bad as Voss. Perhaps he was just a product of his environment. None of that mattered, now.

Hector's red Impala pulled into the driveway of a large ranch-style house, the Wrangler following close behind him. Spiers—being ever cautious—parked the Blazer on the side of the street. Robert pulled up beside him and left his truck sitting in the middle of the road. The former Erda resident got out of his vehicle and walked over to Spiers, who still had his M4 in his hands. Thomas was standing next to the Blazer, staring at the house, and could hear whispering going on between Spiers and Robert. Lee was standing beside Thomas, his revolver holstered and his pack of cigarettes already coming out of his pocket.

"Nice house," the cowboy said as he lit a cigarette.

"Yeah."

"Hope you don't mind coming in," Hector said from the porch, "The poor guy isn't in the best shape. He just barely survived a train wreck."

"Train wreck?" Thomas asked.

"Yeah...couple months back, just south of Utah, in Arizona."

Hector opened the front door and waited for Thomas and his crew to make their way up the driveway. Thomas had left his M4 in the Blazer, but still had his Beretta nestled in his waistband. The bloody claw bar was also hanging from his side. Spiers and Robert still had their weapons; Spiers with his M4 and Robert with his MP5. Mindy and Samantha were in the center of the small group.

"Hope he can tell you something useful," Hector said as Thomas approached the front door.

"Yeah...me too."

Thomas stepped inside behind Hector. The two other men who had been at the store were in the front room, but their weapons were nowhere to be found. Sitting in one of the recliners was a young woman—probably in her mid-twenties—with a sawed-off shotgun in her lap. She was sitting casually, with her chin resting on her hand as if she didn't have a care in the world. Her skin was tan—slightly darker than Hector's—and her hair was was long, straight, and black. Thomas suspected it was Hector's sister. She was absolutely stunning, with soft features that were perfectly proportioned. She wore black, skin-tight leggings and a charcoal gray spaghetti strap shirt. Around her waist was a thick belt that had a holster, and in that holster was some sort of semi-automatic handgun.

"That's Mina," Hector told them, "She's in charge of our weapons. Maintenance, ammunition, etcetera."

"Nice to meet you," Thomas said quietly.

"Who are these people?" Mina asked, rather hatefully.

393

"Found them at the dollar store. They're on their way to Albuquerque, and I told them we have a survivor from there. They want to see what he has to say, maybe it will help them."

"If you steal anything while you're here, I'll cut your throats." Mina's appearance was the complete opposite of her attitude. She was forthright and spoke quickly.

"Charming," Lee said. Mina shot him an ugly glare.

"Where's Voss? And Luke?" Mina asked, completely ignoring Lee.

"Uh, yeah...we need to talk about that," Hector replied.

"What do you mean?"

"Just wait, Mina. I'll explain everything."

"Peter's not going to be happy if they're dead..." Mina told him.

"Right this way," Hector said to Thomas and the others.

The group walked through the wide hall of the house, past the kitchen and dining room. It was a beautiful house, and didn't suit the world they were now living in.

Once they had reached one of the back rooms of the house, Hector poked his head inside and said, "Charles, we have some guests."

Charles? Thomas thought.

The sound of a cane tapping against the hardwood floor could be heard, and after several long moments an older man in his late fifties appeared. He had a healing wound on the right side of his head, and his left arm was in a sling. His eyes were directed down at the floor as he carefully walked with the aid of his cane. Thomas almost collapsed.

"Dad..." he said under his breath.

Charles Briggs lifted his head up and looked at his son, who already had tears in his eyes.

"Dad!" Thomas let out, and took two giant steps forward. He carefully wrapped his arms around his father, trying his best not to hurt him.

"Son...oh my God..." Charles said as he wrapped his good arm around Thomas's back.

Hector stepped away in confusion.

Mindy rushed forward without saying a word and hugged both her father and brother. The three held each other tightly for many moments, and sounds of gentle sobbing could be heard.

"Oh my lord..." Charles began, "I didn't know what had become of you two. I've been beside myself."

"We're here now," Mindy finally said.

Thomas tried several times to speak before finally getting the words to come out.

"We've come so far," he said, "We were so worried we wouldn't find you."

"What about..." Mindy stepped back, "Where's...?"

Charles Briggs let go of his son and gave Mindy a sorrowful look. Tears ran down his cheeks as he took a small step toward her and looked into her eyes.

"Honey..." he said.

"No..." Thomas recoiled back, almost tripping over himself, "Mom..."

"We got on the last train out of Albuquerque," Charles told them, "We had to go north, to find you. But the train derailed before we even got to Utah. I don't remember much, or how long I laid there before I was found. But by the time that happened, your mother..."

Charles shut his eyes and let his head drop down. Tears fell to the floor, and the man could say no more.

"No..." Thomas said again.

Thomas threw his arm against the wall to keep himself from falling down. He felt a hand touch his shoulder, but he didn't know whose hand it was. Slowly, dramatically, he slid down the wall onto his haunches. Lee was standing over him. It had been he who had touched Thomas's shoulder.

Thomas buried his face in his hands and sobbed. After a moment he looked up and saw his sister, who was mortified. Both of her hands were over her mouth and nose, and he could barely see her eyes because they were squinted so tightly. Thomas shook his head and cocked it to the side while staring at his sister.

"Mindy..." he said, "Oh, Mindy..."

Thomas stood and embraced his sister, who threw her head onto his chest and cried. She did not make a sound. No wailing, no bawling. She simply cried. Thomas felt her tears soak through his shirt as he stroked her hair and cried with her. So much had happened to them already, and now this? Surely the Gods must jest.

* * *

Thomas sat alone on the back porch of the house, staring up at the stars. His eyes still hurt from all the crying, and his nose was stuffy. He had cried off and on all day long, and there was no way he could leave in his condition. And why would he leave? Where would he go? His journey was over. They had found his father, and his mother was dead. Of course he had expected such a fate. He had anticipated coming to the end of his journey never even knowing if his parents were alive or not. But they had attained closure. His father was alive, if not recovering from serious injuries, and they knew what had come of their mother. Even though he was stricken with grief, he couldn't help but feel fortunate in a way. At least they still had their dad.

Thomas looked down at his hands, which were clean now. He had washed up and changed his clothes shortly after arriving. The blood that had coated him was only another sign of everything that was wrong. Everything that was wrong with the world, everything that was wrong with *him*.

Thomas heard the glass door slide open behind him. He immediately recognized the sound of Lee's cowboy boots as they thumped across the wooden porch. The older man sat down in one of the reclining patio chairs that sat across the table from Thomas. He leaned back, looking up at the sky just as Thomas was.

"Part of me is jealous," he began, "You traveled all the way from Washington in search of just two people, through a world of undead, and violent human beings who have no one keeping them in check. Out of the millions of bodies—living or dead—you stumbled across one of the people you were looking for. And you didn't even have to go as far as you thought you would. Sure, your mother is gone. But you have two out of your three family members with you now. And here I am, with no one. Yeah pardner, I'd say it turned out about as good as it could have."

Thomas stared at the stars as Lee spoke. When he was done, Thomas turned his head toward him and gave him a soft smile. Lee's eyes glistened in the moonlight, even beneath his cowboy hat.

"You're not alone anymore, Lee. You have someone now."

Lee Granger smiled, his bushy mustache spreading across his face. Thomas stretched out his open hand and laid it on the table. Lee took it and gave it a squeeze before getting up and heading back inside. On his way, Thomas heard him say, "Excuse, miss."

Thomas turned around and saw his sister coming out, arms crossed across her chest. She sat down in the same chair Lee had been sitting in, except she didn't look up at the stars. Thomas sat up in his chair and turned to face her.

"Hell of a trip," he said.

"Yeah."

"At least we found Dad."

"Yeah."

"How are you holding up?"

"I'm better. Like you said, we found Dad. I really wasn't expecting to find either of them. It's just hard to accept that Mom is dead."

Mindy looked down at the table, but her eyes were dry.

"It'll be okay, sis," Thomas said to her, "We don't have to run around anymore. No more fighting, no more killing..."

"I don't believe that," she interrupted, "If anything is certain— if everything we know about this world has taught us anything— it's that there will always be somebody to kill. It was true before, and it's true now. We just didn't have to face it before all this."

Thomas stared at his sister, a feeling of emptiness growing inside of him.

"I'm sorry, sis," Thomas said to her, his words soft and quiet,

"I'm sorry for everything I've done. I promised you I wouldn't turn into...whatever it is I am now..."

"Neither of us are the same anymore, Thomas. We should have known that was going to happen before we ever left Seattle. We were so naive to think any different."

"So you're okay? With the things I have done, I mean?"

Mindy looked up at her brother.

"No. I don't think I'll ever be okay with it. But I accept it."

Thomas looked down, a knot forming in his throat. The realization of what Mindy had said was immediate.

"There's something else..." Mindy began.

"What?"

"Well, Samantha told me something a few minutes ago. That's actually what I came out here to talk to you about."

"What, Mindy?"

"She thinks she's pregnant."

Thomas's jaw dropped. He was speechless. *Pregnant?*

"We have to go back to the store and find some pregnancy tests."

"Pregnant?" Thomas asked.

"Yes."

"But...how? I mean...she's only fifteen..."

"She was raped, Thomas," Mindy reminded him, "Nearly everyday for almost two weeks."

"My god..." Thomas leaned back in his chair and covered his face with his hand.

"I just thought you should know."

"Yeah. Well...we'll have to go back tomorrow. I doubt Hector will have any objection. I also need to speak with him about our living situation. It's understandable if he doesn't want us living here..."

Mindy cut him off, "Considering you murdered two of his people."

Thomas felt an immediate rage flush through him. He almost jumped up and started yelling, but he caught himself. Why was he feeling this way? He never used to have an anger problem.

"Mindy," he said as calmly as possible, but his words were forceful, "That man—those *men*—were trying to come inside and get you. And Samantha. I couldn't let that happen."

"It's just... You did it..." Mindy sighed and looked down at her hands, "It all happened so fast, and it was right in front of me. My *brother*...killing people. It was so violent, so *ruthless*. That's not who you are..."

Thomas stared at his sister for a moment. He leaned forward against the table and his eyes narrowed.

"It's not who I *used* to be. But that person can't exist anymore. Not when it comes to defending those I care about."

"And where does it end, Thomas? You've changed this much... What happens when you keep changing? When you start acting angry and mean toward *me*? Or Samantha? Or Dad?"

"That would *never* happen..."

"Yeah..."

"How can you say such a thing? After all I've done to protect you?" Thomas leaned back in his chair, his eyes still locked on Mindy.

"Thomas..." Mindy shook her head, "Forget it. I'm sorry. I just don't want to lose you."

"You won't," Thomas told her, "I'm not going anywhere anytime soon."

__Epilogue__

Kyle Fields sat in Erda's old ice cream shop, gripping his injured arm. A bullet had torn through it, rendering it completely useless. Worse yet, it was already showing signs of infection. It had been over half a day since the townsfolk assaulted the police station. Luckily he was already wounded when it happened, or he might have been killed in the attack. But now here he was, with his leg shackled to an old radiator and his arm all messed up. It was a wonder he hadn't bled out. Fortunately, Simon Spiers changed the bandage not even an hour before they were attacked. What had come of him? Was he alive? Fields had no way of knowing.

Connor Williams—the other deputy who had been injured in the shootout with the townsfolk—was now laying lifeless on the floor beside Fields. It was horrible, watching him die a slow and painful death from his injury. Even worse when he reanimated and Fields had to crush his skull against the wall with his boot. Poor Williams. But he was sort of a prick, anyway.

Fields winced in pain as he scooted further up against the wall. How much longer would he have to stay here? Were they ever coming back to get him? There hadn't been hardly any activity outside. None that he could hear, at least. Once or twice he had heard people talking, and he thought about calling out to them, but decided that he didn't want to incur their wrath if it was something he wasn't supposed to do. He was getting hungry, though. Very hungry. His stomach was growling. He also really needed to relieve himself. For the past hour, he had held it. But he had held it as long as he could and pissed himself once already, so did it really matter?

Voices...distant voices. They were getting closer. Were they going to walk by again, or were they coming to take him? Kill him, perhaps? Fields couldn't take it any longer. He decided that death was worse than being left I this small room any longer. He called out as loud as he could, straining his neck and hurting his throat.

"Hey! Come get me! Hey!"

Fields continued yelling, unsure about what would happen and not caring. Finally, he heard the front door swing open. The top of the door hit the little bell dangling from the ceiling, and the sound was so out of place for the world he was in today. Fields stopped yelling, listening to the footsteps grow closer and closer. At least two people, he thought.

"Anybody in here?" a female voice called out.

"Back here!" Fields shouted.

The door swung open, and in the dim light Fields saw a slender woman with her hair pulled back in a ponytail. She carried a baseball bat in her left hand, and in her right was a flashlight. She directed the beam of light at Fields, who quickly shut his eyes and turned away.

"Oh my God..." the girl said.

"What? What is it?" This time it was a man's voice.

"Look..."

Fields cracked his left eye open, and the girl aimed the light at his chest instead of his face. A man appeared next to her, and he stepped through the threshold of the doorway.

"Jesus..."

"Please..." Fields said, "...please get me out of here."

He was fairly certain that these two were not part of the angry mob that had attacked the police station. They obviously had no knowledge that he was being kept back here.

"We need a key," the girl said.

"Take Jonathan and go to the police station that's just a couple blocks over," the man said as he knelt down beside Fields.

The girl disappeared, and the man turned on a flashlight of his own. Fields looked into his eyes, letting out a sigh of relief.

"He didn't make it," Fields told the man as he glanced over at Williams' body.

"You're going to be okay," the man said, "We have medicine. We'll take care of you."

"Thank you..." Fields whispered, "...Jesus Christ, thank you..."

The girl returned, this time with a teenage boy, and used a handcuff key to remove the shackle from Fields' leg. The man and the boy helped Fields to his feet and took him out of the store. There was a 4-door truck parked half a block away, which the girl went and got. They placed Fields in the backseat and the man started tending to his wounds.

"My name's Phillip," he said, "The girl is Becca, and the boy is Jonathan. You don't have anything to worry about. We're good people."

Fields nodded his head and looked down at his arm. Phillip was cleaning it, and he was even wearing latex gloves.

"My name's Kyle," he said, "Kyle Fields."

"Nice to meet you, Kyle."

"Just Fields is fine. Thank you so much..."

"What the hell happened here?" Phillip asked.

"It's a long story. I'd rather wait to tell it."

"Understandable. Are there anymore of your friends around?"

"How did you know I had any friends to begin with?"

"Your shirt..."

Fields looked down at his shirt, realizing that it had "SHERIFF" written across it.

"Oh," he said, "Right. I don't know. We got attacked, and the rest of them ran. There was one who stayed, but he surrendered. I'm not sure what happened to him."

"God, it must have been horrible. There was a lot of destruction around here. Blood all over the streets, zombie parts scattered around. The police station looks like a bunker from WWII."

"Yeah, it was..." Fields looked up at the truck's ceiling,

"Where is everyone?"

"We've seen a few people here and there, but they just pretend like we're not even here. Really strange, but I guess it's expected after what this town went through."

"So you haven't found anyone else?"

"Well, we did find one person..." Phillip swabbed some antibiotic cream on Fields' arm.

"Who was he?"

"We don't know. We think he was someone who got caught in the crossfire. He's...he's not doing too well. All burned up. We found him laying in the grass, next to a shed that had caught on fire. He can't speak, or move. Doesn't even have any hair. Becca took care of him the best she could. We used nearly all of our bandages and antibiotic ointment wrapping him up. The burns were pretty bad."

"Can I see him?" Fields asked.

"It won't do any good, my friend," Phillip told him, "You wouldn't be able to tell who he is even if he's your brother."

"Still...can I see him? Please?"

"Yeah, if you really want to."

After Phillip was done tending to Fields' wounds, the four of them drove to the outskirts of town and pulled into an old self-service station. There was one more member of their group, a young man by the name of Henry. Fields was unsure of his age, but he was probably in his early twenties. He, too, was kind and helpful. Fields limped through the station with the help of Jonathan, who was small-framed but strong.

Henry pushed open the office door of the gas station, revealing the horrible scene contained inside. Fields gasped as his eyes looked over the burned man. Parts of his body were so badly burnt that his skin was black, little more than ash. His face had literally melted, and the only part of him that was relatively untouched was his right shoulder and arm. His left hand was shriveled up, the fire consuming most of the flesh and muscle. His left eye was almost completely hidden behind a flap of skin that had melted over it.

"My God..." Fields could hardly believe what he was seeing. As a deputy, he had seen burn victims before. But nothing like this.

"Is he going to live?" Fields asked.

"Probably not," Becca whispered, "But we're doing everything we can. Phillip and I are nurses...we can't leave someone without treatment if we have the ability to help them."

"But how do you..." Fields shook his head, completely aghast at the sight before him, "How do you even treat something like that?"

"It's not easy, even with modern medicine," Phillip told him, "But we're doing what we can. Mostly making him as comfortable as possible."

"Can he hear us? Is he conscious, I mean?"

"We think so. In and out, at least. His body is going into overdrive, between dealing with the pain and trying to repair itself. Luckily, we had some morphine with us to help ease his suffering a little."

"Poor guy..."

Fields couldn't look any longer, and turned away from the burn victim who was surely going to die. The scene represented the entire world, for him. Burning, dying, fading. It was only a matter of time before that flame was snuffed out completely. All of the death and destruction that had happened in the past six and a half months...Fields almost envied those who were already dead. At least they would no longer have to endure the pain and grief and sadness that consumed this new world, this World of the Damned.

www.ingramcontent.com/pod-product-compliance
Lightning Source LLC
Chambersburg PA
CBHW021425240626
47153CB00001B/24